DI AND I

Di AND I

A NOVEL

Peter Lefcourt

Random House New York

Library of Congress Cataloging-in-Publication Data
Lefcourt, Peter.
Di and I : a novel / Peter Lefcourt
p.   cm.
ISBN 0-679-42583-7
1. Diana, Princess of Wales, 1961–   —Fiction.   2. Man-woman
relationships—Fiction. 3. Screenwriters—Fiction.
I. Title.
PS3562.E3737D5   1994
813'.54—dc20   93-38837

Book design by Tanya M. Pérez

Manufactured in the United States of America
2 4 6 8 9 7 5 3
First Edition

For Terri,
who brought pearls to the Russian front

Sing, Heavenly Muse, of fair Diana,
fruit of Johnnie Spencer—scion of Black Jack,
the Seventh Earl Spencer and Lady Hamilton—
and his bride, the beauteous Frances,
issue of the Baron Fermoy
and his conjoint, Ruth, and the unpolluted blood
of noble lords and ladies dating back to Charles I
and farther yet to Hastings and the Dawn of Time.

Sing of her birth amidst the wind-blown fields
of Sandringham 'neath Norfolk's cloud-choked sky
within the time-worn stones of Park House
on that sparkling July day years ago
in simpler times, more clement climes,
the world a safe and bounteous place,
before the . . .

—LEONARD SCHECTER, *The Dianiad*

PROLOGUE

RANCHO CUCAMONGA,
JULY 2, 1994,
1:15 A.M.

It occurs to me, as I sit here naked watching the moon paint the faux tile roofs of the houses on Persimmon Avenue and illuminate the off-beige surface of the rented Ford Taurus in which two men with guns sit watching my house, that only a year ago my life was a great deal simpler. For one thing, I wasn't sleeping with the Princess of Wales.

At the moment she is in one of the two bedrooms of this yellow-and-green stucco house off Interstate 10 between San Bernardino and Los Angeles. She has dropped off to sleep, having taken the latest Danielle Steel to bed with her an hour ago. Next door, in the other bedroom, also asleep, are her sons, Wills and Harry, the second and third in line to the English throne.

Meanwhile, in Room 326 at the Cucamonga Holiday Inn, the boys' father and the Princess's estranged husband is sitting by the phone waiting for news. He and I have spoken by phone several times in the past hour. The conversations have been civil, if a bit strained, given the circumstances. He has told me he would like his sons back. I have replied that it is not my decision but rather his estranged wife's. But you have taken them, he has insisted. I have begged to differ with him. I have explained that I have merely accompanied his estranged wife, a legally separated woman, to Rancho Cucamonga—that it is she who chose to take *her* children with her.

I imagine him, awake and jet-lagged in his room at the Holiday Inn at one in the morning, waiting for developments to take their course, a room-service tray with a half-eaten Cobb salad and an iced tea beside him, the TV turned to CNN. The two men outside my house are MI6 agents, he has told me, waiting for the warrant to come through so that U.S. Marshals can arrive on the scene and reclaim the boys. Wouldn't it be preferable, he has argued, to avoid this kind of unpleasantness? I have agreed with him but have restated my position that it is not my decision. Well, can't you talk to her? he has said. She is sleeping now, I have replied. She has had a very hard day at work. I'll talk to her in the morning.

I get up to stretch my legs. Though the night is warm, a small breeze has begun to rise off the desert, and I feel a chill go through me. I'm exhausted but I can't sleep. Not tonight. Not while my house is threatened by armed men.

I walk down the hallway to the bedroom and stop to peek in on the boys. They lie on their bunk beds, their mouths open, gulping the warm desert air. *Super Mario Bros. 2* still flickers on the TV screen, the music low and cloying, and I go over to turn it off.

In their crew cuts and Bart Simpson pj's, they look like average American kids. I smile and think how adaptable children are. Not long ago they were at the Ludgrove School outside of Windsor, not far from their grandmother's castle, declining verbs in Latin and playing rugby during recess. Now they are at the Millard Fillmore Middle School in Rancho Cucamonga and help out part-time after school at our McDonald's franchise at the Freedom Mall on Eucalyptus Avenue.

Closing the door gently behind me, I move down the hallway to the larger bedroom. The bedside reading light is still on, the Danielle Steel still in her hands. She is fast asleep, snoring quietly in counterpoint with the cicadas outside in the lemon tree. Her eyelids are closed, shielding her pale blue eyes from the sharp pencil of light of the reading lamp. The parallel rows of perfect white teeth are exposed between her lips, which move ever so slightly with the gentle rise and fall of her breath. The nose, her new nose—the nose constructed for her in the middle of the night by a leading Beverly Hills plastic surgeon—stands shyly in the middle of her face, redeeming it from the burden of Grecian perfection.

She has gone to bed in her baby-blue cotton shortie nightgown, which rides up high on her stately, almost Doric, thighs. The contrast of the pearly whiteness of her flesh and the colored print of the Snoopy sheets is dramatic, not to mention erotic. If there were not two gunmen in a car in front of my house, if there was not a threat of U.S. Marshals at my door at any moment, I would be inclined to pick her up and carry her still asleep to the floor beside our bed and wake her with my kisses.

I don't think I have ever loved her as much as I do at this moment. It is not just the whiteness of her thighs, the fine hair on her legs that she shaves so painstakingly with her Lady Schick in the shower every morning, the softness of her mouth as it veils the white enamel of her teeth, brushed to an almost brilliant shine with her Interplak electric toothbrush—it is the sum of the parts that is overpowering.

I bend down and let my lips softly brush her forehead. She stirs. But only for the briefest of moments. And then she returns to the land of her dreams, wherever that may be. Perhaps back to the Norfolk of her childhood, the Althorp House of later years, the flat in Earl's Court of her Sloane Ranger London days, the Kensington Palace of her apotheosis, the Highgrove House of her long purgatory, or here in this tract house on the edge of the desert with me.

I do not know exactly where Di lives these days. We don't often talk of the past. We live in the simplicity of the present. We feed off our own love, like bears feeding off their fat in winter. We are disgustingly happy.

I think of all this as I watch her sleep. And I try to forget about the men outside and the Marshals and the Prince of Wales in his room at the Holiday Inn. I try to remain in the present, in the immediacy of the moment, 1:15 A.M. of the morning after her thirty-third birthday.

Earlier we had a cake with candles at the restaurant, and we all sang "Happy Birthday" to her. The staff gave her a Brunswick Lady Pro bowling ball and an apron with SANDY written on it. She thanked everyone personally, going up to each person with that exquisite charm with which she used to grace state occasions and telling them how much the cake and gifts meant to her and how wonderful a job they were doing.

It is this human touch, this sensitivity to people that I adore. That and the touch of her lips against mine and that soft, reckless cry of abandon that she utters just before . . .

The phone rings. I hurry out to the kitchen to grab the phone before it wakes her. I get it on the third ring, and stand there, my bare feet against the cold floor. "Hello."

"Charles here."

I recognize the voice by now. "Your Royal Highness . . ."

"Sorry to trouble you again, but I thought it might be useful if you and I had a little chat man-to-man."

"Sure."

There is a long silence on the line. Then: "I mean tête-à-tête."

"I don't think that would be a very good idea. Di is asleep and so are Wills and Harry. But they could wake up at any moment."

"Perhaps you could come here, then. I'm afraid the bar is closed, but I suppose we could hunt up a bottle somewhere and sit by the pool."

"How do I know that those two guys in the Ford Taurus out front won't come in here while I'm gone and take the boys?"

"I shall give you my word of honor."

I think about what the word of honor of the Prince of Wales is worth in Rancho Cucamonga. I think about it for long enough so that Charles says: "I'm afraid you are doubting my word of honor."

"Tell you the truth, it occurred to me. I mean, we're in San Bernardino County here. It's a different ball game . . ."

"I beg your pardon?"

"Context."

"I see. Well, suppose I tell the men in the car to go away. In fact, they could run you here, and stay here, and run you back when we're finished. What do you say?"

What do I say? I really don't know. I stand here in our spotless kitchen, staring at the drawings that Prince Hal made in school, held by kitchen magnets to the refrigerator door, thinking hard. What is it that I have to say to him? That he has no jurisdiction, moral or legal, in this part of the world? That I am in love with the woman he scorned? That the story of our life moves in its own ineluctable pattern, a pattern that we may never fully understand?

And so I don't reply. Instead I go to the refrigerator and take out a can of Coors. Then, leaving the phone dangling, I sit down on a kitchen stool and try to remember just how all this began.

DI AND I

CHAPTER

1

"Is that your signature on the check, Mr. Schecter?"

I was looking at a copy of a check that I had written to the Southern California Edison Company two years before. The signature was undeniably mine. I had, in fact, written the check. The correct answer was yes. But I didn't respond immediately to the question asked by my estranged wife's lawyer. My mind was elsewhere. I was thinking about Rivera.

Even though he was no longer present in the courtroom, Jesus Rivera, my fellow defendant and brother, was still there in spirit. Earlier I had watched him being questioned by the court-appointed attorney for *his* estranged wife, Guadalupe Rivera. Jesus Rivera had sat there in his Kmart sports jacket, his shrub-scarred hands tightly wound around each other, listening as the court translator asked him, in Spanish, if he had, in fact, spent only $125 on retread tires for his 1976 Chevy pickup instead of the $750 for new tires that he had written off as a legitimate business expense. He, too, had been confronted with a check bearing his signature and asked to verify it.

I had watched Jesus Rivera look at the check, then look down from the witness stand at Guadalupe Rivera, sitting with a smug look of satisfaction on her face. It was clear to me that at that moment Jesus Rivera wanted to kill his estranged wife, that if he hadn't been in a courtroom with an armed bailiff a few feet away, he would have risen from the witness stand and attacked her. And then, when she was a millimeter away from death, when there was only the merest flutter of life left in her, he would have released his hands from her jugular and thrown his body across her ample breasts and cried that he loved her. Forever.

I did not want to strangle my estranged wife. I just wanted her to go away. My divorce was not about passion. It was about accounting.

Sitting down below me in the spectator seats, where I had sat and watched Jesus Rivera earlier, were the accountants. Hers and mine. They sat beside their hand trolleys bearing cartons full of bank statements, canceled checks, tax returns, phone bills, insurance re-funds—the effluvia of our lives for sixteen years. They had nearly identical dark suits on, their trouser legs perfectly creased, their shoes impeccably shined, matching looks of profound indifference on their faces.

"Mr. Schecter, would you please answer the question?" This was the judge's baritone, a deep, virile drumroll of a voice.

I looked blankly at him. The question, as far as I was concerned, was whether Rivera's attempted strangulation of his estranged wife was justifiable under the circumstances. And so I said yes.

My estranged wife's lawyer then said, "Will the record show that Respondent has identified the signature on this check as his. I am entering a copy of this check as Petitioner's Exhibit Forty-three B."

She then returned to the counsel's table, where the Petitioner nodded with satisfaction, took out a Kleenex from her navy-blue Coach leather pocketbook, and demurely blew her nose, one nostril at a time. She was enjoying herself. And why not? This party was on

me. The morning's interrogation was costing me well over a grand
an hour, given the fact that I was paying not only my lawyer and my
forensic accountant's fees but hers as well. It was so stipulated by the
court in view of the fact that the Petitioner had no income other than
the exorbitant temporary support I was already paying her.

At these prices I might as well have a good time. So when the
Petitioner's lawyer returned to ask me about a trip I had taken to New
Orleans supposedly to research a script on Dixieland jazz but actually
to see the Super Bowl, I said it was because there was no passion in
my life. My lawyer suggested that this might be a good time to break
for lunch.

She whisked me away to the ninth-floor cafeteria, and as we sat
there surrounded by more lawyers and accountants with hand trolleys, she reviewed my performance on the stand.

"You were terrible."

"Thank you."

"You know, this judge doesn't like wiseasses."

"I'm sorry."

"How many times have I told you, just answer the questions yes
or no?"

"Can't we just get this over with?"

"Sure. We can agree to give her everything she wants, and
we're out of here."

"She pretty much has it all anyway."

She took a bite of her tuna-and-sprouts sandwich and then
looked at me without compassion. "You know what your problem
is?"

I blinked, knowing she was going to tell me. I have never met
anybody as opinionated as my lawyer. Not to mention tactless. She
has absolutely no bedside manner.

"You're making too much money."

"That's a problem?"

"Uh-huh. Look, this whole business is strictly about numbers.
The judge doesn't have time to read all the declarations. And frankly
he doesn't give a shit that your ex-wife didn't wait on tables to put

you through medical school. All he cares about is what's in the bank and what's coming in. So all we can do is fight about the numbers, and, in your case, the numbers look lousy. One way or the other, you're probably in for twenty percent of your gross."

"Twenty percent of my *gross*?"

She nodded dispassionately, took a sip of her diet Coke. "We can waltz around your business deductions for a while, but we all know that half of them are bullshit. You want the IRS down here auditing your returns for the last seven years? You might as well pay your wife. At least it's deductible."

"If I give her twenty percent off the top, and I give the government forty-one percent state and federal and my agent ten percent and my business manager seven percent, I'm working for twenty-two cents on the dollar."

"You could take her back."

"What?"

"Then you'd be up to forty-two cents on the dollar. That's not too bad."

"What kind of legal advice is this?"

She opened her bag and took out a Casio portable organizer. She hit a few buttons, then some more buttons, then put it back in the bag.

"Billing hours?" I asked.

"There is no free lunch, Leonard."

"So basically that's it. I'm fucked, one way or the other."

"You could always go broke."

"What?"

"The judge can't force you to give her money you don't have. You can't get blood from a stone, right? So maybe she'll be motivated to go out and get a job or find a new husband to support her, and then you'd be off the hook."

"Great."

She looked at her watch. "We have to be back downstairs. Let's go."

I didn't want to move. I didn't see any point in going back down there and subjecting myself to more humiliation if it was all futile anyway.

"Look on the bright side, Leonard. You don't have any kids. If you did, you'd have to give her thirty percent of your gross, and then you'd be working for twelve cents on the dollar."

Later, driving back on the Hollywood Freeway in rush-hour traffic, I thought about the day I had just spent in Section 29 of Los Angeles County Superior Court. I thought about going broke. And I thought about Rivera.

Going broke was a tactical matter. I simply instructed my agents to stop soliciting writing assignments. They would balk, of course. Why now? Why walk away from the table when the cards were hot? I could hear the whole committee of them wailing like a Greek chorus. They were a collectivity, my agents. I thought of them in the plural. Different ones called me all the time. I couldn't tell one from another.

I would move out of my rented house, get a cheap apartment, and live frugally while the Petitioner tried to manage the life she had grown accustomed to without her large support checks. I had to admit that I could take a certain degree of kamikaze pleasure in that idea after all she had put me through—the subpoenas, the motions, the months of discovery . . .

Discover *that.*

I wondered if Jesus Rivera was considering going broke, too— giving up the gardening business and letting Guadalupe try to get blood from a stone. I'd give him a call, suggest we get together. We could become renegades, living off Coors and Kraft macaroni-and-cheese dinners, safe from the attacks by our estranged wives' lawyers . . .

These thoughts were interrupted by the car phone—a high-pitched little whiny ring that reminded me of the Petitioner's lawyer's voice. I was sorely tempted not to pick up. It was undoubtedly my lawyer with more bad news.

"Hello?" I said noncommittally.

"Len?"

Very few people called me Len, and I didn't like any of them.
"Who's this?"

"Brad."

"Brad?"

"Brad Emprin. At GTA."

One of the members of the Greek chorus. They all sounded alike
to me—bland, inflectionless voices attached to lithe, jogging-honed
bodies.

"Hey, Brad, how're you doing?"

"Great. Terrific. Listen, we got a call for you this morning."

"Oh yeah?"

"Uh-huh. From Charlie Berns."

"Who?"

"Charlie Berns."

"Who's Charlie Berns?"

"You don't know who Charlie Berns is?"

"If I knew who he was, I wouldn't have asked you the question."

"Charlie Berns produced *Dizzy and Will*."

"No shit."

"The guy won an Academy Award. Three years ago."

"No shit."

"You know what he wanted to talk about? Princess Di . . ."

"No shit."

"It's a miniseries, Len. Four hours. They're calling it *Inside Di—
The Real Story*. They want to go after it from the human angle—
Diana as a person, not as a princess or as an international celebrity.
They want to show the Diana that nobody knows, the brooding,
sensitive, misunderstood woman who has been thrust upon the
world's stage unexpectedly. They're talking about Demi Moore."

"Listen . . . Brad, is it?"

"Yeah."

"I can't take the job."

"Huh?"

"I can't afford to make too much money just now."

There was a long silence on the other end of the line. For a moment I thought he had hung up. Then, in a very quiet voice, "You want to run that by me again?"

"It's an accounting decision."

"Accounting decision?"

"Tax brackets."

"Hey, don't worry—they'll defer payment. No problem."

"I really don't think . . ."

"Len, they asked for you specifically. *Specifically.* The head of the network and a producer with an Academy Award for Best Picture. Now what am I supposed to tell them—'Sorry, Len Schecter can't take the job because it pays too much money'? You want me to tell them that?"

It occurred to me there was no way that Brad Emprin could grasp the problem. It was completely beyond the scope of his understanding. It was, quite simply, unacceptable to him that anybody did not want to make money. And so he plowed right over it and kept going.

"Look, do me a favor, will you? Take a meeting. Go see Charlie Berns. Let him tell you about it. Just listen. It can't hurt to listen, can it?"

So that was the beginning—the car-phone conversation with Brad Emprin bumper to bumper on the Hollywood Freeway after a day of being raked over the coals by the Petitioner's lawyer. This strange and wonderful odyssey that has taken me here to Rancho Cucamonga began simply enough with a phone call from one of my bagmen as I drove back from court. If I had been more forceful on the phone, if I had explained more cogently my decision to pursue poverty as the only legitimate defense against the family-law statutes of the State of California, all this may not have happened.

But I didn't. I sat there, one hand on the steering wheel, the other on the car phone, listening as Brad Emprin gave me Charlie Berns's telephone number.

"Are you copying it down, Len?"

"It's all right. I have a photographic memory."

"Well, if you forget it, call me. Anytime. Day or night. I've got a machine. I'll leave his number on the machine."

I got off the freeway and headed west on Sunset. East Hollywood was raw and ugly in the refracted late-afternoon light. I didn't want to see it. I had enough problems. I kept my eyes straight ahead, peering through my dirty windshield, and remembered Charlie Berns and his Academy Award.

Dizzy and Will, a lushly filmed epic about the life of Benjamin Disraeli, starring Jeremy Ikon and Jacqueline Fortier, snuck in as a dark-horse Best Picture a few years ago. I remembered Charlie Berns accepting his Oscar on television—an amorphous man in an ill-fitting tux looking dazed as he stood holding the statuette and listening to the applause. No one had expected the picture even to be nominated, let alone win. The Vegas line was 25–1 against.

But then he disappeared back to that planet of anonymity where most people in the movie business report on a regular basis and where I wanted to be at the moment.

Apparently Charlie Berns was back on earth. And he had a deal to make a miniseries about Princess Di.

As far as I was concerned, we knew far too much about this woman already. You could scarcely walk into a supermarket without being confronted by screaming headlines: DI PREGNANT; DI OFF TO BIMINI WITH SECRET LOVER; DI'S NEW SUICIDE ATTEMPT.

As I drove home that day I thought of the Di who had been thrust upon us relentlessly for years, and I wondered if there was really anything new to say about her. With all the articles and books and movies, was there anything left unsaid, unfathomed, unphotographed?

If only I'd known . . .

But I didn't know. I was just another consumer of the mythology that surrounded her. I didn't know that underneath the Princess Di façade was Sandy Keats—a marvelous and deeply passionate woman. And I didn't know that we would fall in love and embark on a beautiful adventure together.

CHAPTER

2

I didn't call Charlie Berns immediately. Brad Emprin left daily messages of increasing gravity on my machine, but I ignored them. I was focused on my resolution of poverty. The more I thought about it, the more I was intrigued by the idea of getting up and walking away from the table.

I scanned the classifieds for cheap apartments. I bought some Kraft macaroni-and-cheese dinners. I took long walks in the hills. I read Gabriel Rossetti's sonnets. I played with the idea of poverty like a Life Saver on the tip of my tongue. But eventually I made the mistake of answering the phone.

Charlie Berns's voice was quiet and soothing, almost soporific. He sounded as if nothing were very important, least of all this phone call. He asked me if I would come to his house to talk. I explained my peculiar financial problem, and he said, as if I hadn't just said what I had said, "How about this afternoon at four?"

And so only a few days after my vow of poverty I found myself driving to the house of a producer to discuss a job I didn't want. I would listen to him, say thank you very much, and leave. And then I would have one of my bagmen call him up and pass.

Charlie Berns lived in the Beverly Hills flats, in a large, neglected Mediterranean with faded stucco and overgrown shrubbery. The lawn and driveway were littered with eucalyptus nuts and palm leaves. There were a number of uncollected throwaway newspapers on the front walk.

The doorbell didn't work. I knocked softly, then more loudly. Eventually, the door opened, and I was confronted with a sleepy-looking man in his mid-to-late fifties. He wore a rumpled sweater, trousers, argyle socks, and bedroom slippers. A pair of reading glasses was perched precariously on the tip of his nose. They were attached to a cord around his neck, but he didn't remove them, looking over the top instead.

"Glad you could make it," he said.

We walked through a cavernous living room, nearly empty of furniture, to a sunporch that gave on the back of the house. There were bleached rattan chairs that had seen better days and a small TV set that was on without the sound. Through the windows you could see the yard and the greenish, algae-infested pool.

"Sit down, please." He motioned to one of the rattan chairs. I removed a stack of old trade papers and sat down. A small puff of dust rose from the cushions.

Charlie Berns looked at me over his glasses, then nodded to himself, as if confirming something that he or I had said. Then he didn't say anything at all for some time. Finally, I said, "Well, look, I really don't know if this is going to work out. I mean, there've already been a bunch of movies about Diana . . ."

"What do you think about her?"

"Think about her?"

"Yes."

"What do you mean?"

"Does she make an impression upon you?"

"An impression? You mean, as a woman?"

"Yes."

"Tell you the truth, I really don't think of her like that."

"That's my point. Nobody does. Because nobody *knows* her. We haven't had the real Diana presented to us, the one who lives and breathes, the one who has color and dimension. I want to tell the real story, the human drama under the surface. The story that nobody knows—her dreams, her fantasies, her innermost desires, what she eats for breakfast . . ."

We were sitting on shabby rattan furniture on a sunporch looking out at a badly neglected swimming pool. The TV reception was so bad it looked as if Phil Donahue were interviewing transvestites in the middle of a blizzard. Three years after winning an Academy Award for Best Picture, Charlie Berns couldn't afford a cleaning lady, a pool man, or cable TV.

I fidgeted in my chair. It must have been ninety-two degrees in there. Large beads of perspiration were dripping down my back. I was not interested in writing a movie about what Princess Di ate for breakfast.

"It's a fabulous idea. Really. I think it'll be terrific. I just don't think I'm the right writer."

"You are, believe me."

"I mean, of all the writers in this town . . ."

"You're everybody's first choice."

"Well, I really don't think . . ."

"You'll want to get some general background reading done before you go over to London for research."

"London?"

"Absolutely. You've got to be there. You've got to soak up the atmosphere, talk to people, see where she lives, where she eats . . . get to know her habitat, if you will."

"I'm not sure I can get away . . ."

"I've made a deal with Rupert Makepeace, the royal columnist for *The London Herald*. He's going to be the technical adviser on this picture. He'll be at your disposal."

Charlie Berns already had me in makeup. His method was very effective—he merely ignored everything you said.

"Rupert Makepeace has been following Diana since she was a kindergarten teacher. He's spent hours stalking her. He's taken pictures of her from trees and moving cars. He wrote the book on Diana."

"Then why isn't he writing the script?"

"I can't get him approved by the network. So when can you start? I'd like to have you over there next week. The Dorchester okay?"

If it hadn't been so hot on that sunporch, I might have said no more emphatically. I was so desperate to get out of there that perhaps I didn't articulate my response clearly enough. It was definitely my impression, however, that I did turn the job down.

But that wasn't Charlie Berns's impression, apparently.

An hour later Brad Emprin was on the phone wanting to talk about deal parameters.

"Brad, I told the guy I didn't want the job."

"You're kidding."

"No. I said no and left."

"That's really weird, because I just had Charlie Berns on the line telling me you had a fabulous meeting. Len, they really want you. Not only Charlie Berns but Norm Hudris at the network. You're the only one on a very short list."

"Isn't that a contradiction in terms?"

"Huh?"

"Being the only one on a list."

There was a pause during which I could hear Brad Emprin's primordial breathing. Semantics was not his long suit, but it took more than a contradiction to slow him down, and so after a moment he started back up again.

"Look, they want this for the November sweeps. We've got leverage. I can back up a truck."

"I don't need the money, remember?"

"Hey, I told you not to sweat the tax-bracket thing. We can defer, we can stick you into fourth quarter 1994. We can bury it so deep your wife's lawyer won't be able to find it with a Geiger counter."

I sighed deeply, audibly, wondering if I should just hang up and unplug the phone. But I sensed that this would not stop Brad Emprin and his gang of thugs. They would converge upon the house, if necessary, lie in wait in the shrubbery, mount a siege until I relented.

"All right. Let me think it over," I said at last.

"What's to think about? I can get you two-fifty with a hundred production bonus, executive-producer credit at another seventy-five, and maybe even two and a half of the gross, minus distribution fee and negative cost."

"Brad, the guy wants me to go to London. I don't know if I can get away right now."

"Why not?"

"This divorce thing . . ."

"You can't take a couple of weeks? It's work. What're they going to say?"

"I've got another court date on the twenty-third."

"You ever hear of a continuance? Come on, you get on a plane. First class. Reclining seats. Individual TV screens. Champagne and chateaubriand . . . ten hours later you're there. I can get you five hundred per diem to walk around with in London. A secretary, researcher, you name it."

I managed to get Brad Emprin off the phone by promising to discuss things with my lawyer and call him back first thing in the morning. But I didn't call my lawyer right away. That was a hundred-dollar phone call, no matter how fast I spoke. Her billing system did not recognize increments of less than a third of an hour.

Instead I got in my car and drove to Gelson's. Supermarkets comfort me in times of stress. There is something about walking through well-stocked aisles of food that is reassuring. I find solace in cornucopia.

I didn't need anything in particular. Since my separation I rarely ate home. But I filled my cart with packages of frozen lasagna, cans of fruit cocktail, rolls of toilet paper, extra-strength aluminum foil, a box of fabric softener, and a container of drain declogger. Just in case.

As I rounded the corner past spices and seasonings and headed down the next aisle, I saw Rivera over by the beer, loading his cart with six-packs of Corona. "Did they nail you on the retreads?" I called.

He didn't answer, but I could see from the anguish in his eyes that he'd taken a beating. Then he grabbed a Corona, opened it with his teeth, and dissolved into the aqueous fluorescent lighting.

I was hallucinating. In Gelson's. Jesus. It got worse. Di was waiting for me at the checkout counter, staring at me from the newspaper rack. The headline read: DI PREGNANT WITH ANDREW'S CHILD?

I read the article in my car, windows tightly shut in spite of the heat.

When the cat's away, the mice will play. In this case, it's a matter of cozying up to your former brother-in-law. With Fergie off gallivanting with wealthy Texans, Diana has been free to indulge her wildest whims and fancies. She's been spotted a number of times with the Duke of York, her estranged husband's younger brother, most recently at Sandringham, where she was supposedly visiting her mother-in-law, the Queen. House personnel, however, report long walks together in the countryside, tête-à-têtes in the stables, jigsaw puzzles at fireside late into the evening. This all goes a long way perhaps to explain the extra pounds that Diana has been sporting lately. Could it be that there is a new bun in the oven? Is the Princess of Wales keeping it in the family? And will the child be a prince or a pauper? Half-brother to Wills and Harry? And where in the succession will he or she be? After Harry, certainly, but before Andrew? Interesting question. Stay tuned . . .

There was a photograph of her getting out of her Ford Granada Scorpio, in jeans, ski jacket, and boots. She looked as trim and graceful as ever to me. But her pale-blue eyes were tinged with sadness, as if she knew that each time the camera clicked, another part of her would be thrown to the wolves.

I sat there staring at her for a long time. Various people, coveting my parking space, waited patiently behind me in the overcrowded garage, but I didn't move. Something very strange and powerful was occurring. Though I didn't know it at the time, that moment was the first ineluctable step in her direction. There in Gelson's parking lot, with my lasagna melting in the backseat, I took that first awkward, hesitant step toward the precipice.

I abandoned the lasagna and went upstairs to Brentano's. There, between COSMOLOGY and DIVORCE, I found DIANA. She had a whole section to herself. I selected a half-dozen books at random and went home to read.

I read most of that night and the next day. By four o'clock the following afternoon, I had devoured over a thousand pages about Diana, Princess of Wales. I knew all about her—her family, her marriage, her charity work, her children.

In one of the books, there were photos of her as a teenager, with her long-limbed, awkward posture and brooding eyes. Even then you could see what it was that made men fall for her. Underneath the decorous façade—the tartan schoolgirl skirts, the cardigan sweaters, the pageboy haircut—was a feline sexuality that belied the innocence of the picture.

And in my exhausted, emotionally precarious state, I was convinced that those eyes were looking right at me, summoning me to come and rescue her, that I, Leonard Schecter, had been chosen to ride to her castle on my white horse and whisk her away.

I reached over for the bedside phone and dialed my lawyer to ask about a continuance.

She was, as usual, refreshingly direct.

"Sure. We can continue this forever if you want. And meanwhile you'll continue to write her that enormous temporary support check every month. She'll be thrilled. Not even this judge would award that amount on a permanent basis. And what's more, you'll be jacking up your income figures for the year so that when we income-average, you'll come out worse."

"What if I deferred the money?"

"Are you kidding? Her lawyer'll smell that out in no time, and then you'll be looking at three pages in the brief on intent to defraud. This judge already doesn't like you."

"Am I allowed to leave the country?"

"Leonard, as long as you keep writing those checks every month, you can go to Mars as far as she's concerned."

"Thanks."

"Anytime."

She clicked me off her speakerphone, activating the automatic billing machine, which measured the duration of all phone calls, incoming and outgoing, and cross-referenced it with the client number.

I got out of bed—demented, groggy, my eyes strained—and walked to the window. I looked out at the early-summer light, the dull, brown water-parched hillside, the flat contours of Southern California. It looked stale and without dimension to me. There was no magic here. There was only the smog-gray sky and Section 29 of the Los Angeles County Superior Court.

There was nothing here for me at the moment but a lot of macaroni and cheese. I thought of Rivera and what he would do in my frame of mind. I had no doubt that he would get in his truck with the retread tires and head off into the sunset. He wouldn't look back.

I smiled. For the first time in months. Then I picked up the phone, called Brad Emprin, and told him to back up a truck.

CHAPTER

3

The first-class cabin of the Virgin Atlantic 747 was nearly empty. I sat in my recliner, a laptop Toshiba and a pile of books on the seat beside me, and let myself be plied with chateaubriand and champagne. The two hostesses, Alexandra and Phoebe, fussed over me. The co-pilot, Nigel, came out for a chat. The London Philharmonic gurgled in my headphones.

I drifted off into the ethereal hush of the endless polar day. I was thirty-eight thousand feet off the ground, somewhere over Greenland, buoyed by Bernoulli's principle, in good hands. There was nothing to worry about up here. I dozed, lulled by the hum of the Rolls-Royce engines and the cumulative effect of three glasses of Piper Heidsieck.

It is a comment on my life that leaving Los Angeles for an indefinite absence did not require a great deal of forethought. I merely left a note for my cleaning lady, stopped the paper, and called a taxi. I didn't have the stomach to phone my lawyer. Instead I sent her a fax asking her to get me a continuance. Then I wrote out the exorbitant monthly support check to the Petitioner, postdated it, and put it in the mail. Rivera would have tied it to a rock and thrown it through her window.

Brad Emprin had indeed backed up a truck, but I barely listened as he rattled off the deal points in his overaspirated nasal voice. As far as I was concerned, it wasn't really my money anyway. I was just handling it briefly before signing it over.

The paid-up suite at the Dorchester and the five-hundred-dollar per diem were safe from the Petitioner's dragnet. In my wallet were thirty-five crisp hundred-dollar bills, an advance for the first week's meal money, and the office and home phone numbers for Rupert Makepeace.

Before leaving, I was asked to take a meeting at the network. It would be strictly pro forma, Charlie Berns assured me. We sat in black leather armchairs, glasses of Perrier in front of us on the ebony free-form coffee table, and listened to Norm Hudris, the vice president for movies, West Coast, tell us how excited he was about this project.

"This is terrific. I can't tell you how thrilled we are about this. Really."

Charlie Berns smiled and nodded. I smiled and nodded, too. Norm Hudris went on at some length. "There really hasn't been the definitive film on Diana. All the others have been so superficial. They've only touched the surface. We need to know who she is . . . her quirks and vulnerabilities, the inside of her soul . . ."

We continued to smile and nod until it was over and we all walked together to the elevator and were shaking hands. Norm Hudris looked at me and, with an effusion of sincerity, said, "I know you're going to do a terrific job." Then he shook my hand solemnly, as if to seal our bargain with a blood oath.

Charlie Berns walked me to my car. He had said very little during the meeting, but when we got to my car, we stopped, and, for the first time, he said something personal to me.

"A couple of years ago I was making a picture in Yugoslavia. It was a thirty-million-dollar production. The studio was very nervous. The night before we started shooting I got a phone call from the studio in Los Angeles. Do you know what they said?"

"What?"

"They said, 'Charlie, get it over the plate, but keep it low.' "

"No kidding."

"Uh-huh. There you are in the bottom of the ninth. Bases loaded, two outs, the count three-and-two. And they come out to the mound and tell you that. Have a nice trip."

And he turned and walked away. I watched him walk over to an old 560 SEL. Like everything else about Charlie Berns, it looked like it had seen better days.

As I lay back now in my first-class recliner, riding the pleasant champagne buzz, I thought about what Charlie Berns had said about getting the ball over but keeping it low. I wondered if it was profound in a Zen-like sort of way or simply another banal anecdote about show business. I couldn't get a handle on this guy. I kept wondering how, in only a few years, a man went from winning an Academy Award to hustling TV miniseries. In the strange ecology of Hollywood careers, fortunes went in and out like the tide. But you would think that a man could ride the crest of a Best Picture Oscar for a long time. You would think that he could afford to have his pool cleaned.

In any event, Charlie Berns and I were in business together. For better or for worse. We had contracted with the network to deliver the inside of Diana's soul. And I was on my way to do the job, a hitman with a Toshiba laptop and a per diem.

I closed my eyes and drifted. In one of the books I had read, there was a photo of Diana standing at the edge of a field somewhere in the undulant English countryside, dressed in jeans and boots, a ski jacket zipped up tight. Her hands were stuffed deep in the pockets and her hips jutted out slightly to give her tall, leggy frame some relief. Her lips were pursed, her eyes liquid and distant. And there in the middle of that perfect English face was the nose. It was just a tiny bit too big for the rest of her features. A millimeter or two, at most.

I adored that nose. It redeemed the flawlessness of her beauty. It was the sprinkle of garlic in the sauce, the speck in the marble, the tremolo in the flute solo. Without it she would have been Princess Grace—a monument in stone. Her nose gave her back to us.

The throttling back of the engines jarred me from my champagne stupor. It was still daylight. Phoebe was standing over me with a hot towel and a tray of mints.

"Did you have a pleasant nap, sir?"

"Yes. Great. Thanks."

"We'll be on the ground straightaway. Would you buckle up, please?"

At that moment, I would have done anything Phoebe asked me to do. She may not have been Diana, but she wasn't bad. Her nose was trim and small, with a little tinge of redness on the aquiline tip that made her look as if she had a perpetual head cold.

We exchanged smiles. She helped me find my seat belt and return my recliner to the normal position.

I felt the plane descending through the thick cloud layer. I had no idea what time it was. Or even what day it was. My watch was still on L.A. time, and I was trying to calculate the difference when Nigel's mellifluous voice filled the cabin.

"Ladies and gentlemen, in just a few minutes we'll be landing at London's Heathrow Airport, where the local time is . . ."

I reset my watch and looked out the window as we banked over the countryside west of London and came in for an impeccable landing. A light rain was falling from a blotchy gray sky. The jet glided smoothly down the rain-slick runways to the gate. Nigel, Phoebe, and Alexandra wished me a pleasant stay in England.

The customs officer made me turn the laptop on. As I booted the machine up, he asked, "What do you do for a living, sir?" As he chatted away in this amiable tone, his eyes searched my laptop for evidence of plastique.

"I'm a writer."

"So you're a writer, are you? I've always wanted to write myself."

"Then why the fuck don't you."

The words came out of my mouth before I could stop them. He looked up at me sharply, as if he had in fact found a bomb in my laptop.

"Sorry," I said quickly. "It's just that people always say that when you tell them you're a writer, and I'm tired of hearing it. I mean, when you tell people you're a customs officer, do they say, 'I've always wanted to be a customs officer myself'? No. They don't, do they?"

He snapped my laptop closed and waved me through without welcoming me to England.

My cabdriver was a Pakistani in a Rolling Stones T-shirt who drove perilously fast on the M4 motorway into London. I had trouble getting any traction with my ass against the well-worn leather of the seat. When I saw the speedometer top eighty miles an hour, I said, "I'm in no hurry."

He smiled, ignored me, kept the cab at eighty.

"Did you hear what I said?"

He nodded, smiled again, and said, "Dorchester."

"You're going too fast," I said. "Slow down."

"Dorchester, very nice hotel."

I leaned forward in the seat and shouted, "If you don't slow this goddamn cab down I'm not going to pay you."

Apparently this got through, because he slowed down to seventy. I am normally a polite, nonconfrontational type of person, but I had been in England for less than an hour and had already had two altercations. There is something about the indirect, passive-aggressive manner of the British that brings out a mean streak in me.

I leaned back in my seat, watched the gray red-brick suburbs of west London roll by, and made myself promise to relax. I was out of the jurisdiction, for the moment at least, of the Los Angeles County Superior Court, with a room at the Dorchester and five hundred dollars a day to play with. There was no reason to be hostile.

My suite at the Dorchester was enormous. The furniture was Louis something, and there were oils of pastoral scenes on the walls. Fresh flowers and yet another bottle of champagne awaited me.

There was a large TV, a VCR, a CD player, and a fully stocked minibar in the Chippendale armoire.

Charlie Berns certainly knew how to spend other people's money. He had gotten the network to load up Brad Emprin's truck to the hilt.

It was a little past two in the afternoon. I was jet-lagged and hung over from the flight, in no frame of mind to think about working. And I was too wired to sleep. So I bounced the champagne cork off the cerulean ceiling and poured a glass to take the edge off the hangover.

Two glasses later, feeling considerably better, I went out for a walk. The rain had stopped, and the city was ripe with summer smells. The trees were in their full leafy green, a green that you didn't see in California except on Astroturf. The layered light imbued objects with texture and a sense of complexity. Like all great cities, London had its secrets.

I walked over to Green Park, where I found Rivera sitting on a bench eating sunflower seeds. I sat down beside him.

"Good trip?" I asked.

"You kidding? Twelve hours like a sardine." He scowled.

"They send you coach?"

"What do you think?"

"So what are you going to do?"

"Get laid."

And he got up and trudged off in the general direction of Piccadilly. I watched him walk away, his hands thrust deep into his jeans pockets, his sombrero down over his eyes at a rakish angle, until he blended into the greenness and vanished.

I sat there for a long time on that bench and thought about Rivera, the Petitioner, Charlie Berns—and Diana. I could already feel her presence. There, on the other side of the park, was Constitution Hill and Buckingham Palace, where Di's in-laws lived. Next door was Clarence House, where Charles stayed when he was in London. And behind me and to my right was Kensington Palace, where Di lived.

I turned and faced in her direction. She was only a few miles away, across Hyde Park, with Wills and Harry and her equerry, her ladies-in-waiting, her detective, her Elton John albums.

I sat there for a long time, drifting in and out of my jet-lagged stupor, staring vacantly across the green expanse. I felt like Lee Harvey Oswald in the window of the Texas Book Depository waiting for the motorcade. Except I wasn't going to shoot Diana. I was going to deliver the inside of her soul to Norm Hudris.

CHAPTER

4

Rupert Makepeace sounded put out when I telephoned him the following morning. His voice had a peevish tone, as if he were inconvenienced just by having to talk to me. Eventually I would realize that this was his usual way of dealing with people, but after that first phone call in London I wasn't looking forward to meeting him.

"Are you on an expense account?" he asked.

"Yes."

"In that case, we should meet at Waltons. It's one of her favorite restaurants. Of course, she won't be there today. She's off to some leper fund-raising luncheon in Clapham. We're not even sending a photographer. Half past twelve suit you?"

"Fine," I replied. Then, "How will I know you?"

"I'll be the only one besides you who'll be underdressed."

And he hung up. I walked over to the closet and examined my

wardrobe. He was right. The best I could come up with was a lightweight Dacron suit that I had bought on sale at Bullock's. I chose a green silk tie to go with the suit and my only decent pair of shoes, Bally loafers, which, like Charlie Berns's Mercedes, had retained a modicum of elegance despite the mileage.

Rupert Makepeace had assumed that I knew where Waltons was. There was no phone book in the Regency desk or the armoire. Guests at the Dorchester presumably didn't use phone books. I called down to the concierge, who told me that the restaurant was on Walton Street in Brompton.

"Would you like me to book a table for you, sir?"

"Do you think it's necessary?"

"I should think so, yes."

"Two at twelve-thirty. Schecter."

"Certainly, Mr. Spector."

"It's Schecter. S—C—H—E—C—T—E—R."

I arrived at Waltons at twelve-thirty on the nose to find more than half the tables empty. Nevertheless, the maître d' checked his book to confirm my reservation.

"That's Mr. Spector, is it?"

"Schecter. S—C—H—E—C—T—E—R."

"Of course, sir. Right this way, please."

He led me to a small table near the kitchen.

"Is this the best table you have?" I asked.

"I'm afraid so, sir. The others are all booked."

"I'll be joined by a Mr. Makepeace."

The maître d's face darkened perceptibly. It would be the last time I ever mentioned Rupert Makepeace's name in London, for, as I was to learn, Rupert Makepeace was persona non grata in many of the best places.

He was also not very punctual. I sat alone and sipped an uninspiring martini, watching the desultory luncheon conversations at the better tables. Well-dressed women sat over their watercress-and-foie-gras salads and spoke in the limpid, indifferent manner of the bored and wealthy.

It was nearly one o'clock before Rupert Makepeace breezed in off Walton Street, wearing a Burberry raincoat in spite of the heat and carrying a worn leather attaché case. He stood there filling up the doorway with his bulk, scanning the restaurant. The maître d' nodded curtly to him. Rupert Makepeace nodded curtly back and said, in a booming voice, "That's all right, Victor, I can find my own way, thank you."

He walked directly to my table, sat down, and said, his voice still loud enough for the entire restaurant to hear, "Well, I see they've given us the Siberia table by the kitchen. How lovely. We shall be able to smell the food as it comes out the door. Rupert Makepeace. How do you do?"

He offered a large, soft hand across the table. Underneath his raincoat was a tweed sports jacket and a sweater over a shirt and tie. He was dressed for Scotland in December instead of London in June.

"They don't like me here, as you can see. I've been on Victor's shit list for years, ever since I got the table next to Di and Fergie and wrote a piece about their luncheon. Do you know what they were discussing?"

I shook my head.

"Premenstrual water retention. I see you've ordered a martini. I should have warned you. They're rather limp, aren't they?"

"Yes."

He raised his hand peremptorily, and a waiter hurried over. "Bring me a Bass please." Then he turned back to me, and said, "So, you're here to tell all about Diana, are you?"

"Not exactly . . ."

"All has not as yet been told. And may never be. And I'll tell you why. I'm the only one who knows all, and they'll never print a book of mine in England. Every publisher in London has been told by the Palace not to have anything to do with me. I shall have to publish in France. And they pay dreadfully over there. Do you have an agent in New York?"

"I have one in Los Angeles."

"Really. Would he be interested in a book on Diana? The real McCoy, as you say."

"Well, he's a film and television agent."

"Is he? Do they pay well?"

"Very well."

"I shall have to ring him after lunch."

He picked up the menu.

"I suggest the prosciutto and melon or the scallops as an appetizer. The foie gras is from a tin."

We ordered, and as we waited for the food, Rupert Makepeace told me about his history with the Princess of Wales.

"I go back with Diana to the days when she was a kindergarten teacher in Pimlico. I knew the photographer who snapped the picture of her in that diaphanous skirt. He was up a tree and got the sun in back of her to highlight those splendid legs. Apparently this was the photo that got Charles's attention in the first place. He was always a randy little sod, running around dipping the royal scepter into half of London. But it was no doubt the thought of those long legs wrapped tightly around his middle that got him to make a move. They're awfully sex-obsessed, the Windsors, the whole lot of them. They may be German but they're not anesthetized. Even Queen Victoria was voracious. I suspect that it wasn't typhoid that did in poor old Albert but too much sex. How're your scallops?"

"Fine."

"Of course, you could have gotten twenty-five to one against her back then. She was a typical Sloane living in Earl's Court with two friends, making pocket money by flat-cleaning and baby-sitting. She was Andrew's contemporary, actually. Charles barely knew she existed, even though she was brought up on the fringes of the royal family. Her father was an equerry to the Queen, you know. But Diana wasn't taken very seriously at the time. Charles no doubt saw her at the odd regatta or polo match. She was just another one of those vapid, well-brought-up society girls without a brain in her head. Then he saw the photo. And suddenly he was ringing her and inviting her to Balmoral to meet the Queen. Amazing what a shot of blood to the gonads will do to a man, isn't it?"

I nodded, watching him cut small, almost surgical slices of veal florentine with his knife. He was the kind of man who could eat and talk at the same time without seeming to chew, a particularly British skill. He ordered another Bass ale. It was very warm in the restaurant, but he kept his jacket and sweater on.

"Interesting, isn't it, how the entire history of the British royal family was changed by one photograph? As far as I'm concerned it was as important as Nelson's victory at Trafalgar. That depends, of course, what happens next. Nobody knows for sure, but I have my theories. This Berns fellow. Does he pay on time?"

"Sure."

"Well, he's promised me some money, to be some sort of consultant to you. Is that it?"

"Yes. That's why I'm over here. To do research on Diana for a miniseries."

"A miniseries?"

"Four hours, on two successive nights."

Rupert Makepeace put his fork down and looked at me, as if for the first time. Then, "You're not writing a book?"

"No. I'm writing a movie. Didn't Charlie explain that to you?"

"Well, I had this fax from him last week sometime. I don't know that he said anything about a movie. How extraordinary. Do they know who's going to be in it?"

"I have to write it first."

"You know who would be perfect—what's her name, that thin, willowy one with the thick lips . . . ?"

"Julia Roberts."

"Is that her name? She has that badly used look, like the wronged heroine in a Victorian novel. Though I should hardly think of Diana as a victim. She has everything—the title, the money, the palace, and she doesn't have to sleep with Charles anymore. Not that they ever did spend a great deal of time horizontally, mind you. Prince Harry may very well have been the last shot, the Parthian volley, as it were. Shall we have a postprandial cognac?"

"I'll pass. But please go ahead."

"You're not much of a drinker, are you?"

"Well, you know how it is, with the jet lag, you have one drink and you're on the floor."

He snapped his fingers. One of the waiters turned and started to approach, but Rupert Makepeace stopped him in his tracks with a bellowing, "A cognac please. Courvoisier V.S.O.P."

"Well, I suppose you ought to meet her," he said, taking out a pack of cigarettes. "Cigarette?"

"No thanks. Meet her?"

"Yes. Though you'll find that she photographs better than she looks."

"Can I really meet her?"

"It'll take a bit of doing, but I suppose it can be arranged. She's been invited to a cocktail party at the Togolese embassy this evening. She doesn't ordinarily do embassy parties, but she's a friend of the Togolese ambassador and she's doing him a favor, giving his party some cachet. They go to the same colonic-irrigation clinic in St. John's Wood."

"Colonic irrigation?"

"Enemas. At two hundred pounds a crack. She's been doing it for years. I don't suppose you have anything better to wear."

"I'm afraid not."

He looked at his watch, scowled slightly, then said, "Since we only have time for off-the-peg, you'll do best at Harrods."

"Wait a second. I'm going to this cocktail party tonight? At the Togolese embassy? To meet Diana?"

"That depends upon whether Lady Poulstice has found an escort yet. As of last night she had been turned down by at least three men. Even with Diana present, Togolese cocktail parties are not a hot ticket. I shall ring you at the Dorchester before six. In the meantime, you must pop by Harrods and pick something up in navy blue or dark gray."

"What if Lady Poulstice already has a date?"

"Well, then, you'll have a new suit, for which you'll find good use, I should think."

The bill came to £134 with tip. Rupert Makepeace took Charlie Berns's phone number, asked if he could phone collect, and promised to be at my disposal for as long as I needed him.

· · ·

The suit was a dark-gray or light-black Cardin knockoff that the salesman at the Harrods men's shop described as charcoal. At £260, it was the cheapest dark suit in the store, and it fit. More or less. The sleeves were a quarter of an inch too long. I would have to be careful around the dip.

I took a cab back to the Dorchester, hung my suit up, and collapsed exhausted across the bed. An hour later the phone woke me. When I picked up, I heard Rupert Makepeace's cannonade in the earpiece.

"Well, it seems you're in luck. Lady Poulstice is desolate this evening. You're to pick her up at half past seven. She lives in a mews off Eaton Square in Belgravia. Don't eat the hors d'oeuvres with your hands. Use the toothpick."

"What?"

"You Americans tend to gobble up the petits fours with your fingers. Try to refrain from gobbling if you can. Though I'm not at all sure just what the Togolese serve at their cocktail parties. My rule of thumb is don't eat anything shiny or with hair on it."

"Are you going to be there?"

"Oh, heavens, no. I'd never get in the door. Her detective won't let me near her."

"Do I bow to her?"

"Of course. She's royalty. And if you address her, you address her as 'Your Royal Highness' the first time. Afterward as 'Ma'am.' Not *madam*, but *ma'am*. Like John Wayne."

"You mean, I can just go up and talk to her?"

"If you can manage it. Though I suspect you'll have to queue up behind the Togolese. They adore her. They issue postage stamps with her on them. Well, good luck, then."

"Thanks. Listen, I appreciate your help."

"I'm at your disposal. Please don't ring before ten A.M."

And he hung up. I stumbled into the bathroom with the tile sink and the ivory-handled water taps, the neatly folded towels with the raised Dorchester crest, the toilet with the soft foam-rubber seat, the tray full of tiny bottles of perfume, cologne, aftershave, and shampoo.

I showered and shaved and put a dab of eau de cologne behind my ears. I put on a pair of Calvin Klein briefs and a light-blue telegenic shirt.

My new charcoal suit did not look as good on me as it had at Harrods. They had those trick mirrors that made you look taller and slimmer. I chose the only other tie I had with me, a beige-and-blue-striped number with a small but prominently displayed gravy stain. Then I slipped on the Bally loafers, buffed them with a damp towel, and went downstairs to catch a cab.

CHAPTER

5

Lady Poulstice's house in Eaton Mews was one of those Georgian houses with the black wrought-iron fence and the brass door knocker. Lady Poulstice's maid admitted me into a small parlor full of bric-a-brac and guarded by a dyspeptic Scottish terrier who watched me as if to make sure I wasn't going to pocket any of the miniature porcelain pieces scattered about. We glared at each other for a few minutes. Then I lost interest, and so apparently did he. By the time Lady Poulstice made her appearance twenty minutes later, the dog had fallen asleep and was snoring and farting contrapuntally.

"Oh, I see you've met Cecil. I hope he's been behaving. How do you do?" She put out her hand, and I, unsure whether to shake it or kiss it, wound up doing a combination of both.

"Nice to meet you," I said.

She looked me over cursorily and pursed her lips slightly, repressing a frown. She didn't seem thrilled with what she saw. I felt the same way about her. We would both have to do, given the circumstances.

Lady Poulstice, or Gwen, as she announced, was a woman deep into her fifties, with a thin, angular face, distrusting eyes, and aristocratic cheekbones. She spoke with the kind of singsong inflection that made everything sound like a question.

"Well, I suppose we should be on our way? You're parked in front?"

"I came by cab."

"Oh?" she said, her voice dropping an octave. We stood there for a moment, two feet apart in her rococo parlor with her flatulent dog, avoiding eye contact, until she uttered, "Well, I expect we'll find a taxi in the King's Road."

As we walked the several blocks to the King's Road, I tried to make small talk.

"So . . . do you do colonic irrigation as well?"

"Sorry?"

"I thought maybe you went to the same specialist in St. John's Wood that Diana and the Togolese ambassador go to."

"I'm afraid not."

That was the extent of our conversation until the taxi pulled up in front of the embassy. She turned to me with the familiarity of a wife and said, "Let's make this an early evening, shall we? After an hour or so they start playing this dreadful high-life music, and one is asked to dance."

We entered past a row of security people in better suits than mine. They looked me carefully up and down as Gwen displayed her printed invitation and had her name checked against the guest list.

The room was large and already crowded. Diana was apparently a big draw. There were a number of Africans in native dress and an assortment of foreign languages being spoken. Gwen Poulstice navigated us to the bar, where she requested a gin gimlet and I, heeding Rupert Makepeace's advice, asked for a beer.

She introduced me to some friends. "Geoffrey and Annabel.

This is Leonard Spector. He's an American writer. From Hollywood. Isn't that fascinating?"

Geoffrey and Annabel smiled dimly with just a minimalistic movement of their cheek muscles, as if they had food stuck in their teeth.

"So you're a writer, are you?" Geoffrey said.

The evening limped along in a series of tight-lipped rhetorical conversations. At one point I had a discussion with Kodjo Kponvi, the visa-and-immigration officer at the embassy.

"So you're the visa-and-immigration officer?" I said. I was learning fast.

"Oh, yes. Most definitely."

"Do you have a lot of requests to visit Togo this time of year?"

"Oh, yes. Quite. There are the falls at Dapango. Quite lovely, I assure you. Do you know Clint Eastwood?"

"No, I don't."

"He lives in Hollywood, doesn't he?"

"He lives in Carmel, actually. That's up the coast a few hundred miles."

"Splendid. What about Madonna?"

"She lives in New York."

"Splendid."

His eyes, like everyone else's, kept flitting to the door. We all were wondering when she would show up. It was past nine o'clock, and there was still no Diana.

"Do you think she'll be here?" I asked.

"Oh, most definitely. She is quite good friends with our ambassador."

And then suddenly she was there. A hush enveloped the room. All conversations came to an abrupt halt. There was a collective intake of breath as she entered, accompanied by her detective. The crowd made way for her, parting in her path to allow the Togolese ambassador to greet her.

He bowed deeply from the waist, then took her hand in his and said something I couldn't hear. She smiled her incandescent smile and tilted her head slightly. I watched avidly as her tongue brushed gently against her lower lip, a little nervous gesture that I would come to love.

The ambassador led her to the bar. She stopped on the way to greet people she knew. Bows and curtsies attended her. The smile, the tilted head, the few words, the tongue brushing the lower lip.

She was wearing a satin jacket over a lace dress, with a simple strand of pearls. In her heels, she towered over the Togolese ambassador by nearly half a foot. The security people kept their eyes on the guests as we formed a semicircle around her. We all stared as Diana sipped a glass of mineral water and chatted with the ambassador.

Kodjo Kponvi, standing beside me, kept shaking his head and uttering little sighs. Finally the band, which up until then had been softly playing Gershwin and Cole Porter, broke into loud African music. "High life," said Kodjo Kponvi.

The ambassador led Diana to the center of our semicircle. He bowed one more time. Diana smiled and took his hand. We all watched as the Princess of Wales danced the high life with the Honorable Kwami Mbtomo, ambassador of the Republic of Togo to the Court of St. James's.

She swung her hips decorously but not without a hint of naughtiness, as if to say, *I may be married to a Windsor, but I'm not a complete stiff.* The guests loved her. They stood clapping with the music, as Diana and the ambassador danced the "Même Mère, Même Père" high life.

"Many people in Togo are related," Kodjo Kponvi explained. "So when you introduce your brother or your sister, you say, if they are indeed from the same mother and father, '*Même mère, même père.*' "

"Really?"

"Yes. A man may take many wives in Togo. Why not?"

"Why not."

My eyes never left Diana as I listened to Kodjo Kponvi explain Togolese marriage customs. I was mesmerized. My head was swimming. I was a goner from the moment I saw her tilt her head.

When the music ended, there was a smattering of polite applause, and the ambassador led Diana to the place of honor, near the window, where an informal receiving line developed.

One by one, people approached, bowed or curtsied, and exchanged a few words under the scrutiny of the security people. The band went back to Gershwin.

I got in line with Kodjo Kponvi, having lost Gwen Poulstice to Geoffrey and Annabel some time ago.

"You see," said Kodjo Kponvi, "I have a brother named Koffi. That's because he was born on Thursday. If you're born on Monday or Friday your name is Kodjo. That's why there are so many Kodjos. The ambassador was born on Tuesday so he is named Kwami. My brother Koffi and I have the same mother, but not the same father. So he is not my brother *même mère, même père*, you see . . ."

We inched closer to her.

"So Koffi is *même mère* but not *même père*, and so I would call him my brother but not my brother *même mère, même père* . . ."

The security people gave me a very thorough looking over as I stood in the on-deck circle waiting my turn. They undoubtedly picked up on the gravy stain. I had the feeling that if I made a sudden move toward my pocket, they would be all over me.

I did have a concealed weapon in my trousers, but it wasn't what they were looking for. Nor was Diana, I imagine, as I stepped up to the plate. Her eyes met mine directly. I smiled, forgetting to bow, then made a quick, remedial bow and said, "Your Royal Highness."

"Good evening."

"I'm Leonard Schecter."

"How do you do, Mr. Schecter."

She offered her hand, and I took it, held it in mine for perhaps a moment too long. But I wasn't about to let go of that hand and with it my connection to her, flimsy as it may have been, there in front of the hundred odd guests and security people with the band playing Gershwin in high-life tempo and thirty more people behind me waiting their turn. For the moment it was just the two of us, all alone, face-to-face, nose-to-nose.

From close up, the nose was even more adorable than I had imagined. I wanted to reach out and caress it, but the security guys would have had me spread-eagled on the floor with their knees in my kidneys in a matter of seconds. As it was, her detective was starting to stir impatiently as I continued to hold her hand and gaze into her nose.

It was at that moment, the moment when the banal was about to pass into the absurd, that fate intervened. The band broke into a bluesy rendition of "Embraceable You." I took it at face value. I asked her to dance.

There was a suspended moment of reaction, during which the people around her, trained to respond with hair-trigger speed to assaults on her person, attempted to respond to this assault on her sensibility from an American with a gravy stain on his tie. Throats were cleared. Feet were shuffled. Eyes darted back and forth to see who was going to step forward and deal with this situation.

It was her detective, finally, who, clearing his throat once more, said, "I'm sorry, sir, but the Princess is on a rather tight schedule . . ."

"It's all right, Donald. I would be delighted to dance with Mr. Schecter," she said.

And with that she smiled at me and tilted her head. I smiled back at Diana and, as I led her to the center of the floor, I caught a glimpse of Rivera, standing by the bar, drinking tequila from the bottle. I resisted the impulse to wave at him, as I resisted the impulse to wave at Gwen Poulstice, who was standing there watching with one eyebrow raised at least three inches above her forehead.

People parted in our wake as they had for her and the Togolese ambassador. The band started the number from the top. Taking her lightly in my arms, I began a sort of free-form fox-trot. Diana followed my lead superbly.

"Bravo, Mr. Schecter. Didn't you just adore the look on Donald's face?" There was a tone of schoolgirl mischief in her voice. "No one's ever done that, you know. Just asked me to dance in a receiving line like that. Of course, Charles would have had a cow, and, frankly, Donald's not much better. I'm sure to hear about it tomorrow."

We chatted as if there were no one else in the room and not, in fact, a hundred deathly quiet people staring intently at us. It was the most sublime two minutes of my life. It wasn't so much what we talked about that mattered. It was what wasn't said, what was left unarticulated in the interstices of our conversation.

"Now what brings you to England, Mr. Schecter?"

"Leonard, please . . . ma'am."

"Shall we make a deal? Suppose I call you Leonard and you drop the 'ma'am.' "

"Okay."

"Are you working here or just visiting, Leonard?"

I certainly wasn't going to tell her the truth—that I had come over here to turn her life story into a four-hour miniseries for American television. And so once more I took a bold leap into the unpremeditated. I thought of Helen of Troy. Don't ask me why, but at that precise moment, the *Iliad* popped into my mind, and I said, without any forethought whatsoever, "I'm here to write an epic poem."

"Oh, lovely."

"It may or may not have rhyming couplets."

"I see. And what's the subject of your poem?"

"You."

I was improvising fast now, just trying to keep the balls in the air. Words came out of my mouth spontaneously, as if some alter ego were driving me to say these things.

Diana actually blushed. I can't begin to tell you how disarming it was to see a flush of pale pink rise to her cheeks. I could actually feel the heat beneath the satin underneath my fingers.

"I'm going to call it *The Dianiad*."

The band played on. We danced in silence, stealing quick little glimpses at each other. We could have danced all night, but unfortunately "Embraceable You" ground to a stop, on cue from Donald, undoubtedly.

There was another smattering of applause—louder, I believe, than the ovation given the Togolese ambassador when he had concluded *his* dance. We stood together, nodding to the crowd, and

Diana did a little mock curtsy to the ambassador that was greeted with nervous laughter from the crowd.

I returned her to Donald with a little mock bow of my own.

"Thank you so much, Leonard," she said.

"It was indeed a pleasure."

"And good luck with your poem." She smiled and offered her hand once more. I took it and felt the lingering pressure of her fingers around mine. Lingering. Yes. It was more than a pro-forma handshake. I swear.

The next thing I can remember was standing with Kodjo Kponvi and hearing him say, "Nicely done, old boy."

"Huh?"

"Splendid."

"What was that?"

"Your dance with the Princess of Wales. May I make a small suggestion, however?"

"Sure."

"Perhaps dancing lessons would be useful. I would be honored."

He gave me his card and promised to ring me at the Dorchester.

In the cab on the way back to Eaton Mews, Lady Gwen Poulstice was particularly icy to me. I could tell she was pissed because I had become the talk of the party, *her* party, which I had tagged along to. And she did not consider me worthy of being talked about.

As we pulled up to number 61, she said, "Well, I suppose I should thank you for escorting me."

"I suppose you should," I responded.

"I must tell you, however, that your behavior was completely untoward."

"Really?"

"One does not ask the Princess of Wales to dance under those circumstances. You're fortunate that she was in good humor."

"Thanks for pointing that out to me, Gwen. Maybe we can do this again sometime?" She looked at me as if I had asked her for a blowjob and declined my offer to walk her to the door.

CHAPTER

6

Rupert Makepeace's stentorian voice roared at me through the phone. "Did you actually *ask* Diana to *dance* at the *Togolese* embassy last *night?*"

I was still half asleep, befogged in a cloud bank somewhere over Newfoundland. It took me several moments to figure out where I was and what I was doing there. By then, Rupert Makepeace had gone on to say, "I had Gwen Poulstice on the phone shortly after *eight.* Then the paper rang wanting to know just *who* Diana's dancing partner was and was this a *new* beau or someone from the past, and why *I* wasn't at the Togolese embassy last night. And could I *please* get on top of the story . . . What in *God's* name is going on?"

I looked at the digital bedside clock: 8:48 A.M.

"I thought you didn't want to talk to anybody before ten in the morning," I said.

"Leon . . ."

"It's Leonard."

"Leonard, spare me your sarcasm. Please. It's too early. Now what happened? At the very least, I expect an exclusive story."

"I fell in love."

There was a long, breathy pause. For a moment, it appeared as if Rupert Makepeace were at a loss for words. But only for a moment. Rupert Makepeace, as I was to learn, was never at a loss for words.

"Have you had breakfast yet?"

"No. You woke me up."

"The Savoy Grill. In an hour."

"Huh?"

"There may be reporters already watching the Dorchester. Do you know where it is?"

"No."

"It's in the Savoy Hotel. On the Strand."

"Look, I don't really eat breakfast . . ."

"They have excellent kippers and eggs. I'll see you there. By ten, the latest. If you see a reporter outside the hotel, go back up to your room and ring me straightaway. I'll explain to you how to get out through the service exit."

And he hung up. His words still ringing in my ears, I lay back in bed and tried to close my eyes again, but it was to no avail. The fragile memory of the evening was rapidly disintegrating, exploded in the earpiece of the telephone. I did not want to go eat kippers with Rupert Makepeace. I wanted to lie in bed and think about Diana. I wanted to relive our moment, redance our dance, savor the aftertaste of the entire evening.

But I got up, showered, dressed, and took a cab to the Savoy Grill. This time Rupert Makepeace wasn't late. He was waiting for me, ensconced in a small dark booth in the corner of the room, a tabloid newspaper and a pint of Guinness beside him.

"Were you followed?" he asked as I slid into the booth.

"I don't know. I didn't look."

"You have to be very careful."

"I'm a writer doing research for a TV miniseries, not a goddamn CIA agent."

He handed me the tabloid. There was a headline—WHO'S

THIS?—and a photo of me leaving the embassy with Lady Poulstice. The story read:

> At a cocktail reception last night at the Togolese Embassy in Mayfair a mystery man was spotted dancing with the Princess of Wales. They were observed in animated conversation during the dance, a fox-trot, played by the band after Diana danced the usual ceremonial high life with the Honorable Kwami Mbtomo, the Togolese Ambassador. Earlier, as Diana was greeting party guests, the mystery man had asked her to dance, a highly unusual and, according to Palace sources, frowned-upon practice. "One never asks the Princess of Wales or any other member of the Royal Family to dance at a diplomatic reception without clearance through her office in advance," said a spokesman at Diana's Kensington Palace office. Nevertheless, the Princess was asked and accepted the invitation, and the couple danced and chatted tête-à-tête for over two minutes in front of a group of nearly 100 guests. Diana's dancing partner arrived apparently with Lady Gwen Poulstice, the estranged wife of the Third Marquess of Abington, but his name was not on the guest list. Lady Poulstice has not returned calls this morning. According to Geoffrey and Annabel Fitzhugh, who were present at the party, the mystery man is not an intimate acquaintance of Lady Poulstice. He is, as far as they know, an American writer visiting London, who escorted Lady Poulstice to the reception as a favour to a mutual friend. The Princess of Wales's Press Secretary, Maude Connaught, had no comment except to say that the Princess was free to dance with whomever she chose. We, however, are left with the question: Can this be the start of something new?

"Didn't you realize that asking the Princess of Wales to dance at a cocktail party isn't done?"

"Why do they have a band playing if you're not supposed to dance?"

"What did you talk about?"

"Interested?"

His features contorted into an expression of profound impatience. "Leonard, we're working together, remember? We're collaborating."

"Yes. On a movie. But this isn't the movie. This is my life."

"Look, if it weren't for me, you wouldn't even have been at that bloody reception."

"True. Very true. Tell me something, Rupert—how can I get in touch with her?"

"Get in touch with her? Why do you want to get in touch with her? One doesn't *get in touch* with the Princess of Wales."

"Why not?"

"She is the most popular woman in the world. Several million people, if not several billion, would like to *get in touch* with her. Now what would happen if everyone who wanted to *get in touch* with her was permitted to?"

"I bet you know how to *get in touch* with her."

He was in his raincoat and sweater, a tweed cap on his head, a pair of racing gloves beside him on the seat. You wouldn't know from looking at him that he was a reporter for a London tabloid. He looked more like a character actor from a 1950s English comedy, one of those slightly seedy, bumptious racetrack touts drinking a pint in the saloon-bar section of a pub.

When his kippers and eggs arrived, he left them untouched.

"C'mon, Rupert, you must have some inside contact in her entourage at Kensington Palace. Don't you?"

He didn't reply. Instead he continued to sit there with a sour expression on his face.

"If you get a message to her from me, I promise to give you a scoop on the story."

"What story?"

"I don't know yet."

"You don't know yet."

"That's what I'm trying to tell you. Something happened between us last night. It's hard to describe. But it was very strong."

"You're not crackers, are you, Leonard?"

I looked around to make sure that no one was within earshot and then said, "Rupert, she squeezed my hand."

"I beg your pardon?"

"When we said good-bye, she didn't just shake my hand. She *squeezed* it."

"How do you know it wasn't some sort of reflex stress reaction?"

"It wasn't, believe me. She looked me in the eye at the same time. It was an incredible look. I can't even begin to describe it to you."

He took a long pull on his Guinness, stared at me for a moment, then, "I trust that you will behave decently."

"Hey, Scout's honor."

"You understand that if anything happened to her, I would feel personally responsible."

"Of course."

"I scarcely know you. You could be some maniac or terrorist bent on doing her harm, for all I know. And what if you were? It would all eventually be laid squarely at my doorstep. And I would feel terribly responsible because though it may be the case that Diana is, in a sense, grist for the mill, she is nonetheless a sort of national treasure, you understand, a symbol of this country's glory, however tattered that may be at the moment."

He paused, knocked off the pint, then said, "I should expect nothing less than the complete story. Exclusively."

I nodded.

"You speak to no one else but me. Is that clear?"

"Crystal clear."

He burrowed in his raincoat for a pen and a business card. On the back of the card, he wrote a phone number. "Ring this number, ask for Archie. If they say that Archie isn't there, do *not* leave a message. Simply say you'll ring back. When you get Archie on the phone, tell him that I gave you the number. He will get a message to her provided that it is reasonably short and discreet."

"Great."

"Leonard, this is a source that I have cultivated with great care and at no small expense. If you bollix this up for me, I shall be extremely put out."

"No sweat."

"You have my home and office phone and fax numbers. You may call me at any time. Anytime, even the middle of the night."

Archie was not there. An imperious voice asked me if I cared to leave a message, and I replied, as instructed, that I would not care to. I asked when Archie would be available and was told to call back at tea.

Even though I did not know when tea was, I had the presence of mind not to ask the voice on the phone. Instead, I hung up and phoned down to the concierge to ask him the question.

"Tea, sir?"

"Yes, tea. When is it?"

"We serve tea anytime, sir."

"I understand, but when is tea *time*?"

"Tea time?"

Why did they repeat everything I said in this goddamn country? It was beginning to really piss me off. "If someone suggested that you call them at tea time, what time might they be referring to?"

"Well that would depend, sir. There is tea in the literal sense, which is usually taken in the late afternoon, around four o'clock generally, and then there is tea in the figurative sense, which is sometimes used synonymously with supper, and that, of course, can be taken anytime after six in the evening, if not later . . ."

"You've been very helpful. Thank you." I decided to hang up before the conversation got any more abstract.

It was already noon. I was exhausted and exhilarated at the same time. My body clock was still bouncing around somewhere over the North Pole. I felt light, almost giddy, reckless and unrestrained. I had no idea what was going to happen next.

Rivera was sitting in one of the Edwardian armchairs, his feet up on the table, smoking.

I asked him his advice.

"Go and take her," he said.

"You think I can?"

"Sure. She's beautiful. She will drive you crazy. What can you do?"

He inhaled deeply, then flicked an ash carelessly from his cigarette onto the Persian throw rug. I looked at him as he sat there with his deep and beautiful scowl.

"What are we supposed to do, Rivera?"

"Suffer."

Then he turned away, declining further comment. The phone rang. When I picked up, I heard a vaguely familiar voice.

"Mr. Spector?"

"Schecter."

"Sorry."

"It's all right."

"Good day. You made quite a stir last evening. The embassy has been besieged with phone calls . . ."

It took me a moment to identify the musically inflected voice as that of Kodjo Kponvi, the visa-and-immigration officer of the Togolese embassy.

"Are you free for lunch?" he asked.

"Well . . . I'm sort of on a strange schedule . . ."

"There's a foo-foo restaurant in Soho."

"What's a foo-foo?"

"It's a dish from my country. Pounded yams. You will like it. They serve it with a choice of sauces. You can have peanut, pepper, or mango sauce. Would one o'clock be convenient? Splendid. Afterward, we shall have a dance lesson at the embassy . . ."

Même Mère, Même Père was on Greek Street, between a nude-model drawing studio and a Chinese acupuncturist. It was small, crowded, loud, and permeated by a complex mixture of pungent aromas. The walls were covered with African masks and vibrated with syncopated drum music. People shouted at one another in a variety of exotic languages. After midnight, Kodjo Kponvi explained, the restaurant became a discotheque. They removed the tables and danced the high life.

Kodjo Kponvi and I shouted at each other across a tiny table in the rear. Next to us, hanging from the wall, was a shrunken head of a warrior with long wisps of dry hair and a bone through his nose. All this didn't help my appetite, already blunted by jet lag and the lingering memory of Rupert Makepeace's kippers.

"My brother owns this place," he shouted at me.

"Même mère, même père?"

Kodjo Kponvi smiled broadly, like a teacher with an apt pupil. "No. He is my father Koffi's brother Kodjovi's wife's second son's brother-in-law. Kodjovi is little Kodjo, to distinguish him from another Kodjo born in the same family, who is Kodjoga or just Kodjo if there are only two Kodjos."

"What if three brothers are all born on Monday or Friday?"

"Then we pretend that one is born on Tuesday and call him Kwami."

Kodjo Kponvi's half-brother Kosi, a very large man with a colorfully stained chef's apron, came over to the table and shook hands.

"This is Leonard Spector, a good friend of the Princess of Wales," said Kodjo Kponvi proudly.

Kosi turned around and announced the news to the entire restaurant. There was a lot of nodding and buzzing, as the announcement got translated into different languages. People looked at me with admiration. I smiled back, waved, and nodded.

Kodjo Kponvi's pronouncement made me a guest of honor in the restaurant, and, as such, I was treated to a number of dishes paraded out by Kosi and his wife, Kumla, which, I was told, was the name for a female child born on Wednesday.

The foo-foo was the consistency of bread dough. You ate it with your hand, dipping it into a communal bowl of sauce, made of peanut oil, red peppers, tomatoes, and onions, among other things. It was washed down with Senegalese beer and palm wine.

As I sampled the various foo-foo dishes and drank the beer and the palm wine, I began to realize that I was not going to get through this extravagance unscathed. But that would come later. For the moment I ate and drank and shouted back and forth with Kodjo Kponvi.

"When the Princess came to my country," he said, "I had the honor to be in her entourage."

"Really?"

"Yes. She visited the phosphate mines near Sokodé and gave a splendid speech."

"Yes, of course."

"She even visited the lepers and shook hands with them."

"That's Di," I said casually, in the tone of voice one uses for intimate friends.

"We all love her very much," he shouted.

"To know her is to love her," I shouted back.

After lunch, I begged off Kodjo Kponvi's invitation for dancing lessons by saying that I had an engagement for tea. Which was not entirely untrue. At Kensington Palace Archie was waiting for my call.

Back in my room, I dialed the number that Rupert Makepeace had given me. The same imperious voice answered. I asked for Archie once again. There was a pause, then the sound of the receiver being put down on a table.

After what seemed an interminably long time, a new imperious voice said, "This is Archie."

"Rupert Makepeace gave me your number."

"Yes?" The voice was superbly noncommittal.

"I would like to speak to the Princess of Wales."

"Yes?"

"Would it be possible to have her call me?"

"Who is this?"

"Leonard."

"Leonard who?"

"Just Leonard. I'm at the Dorchester. Room Nine-fourteen. I'll be in all evening."

"Will she know what this is regarding?"

"Yes." I decided to leave it at that. I hung up. Kicking off my shoes, I propped myself up on the bed and felt a thrill rush through me. The ball was now in her court.

I would find out if the squeeze of the hand was, in fact, a squeeze of the hand, if the look in her eye was not merely the pro-forma look she gave the Togolese ambassador or the Dalai Lama or Mother Teresa, but a look especially meant for Leonard Schecter.

I lay there and stared at the phone. Within an hour she hadn't called. But the foo-foo and the palm wine had. I managed to make it into the bathroom just in time.

CHAPTER

7

We were paddling up the Atakpamé River in a dugout canoe, Rivera and I, penetrating the dark heart of the Togolese bush in search of the phosphate mines. The heat was so intense that we had to travel by night, inching our way slowly upriver in the dim moonlight. By day we grabbed what sleep we could, moored in the alligator-infested rushes. By night, we headed north into the unknown.

We traveled with the silent complicity of desperate men, driven farther and farther into the terra incognita of our own souls. We had no idea what awaited us at the mines. And, ultimately, it didn't matter. We had gone too far. There was no turning back.

As the canoe sluiced through the turbulent river currents, we began to hear the sound of drums—faint at first, then louder and more insistent. There was movement in the thick bush on either bank of the Atakpamé, and we could feel hidden eyes upon us.

But it wasn't until the eighteenth day out from Port Geoffrey that we saw human life. A canoe appeared behind us, paddled by a dozen painted women. They kept a respectful distance, as if they were escorting us upriver. Then a second canoe and a third. By daybreak we were encircled by a flotilla of canoes, each of them filled with sullen women warriors, their spears tipped with a slow-acting poison made of dried yucca leaves.

It was impossible to land on either bank. They had us surrounded, leading us toward a clearing on the far bank of the river. We could see, in the distance, a crowd of garishly painted women waiting for us. They were naked to the waist and brandished large foo-foo paddles, which they banged rhythmically into wooden pestles.

Our canoe ran aground in the soft mud of the riverbed. We climbed out among the clinging vines and overhanging mimosa branches. There, lying in front of us, awful in the glare of the first rays of morning sun, was the evidence.

Four retread tires lay in a neat row staring back up at us. Beside them was a ticket to the Super Bowl in New Orleans, nailed to the earth with a spear. Petitioner's Exhibit A. Behind this, row upon row of women banged their paddles and chanted a dirge, waiting for the honor of displaying parts of our dismembered bodies around their necks and wrists like jewelry.

The slow, mournful rhythm of their chant became louder as they inched closer to us, tightening the circle.

I looked at Rivera. His teeth ground together. The blood rose in his veins. His fists clenched tightly. His cheekbones strained against the taut leather of his skin. And then a single plaintive and beautiful cry issued from his throat.

¡Putas!

As I awaited the first touch of sharpened metal lacerating my skin, I heard a ringing in my ears. It got louder. And louder. And louder . . .

I lunged for the phone, knocked it off the night table, dove onto the floor, and tried to find it in the twisted mass of bed linen.

"Hello!" I nearly screamed when I finally got the receiver in my hands.

It was a desperate cry from a man under the influence of slow-acting poison. And for a while it seemed that it would go unanswered. But then, at the very last moment, just before I was ready to slam the receiver back into the phone base, I heard her voice—soft, melodic, a little breathy.

"Leonard?"

"Your Royal Highness . . ." I managed to say.

"Oh, come now, I thought we were going to dispense with that rubbish." There was just a touch of coquetry in her voice.

"Yes, of course. I'm sorry. How are you?"

"Very well, thank you."

"That's good. That's great . . . Uh . . ."

I had no idea what to say. I was lying entangled in a heap of bed linens, foo-foo puke on my breath and a vicious palm-wine hangover ringing in my ears.

"Look, I was wondering if . . ." I mumbled.

"Perhaps tomorrow. In the afternoon. I was thinking of popping into Butler and Wilson to have a look at some earrings. It's in the Fulham Road. There's a tea shop two doors down, with a table in the back. Would half past four be suitable?"

"Perfect."

"Lovely."

"Yes . . ."

"I have to ring off now."

"Of course."

There was another moment of breathy silence before she said, "I'd be awfully pleased to hear some of your poem."

"It would be an honor."

"Good-bye."

The line went dead. Slowly, I got up off the floor, disentangling myself from the bed linen. My head ached. My stomach felt as if it had been permanently compromised by an invasion of spices that no mortal stomach should be expected to accommodate. Between the jet lag and the foo-foo and the hangover and the giddiness of falling in love, I was in a very precarious state of body and mind.

Given the circumstances, however, I didn't have much time to lose. An epic poem, or even the beginnings of one, was not something you could count on dashing off in an hour.

I went over to the minibar and looked over the contents. Champagne, Chivas Regal, vintage port, Perrier . . . I decided on a very small hair of the dog.

I took out a bottle of Beck's beer and a bag of potato chips. I cleared the room-service menu and the guide to the highlights of London off the Regency desk, unpacked my laptop, booted up, and waited for the muse to show up.

THE DIANIAD
Invocation to the Muse

Sing, Heavenly Muse, of fair Diana,
fruit of Johnnie Spencer—scion of Black Jack,
the Seventh Earl Spencer and Lady Hamilton—
and his bride, the beauteous Frances,
issue of the Baron Fermoy
and his conjoint, Ruth, and the unpolluted blood
of noble lords and ladies dating back to Charles I
and farther yet to Hastings and the Dawn of Time.

Sing of her birth amidst the wind-blown fields
of Sandringham 'neath Norfolk's cloud-choked sky
within the time-worn stones of Park House
on that sparkling July day years ago
in simpler times, more clement climes,
the world a safe and bounteous place,
before the . . .

Before the *what?* I had been stuck on that line since well before dawn. My idea had been to establish the worm in the apple early in order to foreshadow what was to come and give the work its underlying theme of the ineluctability of fate. Eventually, we would have to deal with tragic events—the unraveling of the marriage, the scenes and squabbles, the lemon peeler, the vomiting, the cellular-telephone tapes, the separation, Camilla, reincarnation as a tampon . . .

I decided to stop here before the poem became lugubrious. I would delete the last line and present it as a sonnet: "An Invocation to the Muse." It was an overture, the statement of themes, the promise of things to come.

Outside, the sky was beginning to brighten. I went over to the window and looked down at the city. A fine mist had settled over Hyde Park. It refracted the harsh morning light and made it gentler, more forgiving. It was more Monet than Turner.

Park Lane was already starting to fill with traffic. The black taxis, like so many ravens, were descending upon the city. An old woman, wrapped in a blanket, pushed a rickety shopping cart full of junk along the edge of the park. She stopped, looked across the street at the hotel, shouted something, and moved on.

Almost due west across the park, beyond the bird sanctuary, across the Serpentine Bridge, and through the Kensington Gardens, was the palace and the second-floor bedroom where she slept on the high four-poster long ago deserted by the Prince of Wales. She slept surrounded by her children and her detectives, not knowing that in a hotel room less than a mile away a poet had been up all night composing verses to her.

I blew her a kiss and closed the black-out curtains. Picking up the phone, I dialed the concierge.

"This is Nine-fourteen. Could you give me a wake-up call at two o'clock?"

"Certainly, sir, but you want the hall porter for that."

"Could you tell the hall porter for me?"

"Certainly, sir. But if you ring your call button, located near the night-reading lamp beside your bed . . ."

"I don't want to ring my call button. I don't want to talk to the hall porter. I just want someone to call this room at two o'clock and wake me up. And I'm communicating that wish to you. You may delegate that task to the hall porter or to anybody else you choose as long as *someone* does it. Okay?"

"Certainly, sir."

I hung up, threw myself across the bed, and slept.

When I was woken at two by the hall porter's discreet knock on the door, I felt, if anything, worse than I had when I'd passed out. I dragged myself into the shower and stood under the spray for a very long time. Afterward I shaved meticulously, brushed my teeth, thought about eating, thought better of it, then contemplated my meager wardrobe hanging forlornly in the closet.

I settled on a PROPERTY OF THE LOS ANGELES RAMS T-shirt, jeans, Reeboks, and a worn silk sports jacket that I had picked up for ten dollars in the Rose Bowl Swap Meet.

Declining the doorman's offer of a cab, I set out across the park with my city map in hand, heading southwest toward Chelsea. Folded in the pocket of my sports jacket was a copy of the "Invocation to the Muse" of *The Dianiad* written out in longhand on the back of a sheet of Dorchester stationery.

Rivera walked along with me, scowling and spitting sunflower seeds onto the immaculate green lawns.

"What's going to happen?" I asked him as we passed along the edge of the bird sanctuary and heard the demented chirping of caged birds in June.

He shrugged, as if the question were absurd. What did one do with women except suffer at their hands?

"I haven't thought this out very clearly."

"Take her," he said.

"She'll probably be accompanied by her detective."

"Kill him."

We walked across the Serpentine Bridge and down past the Albert Memorial in silence. As we left the park and turned onto Exhibition Road, he hopped a 73 bus to St. Pancras.

I continued alone, past the Imperial College of Science and Technology and the Victoria and Albert Museum, then down the Old Brompton Road toward the Fulham Road. It was 3:45. I was early. She would be late.

The tea shop was called Cuppa, a little Victorian storefront with a lace-curtain window giving on the street and a cowbell attached to the door that tinkled dully as you entered. The place was empty except for a very old, very tiny woman studying a racing newspaper.

I closed the door behind me, causing the cowbell to sound

again. It took the old woman a very long time to put down her pencil, close the newspaper, and look up at me, then squint and focus.

"Do you have a quiet table in the back?" I asked.

She looked me over carefully, evidently not liking what she saw because she grunted, "No," and started to open up the racing paper again.

"I'm going to be joined by the Princess of Wales," I said as matter-of-factly as possible.

She put the paper back down and looked me over one more time, then said, in a surprisingly rich and sonorous voice, "Are you now?"

"Yes, I am."

"Really . . ."

"Yes, really."

We looked at each other for a long moment, locked in a stalemate created by intersecting rhetorical questions and answers. Someone would have to break the impasse by saying something of substance, and I knew it wasn't going to be her. So I said, "Do you suppose I could sit down at this table and wait for her arrival?"

More seconds elapsed. It felt as if we were in a time warp. Eventually, the old woman got up, with some difficulty made her way toward the rear of the shop, and parted a curtain, revealing a table and two chairs.

I walked over and sat down. "Thank you," I said.

She said nothing in return, merely shuffled back to her table and her racing newspaper.

Several minutes passed before the cowbell tinkled again, and a man with prominent ears, thinning hair, and a dull green sports jacket entered. He looked around the place carefully, saw me at my table in the rear, and approached.

He took out a wallet and revealed his ID.

> SGT. DONALD F. BELLCHASE
> ROYAL PROTECTION SQUAD
> NEW SCOTLAND YARD

I wondered if I could make a run for it. The Reeboks would give me good traction. He was wearing a pair of shiny black shoes with leather soles. If I could roll the table up and into him, I could create a diversion. Rivera would be waiting outside with the horses . . .

"Terribly sorry to bother you, sir, but we do have to take our precautions, you understand. May I see some identification?"

"Do you know what habeas corpus is?" I replied.

"I beg your pardon?"

"Do you have probable cause for demanding my identification? Otherwise, it's unconstitutional. Unreasonable search and seizure. Fifth Amendment."

By now my accent must have registered because a small smile leaked from his features, and he said, "We don't have a constitution in this country. But we do have security precautions that we take for members of the royal family when they have engagements with people who are unknown to us. I don't suppose you have some ID on you?"

I took out my wallet and showed him my American Express card. He copied down my name and number, then said, "Would you mind standing up, sir?"

"Standing up?"

"I believe you call it a frisk in the States. It won't take a minute."

"You think I'm armed?"

"I very much hope you're not."

"You know, we have the right to bear arms in the States. Second Amendment . . ."

"Sir, if you'd like to speak with the Princess, I'd suggest we get this over with." There was an impatient schoolmaster's tone creeping into his voice. I would learn eventually that Donald was one of the little inconveniences that you had to put up with around Diana. He was harmless, if overly literal and humorless.

So I got up and let the guy frisk me. He must have been watching *Kojak* reruns, because he did a very slick job of it.

"Do I have the right to remain silent?" I asked with a straight face.

"I beg your pardon?"

I let it pass and sat back down.

"The Princess will be along straightaway. Good day." And he turned and exited past the old lady, who didn't even look up from her paper.

About twenty minutes went by, during which nobody entered the tea shop. I sat watching the old lady pore over her racing forms. Somewhere a clock ticked very loudly. A phone kept ringing, but no one answered it.

Then the cowbell tinkled, and Donald appeared once more in the doorway. His ferret eyes checked out every corner of the place, barely bothering with me. Presumably he expected to find my terrorist cohorts hiding under the tables. He held the door open behind him as he did his inspection. Then he stepped quickly aside, and Diana appeared.

She was wearing jeans, boots, a vest over a T-shirt, and a baseball cap. She smiled across the tea shop at me. My heart did a small drumroll. I got up and immediately felt my knees go soft. Grabbing the side of the table for support, I waited as she crossed the small room, stopping for a word with the old lady, who struggled to her feet and dropped a subliminal curtsy.

I remained standing until she arrived at the table. She held out her hand to me, tilted her head very slightly in a gesture that I would grow to cherish, and said, "How lovely to see you, Leonard." I took her hand, held it in mine, felt its warmth.

"Likewise," I mumbled, holding on to her hand. Donald watched my every move, ready to pounce at a moment's notice. In her boots she was over six feet, maybe an inch taller than me, but there was less of a height difference between us than between Charles and her. I thought of all those pictures of her stooping over slightly to minimize the height difference, with Charles's little bald spot glaring out at the camera from between his Mr. Spock ears.

While I was thinking about this, I forgot to let go of her hand. We stood there smiling at each other across the table until she said, "Perhaps we should sit down."

"Yes, of course," I said, releasing her hand.

We sat simultaneously on the rickety chairs and smiled some more until Di said, "Well, here we are."

"Yes. Here we are." I was so taken with her that I was reduced to the British gambit of merely batting back across the net like a Ping-Pong ball whatever someone said to you.

She was wearing a pair of long silver-and-jade earrings that dangled frivolously from half-hidden ears that protruded from the fringe of hair beneath the baseball cap. There was just a touch of makeup—a little blush on the cheeks and some pale-pink lipstick, no eyeliner.

"I like your earrings," I babbled.

"Do you? I just picked them up. Twelve pounds, sixty."

"Great. So . . . here we are," I repeated.

"Yes. Here we are."

The old lady trudged over and looked at Di, ignoring me entirely.

"What will you be having, ma'am?" she asked, her tone less deferential than the words she spoke.

"A cup of your jasmine herb tea and a scone with boysenberry jam, Doris."

The old lady turned to me with a pained expression on her face. She didn't even bother to ask what I wanted, merely raised her chin slightly in a vaguely interrogatory gesture.

"A Bud Light and some chips, guacamole on the side." I didn't even get a blink out of Doris. But Di giggled. A delicious little girlish titter.

"Leonard is an American, Doris. An American poet."

"Is he now?" Doris chirped disdainfully. "Well, it doesn't alter the fact that this is a tea shop and not a pub, does it now?"

"Bring me what the Princess is having, Doris."

She looked at me as if she resented the familiarity and trudged off toward the kitchen.

"And how is your poem coming along?" Di asked.

"Fabulously. It's going to be marvelous. Really."

"I don't suppose you've brought it with you?"

"Well, it's a work in progress . . ."

"Couldn't you recite just a tiny bit?"

"I did bring the 'Invocation to the Muse.' "

"Sorry?"

"The introduction. It's a convention in epic poetry. The poet asks the muse to descend and give him inspiration worthy of his subject."

"Lovely."

"You'd like to hear it?"

"I'd be delighted."

I reached into my jacket pocket to take out the poem. From his table near the door, Donald tensed up, anticipating a concealed weapon. But this was one concealed weapon that wasn't in his antiterrorist-response manual. I unfolded the Dorchester stationery and looked down at what I had written. It didn't seem like much— fourteen lines of blank verse squeezed out in the dead of night on a low-grade beer buzz. But it would have to do.

I cleared my throat, looked at her, smiled. She smiled back, folded her hands in front of her like a schoolgirl, and waited for me to begin.

"Sing, Heavenly Muse, of fair Diana . . ." I read as slowly as possible, enunciating the words, emphasizing the internal rhyming in line thirteen of *times* and *climes*. When I finished I took a moment before I looked up from the paper. I was afraid she might be amused or bored or contemptuous.

What I saw was radiance. She was glowing. It was a look I had never seen on her face before. Never in any of the hundreds of photographs I had looked at had I seen anything remotely resembling the look she gave me upon hearing my "Invocation to the Muse."

"Oh, Leonard . . ." she murmured.

"You like it?"

"It's exquisite. I don't know what to say."

"It's just the beginning, kind of like the overture to an opera."

"To have something like that written about one . . . To have a poet, a real poet, write such beautiful words . . . I can't begin to tell you how thrilling it is."

"It'll probably have at least thirty cantos." I was getting in deeper and deeper.

"You know, I have received gifts from all over the world. Paintings, sculpture, jewelry, dresses . . . But I have never had a proper poem written for me. An epic poem. How lovely."

At this moment Doris showed up and deposited the tea, sugar, jam, and scones on the table in front of us.

"Thank you, Doris," Di said.

"An honor indeed, ma'am."

"Do you have a favorite for Saturday?"

"I'm liking the looks of Hurly Burly, ma'am, if it don't rain. I suspect she's not much of a mudder."

"Hurly Burly. I'll remember that." Di smiled, and Doris returned to her table and newspaper. Then Di turned to me, and said, "Shall I pour?"

"You're probably much better at it than I am."

"Sugar?"

"Three, please."

She poured our tea with expertise, handed me my cup.

"Thanks. Who's Hurly Burly?"

"A horse, I should imagine. Doris loves to bet on the horses." Suddenly her smile faded into a frown. "Ascot on Saturday. How I dread it. I shall have to ride with Charles and the boys in that awful carriage and wave to everyone."

"I thought you were officially separated."

"We still have the odd official duty together. Really, do you think anyone wants to see us sitting side by side in that carriage?"

I shook my head. She took a sip of her tea, then put the cup down. Her eyes were downcast and liquid, and for a moment I thought she was going to burst into tears. Then she looked across at Donald, who was drinking his tea and watching us, and with a sudden flash of anger, she reached up and closed the curtain.

We were now sitting completely alone. She looked at me, took two deep breaths, and blurted, "You have no idea how desperately unhappy I am."

I didn't know whether to nod or shake my head. I did neither. Instead I reached out and took her hand. It was an instinctual gesture. She didn't take her hand away. She left it in mine, warm and moist, and took some more deep breaths. It was, as I would learn, a yoga technique for controlling emotion.

"I've mucked things up awfully, haven't I?"

"What are you talking about?"

"Everything. My whole life. It's a bloody mess . . . I feel so utterly useless . . ."

"Di . . ." The word slipped out of my mouth. It was too late to take it back. I had crossed over into a new and rarefied area of intimacy.

"I have no one to come home to. No one to have supper with and to go for walks with and to curl up with in front of the telly at night . . ."

"The whole world loves you."

"They don't love *me*. They don't even know who I am. Love is cherishing, Leonard. Love is supporting each other . . . holding hands in the dark . . . being there for you when you need someone. Don't you agree?"

I nodded.

We sat like that for what seemed a very long moment. Then, with great sincerity, she said, "Love is never having to say you're sorry."

"Yes . . ."

"Didn't you just adore that picture?"

"I sure did."

"I cried all the way through it."

"Me too."

"Charles hated it."

Her nose wrinkled up a bit, as a touch of humor returned to leaven her emotion.

"Well, I seem to have unburdened myself to you, haven't I? I hope I haven't been too terribly tiresome."

"Not at all."

"One ought to be transparent to one's poet, I suppose."

Taking out a pearl-inlaid compact, she looked at herself in the mirror and shook her head.

"Oh my. The Princess is developing a sty. Beta carotene deficiency. Do you take beta carotene?"

"No. Not yet."

She took out a small vial that contained a collection of odd-shaped pills. "Don't worry. I'm not a drug addict—despite what they say in the papers. These are just vitamins and minerals—A, C, E, B-six, B-twelve, calcium, iron, zinc, phosphorous, iodine, kelp, acido-philus . . . what have you."

She washed down the pills with her jasmine herb tea. Then she put everything back in her purse, turned to me, and said, "I'm afraid I must be off. I have a hospice to visit. This has been a most delightful interlude."

It was as if she had flipped back into her Princess of Wales mode, as if the intimacy that had been established between us had dissolved.

"I'm not quite ready to part with you," I said.

"Oh, Leonard. What a lovely sentiment." She put her hand on mine again, reestablishing contact. "We shall meet again. Soon. All right?"

I nodded. But without conviction.

"I'm afraid of losing the . . . thread of the poem," I said. "It's very fragile. Can we see each other again?"

She thought for a moment, then said, "Well, let's see now . . . would you like to come to Ascot on Saturday?"

"The horse race?"

"Yes. It's rather fun, after we get out of the carriages. I suppose we can get you admitted to the Royal Enclosure. You do have morning clothes, don't you?"

"Sure."

"And it would be preferable if you had someone on your arm. Would that be a problem?"

"Not at all."

She opened up her purse again, took out a card, and handed it to me. It was a formal calling card with HER ROYAL HIGHNESS THE PRINCESS OF WALES printed in raised gold letters over a coat of arms.

"If you show this to the guards at the enclosure, they'll admit you. You're not a convicted felon, are you, Leonard?"

"No."

"They don't allow convicted felons in the Royal Enclosure. They used not to let divorced people in, either, but they've had to change that. So it's settled. Until Saturday, then."

"Yes."

"Oh, lovely." She leaned closer to me and whispered, "Thank you for listening to all that rubbish. I suppose I should say I'm sorry, but I don't think I shall." And she smiled at me conspiratorially, squeezed my hand one last time, and pulled the curtain open.

Donald looked up at us from his table, a vexed expression on his face. You could tell that he did not like being screened from direct visual contact with his charge. He rose as Di walked across the shop.

When Di reached the door, she turned around and waved at me. I waved back.

I stood there basking in the afterglow of the moment. My hand could still feel the warmth of hers. In my pocket was her personal card, which, like a magic wand, would admit me into her proximity when I chose to use it.

I sat for a long moment, staring at the empty doorway as if she were still there waving at me. Then I collected myself and headed for the door. As I passed Doris she said, "That'll be five pounds even."

I reached into my wallet, took out a ten-pound note, and gave it to her. "Keep the change," I said.

"I'd rather not, actually," she replied, handing me back a five-pound note from her pocketbook.

CHAPTER

8

"A *tea shop* in the *Fulham Road*?"

"Yes."

"And it was just the *two of you*?"

"And her detective. But she closed the curtain on him."

"Extraordinary."

Rupert Makepeace put his foot down harder on the accelerator of his vintage Austin Healey, and the speedometer needle nudged past eighty.

We were heading north on the M1 to visit Althorp House, the Spencer family estate outside of Northampton. The top was down in spite of the threat of rain, and between the rushing air and the engine noise we had to shout to be heard. Which was no problem for Rupert Makepeace, for whom shouting was the normal method of communication.

"What did you discuss?"

"Love Story."

"Love Story?"

"Yeah. The tearjerker with Ali MacGraw and Ryan O'Neal. It's one of her favorite pictures."

Rupert Makepeace looked over at me and frowned, then reached into his raincoat pocket for a cigarette, and lit it with the dashboard lighter.

"You realize, of course," he said, smoking furiously, "that it is only a matter of time before this . . . this liaison that you are having with her will become known. And then your life will become a public spectacle, your privacy will be invaded . . ."

"By the likes of you."

"The public has a right to know."

"Yeah . . . and I have a right not to tell."

"I thought we had an arrangement."

"We do. I promised you the exclusive story. When there is an exclusive story. At the moment there is no story. We're just friends."

"You have no idea how difficult this is for me, Leonard. I have spent the past ten years on this woman's trail, tracking down every lead like a bloodhound. I have stood outside flats in the rain, I have waited at airports in the middle of the night, I have been reduced to eating Wimpys in my car like some private detective in the cinema. All for the story. And here I have the story in my car, and he won't tell me."

"I told you—there is no story."

"I beg to differ with you. There *is* a story. Your having tea with her tête-à-tête in the Fulham Road is very definitely a story. Believe me. We could sell a million papers tomorrow with that story."

It wasn't so much that I didn't trust Rupert Makepeace, though I didn't, but rather that it was all so vague and undefined. In a sense, I was right—there was no story. Di and I had met for tea and talked about the meaning of love. We were together for perhaps three quarters of an hour. We held hands and didn't drink our tea. She got up and left. We didn't kiss good-bye.

And so I didn't say anything, and we continued to drive north at a hazardous speed in brooding silence. We got off the M1 at Northampton and drove through the dreary red-brick city and then out onto smaller roads.

The scenery turned picturesque, the rain-washed green of rural England. Eventually Rupert Makepeace relented. The man was incapable of silence for a prolonged period of time.

"Pity old Johnnie Spencer died," he boomed. "During his declining years, he and his second wife, Raine, Diana's stepmother, turned the place into a veritable roadside tourist attraction. They opened it up for tours. We could have tramped through and seen the place. Now, unfortunately, the property has passed to Diana's brother Charles, the Ninth Earl Spencer, and he's rather uncivil to trespassers."

We reached the entrance to the estate and pulled over to the side of the road. Rupert Makepeace shut off the motor, which died with a final, agonized death rattle, and we sat there in the car, enveloped in sudden quiet.

There were closed gates, barring access, and a sign warning against trespassing. Behind the gates was a stately mansion with a white used brick façade. The setting was out of a Jane Austen novel, pastoral and idyllic.

"It was built in the early sixteenth century by Sir John Spencer, a wealthy sheep farmer who was knighted by Charles I. Most of the renovation was late eighteenth century, done by Henry Holland, the famous Regency architect . . ."

I wasn't paying much attention to Rupert Makepeace's lecture on architecture. Instead I was trying to imagine the woman I'd had tea with yesterday, the woman in the T-shirt and Calvin Klein jeans, living in a house like this. I was trying to imagine her bedroom, with the Rolling Stones posters and Elton John albums, the shelves of Barbara Cartland novels, the vanity table with the moisturizer and the cold cream, the bed where she slept with her teddy bears, those long adolescent legs wrapped around the soft fur . . .

"Of course, Diana and her sisters couldn't stand Raine," Rupert Makepeace droned on. "They never forgave her for selling the Van

Dycks, not to mention having it off with their father. Even though it was their mother, Frances, who left Johnnie—for a wallpaper tycoon, no less—they never accepted their stepmother. To this day, they barely speak . . ."

A soft rain began to fall. Rupert Makepeace didn't bother to put up the top. He merely put up the collar of his raincoat and went on talking.

"After Diana married Charles, Johnnie and Raine decided that they were royals now, too. And so the entire house had to be redone. They sold more paintings and furniture to finance the job, stripped the place of priceless objects in order to put gold leaf on the ceilings. It was quite a scandal. Fortunately, her brother got the house back, or what was left of it, when their father died in '92. You may remember Di going to the funeral with Charles. They were barely on speaking terms by that time. It was just months before the separation, after that book came out with the bulimia and the suicide business . . ."

The rain was coming down harder. I was starting to get very wet. "Rupert, do you think you could put the top up?"

"Sorry, but there is none."

"You're kidding!"

"I'm afraid not. But I have an umbrella in the boot."

He got out of the car and went around to the trunk to get the umbrella. While he was doing this, a small blue car approached and pulled off the road in front of us. Two policemen emerged and walked over to us.

"May we be of some assistance?" a tall man with very blue eyes, a sort of road-company Roger Moore, asked.

"We were just taking a bit of a breather."

The cops looked pointedly at Althorp House, then back at us. "Perhaps you'd be good enough to have your breather elsewhere," Roger Moore said.

"Certainly, officer," Rupert Makepeace replied, hurriedly slipping back behind the wheel. The Austin Healey started up with a loud report of badly timed spark plugs, and we continued on down the road in the rain.

"The bloody bastard must have called the cops," Rupert Make-peace said through his teeth. "It could have been worse, I suppose. We could have been shot."

We waited out the rain at a pub in Northampton, eating sausage and chips and drinking beer. We sat in a dark mahogany booth, getting sodden from the beer, thinking about her. At least I was. I didn't know about Rupert.

But I sensed that we were developing a bond. And she was at the center of that bond. We both had an inordinate interest in this woman, if for very different reasons.

"What do you think she's really like?" I asked.

He stubbed out his cigarette, looked at me for a moment, seemed to hesitate. When he spoke, it was in a softer, more confidential tone of voice.

"Well, sometimes I think she's the Mona Lisa or Helen of Troy, and other times I think she's a Sloane Ranger with good legs who got lucky. I fluctuate between the two points of view with some regularity."

"There's this innocence about her, don't you think?"

"Innocence? Rubbish. That woman has the survival instincts of a barracuda. Look what she did to Charles. The poor man has been reduced to locking himself up in his organic garden and talking to his rutabaga."

"She thinks that love is never having to say you're sorry."

He looked at me quizzically, not catching the reference. In spite of all those hours waiting for her in the rain, Rupert Makepeace didn't really know Diana. To him, she was a story. She may have been the biggest story of his life, but she would never be more than that. He would never see the woman underneath.

I knew things he would never know.

Rupert Makepeace had not sat and listened as she spoke to him of her unhappiness, her eyes heavy, her hand moist in his. He was not privy to the loneliness that gripped her. He didn't know that what she wanted most in life was someone to curl up in front of the telly with.

As I sat there in that pub in Northampton drinking beer and thinking about her, I began to suspect the real reason I had come to London. I hadn't come merely to research a miniseries about Diana. I had come to rescue her.

I didn't share this thought with Rupert Makepeace, nor did I tell him about my invitation to Ascot on Saturday. There seemed to be no point in getting him more hysterical than he normally was. He would probably want to put a concealed wire on me.

We drove back to London in silence. He kept the Austin Healey at eighty and smoked while I gripped the underside of the seat for support. It wasn't until we were nearly at the Dorchester that I asked him casually if he was going to be at Ascot on Saturday.

"Yes, unfortunately. We shall need the usual pictures of those silly carriages. Of course, Diana will be stoic and fuss over the boys like a mother hen, while Charles will look as if he has an earache. The Queen will pretend that everything is perfectly normal and sit there with one of those dreadful hats with matching handbags and prattle on about the horses. And Philip will ignore her, as usual. We might just as well use last year's pictures."

"Do the men really wear morning suits?" I asked.

"If they want to be admitted into the Royal Enclosure."

"What exactly is a morning suit?"

He looked at me condescendingly and said, "Really, Leonard, don't you know anything?"

"I'm a second-generation Polish Jew. My grandfather sold herring from a pushcart on the Lower East Side of New York. He didn't have much call for a morning suit."

"Tails and a top hat, with a gray waistcoat."

We pulled up in front of the hotel, and a doorman, wearing, it turned out, a morning suit, opened the door.

"Thanks for the excursion," I said.

"You will keep me posted, won't you?"

"Of course."

"Anything at all from her. A phone call . . . a message . . . a fax . . ."

"I promise."

"Anytime. Day or night. You have my numbers."

I nodded and got out of the car.

There was a message waiting for me at the front desk. But it wasn't from Di.

In my room I dialed the number in California. The phone rang a half-dozen times, and I was about to hang up when I heard the soft, uninflected voice of Charlie Berns.

It sounded as if I had woken him. I checked the clock, deducted eight hours. It was 9 A.M. in L.A.

"It's me," I said. "Leonard. Schecter."

There was a moment of silence, as if Charlie Berns were trying to remember who Leonard Schecter was, then, "Hey, how're you doing?"

"Great."

"You meet with Rupert?"

"Yes. In fact I just spent the day with him. He drove me up to Northampton to see Althorp House."

"What?"

"Althorp House. It's the family estate."

"That's great. There's nothing like verisimilitude, is there?"

"No."

"You think you'll have anything on paper soon, an outline I could run by Norm Hudris?"

"Yeah, probably. As soon as I get the shape of the story—you know what I mean?"

"Absolutely. The dynamic, right?"

"Right."

"You figure you're going to need more than a couple of weeks?"

"I think so," I said. "I've just scratched the surface."

"I'll call over to the network and tell them you're getting the verisimilitude. You can't get that in Burbank, can you?"

"No way."

"So . . . keep the ball low, okay?"

"Okay."

After the booming voice of Rupert Makepeace, you had to make an adjustment listening to Charlie Berns. It was like trying to hit a change-up artist after a fastball pitcher. You had to step forward in the box, lean in, and listen very carefully.

I couldn't get a handle on the guy. Nothing seemed to faze him. It wasn't the kind of laid-back, breezy, vacuum-cleaned patter you got from people in the movie business, but rather a strange sort of ironic detachment. You had the distinct impression that Charlie Berns didn't give much of a shit about this or anything else. You had the feeling that the man had seen it all, sold it all, been to the bank and back enough times to know that it was all one big crapshoot anyway.

Get the ball over but keep it low.

I poured myself a Beck's from the minibar and thought about a morning suit and a date. I decided to tackle the easier problem first.

I called down to the concierge and asked him for the number of the Togolese embassy.

"You can get it through directory enquiries, sir, if you dial nine, then one-nine-two."

"I don't suppose you could get it for me?"

"Certainly, sir. Would you like me to ring you back when I get it or will you remain on the line?"

"I don't know. What do *you* think?"

There was a brief, icy pause, then, "One moment please . . ."

When I got the number, I called and asked for Kodjo Kponvi. He got on the line with his cheerful voice: "Kponvi here."

"Hi. It's me. Leonard Schecter."

"Splendid. How nice to hear from you."

"Likewise. I have a small favor to ask."

"It would be a great pleasure to accommodate you, my friend."

"My morning suit was lost by British Airways. You know, the baggage service on the Concorde is terrible. They apparently shipped it on to New Delhi, and they can't guarantee I'll have it back in time for Ascot on Saturday. And Diana's asked me to be in the Royal

Enclosure. And so I was wondering if I could possibly borrow yours."

"By all means."

"We look about the same size, don't we?"

"I would say so."

"I really appreciate it."

"It would be an honor."

He promised to send the morning suit over to the hotel, and I promised to come by for a dance lesson soon. Then I dialed directory enquiries and asked for the number for Lady Gwen Poulstice in Eaton Mews, Belgravia.

"Gwen, how are you?"

There was no answer for a moment, then a loud, audible sigh, and "Really, Mr. Spector, you have no idea how much embarrassment you caused me the other night. I have had the papers ringing me nonstop."

"I'm terribly sorry about that, honest. Listen, I've got a little proposition to make."

"I beg your pardon?"

"How would you like to accompany me to Ascot Saturday?"

"Thank you but I don't think I'm available."

"Not even for . . . the Royal Enclosure?"

There was another pause, then, "Is this another one of your jokes?"

"Nope. This is the real thing. I have a pass to the Royal Enclosure given to me personally by the Princess of Wales."

"How did you manage that?"

"We had tea yesterday in the Fulham Road. We got on the subject of Ascot and she said, 'Oh, do please come, Leonard. It will be so frightfully boring without you.' So what do you say? Everyone's going to be there."

There was a long, agonized silence. I could hear the gears of her brain meshing. It was a tough call. Then, in a small voice, a voice that was not very proud of itself, she said, "I . . . suppose I could make myself free."

"Splendid. Listen, Gwen, please forgive my asking, but you're not a convicted felon, are you?"

CHAPTER

9

We drove out to Windsor Great Park on Saturday, Lady Gwen Poulstice and I, in a Mercedes 190 that I had rented for the day. I could tell from the way her nose twitched when I opened the door for her that the car was a class or two below the appropriate level for Ascot. It was not unlike the look she had given my morning suit when she had greeted me in her parlor, where I had been sitting with Cecil for half an hour waiting for her.

The suit was broad in the shoulders and tight in the waist. You could tell it had been borrowed from someone a little better put together than I was.

I tried driving with the top hat on, but it rubbed against the roof, and so I tossed it in the backseat. Gwen Poulstice, however, kept her hat on, even though the ostrich feather looked unhappy and constricted inside the small car. She kept her eyes focused directly in front of her, hands folded in the lap of her—she informed me— Victor Edelstein original.

We headed west out of London into a dull blue early-summer sky. Conversation was labored.

"So, Gwen," I said, trying to warm things up, "what do you do in your spare time?"

"I keep myself occupied, thank you."

"Any hobbies?"

"Hobbies?"

"Stamp collecting, bowling, model airplanes?"

"I'm involved with various cultural and philanthropic organizations."

"Are you?"

"Yes."

"Extraordinary."

"I trust," she said, without looking at me, "that you are not going to ask her *to dance* this afternoon?"

I smiled over at her, hoping for an ounce of irony in her expression. There was none. This was all deadly serious business to Gwen Poulstice.

"Do behave yourself," she added. "Please."

She turned away and stared out at the countryside for the remainder of the drive.

There is no valet parking at Ascot. The reason, of course, is that no one of any importance drives himself. Gwen Poulstice had to suffer the further indignity of parking in the car park behind the grandstand and walking among the proletariat to the racetrack.

Security was tight at the entrance to the Royal Enclosure. Besides a half-dozen bobbies, there were a number of heavy-looking guys in dark suits milling around.

I handed my card to one of the dark suits. He examined it carefully, checked the reverse side, ran his fingers over it.

"Your name, sir?"

"Leonard Schecter."

He checked a list of names carefully, then shook his head slowly. "Sorry, Mr. Spector, but I don't seem to have you on the list."

"That's Schecter—Sir Leonard Schecter and Lady Schecter," I said. "We were invited personally by the Princess of Wales."

The suit went over to confer with other suits. They all examined the card carefully. Gwen Poulstice, meanwhile, was turning a variety of different colors. This was beginning to resemble her worst nightmare.

The suit returned and handed me back the card. "I'm afraid, sir, that we'll have to wait for corroboration from the Princess herself. You do understand, don't you?"

"No, I *don't* understand. We drove all the way out here from London. At some expense and difficulty, I should add. Do you think it's fun wearing a morning suit in this heat? Not to mention Lady Schecter's hat, which, you should know, is a Victor Edelman original."

Gwen Poulstice turned a deeper shade of red, but the suit wasn't budging. "If you'll wait outside until after the carriages arrive . . ."

Suddenly I heard a familiar voice from behind me.

"Leonard?" I turned and saw Rupert Makepeace among the reporters and television cameras on a raised balcony above the entrance.

"Rupert." I waved.

It took Rupert Makepeace only a few seconds to grasp the situation. And though he was no doubt furious at me for not telling him I was going to be at Ascot, his reporter's instincts prevailed.

"Let him in, Reggie," he said to the suit at the door. "He's a close friend of the Princess."

Having followed Di around for years, Rupert Makepeace was apparently on a first-name basis with the members of the Royal Protection Squad.

"She'll be very cross if she finds out you made him stand outside," Rupert boomed from the reporters' balcony, loud enough for everyone around us to hear.

This seemed to do the trick, because Reggie handed me back my card and stepped aside.

"Sir," he said through his teeth.

"Thank you, Reggie," I said as I offered my arm to Gwen Poulstice, and we entered the enclosure.

"Well, Gwen," I said. "Here we are."

She grimaced again and removed her hand from my arm. "Yes," she muttered.

"So what do we do now?" I asked.

"We wait for the carriages to arrive," she replied.

There was a bar set up in the corner of the enclosure, but no one was frequenting it.

"How about a drink?" I suggested.

"One doesn't drink until the Queen arrives."

So there we were, Gwen Poulstice and I, standing in a large, enclosed area, among other similarly dressed people, with absolutely nothing to do. I recognized some of the faces from magazine photos—the icy blond features of Princess Michael of Kent; the serious, sensible shopkeeper's face of Princess Anne, who, with her new husband, had decided apparently to forgo the carriages, as had Prince Andrew, who was there with a young thing in a very short skirt and the princesses Beatrice and Eugenie, looking like miniature Fergies with their red hair and freckles and gracelessness.

No one was talking to us. We were, quite simply, not known. Gwen Poulstice stole away to the solace of the powder room, and I found myself standing beside Prince Andrew.

"Lovely day, isn't it?" I said casually.

He turned toward me, looked me over, then replied, "Quite," before turning away again.

I thought that due to his navy service he might be more relaxed around commoners, so I pursued the conversation.

"It must have been pretty nasty down there in the Falklands," I said.

He turned back once more, looked me over a little more carefully.

"Piloting that helicopter with the Exocet missiles going off all around you—I imagine that was quite some experience."

"I'm sorry," he said, "but do we know each other?"

"Leonard Schecter," I said, offering my hand.

He took it, shook it brusquely.

"Are you a rock star?" he said.

"No." I smiled. "I'm a writer."

"So you're a writer, are you?"

Gwen Poulstice emerged from the powder room and hurried over with the air of a mother whose child was about to do something untoward in the sandbox.

"Your Royal Highness," I said, "this is Lady Gwen Poulstice of Eaton Mews, Belgravia."

"How do you do," Prince Andrew said.

She did one of her neat little curtsies and said, "Very well, thank you, sir."

"We were just discussing the Falklands," I said.

"Really?" said Gwen Poulstice.

"The Prince was up in his helicopter flying decoy missions. Talk about courage, there he was, the second in line to the English throne at the time—maybe it was the third—was Wills born yet . . . ?"

"If you'll excuse me," said Prince Andrew and hurried off to be with his bimbo.

Gwen Poulstice exhaled loudly to indicate, no doubt, that I had once again stepped over the line of propriety.

"Just trying to make small talk," I said. She didn't reply. We stood there locked in stony silence until cries were heard from down below in the grandstand.

The occupants of the Royal Enclosure moved forward to get a better view of the track as the first of the royal carriages came into view. Sitting beneath an enormous pink bonnet was the Queen Mother, still going strong at ninety-three. Beside her was the balding and sexually challenged Prince Edward in a morning coat and top hat.

Then came Princess Margaret, riding with a young man.

"Who's he?" I asked.

"Her son, the Viscount Linley."

Then there was a small, dramatic gap in the procession, a sort of drumroll, and a collective outpouring of breath as the carriage with Charles, Di, and the little princes came into view. This was the show that everyone had been waiting for—the ceremonially reunited family of the heir apparent. It was just as Rupert Makepeace had predicted. Charles seemed to tilt his head and smile painfully, as if he did indeed have an earache. Di leaned forward and supervised Wills and Harry, as they all waved perfunctorily to the crowd.

My heart ached as I watched her sitting there beside the man she despised, the man who hated *Love Story*, looking very alone and vulnerable amid the adulation of her subjects. She waved to the crowd with a swanlike, martyred expression, her princess smile on automatic pilot. It was not the smile I knew, the shy stolen little moment in which her insides glowed. This was the official Buckingham Palace smile, the one that went on magazine covers and postage stamps.

Cameras clicked furiously as she disembarked from the carriage and entered the compound. She completely upstaged the Queen and the Duke of Edinburgh, who followed in the final carriage like a pair of chaperones at a college mixer.

All eyes were on Di and Charles. They walked as if any incidental contact between them would be catastrophic, looking to either side, acknowledging the cheers. Wills and Harry trotted along in front of them in their down-sized morning suits and miniature Dickensian top hats.

The procession entered the Royal Enclosure to a polite smattering of applause. The Queen and Prince Philip nodded to the members of their family and distinguished guests gathered waiting for them. She had one of her trademark matching handbags grasped in both hands, which, Rupert Makepeace had explained to me, discouraged attempts to shake hands with her.

"Can we have a drink now?" I asked Gwen Poulstice.

"I suppose so," she replied without enthusiasm.

"What can I get you?"

"Tonic water with a slice of lemon."

"Living dangerously, are we?" I made my way to the bar, which was now doing brisk business. As I stood waiting my turn, I noticed Di talking to Anne and her new husband. Standing a few feet away from Di and the boys was Donald, whose eyes landed on mine for a brief moment. I nodded amiably. Donald did not nod back.

I asked for a glass of champagne. It was extra dry, nonvintage. You'd think the Windsors could have afforded something a little classier. I worked my way back to Gwen Poulstice and handed her the tonic water.

"Shall we have a word with Di?" I said.

"She is occupied with the Princess Royal at the moment."

"Is she?"

"Yes."

A few minutes later there was a gradual movement toward the rear of the enclosure. People began to exit through a narrow opening guarded by more security men.

"Where's everyone going?"

"To the paddock. To look at the horses."

"Are we all supposed to go?"

"Yes."

We followed the Queen and her entourage through a hallway and out into a grassy area between two grandstands. The TV cameras swung over from the other side of the balcony and photographed us as we headed toward the paddock. People hung over the railings gaping at us.

The Queen kept stopping to allow her mother to catch her breath. And we, in turn, had to start and stop accordingly. It was a strange, jerky procession.

Di and the boys were up toward the front, directly behind Charles, who escorted Princess Michael of Kent. I found myself with Gwen Poulstice on one side and Princess Margaret on the other side. The Viscount Linley was up ahead with Andrew's bimbo.

"Hi," I said to the Queen's baby sister.

Margaret looked at me quizzically, then gave me a rather charming smile and said, "Hello there. I don't suppose you have a cigarette."

"I'm sorry, no."

"Well, I've quit, you know, but every now and then I have this extraordinary urge."

"Is one permitted to smoke around the Queen?"

"Oh, I just ignore her. If she expects us to put up with the corgis then she ought to be able to put up with a little smoke, don't you think?"

"Absolutely."

When we arrived at the paddock, we slowed down and waited for the Queen to begin the inspection of the horses. We followed her from stall to stall as she commented on the horses and chatted with the trainers.

The smell of ripe manure merged with the fragrance of expensive perfume. The patter of small talk buzzed around us, punctuated by the occasional snort of a horse.

I lost sight of Di as the line narrowed down and lengthened. All I could see in the distance was Philip's navy hat towering over the group immediately surrounding the Queen. I stared at the horses without interest. They all looked the same to me, nasty brutes with attitudes.

When we got to Hurly Burly I remembered Doris and said to Gwen Poulstice, "That's the winner."

"Really?"

"Uh-huh. The smart money's on Hurly Burly."

"I should think one would want to bet on the Queen's horse, seeing as one *is* her guest."

The line began to double back upon itself to return to the Royal Enclosure. We moved back to make way for the Queen and Philip. As they passed us I issued a small bow.

"That wasn't necessary," Gwen Poulstice whispered through her teeth. "You only bow or curtsy when she first enters a room."

Suddenly there was Di walking directly toward me, holding a prince in each hand. My breath caught. She stopped directly in front of me and smiled. "How nice to see you, Leonard."

I took her proffered hand. "Likewise, Your Royal Highness . . ."

Her hand was soft and pliant in mine. She kept it there several seconds longer than necessary as she gave me a scolding look and said, "I thought we had an agreement."

Then she looked down first at Wills and then at Harry and said, "This is Leonard Schecter."

The two of them gave me perfectly condescending little nods, as if I were a footman. Di gave them each a correctional nudge, and they muttered dutifully, in unison, "How do you do?"

"Fine, thanks. And you know Gwen Poulstice, of course, the former marchioness."

"Yes, of course," said Di, offering her hand, which Gwen Poulstice shook reverentially.

"A pleasure to see you again, ma'am."

"Indeed," said Di. "Well, you'll have to join us in the Royal Box for tea after the race."

"We'd love to," I said quickly.

Gwen Poulstice was speechless. She stood there, mouth slightly agape, as Di and the boys continued back toward the enclosure.

"Gwen," I said, after they were gone, "you feel like having a cup with Liz and Phil?"

Hurly Burly paid thirteen pounds, fifty, and won going away. The Queen's three-year-old, Jodhpurs, finished out of the money. The mood in the Royal Box after the race was appropriately subdued.

A long table was set up along the rear wall for tea. The Queen and Philip sat in the center, their backs to the wall, and from there the seating plan radiated outward roughly in proportion to diminishing status. Gwen Poulstice and I were seated on the extreme left, facing the wall, opposite Andrew's bimbo and Sarah Armstrong-Jones's ex-boyfriend.

Andrew's bimbo, whose name was Sabrina, was a model with acting aspirations. When she found out that I lived in Los Angeles, she became chatty.

"Do you suppose one should have an agent *and* a personal manager?" she asked.

"It couldn't hurt," I replied. "They're both deductible off the top."

"Sorry?"

"They're legitimate business expenses. Of course, you're in for a combined twenty-five percent of your gross."

"Really?"

"Quite."

"Extraordinary . . ."

Photographers were allowed in briefly to take pictures. We turned around and faced the cameras. Those of us in the front row were asked to remove our top hats so as not to block the people in back.

After the photo opportunity, the Queen circulated to greet her guests, accompanied by Philip and an equerry, who made any introductions that were necessary. When they got to us, the equerry stole a glance at his list and said, "Mr. Leonard Schecter and Lady Gwen Poulstice, Your Majesty."

I got up, smiled, and did not bow.

"I should like to present you to Her Majesty, the Queen, and the Duke of Edinburgh."

"I am honored," I said. Gwen Poulstice mumbled something mousy and deferential.

"How nice of you to join us for tea," the Queen uttered. Philip nodded, as if he had a crimp in his neck.

"It is a profound pleasure," I said.

"Lovely day, isn't it?"

"Yes. Though I'm sorry about Jodhpurs."

"Well, one must expect to be disappointed now and again with horses, mustn't one?"

"I bet on him to win."

"Well, then, you are poorer but wiser, Mr. Spector, aren't you?"

"It's all right. I'm on a per diem."

I smiled. There was a moment of bewildered silence as my non sequitur floated through the tea-sodden atmosphere of the Royal Box. Then the equerry, eager to move things along, turned his look to Andrew's bimbo and said, "Miss Sabrina Gorsky, Your Majesty."

Sabrina Gorsky removed the chewing gum from her mouth and smiled at the Queen. Philip crimped his neck somewhat more demonstrably. The Queen clutched her handbag.

.   .   .

I had lied to the Queen. I hadn't bet on Jodhpurs. I had put a hundred quid on Hurly Burly to win. Under the circumstances, however, I thought it better not to cash my ticket immediately.

I had no further contact with Di that afternoon. She disappeared right after tea, apparently, because when I looked for her after my chat with the Queen, her place was empty. And she didn't reappear. But our moment together at the paddock had been captured by several Fleet Street photographers.

When I went to bed that night, I didn't know that the day following the Royal Ascot I was going to become a hot item in the tabloid press. The mystery man from the Togolese embassy had been identified as "Leonard Spector, an American movie producer from Hollywood, here in London to discuss a film career with the Princess of Wales."

The only person who had the story vaguely right was Rupert Makepeace, and he wasn't talking. Yet.

CHAPTER

10

On Monday afternoon, I got a phone call from my lawyer.

"Leonard," she said. "What the hell's going on over there?"

"Going on?"

"I thought you were doing research to write this TV thing."

"I am."

"Well, according to your wife's lawyer, anyone who hobnobs with the British royal family has to have more money than you're declaring."

"What is she talking about?"

"There were pictures of you and Diana at Ascot on *Good Morning America*. They led the 'Show Business Today' segment with speculation that Diana's coming to Hollywood, and that you're bringing her. Your wife thinks you're into something big. She's hitting you with an SDT."

"A what?"

"A subpoena duces tecum. All revenues from all bank accounts worldwide. Sworn affidavits from your agents, stockbrokers, pension-plan managers, bank officers, financial institutions where you have money deposited, cash-value life insurance, jewelry, automobiles, rents, and residuals . . ."

"For chrissakes . . ."

"It gets worse. She's filing for an increase in temporary support."

"An *increase*? She's getting over twenty percent of my gross. My *gross* . . ."

"She's convinced you have money stashed in the Grand Caymans or Switzerland. You don't, do you?"

"No I *don't.* I'm broke except for this per diem I'm getting."

"So do you want me to prepare a brief?"

"Of course I do."

"Actually, you ought to look at this from a cost-effectiveness point of view."

"What the hell does that mean?"

"It means that when you add my fees to her lawyer's fees, which, according to the stipulation in force, you have to pay, until otherwise stipulated, you're looking at some serious change. It may be cheaper just to give her what she wants for a few months until we get into court on permanent support."

"Really?"

"It's your dime."

I told my lawyer I'd get back to her, walked over to the minibar, and helped myself to a Beck's. Then I sat down in the matching wing chair opposite Rivera and looked out the window.

There were paparazzi out there with loaded cameras waiting to ambush me. Back in Hollywood there were people expecting an outline for a prime-time network miniseries, not to mention a subpoena duces tecum.

Under the circumstances, I thought this might be a good time for a dance lesson. I called the Togolese embassy and asked for Kodjo Kponvi. I thanked him for his morning suit and asked if he happened to be free for a lesson at the moment.

"Most assuredly," he replied.

Then I called Rupert Makepeace at the paper.

"Where have you *been*? I have been ringing steadily since Saturday evening," he bellowed into the phone.

"You and every other reporter in this city."

"Well, you could at least have called *me* back."

"I *am* calling you back."

"Leonard, we have to talk."

"Absolutely. But first I have to go to a meeting."

"What kind of meeting?"

"It has to do with the script. Listen, you told me there was a way of getting out of the hotel without being seen."

There was a long pause on the other end. Rupert Makepeace was obviously searching for some quid pro quo for this piece of inside information.

"Dinner tonight?"

"I don't know . . ."

"Leonard, how would you like to have your every step recorded by a relentless phalanx of men with cameras? They will follow you everywhere, even into the loo. Believe me, I know."

"I bet you do."

"There's an Italian restaurant called Cromwell's in Lambeth in St. George's Road near the Imperial War Museum."

"What kind of Italian restaurant is called Cromwell's?"

"Leonard, please. Just do as I say. Eight o'clock. Will you be there?"

"I'll be there."

"Word of honor?"

"Word of honor."

"All right. Now listen carefully. You'll need to be sure not to let the hall porter or any of the chambermaids know when you're going out. They're probably on someone's payroll. Leave your room, look carefully to make sure the coast is clear, then proceed to the service lift at the end of the hallway. Then take that to the basement. You'll get out and walk left past the laundry to a door marked NO WAY OUT. You go through that door and into an alley. Turn right and continue until you reach Curzon Street. Then turn left and follow the street to Berkeley Square, where you will find a taxicab. Have you got it?"

"I got it."

"See you at eight."

"Right."

"One other thing. Take your phone off the hook and put out the DO NOT DISTURB sign before you leave. It makes them think you're still there."

"Why do I want to do that, Rupert?"

"You'll tire them out. Instead of going home and resting, they'll stay on guard. Diana used to do that to us all the time—leave lights and music on and slip out back doors, and we'd stay there, sometimes all night, waiting for her to come out."

"Jesus . . ."

"Whether you realize it or not, dear boy, you are involved in a war of attrition. Your best hope is to tire us out."

With Kodjo Kponvi's morning suit draped over my arm, I slipped out of the Dorchester via Rupert Makepeace's escape route and reached the Togolese embassy without incident.

The visa-and-immigration officer greeted me warmly and took me down to the recreation room in the basement, a large room with a Ping-Pong table, a refrigerator, and a dartboard.

He took a couple of beers out of the refrigerator, uncapped them with his teeth, and handed one to me.

"So we must teach you to dance, *n'est-ce pas?*"

"I thought it would be useful."

"Splendid. What would you like to begin with?"

"What about that dance the ambassador was doing with Diana the other night?"

"Ah, the high life. The dance of dances. If you can do the high life you can do anything. And the beauty of it is that it is so simple. One-two, one-two, one-two, one-one. That's all there is to it."

He turned on a cassette player, and the room filled with music.

Turning to me, he opened his arms and said, "I will lead first. It's simpler at the beginning to follow."

Kodjo Kponvi took me in his arms. "One-two, one-two, one-two, one-one," he intoned and led me gently around the floor.

After a while we switched, and I led. One-two, one-two, one-two, one-one. We were interrupted by the ambassador's wife, Madame Mbtomo, a large, cheerful woman who had heard the music and wandered down to see what was going on. Kodjo Kponvi insisted that I dance with her.

So I danced the high life with Madame Mbtomo. When we were finished, she said, "*Bravo, monsieur.*"

"*Monsieur Spector est un ami intime de la princesse de Galles,*" Kodjo Kponvi said to her.

"*Vraiment?*" Madame Mbtomo exclaimed.

"*Oui. Ils étaient ensemble à Ascot samedi. Vous avez dû voir les photos dans les journaux . . .*"

We took tea in the embassy's parlor, a charming Victorian drawing room with brocade curtains and Persian rugs. Madame Mbtomo excused herself to attend to the ambassador but made me promise that I would return for more high life soon.

"So," said Kodjo Kponvi, "when will you dance the high life with the Princess of Wales?"

"It's hard to say. She's awfully busy."

He looked at me like a big brother and clicked his tongue. "You know what we say in Togo?"

I shook my head.

"*Tcho hamu kpo ga baymah gbava konyo ga.* The arrow sticks in the bow of the lazy hunter."

"Really?"

"It's an approximate translation. Surely, you intend to pursue your suit."

"Well, it's kind of complicated. I'm not exactly sure where our . . . relationship stands."

He gave me another one of his big-brother looks and shook his head. "My dear friend, you are mistaken. One only had to observe you dancing the other night to be confident that she is smitten with you."

"Do you really think so?"

"Most assuredly. A woman's heart is in her legs."

I looked at him blankly.

"More precisely, it is in her knees. When they give a little bit, like a palm tree in the wind, it means that you may be confident of success."

"I see."

"Press on, my friend. Press on with confidence."

I pressed on. As soon as I got back to the hotel, I called Archie at Kensington Palace. The conversation resembled our first one.

When he got to "Will she know what this is regarding?" I added, "Definitely," lest he underestimate the importance of my message.

I left the number and hung up. On the night table was a new stack of phone messages. I now had CBS, NBC, ABC, and CNN wanting to talk to me, in addition to Oprah Winfrey, Phil Donahue, Geraldo Rivera, Barbara Walters, and Ted Koppel, not to mention my guy at the network, Norm Hudris.

I dialed Norm Hudris's office in Hollywood. His secretary patched me through to his car phone.

"Lennie, good to talk to you," he said.

"How're you doing?"

"Great. So it looks like you're doing some firsthand research. Verisimilitude, right?"

"Right."

"Well, listen, we've been kicking things around here with Charlie, and we thought maybe we'd back-burner the miniseries and go for something a little more contemporary."

"What?"

"Well, we were thinking of something along the lines of a memoir, a sort of first-person narrative—you know, like *Beloved*

Infidel or *A Moveable Feast*—a kind of hard-hitting personal recollection of Diana as told from the point of view of someone close to her."

"And who would that be?"

There was a peculiar sound over the line. I couldn't tell if it was traffic on Sunset Boulevard or Norm Hudris's laugh. It turned out to be the latter.

"Boy, you got some sense of humor," he said, chuckling.

"Really?"

"You could write it from the gut. I mean, talk about fresh, raw emotion. So what do you think?"

"Think?"

"We've been kicking around a couple of titles. How do you like *The Princess You've Never Known*? Instead of running it four hours over two nights, we could strip it and run it an hour a night over a week, maybe even run it over two weeks. If it works we roll it into a series, order twenty-two . . ."

When I got Charlie Berns on the line, he was philosophical. "Look," he said, in that quiet, out-to-lunch voice of his, "they're hot on this idea. So why don't we go with it? Suddenly they're talking about twenty-two hours on the air. That's a lot of hours."

"A personal memoir?"

"That's what they're talking about."

"Look, Diana and I just kind of met briefly. We really don't have a relationship . . . yet."

The word *yet* was a mistake. Charlie Berns heard it and seized upon it.

"Hey, that's okay. Take your time. Nurture the relationship. When it's developed, you can start worrying about the conceptualizing."

"That could take months."

"We'll get you an advance in addition to your per diem."

"How do I write about my own relationship . . . assuming there *is* a relationship?"

There was a brief pause over the line, then, "Leonard, anybody can get the ball over the plate. Keeping it low is the trick."

. . .

At a quarter to eight that evening, just as I was about to walk out the door to meet Rupert Makepeace, the phone rang. I almost didn't answer it, assuming it was a reporter. But something made me close the door, go back to the night table, and pick up the phone.

"Leonard?"

She pronounced my name softly, melodically, rolling her tongue languorously over the *l*. My knees immediately began to tremble. Like palm trees in the wind.

"Diana," I answered.

"Would you like to meet?"

"Yes. Of course. When?"

"Straightaway. Trafalgar Square. In front of the National Gallery."

"Isn't that . . . very public?"

"I shall be in disguise."

"Will I recognize you?"

"I shall recognize you."

There was a wonderful, breathy silence, a silence full of unspoken promise, and then she added, "Lovely," and hung up. I stood there transfixed, my heart racing, my mind working a mile a minute.

I tried Rupert Makepeace at his office and was told that he had already left for the day. I would explain it to him tomorrow. I put the DO NOT DISTURB sign on the door and snuck down the hallway to the service elevator.

I followed the escape route to Berkeley Square, got a taxi, and told him to take me to the National Gallery. We drove down Piccadilly into the teeth of the evening theater traffic.

"The National Gallery closes at six, sir," the cabdriver said.

"Really?"

"Yes."

"Extraordinary."

It was ten after when the taxi dropped me in front of the imposing façade of the National Gallery. I looked around, saw nothing but the swirl of traffic. Not knowing exactly where "in front of the National Gallery" was, I chose the middle column in the row of Corinthian columns that made up the façade, put my hands in my pockets, and stared out at Lord Nelson's priapic monument.

Then I saw a woman dressed in a jogging suit get out of a small blue car. She ran right up to me.

"Good evening." She smiled at me, her blue eyes sparkling beneath the hood of the sweatshirt.

I must have done a double take because she said, "It's me."

She put her arm through mine and said, "Come, we shall walk down to the Embankment."

As she led me away, she whispered, "Isn't this exciting?"

"Yes."

"Donald is following along in the car, unfortunately. There is no way to escape Donald. I shall expect him to be buried in my coffin with me."

"I'm glad you called," I said.

"Did you think I wouldn't?"

"I didn't know. You seemed so . . . distant at Ascot."

"We were on display at Ascot. The entire world was watching us. One doesn't want more problems than one already has."

When we reached the river, we turned east into Victoria Embankment. It was full of summer-evening strollers, but nobody seemed to notice the tall woman in the jogging suit and hood, her arm tucked inside the arm of the man in the shabby Bullock's sports jacket.

The sun was still well above the horizon but sinking quickly. The light was magical, bathing the river in the surreal patina of an oil painting. The city smelled of old stone and lilacs.

"And how is the poem coming along?" she asked.

"Splendidly," I lied.

"I have told the Queen."

"You did?"

"Well, we don't want her to believe those dreadful things they're writing in the papers about you, do we?"

"You told her I was writing a poem about you?"

"I said it was about the royal family, actually. She was very pleased. Especially when I said it was an epic poem. With an 'Invocation to the Muse.' She's very fond of poetry."

"Do you think this could lead to a knighthood?"

Her giggle was delightful—a little fluttering sound like a bird's heartbeat—girlish but not without feeling or warmth. I would grow to cherish it.

"You have a marvelous sense of humor, Leonard. Truly. You make me laugh. You have no idea how much I need to laugh these days. It's all so bloody depressing."

"What's wrong?"

"Oh, just about everything. There's Charles and the separation and the lawyers and the newspapers and the boys . . . I don't have fun anymore. Everyone is so dreadfully dull. I miss old Fergie. She's the clever one. She got out. She just picked up and left."

"Where is she?"

"In the States. Prowling Texas for a new millionaire. I had a fax from her last week."

"What did it say?"

"She said how thrilled she was to be free of the Germans. That's what we used to call them behind their backs—the Germans. It's all that intermarriage in the nineteenth century. They talk about fertilizer and castrating horses at tea. It's really quite disgusting. You have no idea what that family is like. She prattles on endlessly at dinner and he sits there and says nothing except to correct the boys' posture."

"It sounds awful."

"It is, believe me. And I must take the boys to see them at Balmoral this weekend. I dread the thought of it. One freezes up there. It's cold even in June, and she's too stingy to turn up the heat. One rides morning, noon, and night and then in the evening one does jigsaw puzzles and plays charades. Charles, of course, is excused. Charles, it seems, is giving a lecture on composting to the Royal Agricultural Society in Chichester . . ."

She gradually ran out of gas and became quiet. We walked

along in silence toward Blackfriars Bridge, the setting sun at our back. Suddenly she stopped, turned to me, and said, "I could become terribly fond of you."

I looked at her and saw moistness in the corners of her eyes. I wanted to lick the tears away. Instead I reached my hand inside her hood and placed it against the side of her face. I could feel the heat of her flesh under my fingers. Her whole body seemed to shudder in a sort of paroxysm of released tension.

It was a defining moment, a watershed moment. In retrospect I see that moment on the Embankment as the first kiss and surrender. Though we did not kiss. Not then.

I could have done many things. I could have spoken some inanity or other. I could have taken her in my arms. I could have licked her tears dry or caressed that wonderful nose. I didn't do any of those things. What I did was entirely involuntary. I recited an as-yet-unwritten quatrain of *The Dianiad:*

> *O that the force of blood revealed*
> *through centuries of wayward time*
> *had fashioned in its sluicing path*
> *this face, this monument sublime . . .*

The words poured out of me. I had no idea where they came from. Suddenly they were on my tongue and I spoke them as if they were written on my heart.

Slowly the creased brow and furrowed eyebrows relaxed, and a rapturous smile overcame her. It was like morning sunlight on a field of daisies.

Then she reached up and put her hand on top of mine, pressed it against her face, and said, "That is so lovely, Leonard."

We stood like that for a long moment. People walked past us without letting their looks linger, embarrassed in their Anglo-Saxon prudery to see two people touching in public. Here on Victoria Embankment, no less, named after a woman who was not amused by extravagant public displays of affection.

Of course, they didn't know who was in that jogging suit. We were just two strangers standing together in the orange light of the setting sun, gazing into each other's eyes.

We parted soon thereafter. There was nothing more to say. We needed to be alone with our thoughts, to mull them over in quiet, to replay the events of the evening in a slow-motion reprise.

She took my hand, held it in front of her face, and put her lips gently against it. A demi-kiss, a gesture of supreme tenderness, more haunting in memory than a kiss upon the lips. And then she turned and jogged off in the direction of the small blue car parked at the edge of Blackfriars Bridge.

CHAPTER

11

The engines of the British Airways Airbus 300 purred quietly as we climbed north out of Heathrow heading for Aberdeen. I was traveling, at Di's suggestion, under the assumed name of John Keats, en route to spend the weekend at Balmoral Castle in Scotland as a guest of the royal family. It had all happened very suddenly.

When I left Di on the Embankment, I hurried to Oliver Cromwell's Italian restaurant to find Rupert Makepeace already gone. He was furious when I finally reached him at his home that night to explain.

"That's it. I am going to write my story. A man is only as good as his word of honor . . ."

I managed to explain to him about Di's last-minute call and invitation. He was only slightly mollified and demanded a full recounting of our walk. I gave him an edited version and once again promised more details as things transpired. I didn't tell him about

Balmoral because I didn't know that I was going to be invited at the time. I didn't know that until midnight, when Di woke me up.

"Leonard," she whispered over the phone.

"Huh?" I was still half asleep.

"I have a splendid idea."

"What's that?"

"I shall ask the Queen to invite you to Balmoral this weekend. I shall tell her you need . . . whatever it is you need for your poem."

"Verisimilitude."

"Precisely. I'll tell her you need verisimilitude. Do say you'll come. It will be so dreary without you."

The fact is I would have gone anywhere with her, even Rancho Cucamonga. But I am getting ahead of my story. That summer weekend, a little more than a year ago, was spent at Balmoral Castle outside Aberdeen in Scotland, a private residence belonging to the Windsors since Victoria and Albert purchased it in 1847. And it was during that fateful weekend in the highlands of Scotland, on the banks of the River Dee, under the endless northern midsummer light, that Di and I walked and talked and told each other our most hidden secrets.

At the airport in Aberdeen there was a tall man in a plaid jacket holding up a sign marked KEATS. I walked over to him and said, "Beauty is truth, truth beauty." He looked at me blankly.

"Mr. Keats?"

"Bobby Burns didn't write that line," I said, handing him my Vuitton garment bag, purchased at Harrods that Friday, and following him out to a black Jaguar sedan, parked in the no-parking zone.

He opened the back door for me, and I slid into the cool leather interior.

"Pleasant flight, sir?"

"Quite."

We drove through the grim industrial suburbs of Aberdeen and out into the countryside. I looked out the window at the rolling farmland and grazing cows and thought, *Leonard, you're not in Cracow anymore.*

Di had gone up the night before with the princes on a Queen's Flight plane. We had spoken several times on the phone since our walk on the Embankment—little stolen conversations at odd hours, full of delightful inanities, giggles, and unspoken promises.

"I'm so terribly pleased you're coming."

"I wouldn't miss it for the world."

"I shall be counting the hours."

In a more practical vein, she had told me to pack warm clothes and a pair of walking boots. And to bring my own shampoo and conditioner.

"She puts out this dreadfully cheap goo for the guests. And never any conditioner. And with the weather being what it is up there, one's hair gets hopelessly tangled."

At Heathrow I had bought a postcard and sent it to Rupert Makepeace.

> Dear Rupert,
>   Going to Balmoral. Sorry but I can't take you. There
> ain't nothing in Balmoral for no monkey woman to do.
>   Keep you posted,
>   John Keats

The allusion would escape him, but at least he wouldn't be given another post-facto report of events.

We went through the town of Ballater, where every other shop displayed the Royal Warrant over its doorway, and back out onto a series of small, winding roads that led to the castle.

The driver took me to a rear entrance to avoid a small group of stringers and tourists with cameras hanging around the main gate hoping for a glimpse of Diana. A man in a cap and hunting boots opened the gate for us, and we drove down a tree-lined road to the castle.

We had to pull over to the side of the narrow road in order to make room for a Land Rover, full of dogs, plowing along at a good clip. I caught a glimpse of a dowdy-looking woman with a kerchief around her head at the wheel.

"The Queen, sir, taking the corgis out for a drive."

We pulled up to the rear of the castle and parked beside a turret. There the driver surrendered me and my luggage to an informally dressed couple, who led me through some winding dark staircases to the guest quarters.

My room was large and round, hidden away in a turret that gave on the opposite side of the castle. The man hung my garment bag in an armoire while the woman laid out fresh towels on the bed.

"If there's anything you need, sir," the woman said, "just press the little button beside the door."

"Does anybody know I'm here?"

"I would assume so, sir."

"Where is the Princess of Wales?"

"She's in Craigowan."

"Craigowan?"

"It's a house on the estate a short way from here. Though I suspect she will be here in the main house for tea."

"What time is tea?"

"Four-thirty sharp, sir. The Queen is quite particular."

They exited, leaving me to the privacy of my turret. It was a little after three. I was presumably on my own until tea.

The welcome was certainly on the minimal side. As were the accommodations. There was a high four-poster bed, the armoire, and a couple of undistinguished oil paintings on the wall. I went into the can to check it out. It was cramped and dark with not much more than the bare necessities. I looked in the shower stall and found the goo that Di had spoken about and no conditioner. There was an electric socket over the sink with a sign that said 220 VOLTS ONLY, and a pull-chain toilet that looked unreliable.

Back in the room, I opened the armoire and the Vuitton and was considering the appropriate wardrobe for tea when I heard a voice say, "Are you the Yank?"

I turned around and saw a kid in designer jeans and Reeboks staring at me from the open doorway. He had blond hair falling over his forehead in that *négligé* English-schoolboy look.

"Yes I am," I replied.

"I'm a prince."

"Really?"

"Mother says she'll meet you at tea."

"You must be Wills."

"I'm Harry. You can call me Prince Hal."

"Where exactly is tea, Prince Hal?"

"In the drawing room."

"I see, and . . . where exactly is the drawing room?"

"Downstairs. We don't get scones in Scotland. We get tarts."

"Sorry about that."

"If you're late, Grandmama gets cross."

And with that he turned and disappeared.

I selected a dark-blue polo shirt, off-the-rack trousers, my Bullock's sports jacket, and my Ballys. As it turned out, I was overdressed. Tea at Balmoral was definitely a come-as-you-are affair.

Though she had removed her kerchief, the Queen was in her driving gear—an old cardigan sweater, plaid skirt, and flats. Philip wore corduroy trousers, hunting boots, and a flannel shirt. Princess Margaret, up for the weekend, showed up in a muumuu with large yellow sunflowers and a straw hat. The princes were in jeans and T-shirts. And Di . . .

Let me back up in order to describe my first sight of her that weekend. I was looking out my turret window, across the expanse of green lawn, when I saw a Mercedes 350 SL drive slowly up one of the side roads that led to the castle. She emerged from the driver's side with the grace acquired from all those exits from official cars that she had made over the years, that is, feet first—red leather boots—then knees, encased in tight baby-blue studded jeans, then the soft swivel of the hips toward the assembled photographers, and finally the unwinding of the tall, willowy frame to its full height.

The fact that there were no photographers and no observers

except me (whom she was unaware of) made no difference to her. She had internalized this maneuver and would never be able to get out of a car again in a haphazard manner. Even when she would emerge from our Ford Aerostar minivan with a bag of groceries from the Alpha Beta, she would do it as if she were facing TV cameras broadcasting around the world. Nobody I have ever known in my entire life can get out of a car the way Di does.

I stood there watching her walk toward the castle, the princes running ahead of her. I waited till she passed directly underneath my window and then called down, " 'He jests at scars that never felt a wound . . .' "

She looked up at me, her pale-blue eyes smiling in anticipation of the face whose voice she had recognized.

" 'It is the east, and Diana is the sun,' " I continued, freely appropriating more Shakespeare. " 'Arise, fair sun, and kill the envious moon, who is already sick and pale with grief that thou her maid are far more fair than she . . .' and so forth."

"That's so beautiful."

"You can never go wrong with Bill."

"Do hurry. You don't want to arrive after the Queen."

"How do I get there?"

"It's in the drawing room, beside the armor room."

I waved and then headed down the dark, drafty hallway to the same staircase I had come up. At the foot of the staircase, I turned into another hallway and followed it for a while until it dead-ended at a locked door. Turning around, I headed back toward the original staircase, looking unsuccessfully for a door.

There was no choice but to go back upstairs and look for another staircase. I ran up the stairs, two at a time, and headed back to my room.

I checked my watch: 4:28. I was cutting it awfully close. I double-checked the hallway but could find no other staircase. Not knowing what else to do, I went back into my room and pressed the panic button. Then I walked over and looked out the window.

Leaning against Di's car was a familiar figure. His eyes, accustomed to scanning the field of vision, eventually caught mine. They stopped and focused.

"Hi." I waved.

Donald did not wave back. Instead he gave me a discreet, undemonstrative nod of recognition.

"You happen to know how to get to tea from here?"

"It's in the drawing room, sir," he said.

"I know but I can't find it."

"It's downstairs, next to the armor room . . ."

I was rescued at that point by the man who had brought in my luggage. He led me down the hallway to the opposite end, where there was a closed, unmarked door, which he opened to reveal another staircase, and we descended together to the ground floor, then through some more hallways, and eventually into the armor room, where Di and the princes were waiting.

"Sorry. I got lost," I explained.

"It's all right. Everyone does."

We passed into the adjoining drawing room, which was empty except for two serving maids, who dropped quick curtsies at Di and the princes. The room was the closest thing to cozy I had seen so far in the castle. There were overstuffed Victorian armchairs, arranged in a semicircle, with little tea tables beside them, and a small fire going in the hearth in spite of the season.

Princess Margaret was right behind the first of the corgis, who ambled in and gave me an indifferent sniff before settling in front of the fire. The Queen's younger sister breezed in, gave her two grandnephews kisses on the cheek, and then extended her hand to me.

"So nice to meet you. I just adore poetry. You must come and visit me sometime in London, and we shall read e. e. cummings together. Are you fond of him?"

"Immensely."

"He's so . . . irreverent. 'I sing of Olaf, glad and big whose warmest heart recoiled at war; a conscientious object-or . . .' What a mischievous little man. Did you know he was a vegetarian?"

"No, I didn't."

More corgis arrived with the Queen and Prince Philip, who sauntered into the room with a businesslike stride as if they were entering an office. The Queen must have been briefed by her private secretary because she came right up to me and said, "How do you do, Mr. Spector?"

I bowed, then turned and bowed to the Duke of Edinburgh, who nodded crisply.

"Mr. Spector's writing a poem about our family," the Queen explained to Philip, as if the presence of this American at tea needed some further explanation.

"Really?" he said.

"Yes."

"So you're a poet, are you?"

"Yes, sir."

"It's going to be an epic poem," Di said.

"Extraordinary," Philip said, barely opening his mouth.

"With an 'Invocation to the Muse,' " Di added.

We had apparently exhausted the subject matter for the moment because there was a prolonged silence. Finally the Queen said, "Well, I suppose we should have some tea. Do sit down please, Mr. Spector."

I chose an armchair away from the fire, but as I approached, one of the corgis jumped up into it and started barking possessively.

"Oh, Daphne, stop it," the Queen scolded.

Daphne didn't stop it, and the Queen looked at me apologetically and said, "Would you mind terribly choosing another seat, Mr. Spector? Daphne gets dreadfully proprietary up here."

I chose another armchair, beside Margaret, and waited for the Queen to be seated. The princes sat together on a settee on the other side of Philip, who ignored them except to tell them to stop fidgeting.

The tea was served in Sèvres china along with lemon and raspberry tarts. The Queen poured. Margaret prattled. The princes fidgeted. A grandfather clock ticked loudly in the corner. Di and I stole glances at each other.

Margaret went on about literature, a subject that apparently did not fascinate the Duke of Edinburgh. He looked as if he were about to doze off. At one point, he turned to me and said, "Spector—is that an English name?"

"Actually, it's Schecter," I said.

"Schecter? Is that German?"

"No, it's Polish. My grandfather's name was Schectowski. He was from Cracow."

"Really?"

"Yes."

"Extraordinary."

It was all out in the open then. His eyes narrowed, and the corners of his mouth tightened, expressing that benign but congenital anti-Semitism of the European upper classes. I stared right back at him. Who the hell did he think he was? The man was a Greek who'd married well.

"Perhaps you'd care to go birding with my husband, Mr. Spector?" the Queen chirped. "I should imagine that birds are an important part of the palette of a poet."

Philip looked at her thinly, obviously not thrilled with the suggestion. "I shouldn't think that Mr. Spector would want to tramp around in the woods looking at birds, my dear," he said.

"That's very kind of you, but I'm sure the Duke doesn't want someone tagging along," I added, hoping the Queen would drop the subject.

"Nonsense," she persisted. "He loves to have someone along to whom he can describe the plumages. He absolutely regaled Mrs. Thatcher a few years back. She told me it was the most entertaining time she'd had in a very long while."

"Perhaps Mr. Spector is a late riser," Philip said, not giving up.

"One doesn't sleep late at Balmoral," the Queen countered.

"I do," said Margaret.

"You are beyond redemption, Margaret."

"Thank god for that."

I looked at Di for help, but she seemed, if anything, amused. She held her teacup delicately between her fingers while keeping an eye on the squirming princes.

"It's settled then," the Queen said. "Six o'clock on the south lawn. Malcolm will knock you up at five-thirty. Do bring a notebook, Mr. Spector. You may find yourself given to dashing off a sonnet."

Di told me later that it was either birding with Philip or riding with the Queen. In the early years of her marriage she had been dragged out of bed at ungodly hours to accompany one or the other of her in-laws in their morning activities. There was simply nothing to be done about it.

"Consider yourself fortunate it's not grouse season," she said.

We were walking together alongside the Dee after tea. Di had sent the princes back to Craigowan with Donald, who had made her promise not to leave the grounds of the estate without telling him.

"Now you know what I'm up against," she said.

"But you're separated, aren't you?"

"You don't separate from this family. They stay with you. One way or another."

We walked in silence for a while, listening to the river rush along beside us. Di seemed moody and distracted. She kept her head down and poked at the brush with a stick. After we had walked for several minutes without speaking, I said, "Are you all right?"

She didn't answer immediately. Shaking her head, as if talking to herself, she muttered something I couldn't hear and then said, "The days are so terribly long this time of year."

"I hope it's not a reflection on the company."

She wasn't in a bantering mood because she passed over that remark and said, "And before long summer will be over. Isn't that sad?"

I nodded rhetorically and waited for more.

"And I am getting older," she went on. "I shall be thirty-two on the first of July."

"That's hardly old."

"One rushes through life so, doesn't one?"

"You've lived a very exciting life."

"Do you really think so?"

"C'mon. You've traveled all over the world. You've met important people. You've been on the cover of every magazine . . ."

"But I haven't really been in love. How can one say one's lived if one hasn't been in love?"

"Not even in the beginning, with Charles?"

"Oh, that wasn't love. That was a fairy tale. I was nineteen. What did I know of love?"

She stopped and sat down on a grassy knoll beside the river. I sat down beside her. She began breaking the stick into little pieces as she spoke.

"Charles would take me here before we were married. To watch him fish. He would stand in the river in those silly boots and fish for hours while I sat here on the bank with a book. When he caught something, he would display it for me, and I would have to look at him with great admiration. That's what Charles wants from a woman. Applause. That's what what's-her-name does. She sits at his feet in a rapture as he drones on about organic rutabagas or architecture or what have you. I would start yawning after a while. That was my crime. I yawned. One doesn't yawn when Charles holds forth. What sign are you?"

It took me a moment to adjust to this rapid change of subject.

"You look like an Aries to me," she said when I didn't reply right away.

"Actually, I'm a Sagittarian."

"Oh, lovely," she said, her face brightening for the first time since tea. "It's a very good sign for a poet. Sagittarius settles down gypsylike where night finds him."

"Really?"

"Could you recite some poetry, Leonard?"

She turned to me with an imploring look. At that moment, sitting there on the banks of the Dee, backlit by the lowering sun, she looked so beautiful that I would not have willingly refused her anything. I would have mounted a horse and ridden off to slay dragons for her.

I closed my eyes, searching for inspiration, clenching my fists and praying for something to come. It took a few seconds, and then it happened again. Just as it had on the Embankment. Like some raging underground stream, a quatrain gushed from within me.

> She sat beside the raging Dee,
> her book in hand, her heart forlorn;
> he turned to her, so proud was he,
> but all she managed was a yawn.

She clapped her hands together like a child and treated me to the four-hundred-watt smile. The real one.

"Oh, Leonard, that's smashing."

"It needs a little work."

"Rubbish. It's wonderful. And you just composed it. Sitting here beside me. How poetic of you!"

"It just happens. Especially when I'm inspired. And you inspire me."

She blushed lightly and unzipped her shoulder bag. Taking out her makeup mirror, she began to examine her face.

"I mean it," I went on. "You make me want to write poetry all the time. You are my muse."

She kept her face averted, fussing with her eye shadow. The lowering sun bathed her in dark yellow-red light. The nose—*my* nose—gleamed like polished marble. If Rodin had happened by, he would have grabbed a chisel and gone immediately to work.

Across the river, Rivera sat glaring into the water. We exchanged a look. He said, "Take her. She wants you to."

I didn't take her. Not there, not on the banks of the Dee with the flies beginning to hum and the smell of hay and cow dung in the air. But I did kiss her.

I waited for her to put the makeup case back in the shoulder bag, then reached over and put my left hand against the right side of her cheek. I kept it there for a moment, resisting the temptation to allow my index finger to wander north and caress the contours of her nose.

I could feel her soft breath on the heel of my hand. Very gently, I turned her face toward mine. She did not resist. Her pale-blue eyes said, *Yes, please.*

Our lips touched so softly, so tentatively, that for a moment I wasn't sure we were actually kissing. Did we in fact kiss there on the banks of the Dee? Sometimes when I look back through the prism of the past I see different colors. So much has happened since then.

If we didn't, then we should have. And so it really makes no difference. Whatever the case, there was a surrender on both our parts. We went through another of those invisible doors that close gently and irrevocably behind you.

And we emerged on the other side with a new sense of each other. We now had a taste in our mouths that we couldn't easily forget. We had sipped at the fountain and would be forever thirsty.

CHAPTER

12

That evening I learned of another one of the royal family's peculiar habits. Tea was usually the only meal they took together when they were *en famille.* Supper was sent up on trays to their private quarters to be eaten in front of the TV.

And so I didn't see Di again that night. When we parted, we were both overcome with a sudden shyness. We could barely look at each other. We walked back along the river, hand-in-hand, until we came in sight of the castle. Then she quickly let go.

"We must be very careful," she said. "We must give them no occasion for suspicion."

"Of course."

"You do understand, don't you, Leonard?"

"Absolutely."

"I shall eat supper with the boys at Craigowan tonight."

"Right."

"You must eat at the castle."

"Sure."

"But I shall be thinking about you."

She turned to me, a far-off look in her eyes. How I longed to put my lips back on hers at that moment—to take her in my arms and inhale her sweetness. But Donald could be lurking anywhere or Philip out watching birds with a pair of high-powered binoculars.

"I shall see you in the morning, after your birding with Philip," she said.

"And I shall see you in my dreams," I whispered.

"Oh, Leonard," she sighed, pursing her lips and blowing me a silent kiss. Then she ran off across the lawn toward the Mercedes. She took long, doelike strides, covering ground like a marathon runner. When she reached the car, she looked back and waved.

I stood there watching until she'd turned the car around and taken off down the dirt road toward Craigowan. As she disappeared from view, I muttered, "*Au revoir,* sweet princess . . ."

And so it was Margaret and I alone at the enormous solid oak table in the dining room. She had changed out of her muumuu and was wearing a dark velvet cocktail dress with a cardigan thrown over her shoulders against the Highland chill.

As soon as we sat down, she asked, "Do you drink?"

"Sure."

"Thank god. Nobody in this family touches a drop."

She called over one of the servants and said, "Malcolm, would you go down to the cellar, please, and fetch us a bottle or two of wine. Something wonderfully rare and expensive."

"Yes, ma'am."

"The last time we had a decent bottle up here was when De Gaulle visited. If it was up to my sister, she would have served him some of that beastly sweet German wine the relatives in Germany send us. Do you have a cigarette, by any chance?"

"I'm afraid not."

"Well, I've given it up, but it doesn't seem to have stopped me from smoking, does it?"

Malcolm returned with a Château Latour '61 and a Pommard '70.

We had the Latour as an aperitif. By the time we got into the Pommard, Margaret was reciting Vachel Lindsay's poem "The Congo." She kept the drum rhythm up with the blunt end of her butter knife.

"Don't you just love that throbbing, primitive Negro energy?" she said when she had finished.

"Yes."

"It's so *African.*"

Dinner was overdone rack of lamb served on Limoges china. Malcolm carved at a side table and kept our Waterford crystal wineglasses full.

"Now tell me about this poem you are writing about the Windsors," Margaret said.

"Well, it's sort of a family chronicle written in verse, an epic, I suppose . . ."

"Really? Are you going to go all the way back to George I?"

"At least."

"Well, if you ask me, all those German Georges were half crazy. I would forget about them. I think this family really begins with Victoria. Now she was *English.* When someone said something she didn't like, she would look at them over her spectacles and say, 'We are not amused.' Isn't that marvelous?"

I nodded, trying, with some difficulty, to stay afloat on the sea of Latour and Pommard.

"So you have come up here to do research, have you?"

"To get verisimilitude, actually," I said.

"Verisimilitude. Splendid. One needs that to write well, doesn't one?"

"Absolutely."

It was during dessert, a runny crème brûlée, that Margaret finally got off the subject of poetry.

"May I offer a reflection, Mr. Spector?"

"By all means."

"Diana is a very confused young woman. And though she is separated from my nephew, she maintains a great responsibility in her role as mother of at least one if not two of the future sovereigns of this nation. Frankly, I don't think poetry suits her."

I looked across the table at her, trying to read her expression through the haze of wine. It was difficult to tell if there was irony in her words. Margaret had a good poker face.

"Really," I said.

"Yes."

"Extraordinary."

It was still dark when I was knocked up by Malcolm. He entered with a tray and switched on the electric candles in the wall sconces, then opened the turret shutters to the blackness outside.

"Good morning, sir," he said, putting the tray down on a night table. "I trust you slept well."

"Yes," I lied. The wine and the lamb and the crème brûlée had combined to cause an agitated night. I emerged from the covers into the dampness of the room, feeling the first dull throbbing in the temples that indicated the onset of a hangover.

"Milk and sugar, sir?"

I nodded dully and watched him prepare my tea. Then he opened the armoire and scanned the contents.

"Perhaps the heavy sweater and the blue jeans would be appropriate this morning."

"Right."

He laid them out over the edge of the bed, then returned to the armoire to select a pair of shoes. There were only two—the Ballys and a pair of Reeboks. He chose the Reeboks without consulting me. Then he laid out my black Calvin Klein briefs.

"You'll be shaving this morning, sir?"

"What do you think, Malcolm?"

"I beg your pardon?"

"Does one shave for birding?"

"Most definitely, sir. I'll prepare your shaving articles."

As he started toward the bathroom, I said, "Malcolm?"

He turned, looked at me. "Sir?"

"Go away."

A hurt expression came over his face. He stood there for a moment, absorbing my words, then nodded curtly, turned, and exited. I forced myself out of bed and took my teacup into the bathroom.

Standing there shivering, my bare feet on the cold stone, I thought of Di. She would still be fast asleep, under a down comforter, no doubt, her arms wrapped around her pillow. Was she thinking about me last night? Did she curl up all alone on the couch and watch the telly? Did she replay our kiss in her mind, as I had done a hundred times already?

Oh, Di . . . what is there that I wouldn't do for you? I am going out into the freezing dawn to gaze at birds with your anti-Semitic father-in-law. Does true love have any greater testament?

I shaved in tepid water, dressed, and made it out to the south lawn just as the sky began to lighten. Philip was there with his detective—a tall, thin man named Ted—and a Doberman pinscher with his ears taped back, who growled at me.

"Good to see you," Philip mumbled.

"Good morning, Your Royal Highness."

Ted handed me a pair of binoculars and said, "I hope you'll find these suitable, sir."

We set off into the chilled blackness, the three of us and the dog, walking in silence over the expanse of lawn and into the fields beyond. As the day brightened behind us, the birds began to make a racket. Which didn't help my hangover any.

We walked single file, with the dog leading the way, followed by Philip, then me, and Ted in the rear. After we had walked for a mile or two, Philip stopped, trained his binoculars on a tree branch, and said, "Tit warbler at eleven o'clock."

I trained my binoculars at eleven o'clock and saw nothing. We walked some more and stopped again.

"Abington red thrush at three o'clock." I raised my binoculars dutifully and again saw nothing.

"Lovely, Mr. Spector, isn't he?"

"Beautiful."

And so forth. We walked. We stopped. We trained our binoculars on trees. Philip identified birds. I pretended to see them. Ted checked the woods for assassins. The dog peed on tree trunks. My temples throbbed.

This went on for an hour or so before we finally turned and headed back toward the castle. The Duke became slightly more expansive on the trip back.

"Where exactly do you live in the States, Mr. Spector?"

"Los Angeles."

"So you're from Los Angeles, are you?"

"Yes."

"Extraordinary. I don't suppose you shoot grouse there?"

"We shoot movies there."

This didn't even get a chuckle out of him. He had, it turned out, something else on his mind.

"My son Charles, you know, is an excellent shot."

"Really?"

"Yes."

"I thought he had given up shooting because of his interest in ecology."

"He just needs to be properly motivated."

We were playing soccer on the front lawn of Craigowan, a nice-sized country home about half a mile from the castle. It was Prince Hal and I against Di and Wills. Donald looked on impassively from the sidelines.

The match was hotly contested. Di had a nasty shot on goal, a slicing line drive off the tapered toe of her black Moroccan leather boots. Wills was passive-aggressive, feigning an indifferent attitude to mask a fierce competitiveness. And Prince Hal, my teammate, ran around shouting, "Give it here, give it here."

Afterward, as we sat on the grass cooling off, Wills added his sentiments to those already expressed by Margaret and Philip.

"My father could play rings around you, you know," he said.

"I'm sure he could."

"He's in Chichester this weekend giving a very important speech."

"So I'm told."

"And he used to play polo—quite well, as a matter of fact. We have dozens of trophies at Highgrove."

It was becoming clear that the Windsors perceived me as a threat. It only remained for the Queen to add her point of view. And that wasn't long in coming. It happened at tea, before I was driven off to Aberdeen to catch my plane back to London.

We were in the drawing room again, all of us and the corgis, and the Queen was talking about a horse she had put to stud recently.

"Of course, one never knows how these things work out, does one?"

Nobody contradicted her, so she went on. "It really is entirely a matter of breeding." She looked right at me when she said it.

"Yes, of course," I mumbled.

"Well, I hope you have gathered a sufficient amount of verisimilitude, Mr. Spector," she remarked as we said good-bye. The implication was clearly that there was no reason to return.

Di and I had only a brief moment alone that Sunday. It was after soccer, when the boys went inside to play Nintendo. We were on the grass in the warming sun, observed only by Donald at a distance.

"Are you glad you came?" she asked.

"Absolutely."

"I'm sorry we had so little time together."

"I understand."

"What happened yesterday . . ." She stopped, embarrassed. My heart stopped with her. I was afraid she was going to disavow the moment, protest that it was merely an aberration, never to occur again. But she didn't. In fact, she did just the opposite.

"It was wonderful."

"Yes."

"Don't abandon me, Leonard. I don't think I could manage without you."

And then, coloring deeply, she got up and hurried off into the house.

CHAPTER

13

Rupert Makepeace was waiting for me at Heathrow. He took my arm as if he were making an arrest and led me toward the parking garage.

"How are you doing, Rupert?"

"Splendidly," he said. "I have spent a delightful Sunday checking passenger lists. You are, strangely enough, the only John Keats flying from Aberdeen to London today."

"Well, beauty is truth, you know what I mean . . ."

As we entered the subterranean depths of the parking garage, I said, "Nice of you to pick me up."

He didn't reply. Instead he steered me along the rows of cars until we reached the Austin Healey.

"Well," I said, "at least I won't have to explain to the cabdriver that I want to be let off two blocks from the Dorchester."

"We're not going to the Dorchester."

"We're not?"

"We're going out to eat."

"We are?"

"Yes. And you're paying."

He fired up the Healey and said nothing more to me until we arrived at Oliver Cromwell's Italian Restaurant in Lambeth. The place was dark and empty, with tapestries on the walls and plastic grapes hanging from the ceiling. It looked like a front for the Puritan Mafia.

Rupert Makepeace did not complain when we were shown to a Siberia table in the rear of the restaurant by a short dark man in a very expensive suit. It was clear that what this restaurant had to recommend it was the fact that nobody went there.

He kept on his raincoat and cap, lit a cigarette, sighed, and then said, in a quieter voice than usual, "All right, Leonard, you have led me on a merry chase. Now it's time to come clean."

I grabbed a bread stick and chewed on it noncommittally.

"It appears as if I am the only reporter in London who has absolutely no idea what is going on between you and Diana."

"I told you, nothing . . . really . . ."

"Leonard, I have a professional reputation to uphold. My readers expect me to have the latest and most accurate information about the royal family, and I find myself in the position of being unable to satisfy them, while all around me things are being written about you and Diana by other reporters on other newspapers."

"What are they writing?"

"An enormous amount of rubbish. But it doesn't matter. The story has taken on a life of its own. It's the hottest story in England at the moment, and Rupert Makepeace, who was instrumental in introducing Leonard Schecter to the Princess of Wales, is, as you say so charmingly in your country, sucking hind tit."

"Can we order something to eat?"

"Not until you talk."

"Are you going to starve me to death, Rupert?"

"No, I shall bludgeon you to death."

He looked like he meant it. His face was flushed, his large beefy hands clenched in a position that could be construed as preparatory to violence. I could quite easily imagine him sitting on my chest and bellowing into my ear until I relented.

"Can I have a drink, at least?"

He called the waiter over and ordered two Bass ales without asking me what I wanted.

"Now," he said after the beer arrived, "what is this rubbish about Diana and the movies?"

I imagined Diana in Hollywood and started to laugh. There would be a feeding frenzy. She'd be offered five-picture deals. Writers would be hired to come up with vehicles for her. She would co-star with Kevin Costner in colonial epics about Indian wars and in melodramas about brain-damaged heiresses. There would be TV series developed for her, sitcoms about divorced princesses living in Pacoima with two kids, in unresolved relationships with their gardeners, wisecracking Hispanics who played the congas in salsa bands.

"What is so bloody amusing, Leonard?"

"I guess you had to be there," I said.

"What does that mean?"

He was chewing on his cigarette, getting progressively more cranky. I realized I had to give him something, but frankly, I was at a loss for what it should be. So I told him about the poem. He did a very neat take, like Ronald Colman being informed by his butler that the police were at the door wanting a word with him.

"A poem?" he said, after a moment. "You're writing a *poem* about Diana?"

"Yes."

"What kind of poem?"

"An epic poem."

"An *epic* poem?" he repeated.

Rupert Makepeace had a great deal of difficulty digesting this information. Then he said quietly, "What about that TV-movie business?"

"That's been back-burnered."

"Sorry?"

"They want to go in another direction. Maybe some sort of

first-person-memoir thing, sort of like *Beloved Infidel*, you know what I mean?"

"Does the Palace know about this?"

"Well, not exactly. You see, they think I'm writing a poem about the Windsors, which is how I got invited up to Balmoral for the weekend. Pretty dreary place, by the way. Have you been?"

"Many times. Though never inside."

"You're not missing anything, believe me. They put me up in this dingy turret with a bathroom that looked like it belonged in a Motel 6. And they don't even put out conditioner . . ."

"Did you dine with the Queen?"

"No, I dined with Margaret. Tête-à-tête."

"Margaret?"

"Yes, she recited Vachel Lindsay's 'The Congo' while beating her butter knife against the table to give the effect of native drums."

"Did the Queen receive you?"

"Oh, yes. We had tea. And I went birding with Philip at the crack of dawn on Sunday. We saw tit warblers and red thrushes. Unfortunately, I had a hangover. Margaret and I had polished off a '61 Latour and a '70 Pommard over dinner the night before."

"Where was Diana?"

"She was in Craigowan with the boys. We played a little soccer together on Sunday. It was Prince Hal and I against Di and Wills. They won."

"Leonard, you're not making this up, are you?"

I shook my head gravely. He looked at me for several seconds, gauging my sincerity, then handed me a menu.

After we ordered dinner, I told Rupert Makepeace everything except the lead story—that Di and I were falling in love, that we had kissed by the side of the Dee.

The food arrived, but he barely touched his. He was too busy scribbling in a notebook. He didn't miss much. My veal parmigiana tasted like it had been frozen for a decade.

"You realize," I said to him, "that you can't print that I'm writing a poem about Diana."

"And why not?"

"Because the family doesn't know. They already don't like me. In fact, while I was up at Balmoral I received veiled threats from everyone, even Wills. If you write about *The Dianiad*, they'll do everything in their power to keep me away from her."

"Well, that's a story in itself, isn't it?"

"Rupert, listen to me," I said. "You already have a scoop with the Windsor family poem and the weekend at Balmoral. You can write about the tea and the birding and all that. Isn't that enough?"

He looked at me, unconvinced, lit another cigarette, and extinguished the old one in his pasta.

"I promise that you'll be the only reporter I talk to," I went on. "You'll have the inside story."

"I believe you told me that once before."

"A lot of things have happened since then."

"And what if I don't agree?"

I took a moment before replying. I wanted him to appreciate the delicacy of the situation. We were locked into a symbiotic relationship in which the leverage kept shifting from one of us to the other.

"Can we talk turkey here, Rupert? I like you. You've been a great help to me. If it wasn't for you, I might never have met Di. But now we have a new ball game, as we say so charmingly in my country. I don't need you anymore to get to Di. All I have to do is pick up the phone."

I let that thought linger for a moment, then cut to the chase. "So here's the deal. I will continue to give you scoops, but you will continue to write only what I approve. Otherwise, I'll call Barbara Walters, who leaves me messages every day, and tell *her* all."

"You wouldn't do that, would you?"

"I would very much like not to have to."

There was a long moment of silence. He stared morosely into his Bass ale, clearly unhappy about the alternatives. I could tell that he was searching for a way to beg the question. But as far as I was concerned, it was a very clear-cut deal. He was going to be my press secretary, in effect. Or else he was going to be out in the rain with all the rest of them.

"Rupert," I said, with a tone of finality, "this is how it is. No *Dianiad*. Not a word about it. Otherwise, it's Barbara Walters. I swear."

A scowling Rupert Makepeace drove me back to the Dorchester at frightening speeds. I couldn't tell whether he wanted to kill us or just get rid of me fast so he could hurry to the office and write his story.

He dropped me two blocks from the hotel and sped away in the general direction of his office. I cut up the alley behind the hotel and in the rear door. The service elevator stopped on the first floor, and a chambermaid got in. She looked at me, puzzled to see me coming up from the basement, and asked, "Can I help you, sir?"

"No thanks."

When I got to my room, I found the message light on the telephone blinking madly. I called down to the desk and asked them to send up my messages. The bellman arrived with an enormous stack that had come in since Saturday morning, when I'd left for Scotland. There were forty or so calls from reporters, including call-backs from Barbara, Oprah, Phil, and Geraldo. On Barbara's message, in parentheses, was her home number. There were also calls from Norm Hudris, Charlie Berns, and Brad Emprin.

I poured myself a Beck's from the minibar, found a *Murder, She Wrote* rerun on TV, hit the mute button on the remote control, and dialed Charlie Berns's number in Beverly Hills.

"Charlie. It's Leonard."

As always with Charlie Berns, it took a moment for the synapses to kick in and transmit the message. He was like a poorly wired fuse box.

"Leonard, guess what," he said after a long moment of silence. "Norm Hudris is offering an on-air commitment."

"An on-air what?"

"An on-air anything. As long as it has Diana in it."

I took a deep breath and looked up at the TV. Angela Lansbury was pointing her finger accusingly at Ricardo Montalban.

"Look, Charlie," I said, "I think they're jumping the gun here.

Diana is not interested in coming to Hollywood to be on television."

"It's been all over the papers."

"They write all sorts of shit about her. It's not true, believe me. I know. I spent the weekend with her."

As soon as the words were out of my mouth, I realized I'd made a mistake. It was throwing a big fat log on the fire I was trying to put out.

"What I mean is," I went on quickly, "I was invited up to Scotland as a guest of the Queen. You see, I had this idea of gathering more verisimilitude about the world Diana lives in. So I told them I was writing a poem about the Windsors, and the Queen invited me to Balmoral."

"A poem?" Charlie said.

"Yeah."

"You shitting me?"

"No."

"Don't shit a shitter, Leonard."

"I'm just keeping the ball low, Charlie."

He laughed. It was the first time I had ever heard Charlie Berns laugh. It was a full-bodied, rolling laugh that went on for some time. When he stopped laughing, I said, "I'm spending a lot of money over here, between airfare and clothes and meals . . ."

"Research material, right?"

"Right."

"What do you need? Ten, twenty grand?"

"Twenty."

"I'll have the network wire it to you tomorrow morning."

After I hung up with Charlie Berns, I dialed Brad Emprin's home number in Encino. He picked up on the first ring, as if he had been spending his Sunday sitting by his phone waiting for it to ring.

"Brad. It's Leonard Schecter."

"Jesus, where have you been? I've been leaving messages for days."

"Working, Brad. I've been working."

"So you don't return your phone calls?"

"I've been out of town doing research."

"Well, listen, put a hold on the whole thing."

"What're you talking about?"

"We have every network, studio, independent producer, and cable company calling us seven times a day. They all want a piece of this deal."

"We have a deal, Brad. With Charlie Berns."

"That's for a TV miniseries. *One* TV miniseries. That's all he bought. What about episodic television, feature movies, sequels, books, theater, interactive videos, computer games, T-shirts? They're all wide open. We haven't even begun to deal on this yet . . ."

Ricardo Montalban was trying to get out the door, but Tom Bosley cut him off. Angela Lansbury grabbed her pocketbook, put it smartly on her shoulder, and told Ricardo just how she'd known it was him all along.

Watching Angela nail Ricardo, it occurred to me that if you were going to fuck around, you might as well do it right. Maybe it was time to put Brad Emprin and his band of thugs to work for me. As the Petitioner's lawyer had argued so forcefully in Section 29 of the Los Angeles County Superior Court, the upside potential for income in the entertainment business was unlimited.

So I told Brad Emprin to go for it. I told him to make deals, stack them up, one behind the other, and make sure there was cash up front. I would deliver Diana's story. I would turn it into TV programs, movies, video games, and T-shirts. Anything they wanted.

I hung up and lay there on the bed, thinking about what I had just done. I had unleashed a band of ravenous vultures into the smoggy skies of Los Angeles. They would pick the town clean and mail me the proceeds, which I would do my best to hide from the purview of the Petitioner and her army of forensic accountants.

Ten thousand miles away, on the shores of the Pacific, an inexorable chain of events would begin to unfold. Phone calls would be exchanged, promises made, deals cut. Diana would go through Hollywood like a tornado.

It all meant nothing to me. It was background noise. I was listening to different music. I was listening to love songs. I was hearing tit warblers in my heart.

CHAPTER

14

Even before Rupert Makepeace's story hit the streets, Buckingham Palace felt it necessary to make a statement regarding the rumors. A spokesman for the Queen denied categorically that the Princess of Wales had any intention of going to America to pursue a career in the entertainment business. He went on to add that Mr. Leonard Spector was not, as had been widely reported, a Hollywood film producer, but rather a distinguished American poet who was writing an epic poem about the Windsors.

This took a little bit of wind out of Rupert Makepeace's sails, but not enough to blunt the impact of the story that ran on page 1 of *The London Herald* under the headline DIANA WITH POET AT BAL-MORAL.

The widely-circulated rumours of The Princess of Wales's liaison with a Hollywood film producer and her interest in a possible movie career were quashed this weekend when the *Herald* learned exclusively that the so-called film producer, Leonard Schecter, is in fact a poet who was invited to Balmoral to meet the subjects of his projected epic poem. Mr. Schecter is in Britain to gather "verisimilitude" for his work—a "lengthy and lyrical recounting of the Queen's family history dating back to George I."

Mr. Schecter spent the weekend at Balmoral as a house-guest of the Queen and the Duke of Edinburgh and dined on Saturday evening with Princess Margaret, a great lover of po-etry. He spent Sunday morning bird-watching with Prince Philip and then returned to London directly after tea.

In an exclusive interview with the *Herald*, Mr. Schecter expressed dismay at the reaction to his visit and to the rumours of a possible romantic liaison with Princess Diana. "We're really just friends," he said. "She has a great appreciation for poetry and wants to be helpful in my research." When asked how he liked his birding expedition with the Duke of Edinburgh, he replied, "It was great. The Duke is a very gracious host. As was the entire family. I couldn't have been more hospitably re-ceived."

Other papers, however, persisted with their stories about Diana and Hollywood. Headlines flashed from newsstands. TV and radio commentators repeated the rumors and the Palace's denials. Oprah, Phil, Geraldo, and Barbara continued to call and leave their home numbers. Outside the Dorchester the paparazzi increased their guard; a small army of people with cameras now stood vigil around the clock, waiting to follow me to Diana and photograph us locked in either a passionate embrace or a venal business deal or both.

It wasn't long before my secret route in and out of the Dorches-ter had been compromised. It had no doubt been the chambermaid in the service elevator who blew my cover. I was on my way to catch a cab in Berkeley Square to meet Kodjo Kponvi for a high-life lesson at the Togolese embassy when I noticed a motorcycle driving slowly along Curzon Street behind me. On it was a young man with several cameras strapped across his chest like ammunition belts on a guerrilla soldier.

I doubled back to Piccadilly, and he followed me. Then I turned against the traffic, forcing him to continue his pursuit on foot. He left the motorcycle on the sidewalk in front of the Athenaeum and followed me west. I slowed down. He slowed down. I stopped. He stopped. Several times I saw him take what must have been a tele-photo from the collection of cameras hanging around his neck and fire on the run.

I reached Hyde Park Corner and ducked into the tube station. Halfway down the escalator I turned and saw him at the top, descend-ing. Then, on the eastbound platform of the Piccadilly Line, I had an inspiration.

I walked over to the large underground map on the wall and studied it. Taking out my pocket street guide to London, I found what I was looking for. Then I waited for the train.

He got in the same car, sat at the other end, took out a newspaper. He followed me off the train at the Holborn station and up Southampton Row to Great Russell Street, all the way to the steps of the British Museum. Just before entering, I stopped and turned full face toward him, making sure I was framed with the plaque beside the door. He fired off a half-dozen fast shots. I even smiled for him.

I entered and followed directions to the Reading Room, where I was told that I would need a special pass. When I explained that I was an American poet doing research on the history of the Windsors, I was handed a form and told to fill it out and bring it to a referee. I had no idea what they were talking about. As far as I was concerned, a referee was a guy in a striped shirt with a whistle around his neck. But I never had any intention of actually reading books on the Windsors. I knew far too much about those people as it was. So I took the form, smiled, and asked for directions to the men's room.

My tail followed me toward the men's room, through a throng of Japanese tourists exiting the Duveen Gallery. Seizing my opportu-nity, I turned abruptly and cut into the middle of the group, squeez-ing between two Japanese in midconversation. I ran past the Elgin Marbles and back out through the Room of the Caryatid.

In the clear for the briefest of moments, I made a dash through Egyptology and back toward the Reading Room, then turned left instead of right and hurried through the King Edward VII Gallery and out the rear entrance onto Montague Place.

Once outside, I felt a sense of exultation. Not only had I slipped my tail but I had managed to provide evidence in support of my cover story—that I was writing a poem about the Windsors. It worked like a charm. In the exclusive story in *The Mail* the next day, there was not only a picture of me on the steps of the British Museum but also a statement from the Reading Room guard that I was doing research on the royal family.

Di remained incommunicado for several days following our weekend at Balmoral. I phoned and left messages with Archie, but there was no call from her until midnight Thursday.

I had been out with Gwen Poulstice having dinner at an outrageously expensive restaurant in Kensington, spending some of the money Charlie Berns had gotten the network to wire me. I had decided to cultivate Gwen Poulstice in the event that I would need a beard again. She had become more amiable after I had become a bona-fide celebrity, and we even managed to have a laugh or two.

"Well, Gwen, when's the last time you got laid?" I had said over brandy that night.

"Is that an offer, Leonard?" she had replied, her eyebrow raised an inch or two above normal.

"Nothing would give me greater pleasure, but I'm saving myself for Diana."

"I should think you'll have a rather long wait."

When Di called at twelve on the dot, her voice was frisky and flirtatious. "Have you been thinking about me, Leonard?"

"All the time. Where are you?"

"In KP."

"I mean, where exactly?"

"In my bath."

"What are you wearing?"

She laughed. I adored that laugh. Then: "Are we going to talk naughty?"

"Why not?"

There was a pause, during which I could actually hear the water splashing in the tub, then she said, "Are you in bed?"

"Yes," I lied. I was actually sitting on one of the wing chairs playing gin rummy with Rivera.

"What are *you* wearing?"

"My Calvin Klein briefs."

"Is that all?"

"That's all. Would you like me to describe them to you?"

"All right."

I described them. Then I said, "Di, can we see each other?"

"I'd like that very much."

"Let's go dancing."

"Dancing?"

"How about the high life? I know this African place in Soho."

"Lovely."

"The trick is not to have dinner there."

So at midnight Friday, I found myself once again standing in front of the National Gallery in Trafalgar Square waiting for Di. We had a rendezvous to go dancing at Même Mère, Même Père. I had told only Kodjo Kponvi about it and had sworn him to secrecy.

The British Museum story had cooled off the paparazzi for the moment, and I was once again able to enter and leave my hotel by the front door. Oprah, Phil, Geraldo, and Barbara had stopped calling. Even Rupert Makepeace was quiet, boxed in by his own story. He had gone off to Juan-les-Pins for a few days to cover the latest Fergie escapade. The Duchess of York had been caught on the beach at 3 A.M. allegedly topless with members of a Finnish rock band. *Paris Match* featured it on its cover. Rupert Makepeace wrote a jaundiced account for the *Herald* under the headline FERGIE FROLICS WITH FINNS IN FRANCE.

Norm Hudris had called, wondering if I could somehow incorporate the latest Fergie furor into whatever it was I was doing with Di. "We could call it *The Naughty Women of Windsor*," he suggested. I said I'd see what I could do.

My life had been relatively peaceful for several days. I had spent my mornings working on *The Dianiad*, my afternoons walking around London, my evenings at expensive restaurants, and my nights dreaming about Di.

I had dreamt about Di a great deal. I dreamt of her in her jogging suit on the Embankment. I dreamt of her sitting beside the Dee, backlit by the setting sun. I dreamt of her in bed, surrounded by lace pillows. I dreamt of her in the bathtub, the tips of her knees emerging from the warm water like mountain crests . . .

Now she was behind the wheel of a small dark-blue Mercedes, her detective in the backseat. Pulling up in front of the National Gallery with the liquid squishing of disc brakes, she opened the passenger door for me with a resplendent smile.

I got in, and she threw the Mercedes smartly in gear and took off. She looked like a typical Sloane Ranger out for a night of disco dancing—a short skirt, tights, and a fishnet blouse.

"How're you doing?" I said to Donald, who was sitting there vigilantly, hand on weapon.

"Very well, thank you, sir."

Di explained that when she went out in London, it was standard procedure for her to drive, leaving Donald with his hands free to respond to attacks. When she first became engaged to Charles, she said, she had been given the complete antiterrorist defensive-driving course at the police track in Wembley.

"I can do an evasive-action skid stop. Would you like to see it?"

"I would not suggest it, ma'am."

"Just joking, Donald."

Di drove quickly and well. She told me that the Mercedes was just one of the security cars she used when she went out in London and didn't want to be recognized.

"We change the number plates to fool the reporters," she said with a certain satisfaction in her voice.

The presence of Donald inhibited intimate talk, and so we

chatted blandly until we pulled up in front of Même Mère, Même Père. High-life music drifted out onto the sidewalk, but there were no reporters or crowds outside the door. Kodjo Kponvi had kept his word.

Donald insisted on going in first to check the place out, leaving us alone for the first time that evening. We sat together in the front seat, suddenly shy with each other. There was so much to say and so little.

"I've missed you," I said finally, to break the silence.

She looked away for a moment, color rising to her face. Then she went for her makeup bag, a gesture that, I would learn, she adopted when she was nervous. Bending the rearview mirror down in her direction, she touched up her nude-tone lipstick until Donald returned.

He leaned in the window and said, "I'm not particularly happy with this, ma'am."

"What seems to be the problem, Donald?" There was impatience in Di's voice. They were like an old married couple who kept having the same disagreements over and over again.

"There's only one door in and out, for one thing. In the event of a disturbance, it would be very difficult to get you out of there. Moreover, the place is small and crowded. You could quite easily be injured while dancing, and there would be a problem evacuating you . . ."

"Oh, Donald, stop it. Really. I shall survive very well, thank you." And she got out of the car, effectively cutting off further discussion.

Kodjo Kponvi was waiting for us at the door. He bowed low to Di, then rose with a big smile.

"Welcome to Même Mère, Même Père, Your Royal Highness."

"Thank you so much," Di said.

Madame Mbtomo was there, as well as Kodjo's half-brother Kosi and his wife, Kumla, and about a hundred other people jammed into the small room. The music stopped temporarily as Di, with that superb grace she demonstrates in situations like these, greeted people.

Kodjo Kponvi walked around with us making the introductions. When we were finished, he turned to us and said, "Well, then, splendid. I suppose you have come to dance, *n'est-ce pas?*"

He signaled to the band, a four-piece ensemble crowded into one corner, and they immediately started playing an up-tempo high life.

I took Di in my arms, waited for the upbeat, as Kodjo Kponvi had taught me, and started to dance. It was like a wedding. People watched and clapped for a few moments as the bride and groom danced the first dance, then gradually joined in. First Kodjo Kponvi and Madame Mbtomo, then Kosi and Kumla, and finally the whole place.

Donald stood at the side, arms folded, his eyes never leaving us. A few of the women tried to get him to dance, but he shook his head adamantly.

We danced all night. Or just about. At four in the morning, Kumla insisted on cooking us a meal. Suddenly the place was cleared out and reassembled as a restaurant, and we found ourselves sitting at a long table, *en famille*, with Kodjo Kponvi, Madame Mbtomo, Kosi, and Kumla eating foo-foo and drinking beer.

We saw the sun come up from a bench in Kensington Gardens. As an unhappy Donald looked on from a discreet distance, Di and I threw caution to the wind. We sat, hands entwined, and watched the morning light paint the grass in halftones. A passerby would have assumed that we were just another pair of lovers reluctant to part after a night together.

Several times during that exquisite hour we turned toward each other and kissed. They were shy, importunate kisses, innocent and hungry, in search of greater connection. Her mouth was fragrant with breath mint and foo-foo. Her lips were lubricated with lip gloss.

We were slowly drifting toward the edge of the cliff, restrained at the moment only by the fact that we were sitting in a public park a half-mile from Kensington Palace, observed by a member of the Royal Protection Squad.

"Oh, Leonard," she whispered, "what shall we do?"

"We shall fall in love," I replied nonchalantly.

Her eyes went moist. I reached into my pocket for an unused Kleenex and handed it to her. She blew her nose with dignity.

We parted when the morning joggers began invading the park. A last stolen kiss, a squeeze of the hand, a murmured promise, and she was gone, jogging off toward Donald in her dancing flats.

CHAPTER

15

Somebody from Même Mère, Même Père must have talked to reporters because the vultures were back in full force in front of the Dorchester when I returned that morning. I waved to them cordially as I entered the hotel a little after eight, and smiled for the cameras.

As I walked by my friend the concierge on the way to the elevator, he said, with his tight little sardonic smile, "Up early this morning, sir?"

"Yes, as a matter of fact."

"Out for a walk, were you?"

"Actually, I've been necking with Diana in Kensington Gardens."

To his credit, the man didn't flinch. Not even a raised eyebrow.

Upstairs, I drew the blackout curtains and climbed into bed. Just before I dropped off, the phone rang. Thinking it might be Di, I picked up.

"Hello?"

"I trust you had a pleasant night with Diana . . ."

"Rupert, I was going to call you later."

"Yes, of course. After all the other papers have hit the streets and I'm sitting here, once again, with my thumb up my bottom . . ."

"We just went dancing, that's all."

"Dancing? From midnight till after *four* A.M. at an African *high-life* disco in *Soho*?"

"We stayed for some foo-foo."

"Foo-foo?"

"Foo-foo. It's a Togolese dish. It's not bad if you lay off the green peppers."

"Leonard, tell me something. How do you expect me to handle this?"

"What do you mean?"

"How does one explain what a man, supposedly in London to research a poem about the British royal family, is doing dancing all night with the Princess of Wales in an African disco in Soho?"

"Perhaps you can say something about the Windsors' love of dancing . . ."

"Leonard!"

There was a moment of silence, then, in a quieter voice, he resumed. "You have a media problem, Leonard. We shall have to talk."

"Okay, but I need to get some sleep. I'll call you back."

Another deep sigh, then, "If I don't hear from you by three this afternoon, I shall personally come to the Dorchester with my photographer and gain access to your room, photograph you in your underdrawers, and run the pictures on the first page of the *Herald* along with a story about how you insinuated yourself into the Princess of Wales's presence and took advantage of her trusting nature. In short, I shall crucify you."

"How would you get in my room?"

"Leonard, I know how to do these things. Please believe me."

I believed him. I hung up and took the phone off the hook. Sleep was out of the question. I was being terrorized by Rupert Makepeace.

I needed to talk to someone besides Rivera. I needed some advice. In the drawer of the night table were a hundred phone messages. I took them out, sifted through them, found the one I was looking for.

I picked up the phone, hoping she was a very early riser.

"I feel like Wallis Simpson, you know what I mean?"

"Yes, I do." Her voice was soothing, accepting, empathetic.

"Look what they did to *her*. They practically ran her out of the country. And the King with her."

"But people eventually grew to understand that theirs was a love story, a splendid love story, perhaps the most beautiful love story of the twentieth century."

"Well, we're just sort of beginning."

"I understand."

"I mean, she's really very different from what people think. She's very shy, actually, and very kind, and she has this wonderful little smile that lights up her face. Frankly, I can't imagine her married to that sourpuss for so long. He didn't appreciate what he had, for chrissakes . . ."

"Tell me, Leonard, how does it feel to be involved—is that a fair word?—with the world's most well-known woman?"

We had been talking for over an hour, me at the Dorchester, her in her apartment in Manhattan. Right from the beginning she had been friendly, taking the phone call from her maid, even though I suspected she had been asleep. She told me how happy she was that I had called, how thrilled she was to be hearing my story personally.

I told her just about everything. She promised she would repeat nothing until I sat down with her and her camera crew and we could do a real interview. Just the two of us. For an entire hour. She would let me tell the real story to the world.

"Do you have any plans?" she asked.

"No."

"What does your heart tell you?"

"To finish *The Dianiad*. To sit at her feet and recite it to her."

"That's beautiful."

By the time we hung up, I felt a great deal better. Someone, at least, knew the real story. I felt like a threatened man who leaves a letter with his lawyer with instructions to open it if anything happens to him. I would use this as a bargaining chip with Rupert Makepeace and his fellow vultures should it come to that.

It did. And sooner than I'd thought. I had a hot bath and a Beck's and passed out naked on the bed. It wasn't long before I was back on the Atakpamé with Rivera, paddling for my life. We were being pursued by war parties in canoes, and there we were, Rivera and I, in a 1978 Chevy with bad tires.

"If you have to die," I shouted to him above the roar of the rushing current, "this isn't a bad way to go, is it?"

He didn't answer. But I could tell from his scowl that he wasn't happy. Before he went, he wanted another shot at Guadalupe. For my part, I would have to be content with the thought of the Petitioner being tied up in probate before getting her hands on what was left of my estate.

The Chevy ran aground on the soft mud of the riverbed. Rivera gunned the engine but there wasn't enough traction from the worn tread on the tires. It looked like poetic justice. We were going to die because Rivera had spent community-property assets on retreads. And I was going down with him, an accomplice . . .

"Leonard!"

I opened my eyes, expecting to meet my maker, and was greeted by an explosion of bright light. And then another and another.

I turned over and looked up at Rupert Makepeace and a photographer standing over my bed at the Dorchester snapping pictures of me.

"Jesus Christ!" I screamed, covering my nakedness with the bed sheets.

"That'll be it, Seamus," Rupert Makepeace said to the short, balding man in a shabby sports coat and sneakers. The man lowered the camera and put it back in his shoulder bag.

"How the fuck did you get in here?"

"The same way you get out."

Then he turned to his photographer and said, "Lock the proof sheets and negatives in my safe. I'll have a look at them tonight." He took out his billfold and handed the photographer a twenty-pound note.

"Ta," said Seamus, who took the money and, with a little nod to me, muttered, "Pleasure to make your acquaintance, sir," and left.

Rupert Makepeace walked over to one of the wing chairs, sat down opposite Rivera, and lit a cigarette.

"Don't you have any sense of decency?"

"Decency, Leonard, is a luxury I cannot afford in my line of work."

"What are you going to do with nude pictures of me, Rupert?"

"That depends on you, my good man."

"Are you blackmailing me?"

"I wouldn't be so crude as to call it blackmail. Think of it rather as an incentive for you to be candid with me."

"I have been candid with you."

"I am tired of learning about things after they occur. From now on I would like to be alerted before they occur."

"I never know in advance myself."

"Rubbish."

"Just out of curiosity, Rupert, what will you do with those pictures?"

I think it was the first time I had ever seen him smile. It was a flat, sarcastic smile, highlighted by nicotine-stained teeth.

"I could pick up that telephone right there," he said, indicating the pseudo-antique phone on my night table, "make one phone call, and have five thousand pounds in my pocket by tonight."

"Who would want a naked photo of an American writer?"

"An American writer who is having a liaison with the Princess of Wales, let us not forget. And who is writing an *unauthorized* poem about her."

And so, once again, I let myself be extorted by Rupert Makepeace. This time his terms were stiffer. I was to call him immediately after every single phone call from Diana. I was to tell him where we were going and for how long. I was to aid and abet the taking of photographs of us together and then report to him directly afterward what we did. And I was not to have advance approval of what he wrote.

It was definitely a draconian deal. But a man in love is always vulnerable to blackmail. There is no defense against the threat of harm to the beloved. I saw that very clearly as I stood there watching Rupert Makepeace and Rivera blow smoke into each other's faces.

When he left, I slumped down into the wing chair and rubbed my eyes. I was no longer merely a man being hounded by his ex-wife for a large chunk of his pre-tax income. I was now a man in an exquisitely ineluctable relationship with the world's most desired woman being hounded by a venal and enterprising reporter and the mongrel hordes outside my hotel.

"Veracruz," Rivera muttered.

"Huh?"

"We'll go to Veracruz."

"What the hell's in Veracruz?"

"Cantinas."

"Cantinas?"

"Cantinas with whores. Big whores with almond eyes and voices that will make you scream in the moonlight."

CHAPTER

16

Barbara and I spoke by phone several times over the next week. I would call her from the Dorchester, lying in bed like Proust, my manuscript scattered over the covers, the TV on without the sound, munching on jars of pistachio nuts and candied cashews washed down with Beck's. She would be in her gold brocade bathrobe with her fluffy white slippers, lying on her couch beneath the Rauschenbergs, sipping cappuccino as the sun rose over New York.

We were like a couple of teenagers dishing across the Atlantic. The agreement between us was implicit. It was all still off the record, deep background for the interview we would do in prime time as soon as things solidified.

Meanwhile, Brad Emprin had gone trawling with a large net. He'd managed to extort enough money in advances to ensure that I would be financially secure for the foreseeable future. It was all tucked away in a new bank account in Zurich. All this, naturally, was making Norm Hudris nervous. I assured him, however, that he was still my number one priority.

"Don't you think it's time to get something on paper?" he said to me, breathless from his Exercycle.

"Norm, I'm this close to something very big. The worst thing we could do right now is rush into print. I'm moving beyond verisimilitude. Into passion."

"Passion?"

"Yeah. This is a very passionate story."

He liked *passion*. It replaced *verisimilitude* in his imagination and, no doubt, on the weekly status reports he filed with his superiors.

Meanwhile Di and I spent hours on the telephone. She had given me the number of her private line, the pink bedside Princess phone, and so I was able to bypass Archie and speak to her late at night in bed. Our conversations were full of long breathy pauses and fitful giggling. We whispered titillating nonsense to each other. We had gotten to the point of blowing kisses to each other before hanging up.

Several days after my high-life dancing excursion with Di to Même Mère, Même Père, I received an invitation from Margaret to attend a poetry reading at her apartment in Kensington Palace. The invitation, on embossed stationery and hand-delivered to the Dorchester, was brought up to my room by the concierge himself.

"This just arrived for you, sir." He handed me the sealed envelope with the Kensington Palace return address from a silver tray. "Seeing as it is from Kensington Palace, I thought you might want to have a look at it straightaway."

"That was very astute of you," I said, taking the note from the tray and replacing it with a fifty-p coin. He looked down at the tray as if I had deposited a used Kleenex on it, and, with great composure, managed to say, "Very kind of you, sir."

"There's a lot more where that came from," I replied and winked at him.

Scribbled on the printed invitation card was a note, presumably written by Margaret herself, which said, *Bring your own poems. I'm reading Walt Whitman. Please do come—M.*

I called Di immediately to tell her about the poetry reading. There was a long pause, then:

"Poetry reading?"

"Yes. Margaret is going to read Walt Whitman. Why don't you come?"

"Well, I haven't been invited."

"Just drop in. You're right across the courtyard, aren't you?"

"Yes, but . . ."

"Oh, please, Di. I want to see you. And we can be together without the reporters or Donald around."

"Are you going to read my poem?"

"Oh, no. Your poem isn't finished yet. And when it is, you will be the first to read it."

"Promise?"

"I promise."

At seven-thirty the following evening I was standing in front of the sentry box at Kensington Palace having my invitation from Margaret Rose Armstrong-Jones scrutinized. Two uniformed policemen eyed me closely while a third examined the anthology of English poetry I was carrying before picking up a phone to verify that a Mr. Leonard Schecter was, in fact, on the guest list. Even though I had blown a few thousand pounds on a new wardrobe, the security people still looked at me as if I had explosives strapped to my chest.

"It's One-A Clock Court, Mr. Spector, at the end of the north courtyard, beyond the clock tower." I was handed back my invitation and my book with a curt nod.

"Thanks, old boy," I said. "My friend will be along any minute now with the car bomb."

"Beg your pardon, sir?"

I smiled pleasantly and started down the gravel path that led past the apartments occupied by the Queen's free-loading relatives. The gas lamps were lit, even though the sky was still bright with mid-summer evening light. The walls were covered with overgrown rose vines, already past their season, and there was the cloying smell of aging flowers in the air. I walked past the Duke and Duchess of Gloucester's thirty-five-room spread and then beneath the clock tower and into the courtyard, at the far end of which Di and the princes lived, in apartments 8 and 9, next to Prince and Princess Michael of Kent.

It was the Windsor family compound, full of Germans and Greeks. It would take at least another century to bleach the Hohenzollern and Battenberg blood out of the British royal family.

I entered 1A Clock Court, arriving unfashionably early. In fact, I was the first one there, ushered into a spacious and eclectically decorated salon by a well-built Indian in summer mufti.

"Her Royal Highness will join you straightaway, sir," he said, leaving me to admire the Benin bronzes and minor Impressionists scattered about. There was a baby grand piano in one corner, a suit of armor in another corner, and a piece of modern sculpture that looked to be a serpent screwing a mongoose, or vice versa.

Moments later Margaret swept into the room.

"Mr. Spector. How good of you to come."

She was wearing a long black skirt, with a black shawl thrown over her shoulders and a turban wrapped around her head like Edna St. Vincent Millay.

"Besides Dudley Fitts, you will be the only bona-fide poet in the group tonight. The rest of us are just amateurs. Will you read from your own work?"

"I never read my own work. Confusion of voices, you understand."

"Of course."

I flashed my anthology and said, "I was thinking about reading 'Tintern Abbey.' "

"Splendid."

"You can't go wrong with Bill Wordsworth. I don't suppose you have any '61 Latour around . . ."

"What an excellent memory you have," she said with a girlish smile. "I shall see what we can hunt up."

It wasn't long before the other guests began to arrive—an

assortment of minor royalty, second-rate literati, aging rock stars, and freelance psychics. I mingled and kept an eye out for Di.

I had a chat with Elton John about the effects of acidophilus deficiency in your diet.

"It's something you don't want to neglect," he said.

"Really?"

"Do you know what could happen?"

"No."

"It could fall off."

"You're kidding?"

"I'm afraid not."

By eight-thirty Di still hadn't shown up. Margaret banged on a Ming vase with a spoon and called the reading to order.

The Indian put out some folding chairs to supplement the available seating. Each of us was assigned a number to indicate the order in which we would read. We began with Lady Pamela Choate-Harkness, a militant preservationist and paraplegic, reading "The Charge of the Light Brigade" from her wheelchair.

Into the Valley of Death rode the four hundred. Then we had the Viscount Linley reading Matthew Arnold's "Dover Beach," followed by his mother doing a stirring rendition of Whitman's "O Captain! My Captain!"

> O Captain! my Captain! our fearful trip is done.
> The ship has weathered every rack, the prize we sought is won . . .

It was a hard act to follow. George, Earl of St. Andrews, did Yeats with an affected Irish accent, and Princess Michael of Kent read Rilke in the original German. Then, suddenly, it was my turn.

Following Margaret's introduction of me as "one of America's leading poets," I walked up to the makeshift podium and plunged into "Tintern Abbey."

> Five years have passed; five summers, with the length
> Of five long winters! and again I hear

> *These waters, rolling from their mountain-springs*
> *With a soft inland murmur. Once again*
> *Do I behold . . .*

And on that very word *behold*, she made her entrance—as if on cue, slipping into the room unobtrusively and finding a seat near the door. She was in a silk blouse and pair of tight rhinestone-studded jeans tucked into white leather boots.

I stumbled over the next line, groped around for composure while trying to find my place and continue reading. She smiled at me from across the room. I trembled and dove back into Wordsworth.

> *. . . these steep and lofty cliffs,*
> *That on a wild secluded scene impress*
> *Thoughts of more deep seclusion . . .*

But I was lost. From the moment she had walked into the room I had left the Abbey. For good. I plowed my way through the rest of it as quickly as possible and sat down to the polite applause of Margaret and her guests.

The rest of the reading was interminable. I was sitting toward the front, my back to Di, unable to see her. Reader followed reader endlessly. And as the pièce de résistance, the Duchess of Gloucester treated us to the entire "Rime of the Ancient Mariner."

When it was over at last, I turned discreetly around, fearful that she had gone. But she was still there, chatting pleasantly with Angus Ogilvy.

Di introduced me to the Queen's cousin by marriage.

"I enjoyed your Wordsworth," he said.

"Thank you. I never travel without a copy of 'The Prelude.' It helps me sleep on airplanes."

"Really?"

"Quite."

"Extraordinary."

When Di and I were finally alone, I said to her, "I'm glad you came."

"So am I." She smiled. I smiled back. She took a hit off her Perrier. "That last poem was dreadfully long, don't you think?"

"Yes."

We stood there nibbling our watercress sandwiches, uncomfortable. We wanted to be alone and, at the same time, were afraid to be alone. There was an unspoken sense of impending complication. All the giggling and the phone chatter, the kissing and the blushing repartee, was moving us inevitably toward the terra incognita of greater intimacy.

Shortly before midnight I escorted Di across the courtyard to her apartment.

She said to me, quite casually, as we reached her door, "Don't kiss me good night."

And then, seeing my crestfallen expression, she quickly whispered, "It's not that I don't want you to. But we're on television. They've got surveillance cameras here day and night. It's an awful bother."

Then, just as I was about to abandon hope, she whispered, "Would you like to come up for a cup of tea?"

"I would."

"Walk back as if you were leaving the compound. As soon as you get across the courtyard, get down on your knees and crawl back across. The door will be open."

"Crawl?"

"Yes. You'll be under the scope of the cameras. Sorry. It's a bit hard on the knees, but it's the only way. Otherwise, we shall have Donald down here snooping about."

Then she offered her hand. We shook hands formally for the cameras, and she turned, unlocked the door, and disappeared.

I walked slowly back across the cobblestones, my heart racing. Once across the courtyard, I knelt down, turned around, and started to crawl back toward her door. My knees soon began to hurt through the thin fabric of my new two hundred-pound linen trousers. A small price to pay, I thought, as I crawled on, covering the fifty feet of cobblestones to her door as if it were a minefield.

Then like a dog with the morning paper between his teeth, I pushed open the door and went inside. I found myself in a spacious entry hall, on a green-and-gray carpet with the Prince of Wales's feather motif, staring up at a magnificent Georgian staircase, at the top of which stood Di.

She put her finger to her lips to indicate I should be quiet, then beckoned me to follow her. I got up, dusted off my knees, and walked up the staircase.

When I reached the top, she grabbed my hand and led me straight into the drawing room, closing the doors behind us. As soon as the large oak doors were shut, we were all over each other. Lips and hands groped in the diffuse light of the wall sconces. It must have been two solid minutes before we came up for air, and when we finally did it was just for a few seconds to catch our breath and dive under again. We thrashed around some more until Di put her hand on my lips and whispered, "I'll put the kettle on."

She tiptoed away into an adjoining room while I stood there smoking like a hastily capped volcano. I looked around me at the elegant furnishings of the Princess of Wales's drawing room. The walls were covered with yellow silk, adorned with old tapestries and paintings. On either side of the marble fireplace were down-filled salmon-colored sofas, looking homey amid the formal elegance of the room. In one corner was a broadwood grand piano, with Beatles sheet music on it.

The windows were open to the warm summer night. The air wafted in from Kensington Gardens, carrying fragrant promises. Somewhere in the house a clock struck the quarter hour. Otherwise, all was quiet in the west end of London.

When she reappeared, carrying a sterling-silver tea service, she was barefoot. Putting the tea tray down on the ebony end table, she walked over to an armoire against the wall, and opened it, revealing a state-of-the-art sound system. She slipped a CD in the player, and in a matter of seconds I heard the opening strains of "Embraceable You."

It was our song. She had remembered our first dance at the Togolese embassy.

I took her in my arms. Without her boots, her chin rested on my shoulder, her free hand light on my back. I inhaled the scent of Diorissimo and hair conditioner. I could feel the soft tickle of her breath on my neck.

We danced on as the tea steeped. As the night deepened. As the moonlight wafted in from outside and as Sarah Vaughan's liquid voice caressed every syllable of every song on that CD. Di's lips began to nibble on my ear. My hand inched down below the small of her back. Our bodies began to melt into each other.

We didn't get around to having tea. Instead we wound up in the bedroom with the enormous mahogany four-poster bed that Charles had brought especially from Buckingham Palace before abandoning it unceremoniously for polo and organic gardening.

Our clothing fell in disorderly heaps on the deep-pile carpet. We were clumsy in our excitement. Buttons were wrenched, zippers pulled, underwear nearly ripped to shreds.

And then we were suddenly shy as we confronted each other's nakedness in the ebbing moonlight. I could see the color rise to her cheeks as her innate modesty battled with her passion. I loved her all the more for it, and took her in my arms and held her very close, waiting for the up beat. And when it came, I attacked with vigor, as Kodjo Kponvi had taught me.

While Di and I danced through the night, the rest of the palace slept. Upstairs in their rooms, the heirs apparent dreamed of scones and strawberry jam while their nannies slept the sleep of the righteous in adjoining rooms.

It was almost five when she woke me with a kiss.

"I'm afraid you must slip out now," she whispered. "The boys are up early."

I nodded, barely awake, wanting only to take her in my arms again for one more slow dance.

"I could have danced all night," I said.

She laughed delightedly and ran the edge of a fingernail, with its discreet opaque beige polish, against my chest.

"Me too."

We kissed once more, hungrily, and, as we began to drift again into each other's wetness, she whispered, "Please, Leonard, you really must go."

"Parting is such sweet hell," I whispered back. "Out, out brief candle! Life is nothing but a long good-bye . . ."

"Oh, Leonard . . ."

She lay there, the covers around her, and watched me climb out of bed and gather my clothes. When I was dressed, I returned to the bed and sat down. She moved into my arms, and we kissed again.

"Thanks for popping up for tea," she said, an impish smile on her face.

"Anytime."

"I'm sorry you can't stay . . ."

I put my fingers to her lips and said, "Love is never having to say you're sorry."

She sighed deeply, kissed me again, then, "Do be careful, Leonard. Have the guards at the gate call you a taxi."

"Won't they know I've been here all this time?"

"Not if you crawl under the cameras again. They'll think you've been at Margaret's all this time. Isn't that lovely?"

And she giggled and sent me on my way.

CHAPTER

17

Only the sleaziest tabloids went with the story. Even Rupert Make-peace had the decency not to suggest that the American observed leaving Kensington Palace shortly after five o'clock the morning following Princess Margaret's poetry reading had spent the night with the sixty-three-year-old Princess.

A few of Fleet Street's sub-gutter-level publications, however, speculated that since the American was the same Hollywood film producer who had been in London trying to arrange for Diana's film debut, it would be safe to assume that the Queen's younger sister was contemplating a career in the cinema as well. Or perhaps "in the Sin-ama," they suggested, given the early-morning hour that the American was seen leaving the compound.

Margaret considered it beneath her dignity even to comment on the rumors. And Buckingham Palace responded with one terse sentence: "The rumours are patently absurd."

Rupert Makepeace, as usual, was hysterical. In accordance with our agreement, I had informed him that I was invited to the poetry reading at Margaret's, but I hadn't said anything about spending the night. I told him that I'd had too much to drink and had passed out on a couch in Margaret's apartment.

He didn't believe me, but there was not much he could do about it. Since there had been no reporters at the reading and since Diana's impromptu appearance was not public knowledge, there was no way to trace the story.

Di and I were in the clear. For the moment, at least. And we took advantage of it, at poor Margaret's expense. As they increased their surveillance of her activities, following her everywhere in anticipation of her meeting me for a tryst, there was a greatly reduced force available to spy on the Princess of Wales.

I felt so bad about Margaret that I sent her a note saying how sorry I was that she was the victim of such malicious gossip and assured her that I had stated unequivocally to anybody who asked that there was absolutely nothing going on between us. I received no reply.

So Di was free to move about London with relative ease, burdened only by Donald's constant presence. And though the detective was not the most convivial sort, he was the soul of discretion.

We had two allies in our dalliance—Gwen Poulstice and Kodjo Kponvi. The former marchioness and the visa-and-immigration officer of the London embassy of the Republic of Togo became our facilitators, one reluctantly, the other eagerly.

I would leave the Dorchester through the front door and lead my posse of reporters straight to Lady Poulstice's house in Belgravia, where I would have a quick cup of tea with Her Ladyship before slipping out the servant's door in the rear. From there I would grab a cab to the Togolese embassy, where Kodjo Kponvi had made a room available for Di and me.

It was a low-ceilinged third-floor room, accessible by a rear entrance and private stairway, intended for the use of people requesting asylum. As yet, however, no one had taken advantage of the extraterritoriality of the townhouse in Mayfair to avoid political persecution. There was a bed, two armchairs, a refrigerator, a CD player with high-life records, and an electric tea kettle. It was like a cozy little flat in the middle of London. No one in the embassy, except Kodjo Kponvi, even knew we were there.

Di and I met there in the late afternoons to while away the hours in each other's arms. Afterward, she would make tea for me with the electric kettle and serve it with a pastry she had appropriated from one of the trendy Chelsea restaurants she lunched in. She would talk about her day shopping and lunching or her charity work with the homeless and the infirm. She would gossip freely about her relatives, feeding me the latest on Fergie, Andrew, Charles and Camilla, Princess Anne, King Juan Carlos of Spain, and, of course, poor Margaret, who continued to be hounded by the press during the month that had passed since her poetry reading.

We were insanely happy those late-summer days, drunk with the newness of our love. We could not have too much of each other. We partook like gluttons and came back for more. We frolicked and played, singing and dancing like children.

I wrote canto after canto of *The Dianiad* in the mornings and read them to her in the afternoons. She would lie there naked, her pale white skin reflecting in the rays of the setting sun, listening to my verses. Then she would clap her hands in joy and open her arms to me.

Did any poet ever get such instant gratification? Did any poet ever have so fair a muse to inspire him?

And all the while I marveled that, of all the men on this planet, I had been chosen to be her lover. I felt as if I were a surrogate for the entire male race, as if it were my responsibility to appreciate the woman whose face graced a thousand magazine covers.

If only the world knew. But it didn't, and we were left in peace to love each other.

And then one Wednesday afternoon in September, as we were having tea, she suddenly looked at me and said, "Oh, Leonard, why can't we just vanish?"

"Where?"

"Someplace where nobody knows who I am. Someplace where we can live our life, the two of us and the boys, without all this other rubbish. Wouldn't that be lovely?"

"Yes . . ."

"If only we could become invisible. If only we could have a little house someplace with a yard and a swimming pool, someplace warm where it doesn't rain all the time and where people don't climb trees to take pictures of you and you don't need a detective in your car and ladies-in-waiting and equerries and a press secretary . . ."

I nodded. I was way ahead of her. In the febrile recesses of my inflamed imagination, we were already gone. We had ridden off together into the sunset, never to be seen again.

My patrons, meanwhile, were getting very restless. The network had demanded something in writing by the first of September, claiming that three months of research ought to be sufficient for any project. I sent them a proposal for a TV series about the royal family called *Backstairs at the Palace*, a situation comedy about the antics of a fictional royal family called the "Windhursts," with a steely half-German matriarch at the head and a bunch of dysfunctional but lovable heirs, each one less worthy than the next to inherit the throne. If we wanted to heighten the stakes, I suggested in my proposal, we could even have one of them attempt to assassinate the sibling or siblings directly ahead in the line of succession.

I got a five-page memo back from Norm Hudris explaining that a situation comedy was *not* what the network had had in mind when they sent me over to London, at considerable expense, to research a story about Princess Diana. What they wanted was verisimilitude and passion, just as I had been promising.

Norm Hudris went on to threaten to cut off my charge at the Dorchester and ask for a return of the advance if I didn't deliver something soon. Brad Emprin told him he would be only too happy to accommodate him, as he had the other two networks, Fox, HBO, Showtime, and USA cable lined up to take the deal over—at significantly better terms, he might add. That shut Norm Hudris up for a while.

Charlie Berns, on the other hand, seemed, if anything, amused at the way things were developing. There was a bemused chuckle in his voice, an innuendo that seemed to suggest that he was onto me. "You're certainly keeping the ball low, Leonard," he said over the phone late one night. "So low that nobody can see it."

"Huh?"

"You have this whole town running around in circles, and you're over there, living high off the hog, and throwing curves in the dirt."

"What're you talking about?"

"Baseball is a metaphor for life."

"Really?"

"Yes."

"Extraordinary."

My lawyer called regularly with updates on the ongoing litigation. The Petitioner was now coming after me with heavy artillery. She was no longer content, it appeared, to cash her exorbitant monthly support check. Now she wanted me nailed to a cross beside the HOLLYWOOD sign.

"You haven't replied to her duces tecum subpoena."

"How can I? I'm in London."

"The court doesn't care where you are."

"What the fuck does she want now?"

"Verification of additional income. She's subpoenaed your agent for copies of employment contracts. It seems you're making a lot more money these days, Leonard."

"Am I?"

"Yes. According to *Variety* and *The Hollywood Reporter*, you've signed a number of film, TV, and book deals worth several million dollars. You know, it would be nice if you kept your lawyer informed about this type of thing. It's very difficult to go into court and file for dismissal when the other side has evidence that you're earning about five times what you've declared in your moving papers."

"It's just some odds and ends."

"Leonard, perhaps we should talk a little about perjury . . ."

As if all this weren't enough, my confidante in New York was starting to put the squeeze on me as well. No longer content with our phone chats, she was talking about coming over to London with a film crew to do an interview with the two of us.

"It would be like Donald and Ivana or Dick and Liz—great love stories of the twentieth century."

"Let me think about it."

"We could air it before *Monday Night Football*. It's a fabulous time slot. We'll promo it during the Dallas-Washington game."

I was clearly overextended on all fronts. Even Rivera was starting to lean on me. He wanted to go back to Pacoima and get his truck out of impound. Then he would make a run for the border, stopping only to slice up Guadalupe's laywer.

It was at this point, in the middle of September, that I decided to go underground. I was tired of the threats, subpoenas, demands for interviews, scripts, novels, magazine serials, not to mention the daily escort of paparazzi. I was tired of having tea with Gwen Poulstice and her flatulent Scottish terrier.

I flew to Zurich and filled a Hollywood YMCA tote bag with Swiss francs and chocolate bars. Then, to everybody's great relief, I checked out of the Dorchester. I scattered money about liberally to the chambermaids and the hall porters, giving the concierge an autographed copy of my phone message from Oprah Winfrey.

"Leaving us, are you, sir?" he said as I was on my way out the door.

"Yes, as a matter of fact."

"I hope you enjoyed your stay."

"I can't begin to tell you how fabulous it's been, Frederick. Do keep in touch."

I had the two suitcases containing my new wardrobe put into a cab and, waving good-bye to the assembled doormen and reporters, had the taxi driver take me to Eaton Mews. We drove through London traffic with the usual tail of motor scooters and Austin Minis.

Gwen Poulstice's face dropped when she saw me on her doorstep with valises.

"Don't worry, Gwen. I'm in and out. Fire up the tea kettle."

"Where are you going?" she asked.

"It's better if you don't know," I replied. "This way you won't reveal anything under torture."

An hour later, carrying my suitcases and money, I climbed over Gwen Poulstice's hydrangeas and through her neighbor's yard. By noon I was safely ensconced in my third-floor room in the Togolese embassy, thereby becoming the first person in the history of the embassy to be granted political asylum.

CHAPTER

18

And so began my life as an underground refugee and lover of the Princess of Wales. I was able to leave the embassy and move around London at will, as long as I steered clear of Kensington Palace, Gwen Poulstice's place, the British Museum, or any of the trendy restaurants where Di lunched.

Speculation on Fleet Street was that, having seduced both Di and Margaret, I had returned to the States to pursue my sinister life in the demimonde of Hollywood. News of my various film and publishing deals had leaked, and the theory now was that I had insinuated myself into the inner sanctum of the royal family with a bogus story of writing a poem about them, which, of course, was not too far from the truth.

I did not bother informing Rupert Makepeace of my whereabouts, though I did have the courtesy to call him from a phone booth and tell him that I was checking out of the Dorchester and would keep him posted as things developed.

"Where are you *going*?"

"I can't tell you, Rupert."

"What do you mean—you *can't* tell me? You agreed to tell me *everything*."

"Well, that deal is inoperative."

"Sorry?"

"It's what Ron Ziegler used to say to reporters."

"What in god's name are you talking about?"

"Ziegler was Nixon's press secretary during Watergate. Whenever he was caught in a contradiction, he would simply explain that his previous statement was inoperative. I have to go now, Rupert."

"Leonard, must I remind you of certain photographs . . . ?"

"Sell them to *Playgirl*."

I hung up and carefully wiped my prints from the receiver.

In late September Di had to go to Nepal, where she was photographed shaking hands with various government officials, having tea with lepers, and pensively contemplating Mount Everest. She looked marvelous in her new fall wardrobe, the tasteful prints and patterns set against the splendor of the Himalayas. I sat in my room in the embassy, looking through the various magazines that had covered her trip, warm tears running down my cheeks as I thought of my beloved thousand of miles away representing Her Majesty's government with grace and dignity.

While she was gone I got a television set for the room so that Di could watch some of the soap operas she liked to keep abreast of. She was so thrilled when she saw it that she hugged me for a full minute.

We were sitting in our armchairs, after tea one afternoon in early October, watching *Neighbours*, when she mentioned that she and the boys were going to the Bahamas for a week during a school vacation later that month.

"Really? Where to?"

"Bulba."

"Bulba?"

"Yes, it's a private island owned by Juan Carlos. He's invited us for a holiday. . . . I was thinking how smashing it would be if you came with us."

My heart leapt, but I did my best to look a little reluctant, and said soberly, "Do you think it's wise?"

"No one will know, except the boys and Juan Carlos and Sophia. They're quite discreet. And they don't allow reporters anywhere near the island. Oh, please do say yes. We could take long walks on the beach and watch the sun set and have barbecues . . . wouldn't that be lovely?"

I looked at her—curled up in the armchair with a teacup and a high-fiber blueberry muffin, her painted toenails tucked beneath her, a far-off Grecian look in her eyes. I would not have refused her anything at the moment, certainly not a week in the sun on Bulba.

I got out of my armchair and knelt down in front of her. My hands reached out and slid beneath her haunches, pulling her toward me. My nose nuzzled against the warmth of her belly button, my tongue wandered through the crevice left by an open button of her paisley man-tailored shirt.

It wasn't long before we were entangled on the floor. With *Neighbours* playing over our exertions, we rocked back and forth as night fell, sailing off into uncharted waters.

> *My lady sings to me with music sweet,*
> *the failing light upon her shoulders bare,*
> *that I was born her praises to repeat*
> *and worship in the gardens of her hair . . .*

Bulba is a tiny island, seven miles square, in the Agua Fresca Archipelago of the Grand Bahamas, about forty-five miles northwest of Nassau. It was discovered by Columbus in 1492 and first colonized by the British in 1625, then the French in 1649. Much smaller and less strategically situated than the other islands in the chain, it was passed back and forth between the British and the French as a sort of throwaway item in various peace-treaty settlements during the wars of the late seventeenth and early eighteenth century, and finally abandoned and left to its own resources at the Treaty of Paris in 1783.

Though possessed of a benign climate and beautiful beaches, the island was minuscule and lacked a deep-water harbor or any natural resources, and so it had the distinction of being one of the only unclaimed pieces of land on the entire globe during the nineteenth-century colonial land rush. The Spaniards finally decided to stick a flag in the ground in 1826, and, when nobody contested their claim, Bulba passed into the possession of the Spanish royal family.

I learned all this from a copy of the *Encyclopédie Géographique du Monde*, which I found lost among the leather-bound editions of Balzac on the shelves of the embassy's library. There was one other significant fact I learned from the encyclopedia: Bulba is only 298 nautical miles from Miami.

Several days later I was having a beer with Kodjo Kponvi during a break from a Ping-Pong game in the recreation room and asked him if he had ever heard of Bulba.

"Oh, yes. It's a private island belonging to the King of Spain." Kodjo Kponvi, an avid reader of *Tatler* and *Paris Match*, was up on the doings of the various royal families of Europe.

"Is there anything else on the island beside Juan Carlos's house?"

"Nothing. Not even a hut on the beach. This way no journalists can come. Juan Carlos doesn't like journalists. He had Stephanie of Monaco there recently."

"How do you get there?"

"You fly to Nassau. Then you take a helicopter or a yacht. Otherwise you must take a parachute . . ." He laughed with great enjoyment at his own joke.

The plan came together very slowly, incrementally, but never completely until the final moments. In my own defense, I believe that what happened was not entirely premeditated. It was, in essence, a *crime passionel*, and should I ever be asked to answer for it, in this or any other life, I would staunchly make that claim.

And so I didn't discuss the plan with Di. I was afraid that it would dampen the joy of our afternoons together. I was afraid she would run for cover and never come out again. And, frankly, I didn't really know how the hell I was going to pull it off.

We discussed the holiday on Bulba like a couple planning a family vacation. Di assured me that Juan and Sophie, as she called her, were quite informal on Bulba.

"They don't dress for dinner," she said. "It's mostly shorts and bathing suits. Do you have tennis whites?"

"Of course," I lied.

"You do play, don't you?"

"Passionately."

"Juan has a nasty service. She double-faults a great deal, and they have rows all the time."

I snuck out the next day and took a bus to Harrods to buy tennis whites and a bathing suit. As I was walking back up the Brompton Road, talking to Rivera about the colonial history of Bulba, I was frozen in my tracks by a familiar sound. It had been a while since I'd had to deal with a Fleet Street goon, and my reflexes were slow. I didn't react immediately to the click of the camera shutter. Instead I stood there dumbly and let him fire round after round at point-blank range from his high-speed Japanese weapon.

Eventually, I did an about-face and started back toward Harrods. He stayed right on my tail as I weaved in and out of pedestrian traffic, increasing speed. A block later, I broke into a run. He broke into a run right behind me.

I ducked into Harrods and trotted up the escalator. He stayed about fifty feet behind me as I made my way through Home Furnishings and Gardening Implements, went up another escalator, cut across Gentlemen's Clothing and down again to the second-floor Book Shop.

My months of sedentary living in London had not done much for my stamina, which wasn't terrific to begin with. So I said fuck it and turned around and waited for him. I stood there, fists clenched, shoulders arched, breathing heavily.

He skidded to a stop ten feet away, panting. He was a flabby, balding middle-aged man with bad teeth. He didn't look to be in much better shape than I was.

We stood there for a long moment, trying to catch our breath, not saying anything. Though he had the feral instincts of a hunter, you could tell he had no idea what to do when he was actually face-to-face with his prey.

It was a peculiar standoff, there in the Harrods Book Shop, beside a stack of remaindered novels. "Shall we step into the gents'?" I said.

He looked at me suspiciously, unsure of how to respond to this invitation. Not waiting for an answer, I walked off in the direction of the restrooms. He followed at a cautious distance.

The men's room was empty. There was a row of gleaming white urinals, and I decided to avail myself of the occasion. It was an old LBJ trick to make reporters ill at ease. He would lead them into the john and take a leak while he was talking to them.

"Would you like a scoop?" I asked as I unzipped.

"Yes," he said, his voice high-pitched and inelegant.

"This is the skinny."

"Beg your pardon?"

"The skinny. The real thing. I expect you to write it straight, all right?"

He nodded, taking out a notebook and a pen.

"Put your notebook away. You're going to have to do this from memory."

He put his notebook away.

"I'm in love with Princess Michael of Kent."

"What's that?"

"Princess Marie-Christine and I. We're madly in love. We're going to elope to . . . I suppose you want to know where, huh?"

"Yes."

"Take a leak."

"What?"

"Come over to the urinal next to mine. Take out your schlong and start to pee. And I'll tell you."

"You some sort of queer, are you?"

"Hardly. This is just the way I like to do business. The great equalizer. I find a man is more honest with his bladder open."

"I'd rather not, actually."

"Suit yourself."

I finished, rezipped, turned to him. "See. I'm done. I have no intention of attacking you."

He watched me carefully as I walked over to the sink and washed my hands. He was trying to figure out, no doubt, if I was crazy or perverted or both. In the end his curiosity got the best of him.

He approached one of the urinals and unzipped. I moved beside him, waiting for him to begin.

"I don't hear anything."

"It takes me a moment to begin," he muttered.

"The old prostate acting up?"

He didn't answer. After a long moment, I heard the sound of his stream against the deodorant blocks. I figured it would take him almost as long to stop as it did to start.

I ran for the door. I had a five-second edge, and it was all I needed. I was across the Book Shop and down the escalator in no time.

As the taxi pulled away, I caught a glimpse of him through the rear window as he ran out of Harrods and looked madly around. I told the driver to take me to the Tate Gallery and step on it.

"I thought I'd have a look at the Pre-Raphaelites. And they're not going to be around forever, are they?"

"I wouldn't know, sir."

"Nobody's getting any younger," I said, leaning back in the seat and waiting for my heart to stop pounding.

We were at Même Mère, Même Père that evening, Kodjo Kponvi and I, sharing a plate of foo-foo, when I asked him a seemingly casual question: "Tell me, what does it take to get a Togolese passport?"

"You have to be a Togolese citizen."

"Of course, but how do you actually go about doing it?"

"You must take your *acte de naissance* to the Hôtel de Ville in Lomé or in another city in Togo, and they will issue you a passport."

"What happens if you're abroad and you lose your passport?"

"Then you go to a Togolese embassy with proof of your citizenship."

"And see the visa-and-immigration officer?"

"Precisely."

"And he issues you a new passport?"

"Oh, yes. But you must bring a new passport photo."

I ordered us another two bottles of beer, and we ate some more foo-foo, washed it down with the beer, ordered some barbecued lamb, washed that down with more beer. Soon we were sloshing around on a pleasant beer high.

"Kodjo, I need your help."

"Anything, my friend. Anything at all."

"It involves Di and me."

"Of course . . ."

"And her sons, too, I think."

His brow furrowed just a bit, causing his tribal markings to bunch on his cheeks. I looked around me carefully and lowered my voice. "I need four Togolese passports," I whispered.

To his credit, Kodjo Kponvi didn't even blink. He merely nodded, smiled, and said, "Yes."

"Can you really do it?"

"Why not? You'll have to get me photographs and tell me the names and addresses you want on the passports."

"I think I can do that."

"Splendid."

We sat there for a moment saying nothing, as the import of what had just been said sank in.

Then Kodjo Kponvi smiled his big smile and said, "It will be a beautiful adventure, Leonard."

"Do you really think so?"

"Most decidedly. My heart rejoices for you."

Late that night I was sitting in my room and cutting out head shots from pictures of Di and the princes culled from various magazines and books, trying to decide which would be the best ones to convert into passport photos, and explaining to Rivera about the trip to Bulba. He was sitting in the other armchair leafing through a magazine called *Jugs*, which he'd picked up in Soho. He had not been particularly happy about moving out of the Dorchester with its wing chairs and well-stocked minibar and was even less thrilled about the Bahamas.

"All right," I said, "so it's not Veracruz, but there's a nice beach and a tennis court."

"You're so pussy-whipped, man, she got you wearing white shorts."

"I'm in love with her."

"She gonna take the rest of your money—what the other one didn't take."

"I don't think so. This one's very rich."

"It don't make no difference. She get a good lawyer, screw you to the wall, man."

It was close to three before I went to bed. After choosing the pictures, I sat with a yellow pad, the same pad that I used to compose verses of *The Dianiad*, and carefully wrote out names to put beside the pictures. I wrote down close to a hundred and thought about each one carefully. It would be a name I would have to live with for a long time.

In the end I decided to go with Chuck Keats, a variation of the nom de guerre I had used for the plane trip to Balmoral. Chuck was married to Sandy. And their two sons were Timmy and Jimmy, both of whom had been born in Lomé, Togo, where their parents, naturalized Togolese citizens, had been working as Peace Corps volunteers. One day they hoped to return to the States and start a small family business.

CHAPTER

19

To avoid publicity, Di and I traveled separately to RAF Benson, where the Queen's Flight planes are hangared. She gave me another one of her gold-embossed cards as a laissez-passer and suggested I take a cab up to the air base in Oxfordshire.

Di had told no one except Juan Carlos and Sophia that she would be bringing me along. In order to use the Queen's Flight planes, one needed the permission of the Queen, and Di thought it tactful not to mention to her estranged mother-in-law that she would be accompanied to Bulba by the man who had compromised her sister's reputation.

The night before we left, we made final plans on the phone. I was downstairs in the embassy rec room, talking softly, and she was, as usual, lying among her pillows, speaking into her bedside Princess phone.

"Do Juan and Sophie put out conditioner, at least?" I asked.

"Oh, Leonard, do please stop your joking. Really."

There was an edge to her voice. She had seemed tense at tea the day before, as well. I had chalked it up to the fact that she was having her "monthly," as she put it, but I was beginning to wonder whether Di didn't sense, on some level, that she was about to embark on a perilous journey.

"I just want to know what to pack," I said.

"I'm sorry. I tend to get a little tetchy before a trip. There's so much to think of. All my clothes, and the boys' things. And Wills has the sniffles."

"Are you packing a tiara?"

"This is not a state occasion."

"I want to make love to you on the beach with you wearing nothing but your tiara."

"Oh, Leonard . . ."

We blew kisses to each other and hung up. I decided to make one more call that night. I dialed Rupert Makepeace's home number and woke him up.

"Yes," he growled groggily into the phone.

"Rupert, it's Leonard."

There was a beat of silence, then, "I'm no longer talking to you."

"What do you call this, Rupert—skiing?"

"I must warn you that nothing you say is off the record. Anymore."

"Fine with me."

"Where are you calling from?"

"Togo."

"Where?"

"Togo. It's a small country in West Africa. Underneath Upper Volta . . . Listen, I just want you to know that a very big story is going to break in a few days. Maybe the biggest story since Edward VIII's abdication. And I may be calling you from time to time with some news."

"Leonard, are you having me on again?"

"No, Rupert. I'm just trying to give you a leg up."

"Does this involve Diana?"

"Sorry. No details yet . . ."

"She's leaving for Juan Carlos's place on Bulba tomorrow. It's in the middle of the bloody ocean. You won't be able to get near her."

"Rupert, I've got to run. Ta ta."

As I hung up I could feel the telephone line vibrating with his invective. I stood there for a moment, at the knotty pine bar with the Ewe hand-crafted ceramic peanut bowls, and said a silent farewell to the Republic of Togo. I would be eternally grateful for its sanctuary. Earlier I had said my good-byes to Kodjo Kponvi. He had given me the passports and a bon-voyage present—a CD with high-life music.

"For you and your princess to dance under the moon."

"Thank you."

"You will send me a postal card?"

"As soon as we're settled."

"*Kwa gdivi ga fofogo ka mnimja lakala mi.*"

"I give up."

"May the wine from your palm tree be sweet and flowing."

"That's beautiful, Kodjo."

We embraced and said good night. He never asked where Di and I were going.

At seven the next morning I was in a taxi driving north out of London with a garment bag containing two tropical suits, tennis whites, a Malibu Beach surfer's bathing suit, a shoulder bag with four Togolese passports, and $850,000 in cash. The driver had accepted a hundred pounds flat for the trip to RAF Benson, and he drove smartly through the deserted early-morning streets and out the M40 motorway toward Oxfordshire.

The city was shrouded in early-morning fog. It looked soft and mysterious, a veiled woman in uncertain light, and I felt a pang of melancholy as I realized I would not revisit it for a long time, if ever again. I was burning one more bridge behind me.

Arrivederci, London.

The scene at the guard gate at RAF Benson was not unlike the scene at the Royal Enclosure at Ascot. The sentry picked up the phone and called his superior, who drove down in a Jeep and scrutinized my laissez-passer very carefully before looking over at me, in the rear seat of my London taxi, and saying, "Come up from London, have you, sir?"

"No, actually, we've come over from Vladivostok. We've been driving for weeks. The meter's up to four hundred thousand rubles. I don't suppose you can change a five-hundred-thousand-ruble note?"

He looked from me to the driver, who shrugged, having no idea whatsoever what was going on.

"Look, I got a plane to catch. At Hangar A-Thirty. Can we speed this up?"

The supervisor got on the phone and mumbled a few words, and we had a very sour-looking Donald down at the guard gate in a matter of minutes.

"Good morning, sir," he said between gritted teeth.

I retrieved my garment bag from the trunk and followed Donald into a dark-blue Ford Escort. He got behind the wheel, and we drove off.

"Taking a bit of a risk, are you?" I said.

"Sorry?"

"What if we got attacked by a terrorist? Your hands wouldn't be free to respond."

"We are on a Royal Air Force air base, sir. And I might add that clearance should have been arranged for you at a somewhat earlier moment."

"Well, you know the Princess. She's just so spontaneous."

We arrived at a small building beside a hangar from which I could see the gleaming nose of one of the two BAe 146 jets in the Her Majesty's air fleet. Inside were Di and the princes, surrounded by a mound of luggage. Nearby were two nannies and a lady-in-waiting, who would be accompanying us to Bulba.

"Say good morning to Leonard, boys," Di said.

The princes, in their Ludgrove School blazers, gave me their usual sullen, barely audible greetings. Wills sniffled loudly and blew his nose into a wad of crumpled tissues.

"Excuse me, ma'am," said Donald. "I'm going to ring BP."

"Why are you going to do that, Donald?"

"I believe it's customary to inform the Queen of any passengers on a Queen's Flight aircraft."

"Is this a security matter?"

He didn't answer immediately, and Di continued, "If you recall, Donald, Mr. Schecter was cleared by security some time ago. The matter of his flying with us is a purely personal one, between my mother-in-law and me, and I will not have you meddling in it."

She turned away from him dismissively and toward the princes. "Now, has everyone got what they want for the flight before we have the luggage stowed?"

Forty minutes later we were in the air, gaining altitude over Oxford and banking south toward Cornwall and the Atlantic. Wing Commander E. B. Wickham was at the controls. He was, Di informed me, the Queen's personal pilot and a decorated combat veteran. When we reached our cruising altitude, he came out to greet his passengers.

"Good morning, Your Royal Highness."

"Good morning, Wing Commander," Di said, smiling. "This is Mr. Schecter."

"A pleasure, sir," he said.

"Likewise."

"You haven't flown with us before, have you?"

"Not that I recall."

The wing commander looked at me blankly, as the irony bounced off his broad forehead, then he cleared his throat a few times before saying, "If there's anything we can do to make the flight more agreeable, do let us know."

He went back to the cockpit, and in a few moments a steward came out to serve breakfast—grapefruit, muesli, yogurt, bran muffins, and low-fat milk. The princes picked their way unhappily through the spartan breakfast.

"Must we really eat this, Mother?" Wills complained.

"Yes, Wills. It's good for you."

"But it tastes dreadful."

"Sorry, but that's all we have."

"Rubbish. They carry scones and jam for Grandmama, don't they?"

"Shall we have a rubber?" Prince Hal suggested.

"We don't even know if Leonard plays."

Prince Hal turned sharply to me. "You do play, don't you?"

"Play what?"

"Bridge."

Di looked at me and smiled by way of explanation. "Charles taught them."

Prince Hal and I were partners again, as we'd been playing soccer at Balmoral. He shuffled the cards and asked me, "Do you use Blackwood?"

"Not that I know of."

"At four no trump one asks for aces. Five clubs for one, five diamonds for two, and so forth."

"I see."

"I hope you're not going to overbid. Auntie Anne does it all the time, and it's very tiresome."

As the plane headed southwest across the Atlantic, the four of us played bridge. I consistently underbid my hands, not wanting to incur my partner's wrath. Di, for her part, played indifferently. You could tell that she had spent more time than she'd cared to playing bridge. Wills was intense and combative. He slammed his cards down on the table and swept up the winning tricks triumphantly, almost vindictively.

In less than an hour, Prince Hal pronounced me a hopeless underbidder and went back to his Game Boy. Wills sat sulkily by the window, keeping an eye on Di and me, making sure we didn't do anything untoward. Frankly, I wouldn't have minded.

Di looked delicious in black spandex pants and a light-blue cotton sweater, sitting with her feet up and her Danielle Steel in hand. I dozed intermittently, trying not to think about doing anything untoward, spandex notwithstanding.

About an hour before landing, Di went back into the rear cabin to change her clothes. There would be reporters and local dignitaries when we landed in Nassau, and she would be expected to say a few words and inspect the troops.

"I shall make it as quick as possible," she assured me.

As we descended through the cloudless sky to Nassau, capital of the Commonwealth of the Bahamas, Di explained the procedure to me. She and the boys would deplane first. I would wait on board with the crew until the ceremony was over. Then I would deplane with them as if I were part of the crew.

"You do understand, don't you, Leonard?"

"Certainly."

"We don't want nasty things being written in the papers."

"Of course not."

And so I had a good view through the plane window of Di and the princes' arrival in Nassau. Waiting for her was a large crowd of people waving little British flags, and a squad of Royal West Indian Grenadiers in full dress uniforms wilting under the sun. She descended the gangway with the same grace with which she exited an automobile, floating downward without any apparent effort, a prince on either side of her.

She received bouquets of flowers from some local children, then shook hands with the commander of the Grenadiers. She and the commander proceeded down the line of soldiers, chatting amiably and glancing with practiced indifference at the men.

I wondered how it felt for a woman to walk past fifty men standing at attention with their rigid weapons pointing skyward. It is, when you think about it, the ultimate homage.

I sat there, my nose pressed against the glass, and marveled at her poise. After inspecting the troops, Di said a few words to the assembled crowd and then entered the VIP lounge, such as it was, at the Nassau airport.

A few minutes later I followed with the wing commander and his crew. It was there that we hit a snag—a snag, I realized later on, that turned out to be propitious in that strange way life has of throwing fastballs at us disguised as sliders. Or vice versa.

There was a mechanical problem with the Royal Navy helicopter that was supposed to take us on the short hop to Bulba. Rotor torque insufficiency, I was told. There was a long discussion as to whether it was preferable to wait till the problem was corrected or to send for another helicopter from the British fleet in port on Grand Bahama Island. In either case we would be laid over for at least two hours.

I suggested that we hire a helicopter from one of the commercial rental places at the airport. Donald looked at me indulgently, the way one looks at a child who asks a very naïve question.

"I'm afraid that's impossible, sir," he said.

"And why is that?"

"All aircraft that the Princess and the princes travel in must be given a thorough security check."

I looked at Di, but she didn't intervene. There were certain areas, apparently, in which Donald could not be overruled. We were served fresh lemonade and cookies and waited for the mechanics to restore sufficient torque to the rotors. Di went back to Danielle Steel, and the princes went back to their Game Boys. I excused myself to stretch my legs.

There was a tea shop and a bar, both nearly deserted at this hour. I walked into the bar, sat down on a bamboo bar stool, and ordered a beer. A few minutes later a guy came in, sat down a few stools away, and ordered a margarita.

He was fiftyish and tanned, with a graying beard, and wore a Grateful Dead T-shirt. My take on him was an aging hippie, gone down to the islands to burn out what was left of his brain. So I was surprised when the bartender asked him if he had any customers for his plane that afternoon. You would think the fact that he ordered a margarita would have made that question unnecessary, but it didn't, apparently, in Nassau. The man shook his head and dove into his drink.

"The business not so fine?" the bartender said in his bouncy West Indian accent.

"It's shit, man."

"Soon it'll be tourist season. The winter will be getting better, won't it?"

"If I can last that long. You want to buy a plane, Walter? I'll sell it to you cheap."

"What do I do with a plane?"

"Put a straw and umbrella in it and serve it," and he laughed a gravelly, cigarette-honed laugh that was somewhere between a cough and a chuckle. "Instead of tourists, we get the fucking Princess of Wales with her own fucking helicopter."

"Which isn't working at the moment," I interjected.

The man turned and looked at me. It was the kind of paranoid look that old hippies give you, a sort of posttraumatic-stress-syndrome reaction from the days when narcotics agents were infiltrating their ranks.

"What's wrong with it?" he said after a long, suspicious pause.

"Rotor torque insufficiency."

"No shit."

"We're on the ground for two hours."

The *we* intrigued both of them, but neither of them was going to ask me directly, so I volunteered the information.

"We're en route to Bulba."

"That so?"

"Uh-huh. As soon as we get some transportation."

"Five hundred bucks U.S. round trip plus gas," the man said, barely looking at me.

"She's not allowed to travel in unauthorized planes . . ."

"I'll throw the gas in."

"Sorry, but the security people won't approve it."

He nodded, went back to his margarita.

"What kind of plane do you have?" I asked.

"Cessna 310."

"How many people can it carry?"

"Four. Six if you don't mind sitting two on the air mattress."

"What's its range?"

"That depends on the head winds. Little luck I can make Jacksonville and back with a reserve tank on board," he said, finally draining his margarita and signaling for another one.

"How about Miami?"

"I can do Miami in a goddamn gale."

I took my beer and moved down the bar next to him, extending my hand. "Leonard Schecter."

He hesitated a moment, then took it. "Carl Webb," he said.

"Carl, how would you like to make a lot of money?"

CHAPTER

20

As our helicopter hovered over Bulba, I remembered reading in the *Encyclopédie Géographique du Monde* that Bulba was named for its bulbous shape—*sa configuration bulbeuse*—which was readily apparent from the air. Navy Commander Adam Hewitt overflew the island to get a favorable wind, then banked low over the waves and brought us in for a smooth landing.

Juan and Sophie's palace, a sprawling white-stucco compound, dominated the west end of the island. It was surrounded by high walls covered with bougainvillea and towering coconut trees and would have been virtually impregnable even if it had not been on an island that was accessible only by helicopter or boat.

The Spanish royal family greeted us in shorts and sandals. They waved as our helicopter lowered itself onto the helipad in the rear courtyard. Once again, Di and the princes deplaned first, ducking under the rotor wash with practiced nonchalance. I stood and watched them all kiss one another on both cheeks.

Then Di turned to me and introduced me. She had told me that bowing was not necessary on Bulba, but I couldn't resist a little half-bow as I shook hands with King Juan.

"How nice of you to visit with us," he said in perfectly inflected English. "Did you have a pleasant flight?"

"Not too bad. Except for a little rotor torque insufficiency in Nassau."

"Really?"

"Yes."

"Extraordinary."

Di and I were given rooms in the guest wing. The princes and their nannies were sent off to the children's quarters on the other side of the palace. As I unpacked my Harrods tropical wardrobe, I looked around at the spacious Moorish-style room, its windows open to the sea breeze, and I felt a surge of excitement as I realized that for the first time, Di and I would be able to spend the whole night together.

We had lunch with Juan and Sophie on the terrace, under the shade of baobab trees, imported, I was told, from Málaga. The children ate inside with the nannies, and it was quiet on the terrace, with only the sound of forks and knives and desultory conversation.

"So, Mr. Spector, you are American, Diana tells us," Sophie said.

"It's Schecter, but you can call me Leonard."

"Is Schecter a German name?" interjected Juan.

"It's Polish."

"Leonard's family is from Poland," Di said.

"Really?"

"Cracow. Have you been there?"

"No, I'm afraid I haven't."

"Neither have I."

We ate our smoked salmon and caviar with a very dry and delicious Pouilly-Fumé. As usual, Di drank mineral water. She and Sophie got caught up on royal gossip, while Juan and I fished around with some difficulty for a topic of common interest.

"Tell me, Mr. Spector, do you play tennis?"

"Not so as you'd know it."

"I beg your pardon?"

"I've got no backhand."

"That could be a problem, I suppose . . ."

"Not if you hit it to my forehand."

The conversation continued like this, lurching forward in fits and starts, as we broached and quickly exhausted subject after subject. Frankly, I wasn't paying too much attention, more interested in Di and Sophie's conversation about Princess Caroline's love life.

Lunch finally over, it was siesta time. We would reassemble on the tennis court in two hours. Di and I withdrew to the guest wing, and, as soon as we were out of sight, we fell into each other's arms. It was like that very first night at Kensington Palace. We were all over each other standing up in the hallway.

We barely made it up the stairs. We bolted the door of Di's room and shed our clothes. Though there was a big comfortable bed, the covers turned down for siesta, we didn't use it. We sank to the floor, under the open window, and went at it like alley cats.

Her thighs thrown over my shoulders, her arms around my neck, she whispered breathy, inarticulate phrases into my ear. Her nails dug into my neck as she pulled me down deeper into her embrace. We danced for what seemed like hours on the soft afternoon breeze before collapsing into each other like an airplane wreck.

We were asleep, wrapped around each other on the floor, when a servant knocked at the door to remind Di that she was due on the tennis court in fifteen minutes.

I staggered out of the room and made my way down the hallway to put on my tennis whites. I sat on my bed trying to work up the energy to bat a tennis ball around. As far as I was concerned, I'd already had my exercise for the day. I might not have had a backhand, but I had one hell of a forehand.

"Love forty," Juan announced as the ball went quietly into the net. There was a note of self-satisfaction in his voice. Di and I were getting badly beaten in spite of Sophie's double-faulting. We had dropped the first set and were down four games to one in the second.

I stood at the service line and waited for the ball boy, a security guard who had been pressed into service, to bounce the balls to me. Di was at the net looking scrumptious in her Givenchy tennis outfit. I wanted to go back up with her to the floor under the open window instead of serving to the tall, athletic man on the other side of the net waiting to annihilate anything within his reach.

Rivera was sitting under an umbrella on the sidelines with the sangria. Every time I missed a shot he spit a sunflower seed across the lawn. He had already helped himself to one of the Castilian chambermaids, taking her standing up in the linen closet.

I stood bouncing the ball against the baseline, trying to hit the chalk squarely. After a moment Di turned around to see what the problem was. I smiled at her, a wistful smile, tinged with lust. She smiled back her lovely Princess of Wales smile. A thrill of pleasure overcame me as I realized that we were on a speck of land in the middle of the Atlantic, in whitewashed rooms beside the sea, smoked salmon and Pouilly-Fumé at our disposal, crack security guards patrolling the perimeter. And no one knew we were there together except the King and Queen of Spain, Donald, and the crew of the Queen's Flight . . .

"It *is* your service, is it not?" King Juan called to me. He was standing at the net, twirling his racket with some impatience. Queen Sophie waited at the baseline to receive my serve. She had on wraparound sunglasses and a pair of designer tennis shoes. Her hair looked as if it had been flown over to Paris and back just for the day.

They were all waiting for me. Even Donald, who was standing in back of Rivera, wearing one of his plaid sports jackets in spite of the heat, his eyes scouring the horizon for kamikaze planes.

"Is there something wrong, Leonard?" Di asked.

"No. Nothing at all. I was just thinking . . ."

"Thinking?"

I was just thinking about those long, beautiful legs of yours, Di. I was thinking about how deep inside you took me, about how you stopped breathing and left your body to float above it with me . . .

Blood coursing through me like a power surge, I tossed the ball into the air and served an ace. The ball hit deep in the service box and kicked up with vicious topspin. Queen Sophie never even saw it.

The three of them looked at me in amazement. It was my first and only ace of the match.

"Bravo," said King Juan.

It did little good. We lost the next point and the next game and then went to tea. After tea we had a splash in the pool with the princes and then were left alone till dinner.

Di and I took a walk along the beach to the far end of the island. With Donald trailing at a discreet distance, we walked hand-in-hand and barefoot in the surf.

"It's lovely here, isn't it?" Di said.

"Anyplace would be lovely with you."

"Oh, Leonard." She squeezed my hand. We walked for a while in silence. Then she said, "I wish we didn't have to go back."

"We don't." The words came out of my mouth before I could stop them. And as soon as I'd said them my heart froze.

It seemed like forever before she stopped in the surf, turned to me, and said, "What do you mean?"

"I love you, Di," I blurted. "And I want to be with you forever."

Tears suddenly flooded my eyes. I could barely see her through the wetness. "Oh, Leonard," she murmured and began to kiss my tears away. Her lips sponged my eyelids until they were no longer wet from my tears but from the moisture of her mouth.

We sank down into the wet sand and held each other. The waves lapped up around us, but we didn't move. As Donald looked on blandly from a distant sand dune, Di and I whispered words of devotion to each other and promised we would never be apart, no matter what happened.

Dinner was an ordeal. I could barely wait to be alone with her again. I had not gotten specific on the beach, fearful that Donald might be employing some high-tech surveillance device to pick up conversations at a distance.

And so we sat through an endless dinner in the dining room, course upon course of delicacies cooked by Juan's Milanese cook, Gianfredo, who came out to take bows between courses. The conversation centered largely around real estate prices on the Costa Brava.

At one point, Sophie, trying to be polite and include me in the conversation, asked me if I was fond of García Lorca.

"I liked him a lot. Too bad he was shot by the man who put your husband in power."

That quieted conversation only for a brief moment. King Juan simply pretended that I hadn't said anything and asked how I liked the tiramisu.

"Terrific," I said.

"Gianfredo has stolen the recipe from Jacques Taillevent."

"Really?"

"Yes."

"Extraordinary."

After dinner, Di went to put the princes to bed. I sat on the terrace with King Juan, puffing on a Davidoff and listening to the surf pound the shore.

We had sat in silence for a long moment before he said, "I wasn't even born when Franco took power, you know. And I never cared for him. But one had no choice. He had a grip on the Spanish people. We did our best to resist him. I didn't ask to be named his successor. I was only nine years old at the time."

I nodded and smiled beneficently.

"Of course, one had to look at the larger picture," he went on. "The country was in shambles after the Civil War. We needed a strong force to unify us and to rebuild. And let us not forget about all the military aid *your* government gave him in the sixties . . ."

"You know what I think, Juan?"

"Yes?"

"I think it's a lot of water under the bridge. Nobody bats a thousand. When you get down to it, the trick is to get it over the plate and keep it low, isn't it?"

An hour later Di and I lay naked on the big bed in my white-washed stucco room, having taken the measure of each other's passion. The ripe ocean breeze dried the perspiration from our skin. Our breathing had died down from a crescendo to a pianissimo; our arms and legs were languid, our bellies tingling with wine and risotto.

"Di," I said softly.

"Ummn," she murmured, her eyes still closed, her hands clasped beneath her head.

"Do you remember what I said on the beach?"

"Ummn . . ."

"About . . . not having to go back if you didn't want to?"

"Ummn . . ."

"I have a plan."

She turned to me and opened her eyes. "A plan?"

"Yes."

"Do you really?" she said, suddenly alert.

I nodded.

"What sort of plan?"

"It's not entirely worked out yet."

"Tell me."

"If you say no, I'll understand. It involves you giving up pretty much everything. And I really don't have that much to lose, but you . . ."

"Leonard."

"Yes?"

"Just tell me. All right?"

I got up and walked over to the armoire, where I had hidden my shoulder bag under the spare bedding. I found the passports and brought them back to Di.

She opened them and looked inside, saw her picture and the name of Sandy Keats, born July 1, 1961, domiciled at 14, rue de la Révolution, Lomé, Togo. She quickly looked through the others, belonging to Chuck Keats and Timmy and Jimmy Keats.

Then she went back to her passport, looked at the photo again, and said, "It's really not a very good likeness, is it?"

"I took it from *Modern Royalty.*"

"I never cared for their photographer."

"Di, what do you think?"

There was a tone of irritation in my voice. I was standing in front of her, naked, my entire future in her hands, and she was going on about photography.

"Where are we going to go?"

"Florida."

"Florida?"

"First. Then we can go anywhere you like."

"How are we going to get there?"

"There's a plane and a pilot standing by for us at the airport in Nassau."

"And we shall fly into some marsh like gunrunners . . . is that it?"

I nodded, then shrugged, then nodded again.

"Togolese gunrunners?"

"I'm sure they have them."

She took another look at her passport, murmured, "Sandy Keats?"

"It's a good name. Very poetic."

"So it is . . ." She looked up and sighed, then reached for me and pulled me onto the bed. As her legs wrapped around my hips, she whispered in my ear, "You're crackers, Leonard. Completely crackers."

We wound up on the floor again, the bed linen twisted around us. We made so much noise that I was convinced the entire palace could hear us. As I lay there panting, my lips buried deep into the flesh of her shoulder, I heard her say in her very small Diana voice, "Leonard?"

"What?"

"Let's do it."

CHAPTER

21

We stayed up far into the night planning—Di sitting on the bed cross-legged, drinking Perrier straight from the bottle, and I pacing back and forth like a writer in a Hollywood story meeting. As I looked at her sitting there, I was reminded of the pictures I had seen of her as a schoolgirl, the long-legged, sultry adolescent with the pouty lips and dreamy eyes. I imagined her at nine, in her nightie in the Riddlesworth Hall dormitory, planning a raid on the pantry.

She looked at it as a romantic adventure, while I, with my Eastern European cynicism, looked at it as a flight into a newer, less oppressive world. She fixated on details—what to pack, what to tell the princes, what the weather would be like this time of year in Florida. The big picture did not seem to concern her, at least for the moment.

"It will do the boys good to have a holiday," she said. "They are being smothered. They have never been out in the world with real people, doing real things. And Charles's family will have them grow up in a hothouse just like those bloody organic vegetables he fawns over."

I hesitated for a moment, then asked, "What about Charles?"

"Oh, bugger Charles. He probably won't even know they're gone. He spends precious little time with them as it is." She paused, lost in thought. Then: "I just had a splendid idea."

"What's that?"

"We can visit Fergie in Texas."

"Sure."

"Oh, Leonard, we shall have such fun. We shall take the boys to Disney World and eat in hamburger stands and play minigolf. Just like real people. I adore minigolf, don't you?"

Then her eyes screwed up narrowly and her brow creased. "We must find a way to deal with Donald."

"Does he have any weaknesses?"

"He doesn't even go to the loo."

The next morning, after breakfast, Di announced that she wanted to go shopping with the boys in Nassau. Donald's features tightened noticeably when she asked him to have the helicopter come fetch them at noon.

"I'll need to know your itinerary, ma'am."

"I'm going shopping."

"It's standard procedure, as you know, to notify the shops of your arrival so that proper security precautions can be taken."

"Donald, I simply want to spend an hour or two in the shops. And I don't know which ones. So I don't see how you can ring them. And if you do alert the local police, you know they will leak it to the press and we shall just have an awful bother. Now if we simply pop in unannounced it will all go quite smoothly."

Donald gave her one of his gray looks, clearly unhappy. "What about the helicopter? We've given them no advance warning. Perhaps the helicopter isn't available this afternoon . . ."

"Well, if you ring them straightaway they will have enough time to make it available, won't they?"

After dealing with Donald, Di turned her attention to the princes, who were less than thrilled with the prospect of going shopping. They had been invited to go waterskiing with King Juan and now dug in for a battle.

"I shall need you to try things on," Di explained.

Both heads shook simultaneously. We were faced with a united front. Di looked at me for help.

"Hey, how'd you guys like to hit McDonald's for lunch? Couple of Quarter Pounders with fries. What do you say?"

The princes weighed their leverage for a moment. Then, weakening, Prince Hal said, "You don't suppose they have Happy Meals there, do you?"

"Hey, is the pope Catholic?"

"That's a rhetorical question," Wills said.

"Right . . ."

"You know, that's why we broke off and formed the Church of England," he continued. "The pope refused to recognize Henry VIII's divorce."

"Really?"

"I don't suppose you know what the Reformation was?"

"I haven't a clue."

Wills appeared to have his father's Germanic sense of literalness. He proceeded to give us a dissertation on the Reformation in England. They had trained him well in his little hothouse at Ludgrove.

Since the helicopter wasn't due on Bulba till noon, we had a few hours to kill. Di seemed extraordinarily calm. She and Sophie sat around the pool doing their nails and reading movie magazines. I excused myself, saying I had some work to do.

I slipped into Juan's study, closed the door, and dialed the number that Carl Webb had given me. Sitting there, twisting the cord manically, I glanced at the photographs on Juan's desk of him and Sophie with the Windsors, the Grimaldis, the Mountbattens. The phone rang ten times.

Carl Webb picked up on the eleventh ring.

"Yeah?"

"Carl, it's Leonard Schecter," I whispered.

"Who?"

"Leonard Schecter. I hired you to fly me to Florida, remember?"

"Oh yeah, what's going on, man?"

"Carl, have you been drinking?"

"What's your name again?"

I took a deep breath, trying to keep the panic out of my voice.

"Leonard. Schecter. We met at the airport yesterday. I hired you to fly me to Florida. I gave you three thousand dollars in advance to stand by, remember?"

"Oh, yeah, man. How you doing?"

"I'm fine, Carl. The question is how are *you* doing?"

"Pretty good. What's up?"

I lowered my voice even more. "I need you to be ready to leave this afternoon."

"No problem. What time?"

"Sometime between noon and four. Just be fueled up and ready. I'll meet you in the bar . . . no, not the bar. I'll meet you at . . . the Hertz counter."

"Ten-four."

"You got that, Carl?"

"Hertz counter, between noon and four."

Di had managed to stuff a number of things into her enormous Rodier shoulder bag. Besides the tiara, which I asked her specifically to bring, she slipped in the princes' Game Boys, her address book, her astrological chart, and her favorite bedroom slippers—all items that one would not normally bring on a simple shopping trip to town.

I was taking nothing but my toothbrush, the passports, and the $850,000, which was in fifty rolls, each with 170 one-hundred-dollar bills tightly bound with rubber bands. The princes were in baggy Daniel Hechter shorts, earth-toned Lacoste T-shirts in complementary colors, and Reeboks. Di was wearing a sleeveless blouse, blue slacks, and flats. Donald was wearing a wash-and-wear beige suit with a solid brown tie, off-white short-sleeved shirt, and his light-weight tropical shoulder holster.

At exactly five minutes to twelve we heard the chopper blades to the east. We all went out to the helipad to watch the landing. Commander Hewitt put the big bird down on the dime, and we waved good-bye. Juan and Sophie waved back and shouted that they'd see us at dinner.

"*Viva la quince brigada,*" I shouted back, but was drowned out by the rotor blades.

We stayed low over the ocean for the forty-minute hop to Nassau. Di made pleasant small talk with Commander Hewitt, chatting as if this were just another shopping run and not the first leg of a flight into the unknown. I marveled at her poise. She did not seem the slightest bit nervous. The plan was contingent on Di's ability to get Donald to leave us alone for a few minutes. After shopping, we would go to the local McDonald's, where Di would send Donald off on an errand. And then we would take advantage of this narrow window of opportunity and make a run for the airport.

When I had asked her how she was going to get Donald to abandon his post, she told me not to worry. "I shall think of something," she assured me blithely.

Not having alerted the local police, we had nobody waiting for us when we landed. We simply climbed out of the chopper and entered the terminal building like ordinary people. There were no bands playing or troops to inspect this time, only the maintenance crew of the Royal Navy helicopter, who bowed to Di and the princes.

In order to minimize security leaks, Di had told Donald not to arrange for a car. We would get a taxi to drive us into town. We would capitalize on the element of surprise. A blitzkrieg. Before the guerrilla army of paparazzi got mobilized, we would already be gone.

The airport was nearly empty at this hour, with only a few airline and rental-car clerks sitting and half-dozing in the midday heat. As we passed quickly through the main terminal I stole a glimpse at the Hertz counter. Carl Webb was not there. It was 12:45, and he was nowhere in sight.

I didn't have time to worry about Carl Webb, though. We were moving precipitously across the terminal and out toward the taxi stand. Donald walked in front, like an Indian scout, checking for potential ambushes.

I noticed how adept Di and the princes were at the quick-step. They were used to moving hurriedly through public places, walking fast enough to escape recognition but not so fast as to attract attention. It was not unlike the walk that tourists in Mexico use on their way to the bathroom.

We made it through the main door of the terminal unmolested and were outside in the sudden non-air-conditioned humidity. There was only one cab parked in front, a two-toned, rusted Ford Galaxy, circa 1975. The driver was asleep behind the wheel. Donald looked at the vehicle and made one of his unhappy faces.

"What's the problem now, Donald?" Di asked pointedly.

"I'm not happy with the vehicle, ma'am."

"We are only going a few miles. We don't need a Rolls-Royce."

"It looks rather unsafe . . ."

"Oh, bother," she said, and, not waiting for his permission, she opened the rear door and ushered the princes in. "Scoot over," she said. Donald and I got in the front with the driver.

We were all inside the cab before the driver awoke. He looked around, yawned, and said, "Yes, sir. Yes, ma'am."

He turned the key. We listened as the Galaxy sucked air and wheezed to life.

"Would you be good enough to take us to Banana Republic," said Di in her sweet Princess of Wales voice.

"Yes, ma'am," the driver said, and, stealing a glance in the rearview mirror, repeated, more loudly this time, "Yes, *ma'am*."

The Galaxy was not only unsafe, it was uncomfortable and hot. The princes began to get difficult, complaining about the heat and the bumpiness.

"We shall be there in no time at all," Di said firmly, cutting off further whining from the heirs apparent.

I sat in the front seat, wedged uncomfortably between the

driver and Donald. It would have been so much easier to grab the gun from the shoulder holster and shoot Donald. Then we could have dumped the body out of the car, had the driver do a U-turn, and returned to the airport in plenty of time to drag Carl Webb out of the bar and take off.

It was 1:15 when we pulled up in front of the Banana Republic on Nassau's fashionable shopping street. We piled out of the cab like passengers disembarking from a channel steamer after a rough crossing. Donald paid the driver. I waited for him to move up ahead, to do a reconnaissance of Banana Republic, then said to the driver, "Don't go away."

"Yes, sir."

Di bought the princes each a soccer shirt, a bathing suit, and a pair of lightweight summer walking shorts, which Wills swore he would not be caught dead in.

"They're vulgar," he said.

"Nonsense," Di replied. "You can wear them at Balmoral. Your grandmother will adore them."

Donald paid, and we were out of there and on the way across the street to Gucci before the sales staff could get on the phone and call in the photographers.

At Gucci, the princes took out their Game Boys again as Di examined some scarves. Holding up a large diaphanous one, she asked my opinion.

"It's great," I said.

"Lovely." She smiled. "I shall wear it with my lavender coat dress."

As we prepared to leave Gucci, I suggested we take a break and hit the McDonald's. I had the full support of the princes, who simultaneously cried, "Oh, yes." And they were out the door before Donald could stop them.

We trooped down the street to McDonald's, a restored stucco colonial building with an anachronistic golden arch and a sign that said TRY OUR McNASSAU SHAKE. Glancing over my shoulder, I saw the Galaxy pull out into traffic and follow us. Still no reporters. It was only a matter of time before we were spotted. But for the moment, at least, we remained anonymous—your typical tourist family and their slightly demented Uncle Donald.

It was past lunchtime, and the McDonald's was not crowded. Our entrance went unnoticed. I suggested that Donald and I order while Di and the princes took a seat. Donald, of course, found this unsuitable. It was decided that Wills and I should take the orders while Donald accompanied Di and Prince Hal to a large booth in the rear.

Prince Hal ordered a Quarter Pounder with cheese, large fries, and a chocolate shake. Wills ordered a Big Mac, large fries, and a root beer. Di ordered a side salad and an iced tea. Donald ordered nothing.

"So that's why you never go to the can, Donald," I remarked.

"I beg your pardon, sir?"

"Nothing in, nothing out."

Wills and I got the food and brought it back to the table. Di supervised the distribution of the ketchup and napkins, making sure that the princes had their laps properly covered so as not to stain their shorts. Though I wasn't the slightest bit hungry, I had ordered Chicken McNuggets, and I picked indifferently at them, as the princes sucked up their food like vacuum cleaners.

Di casually ate her salad, looking unconcerned, as if she were indeed merely a mother out at McDonald's with her kids.

"Chew your food, Hal," she said. "You don't get the benefit of any of the nutrients when you eat fast."

Prince Hal frowned and made a token stab at slowing down.

"And, Wills, sit up straight."

Wills edged up a little in his seat and went back to his fries. I was starting to get panicky. The window of opportunity was sliding shut.

"Di, are you feeling all right?" I said finally.

She looked at me with annoyance, the way a kid does when you coach her too openly. She waited a moment, then said, "Excuse me. I'm going to the loo."

Donald got up, but before he took two steps, Di turned back to him and snapped, "Donald, there is nobody between here and the loo. And you are not going in with me."

He backed off and watched her cross the restaurant and enter the ladies' room.

"Tell me about your toilet training, Donald."

He looked at me without answering.

"It must have been overly strict. Am I right?"

That was the extent of the conversation until Di emerged from the ladies' room and returned to our table. She sat down, looked at Donald, and said, "I have a problem."

"Ma'am?"

"I need some sanitary towels."

"Sanitary towels?"

"That's what I said."

"Perhaps Queen Sophia has some on hand . . ."

"Donald, you don't seem to understand. The problem is imminent."

Prince Hal looked up from his milk shake and said, "I know what *imminent* means."

"Yes, sweetheart, you do. And we talked about a woman's menstrual cycle, remember?"

He nodded proudly. Then, "Are you having a menstrual cycle presently, Mother?"

"Yes, I'm afraid I am, Hal."

Di turned back to Donald and said, "I'd greatly appreciate it, Donald, if you would fetch me some. There's a chemist down the street."

Donald looked at her unhappily, folded his arms, and said, "Perhaps Mr. Schecter could oblige you."

"Mr. Schecter is here having a bite with the boys and me. Whereas you, Donald, are not eating."

"As you know, ma'am, my instructions are not to leave you unattended—"

"In the face of a security danger. There is no security danger at the moment. We are sitting in a quiet restaurant. No one knows we are here. We are not menaced or badgered by anyone. In the event that someone should recognize me, I shall smile and sign their menu, and we shall all get along quite nicely. Now, please, run along to the chemist. As I have said, the problem is imminent."

"Her egg is unfertilized," said Prince Hal.

Di smiled and patted him on the head as Donald reluctantly rose and, before exiting, said, "It goes without saying, ma'am, that you should remain here until I get back."

"Yes, Donald," she said wearily.

Donald took a last look around the McDonald's, then strode to the door and exited. After a moment, I got up and followed him, stopping just inside the door.

"Where's he going?" Wills said.

"Nowhere, Wills. Wipe your mouth. You have a ketchup stain."

The Galaxy was parked outside, the driver fast asleep again. Donald crossed the street and walked toward the drugstore.

As soon as he was inside, I motioned to Di. She got up, gathered the food wrappers on a tray, and deposited them in the trash can. Then she said to the princes, "Come, boys, we shall wait for Donald outside."

"But what about your menstrual cycle?" Prince Hal protested.

"It's doing better, actually."

Wills looked at her and then at me, his suspicions beginning to crystallize.

"What's going on here?" he demanded.

"We are going to have a little adventure, Wills. Now, come on, move along."

Wills didn't move. I realized that extreme action was necessary. Donald could be back out the door in less than a minute.

"The cab's outside," I said to Di. "You and Hal wait for us there."

She nodded and, taking Hal's hand, exited past me. I walked over to Wills and said, "I'm going to be very brief, Wills. You've got ten seconds to get up and get out the door. Otherwise, I'm going to carry you out."

"You can't push me around. I'm second in line to the throne of England."

"Watch me."

I counted out loud, starting from ten and moving backward. At two, he got up and trudged sullenly toward the door. I grabbed his arm just in case he decided to make a run for it, and got him into the taxi, putting him in the backseat with Di and Prince Hal. Then I got in on the passenger side and said, "The airport. And step on it."

"Yes, sir."

Taking me literally, the driver pressed the accelerator down to the rusted floorboard of the Galaxy. We lurched forward and roared off down the street right past the drugstore.

"This is highly irregular," said Wills.

"Yes, sweetheart, it is," Di said.

"It is a security violation of the first order."

"I know, Wills, but it's necessary, believe me. We shall explain it all to you later. As soon as we take off."

"Take off? Where are we going?"

"We're not exactly sure."

We were doing close to eighty. The Galaxy was making so much noise that I thought it was going to self-destruct. Prince Hal said he was going to throw up. Di asked him to try to hold it in until we got there.

The little prince showed his breeding, hanging on until we screeched to a halt at the entrance to the terminal. Di opened the door, and he tossed his cookies on the pavement.

As Di took tissues from her purse and cleaned up her son, I paid the driver. All I had was U.S. currency. I gave him a hundred-dollar bill. He smiled and asked if Di would sign the bill. She obliged, and, as we staggered out, I whispered in my best Efrem Zimbalist, Jr., voice, "Not a word of this to anyone. It's top secret."

"Yes, sir."

Carl Webb was not at the Hertz counter. I looked at my watch: three-thirty.

"Wait here for me," I said, surrendering Wills to Di and heading for the bar.

I heard him before I saw him. He was slouched over the bar, his back toward me, talking to himself. "I had a Creole woman in New Orleans once. Kept me hard for three days . . ." And then he laughed his phlegmy laugh and started to light a cigarette.

I walked up and looked at his face. What I saw was not reassuring. His eyes were liquid and unfocused, his mouth loose.

"Carl, are you all right?"

"Out of sight, man."

"Can you fly a plane?"

He looked at me, blinked, then said, "Let's go." Then he blinked again, looked at me, and asked, "Who are you?"

I sat down on the stool beside him. "Carl, I came in here yesterday and hired you to fly me off this island. I gave you three thousand dollars to stand by. You promised you would be ready. You even said you'd sleep in your plane. I called you this morning to remind you. I asked you to be ready between noon and four in the afternoon, to wait for me at the Hertz counter. It is now three-thirty, which is between noon and four, and not only are you not waiting for me at the Hertz counter, you're sitting in the bar getting tanked."

He took all this in without flinching, then got up from his bar stool and said in a remarkably sober voice, "I'm ready."

"Are you sure?"

"Man, I've been fucked up worse than this and gone in over the Everglades in a hurricane."

Carl headed for the door, and I followed him. When we got to the Hertz counter, I said, "Carl, this is my wife, Sandy, and our sons, Timmy and Jimmy."

Carl Webb looked at them and said, "You trying to shit me, man? That's Princess Di and her kids."

"How do you do?" said Di, smiling.

"I read the *Enquirer*."

"A pleasure to meet you." She offered her hand, and Carl Webb took it.

"Likewise. You look great in person, you know that?"

"Thank you, Mr. Webb."

"Any luggage?"

"I'm afraid we're traveling rather light."

"Where's the plane, Carl? We're running late," I said.

"Follow me."

He started walking toward the security checkpoint.

"Is he a pilot?" Wills said.

"Yes."

"He doesn't look like a pilot."

"He's a decorated war veteran."

Di and I, a prince in each of our hands, followed Carl Webb to the checkpoint. There was a young woman security guard on duty, whom Carl greeted familiarly.

"Hey, Doris, how're you doin'?" Carl Webb said as Di, keeping her face averted, put the Rodier bag on the conveyor belt, and I put the airline bag full of money right behind it.

"You want to come by my place tonight, sit on my face?"

"You're a bad boy, Carl," she scolded playfully, as we trooped through the metal detector and retrieved our hand luggage. Doris barely looked at us, or at the X-ray machine, where, if she had, she would have seen $850,000 and a diamond tiara.

We followed Carl Webb down a long corridor, past departure-gate counters, empty at the moment, to a door that said AUTHORIZED PERSONNEL ONLY. Carl opened the door for us, and we all walked down a flight of stairs and out onto the tarmac.

"Isn't this fun?" said Di, as we followed Carl Webb past a jumbo jet toward an area where a number of small planes were parked.

"I would like to know where we're going," said Wills.

"To Disney World," I replied.

"But that's in the States."

"So it is."

"Where's Donald?"

"He's taking our packages back to Juan and Sophie's for us."

Wills was scowling darkly by the time we arrived in front of the Cessna 310, standing off by itself, looking lonely and forlorn.

"Well, here we are," said Di, with just a hint of concern in her voice.

"Has this aircraft been checked out by RAF flight mechanics?" Wills asked Carl Webb.

"Kid, this plane runs like a June bride."

"And how is that?" Wills persisted.

"I wish I knew." Carl Webb broke into one of his coughing laughs.

Di looked at me and took a deep breath, as if to say, "Do we really want to do this?"

Frankly, at that moment, I was no longer sure. The plane looked small and fragile. Even stone sober, Carl Webb would not have inspired my confidence. The sun was starting to sink, and a chilly wind was picking up.

As I stood there, I thought of the Petitioner's lawyer with her computer printouts of my tax deductions. I thought of Rivera being restrained by the bailiff from strangling Guadalupe. I thought of Rupert Makepeace standing over my bed at the Dorchester taking nude pictures of me. I thought of Ahab lashed to the bow of the *Pequod.* I thought of Di above me on the bed, her head tossed back, her white skin stretched across her throat . . .

"Let's do it," I said. And, as we climbed into the Cessna, I remembered that those were Gary Gilmore's last words before the Utah State Police firing squad put him out of his misery.

CHAPTER

22

Carl Webb did not bother filing a flight plan with the authorities at Air Traffic Control in Nassau. He merely fired up the engine, taxied out onto the runway, and asked the tower for clearance. When he got it, he turned back to us and said, "Seat backs and tray tables in their upright positions."

I tried not to close my eyes. Di was in one of her meditative trances, her eyes lightly closed, her palms turned up in front of her. Wills was glaring morosely out the dirty window. Prince Hal looked as if he were going to throw up again.

The Cessna rattled down the runway, gaining velocity. I could hear the rivets in the fuselage straining. I uttered a silent prayer as we lifted off the ground. The Cessna climbed unsteadily above Andros Island and banked sharply west into the sun. Then Carl Webb turned back to us, and, like a cab driver, asked, "Where to, folks?"

"Aren't we going to Disney World?" Prince Hal said.

"Maybe tomorrow," Di said.

I got out of my seat and moved forward in the cramped compartment. I knelt down beside Carl Webb and whispered, "What do you think?"

"How hot are they, man?"

"Pretty hot. Listen, is there a small airport we can get into, where we can sort of just wander off without attracting any attention?"

"With her face—where's she not going to attract attention?"

"Is there, like, a landing strip somewhere that's not patrolled?"

"Hundreds of them. The thing is the DEA watches them. It's like Russian roulette. They can't watch them all, so you take a shot."

"A shot?"

"Yeah. It's about three to one in your favor. Not bad odds. Better than you get in Vegas."

"We need to land someplace where we can walk to a motel or something. It can't be in the middle of nowhere."

"Boy, that gets tougher. You didn't think this out so good, huh?"

"It was a spur-of-the-moment thing."

Carl Webb didn't say anything for a moment. He sat there, stroking his chin with one hand, flying the plane with the other. Then he smiled and said, "I think I got the place for you."

"Where?"

"It's a strip on an abandoned army base just east of Naples. You're about a mile from the interstate. You walk along the interstate, you're bound to find a HoJo's."

"Are you sure?"

"Unless the strip's grown over. I haven't put down on it for a couple of years. We'll go down and have a look-see."

"What if the . . . look-see isn't good?"

"We'll abort."

"Can you do that?"

"Depends on the tree line."

"What if the tree line isn't . . . good?"

"Then we'll land . . . one way or another." He lit another

cigarette, leaned back in his seat, and said, "I'm going to pop up over Marathon."

"What?"

"Pop up. What you do, see, is come in low under the DEA radar, and get into the Marathon landing pattern. Then just before you put down, you pull up on the stick and gain altitude. This way you show up on the radar as taking off from Marathon, and the DEA doesn't track you."

"I see. Have you done this before?"

"Lots of times."

"You ever get caught?"

"Once."

"That's reassuring."

"I did eighteen months in Pensacola. I was out in thirteen. It wasn't bad. I built up my upper body, though you'd never know it looking at me, would you?"

I declined comment and moved back to take my seat beside Di.

"We're going to Naples," I announced.

"Naples? Isn't that in Italy?"

"Not this Naples. This Naples is in Florida."

"Lovely," said Di. "Naples without ruins. How refreshing. Charles insisted on dragging me through all these dreadful archaeological sites."

"Will there be a band waiting for us when we land?" asked Prince Hal.

"I don't think so," I replied, as we suddenly dropped altitude sharply, sinking straight down like we were dead weight. My heart contracted as my stomach strained against the seat belt. I looked over at Di, who was silently reciting her mantra.

"Carl?" I called a little shakily. "We okay?"

"No problem. I'm just getting down to a hundred and fifty feet to get under the DEA radar balloon."

"What's a DEA radar balloon?" asked Wills.

"It's an amusement-park ride. We'll go on one in Disney World."

We continued low over an ocean illuminated by the thinning

rays of the dissolving daylight. It would have been beautiful if it weren't so terrifying. It was like waterskiing just above the surface of the water. In the distance, like a strand of costume jewelry, loomed the Florida Keys.

"We're coming into Marathon," Carl Webb announced. "Hang on to your hats."

Carl Webb took the Cessna in over a stand of palm trees, and we could see runway lights in the distance. He got on the radio and said, "Marathon, this is Cessna one-nine-seven-six-six-nine-eight-A taking off on One north-northwest."

"We're not taking off," said Wills. "We're landing."

"Shhh, Wills," said Di. "Don't distract Captain Webb."

There was a crackle on the voice box and a garbled command from the tower. Suddenly we were gaining altitude again, climbing sharply toward the beach and ocean in the distance.

"Ten-four, man," said Carl Webb with one of his rolling, thunderous laughs. And then he announced to his passengers: "Ladies and gentlemen, this is your captain speaking. Our flying time to Naples is approximately one hour. As soon as we reach our cruising altitude of six hundred and fifty feet, flight attendants will be through the aisles with drinks and a meal. Our full-length feature film today is *Key Largo*. Have a nice day."

Though we took no casualties, the landing in Naples was not unlike the Anzio beachhead in 1944. It was dark, cold, and hair-raising. Because there were no lights on the abandoned strip, Carl Webb had to go down with only the Cessna headlight to illuminate the landing surface.

Di remained amazingly calm through it all. She tried to comfort her anxious children by chatting away about our plans for fun in Florida. By this time they were both aware that there would be no brass band when we landed.

Wills was livid. He merely glared at both of us and brooded, his fists clenched. Prince Hal sat there with a postvomit pallor on his face, humming quietly to himself. At the controls, Carl Webb smoked and coughed like a man in the latter stages of emphysema.

It was so dark that we didn't even know we were on the ground until we felt the wheels hit the surface of the airstrip. What followed may have been the scariest fifteen seconds of my life. The Cessna careened through the darkness, weaving back and forth like a drunken sailor, its wing flaps and brakes doing their best to slow us down. My foot frantically pumped an imaginary brake pedal. My hands gripped what passed for an armrest. I kept expecting to hear the screech of metal and feel the heat of the explosion as we collided with whatever was in our path and burst into flames.

My whole life did not pass in front of my eyes. Only a small portion of it. I was back at the Togolese embassy in London, dancing with Di to "Embraceable You."

"Now what brings you to England, Mr. Schecter?"

"Leonard, please . . . ma'am."

"Shall we make a deal? Suppose I call you Leonard and you drop the 'ma'am.' "

"Okay."

"Are you working here or just visiting, Leonard?"

"I'm here to write an epic poem."

"Oh, lovely."

"It may or may not have rhyming couplets."

"I see. And what's the subject of your poem?"

"You. . . ."

For several moments nobody spoke. We all sat there in the darkness, feeling our hearts pound. Then Carl Webb said, "Welcome to Naples, ladies and gentlemen, where the local temperature is . . ." He opened a side window in the cockpit, stuck a finger out, and said, "Sixty-five degrees Fahrenheit."

It was, in fact, an old airstrip, now badly overgrown with weeds but apparently still serviceable for a small enough plane. Carl Webb had left the headlight on, and we could see only straight in front of us. To either side, all was blackness. It was dead quiet except for the croaking of frogs. We all slowly deplaned, looked around into the darkness.

"There's nothing here," said Prince Hal.

"I know, sweetheart," said Di. "We're going to have to walk to our hotel."

"Walk?" said Prince Hal, as if the idea were entirely preposterous.

Carl Webb took his flashlight and moved it in a slow, 360-degree arc. There was an abandoned hut off in the distance, and, according to Carl Webb, a road that led to a larger road that led to the interstate.

We found two old blankets and gave them to the princes. Carl Webb took off his World War II army-surplus flight jacket and gave it to Di.

"Oh, I couldn't," she protested.

"I insist," he said.

Then he and I set off with the flashlight to scout the road behind the hut. When we were about fifty feet away, he said, "You fucking her?"

"Carl, that's personal, all right?"

"Just curious to know what she's like with a cock in her. No offense."

Behind the hut there was indeed a road. Of sorts. Like the airstrip, it was overgrown and abandoned. He shone the flashlight in the distance and said, "If memory serves me, you got about a half hour till you hit a two-lane. Then you go either left or right, I forget, to the interstate."

"You really can't remember if it was left or right?"

"Man, I used to smoke a lot of dope back then. Left, right—it was all the same to me, you know what I mean?"

We went back to Di and the princes and told them we had found the road.

"Is there a McDonald's?" Prince Hal asked.

Carl Webb chuckled loudly and said, "You kidding? You can't take a dump without hitting one these days."

"Are you going to come with us?" Wills asked.

"Afraid not. Previous engagement." He handed me the flash-light and said, "Take good care of this." Then he bowed to Di and said, "Your Highness," and to the princes, "Guys . . ." and climbed back into the cockpit.

We moved back out of the way and watched as he turned the Cessna around in the weeds. He gave us a thumbs-up through the cockpit window and rattled down the strip and took off. From where I stood, it looked like he cleared the tree line by inches.

"Well, shall we get going?" I suggested cheerfully.

"Where?"

"This way." And I shone the flashlight in the direction of the hut.

"But there's nothing there," complained Prince Hal.

"There will be. Soon. I promise."

We walked along, Wills and I in front with the flashlight, Di and Prince Hal behind. The road was narrow and rutted and bordered on each side by thick woods. There was no moon to speak of, only the dim illumination of the flashlight, which seemed to be weakening as we went.

The mosquitoes were feasting on our ankles. It was getting chillier. Several times Prince Hal stopped, said he couldn't go on, and burst into tears. And each time Di spoke to him soothingly and gently and got him moving again. Wills said nothing, but you could hear his teeth grinding as he trudged along wrapped in his blanket.

The road was more than a half hour away, closer to an hour. But when we reached it, there was a sense of deliverance. Our expedition had emerged from the bush to the relative safety of a small country road.

The princes sat down on a patch of grass at the side of the road as Di and I walked off a little distance to discuss our next move. I put my arms around her and felt the warmth of her body through the flight jacket. Her lips nibbled my earlobe playfully.

"Oh, Leonard," she whispered, "this is utterly mad, isn't it?"

"Yes."

"Charles would never do anything like this. And . . ." She started laughing.

"What's so funny?"

It took her a while to stop laughing and then she said, "I was imagining Donald—with his . . . paper sack . . . full . . . of . . . sanitary . . . towels . . ." She could barely get the words out, she was laughing so hard.

"Are you all right, Mother?" Wills asked.

"Oh, yes, Wills, just splendid."

She finally stopped laughing, looked at me, and asked, "Where shall we stay?"

"The interstate's not far away. There should be something there."

"Which way is it?"

"Either left or right."

"Sorry?"

"Carl Webb didn't remember."

I looked up at the night sky. There were stars everywhere. But it had been thirty odd years since I had been a Boy Scout, and it all looked like spaghetti to me.

"You happen to know anything about astronomy?" I asked Di.

"Oh, heavens, no. But Wills does. He's got his own telescope."

I walked over to Wills and sat down beside him. He was scratching his mosquito bites and looking very unhappy.

"Wills, I bet you can't tell me where the North Star is."

"Why do you want to know?"

"Just checking."

"Do *you* know?"

"Of course. But I want to see if you know."

"I'll wager that you don't know. And that you're lost and that you want me to tell you where it is so you'll know which way to go."

I smiled indulgently at the future King William V. Sitting there wrapped in his blanket, his long English schoolboy hair falling in his face, he exemplified the House of Windsor even in south Florida. They were bullheaded, the whole lot of them, as far back as George III, with his Stamp Act.

"Wills," I said, "this is the way I see it. We can spend the night here and let the mosquitoes eat us alive, or we can find a hotel and have a bed and a shower and TV and room service. Which would you prefer?"

"What happens after we find a hotel? What happens tomorrow morning? And the morning after that?"

"We'll get a car, go to Disney World, play miniature golf."

"Yes, and then what? When shall we be returning to England?"

I didn't know what to answer so I said nothing.

"We are in the middle of Cicero at school. There's an exam Monday week on the orations."

"Maybe you can make it up."

"They don't permit makeups at Ludgrove."

Di sat down on the other side of Wills and put her arm around his shoulders. "Sweetheart, wouldn't it be lovely if we had a bath and some tea?"

"He doesn't know where the North Star is. And he doesn't know what we're doing tomorrow. And I suspect this shall end badly."

"Oh, no, Wills," said Di. "We are having a holiday, that's all. Isn't this fun?"

"I am not having fun," said Wills adamantly. "I should like to go home."

"Okay," I said, getting up and stretching, "let's go."

"Where?"

"Since you don't want to tell us where the North Star is, I'll just hazard a guess." And I pointed to my left and started walking.

"That's east," announced Wills.

I stopped and turned around. "Is it?"

"Yes. If you extend directly upward from the right end of the Big Dipper, you'll have Polaris, which is always due north from the observer and will be until the year A.D. 12,000 when the star Vega in the constellation Lyra will be the polestar."

"I don't think I can wait that long. Shall we go?"

.   .   .

We walked west into the night. A few cars passed us, but hitchhiking was a last resort. Until I got Di a wig and dark glasses, and the princes a haircut, they were too recognizable. We would go as far as we could on foot and under the cover of night.

The long march lasted a little less than two hours. It was nearly eight o'clock when we saw the first glow of the interstate faintly in the distance. As we got closer I could make out the comforting neon letters of a Howard Johnson motor lodge.

We let out a little cheer as we got close enough to the HoJo's to see the VACANCY sign. I had Di and the princes wait in the parking lot, as I went into the office with my airline bag full of money. I plunked down forty-nine dollars in advance for a nonsmoking room with two double beds and signed the register Mr. and Mrs. Chuck Keats and family, Tenafly, New Jersey.

"There's a complimentary breakfast in the Everglades Room starting at six-thirty," the clerk told me.

"Great." I smiled wearily.

"Long drive?" he asked solicitously.

"You wouldn't believe how long." I took my room key and went outside to fetch Sandy and the kids. We went upstairs and hurried through the empty hallway to our room.

It wasn't the Dorchester, but it would do. The princes immediately turned the TV on, and Di headed for the shower. When I returned a half hour later with sandwiches and Cokes, Di was fast asleep under the covers on one bed while the princes were on the other bed watching Barbara Walters interview Kevin Costner.

I sat down on the edge of Di's bed, the food in my lap, as Barbara asked Kevin, "How does it feel to be Kevin Costner?"

Kevin Costner shrugged and gave his road-company Gary Cooper smile and said, "I don't know. How does it feel to be Barbara Walters?"

I closed my eyes and imagined myself sitting in Kevin Costner's seat as Barbara leaned casually toward me.

"Tell us, Leonard. How does it feel to have spent the night with the world's most popular woman in a Howard Johnson's motor lodge in Naples, Florida?"

"It was exciting, Barbara. Very exciting. But you should have seen us landing on an abandoned airstrip in the middle of nowhere and navigating by the light of the North Star through mosquito-infested wilderness with only the aid of a flashlight."

"Tell us about it."

"Well, it all started some time ago at the Togolese embassy in London . . . the band was playing 'Embraceable You' . . ."

CHAPTER
23

Later that night I ran into Rivera at the ice machine. He had a rum and Coke in one hand and an empty ice bucket in the other.

"*¿Qué pasa, coño?*"

"I don't know. I've got to go out tomorrow and buy a wig and dark glasses and a car. And some clothes. And figure out what to do. Do you think they'll be looking for us at Disney World?"

He shrugged his Rivera shrug and said, "*Quién sabe?*"

"Where are you staying?"

"One-nineteen. With a Mexicana stewardess."

"Really?"

"Used to be Miss Tampico."

"Great."

"Like a machete into a ripe melon." He gestured to make his point, filled his bucket with ice, and walked away.

I returned to the room and poured some ice into what was left of my diet Coke. I turned the TV on without the sound, and while Cher sold hair products, I waited for the sun to rise.

Di and the princes slept soundly in their beds. I dozed intermittently in my chair. It was close to eight before Prince Hal got up and padded to the bathroom in his bare feet. When he emerged and saw me in my chair, he looked puzzled for a moment, and then, apparently forgetting the events of the previous day, asked, "Are you our new detective?"

"Go back to sleep, Prince Hal," I said softly. He climbed obediently in beside his brother and went back to sleep.

About an hour later Wills was up. He looked at me in the chair, then over at his mother sleeping alone in the other bed, and nodded, as if to say, *Good thing you didn't try anything.*

"What is your plan?" he asked peremptorily.

"Why don't we wait till your mother gets up."

"She sleeps rather late, you know. Especially on holiday."

This conversation woke Prince Hal up. He sat up in bed, rubbed his eyes, and said, "What's for breakfast?"

I opened the room-service menu. "How about some flapjacks?"

"Sorry?"

"Pancakes."

"Do you suppose we can have kippers?"

"I don't think so . . ."

"When can we eat? I'm ravenous."

"As soon as your mother gets up."

Prince Hal went over to the adjoining bed and started tickling Di. She stirred, opened her eyes, and sighed, "Oh, Hal, must you?"

"We're hungry, Mother. And our detective won't let us have breakfast until you get up."

Di looked across at me in my chair, smiled, then turned back to Prince Hal. "That's Leonard. And he's our friend, not our detective."

We ordered breakfast and while we waited for it to arrive, I explained that I would go out and get a car, some clothes, toothbrushes, and a number of other things, and then we would be able to take off for Disney World.

There was some discussion of the type of car we should have. Di wanted a Jaguar. Prince Hal wanted a camping car. Wills wanted to go straight to the police and turn ourselves in.

"But we haven't done anything wrong, Wills," said Di.

"Then why are we in hiding?"

She sat down on the bed beside her older son, putting her arm around him. "Well, you see, Wills, we don't want the papers to know about this holiday. They would write about it and we would have them badgering us all the time and it would be an awful bother, wouldn't it?"

"We are not supposed to be without a detective, Mother. You know that."

"Sweetheart, we only need a detective if people know who we are. And nobody does."

"What if someone finds out?"

"We shall be very careful . . ."

There was a knock at the door.

"Everybody into the bathroom," I whispered.

"This is highly irregular," Wills grumbled as Di ushered him and his brother into the bathroom.

At ten o'clock, I went into the office, said I was having car trouble, and asked the clerk to call a cab.

"What sort of trouble, sir?" she asked.

"It won't start."

"Would you all like me to ask our maintenance man to have a look at it? Maybe it just needs a jump."

"No thanks. I better go to an authorized dealer. It's still under warranty."

"What type of car is it?" Her eyes looked down at the register, then back up at me. "The night clerk didn't get your car and license number. Why don't you give it to me—just in case."

"Just in case what?"

"Well, sir, sometimes we get unauthorized people parking in our

lot. And we have to call the tow truck. And you all wouldn't want
to have your car towed by mistake, now, would you?"

"It's a Ford. New Jersey plates G-two-three-four-seven-H."

"My, you are a long way from home, aren't you?"

I nodded, smiled.

"Whereabouts in New Jersey?"

"Tenafly."

"That anywhere near Parsippany?"

"Not too far."

"My sister's husband's family lives up there. They're in the
coin-laundry business . . ."

I read *USA Today* and *The Fort Myers Journal American* waiting
for the cab to arrive. There was nothing yet about the disappearance
of Di and the princes. The story must have broken after the previous
day's deadlines. By this morning it would be all over the world. I had
a twenty-four-hour start on a mustache. I would let it grow.

I asked the taxi driver, a large woman with a T-shirt that said
CALL ME BABS, to take me to the Ford dealership.

"Don't have one," said Babs.

"You got a Chrysler dealer?"

"That would be Bud Grover. Mount Vesuvius Chrysler-Plym-
outh on East Main."

We got on the interstate for one exit, got off at DOWNTOWN
NAPLES—CITRUS MUSEUM. There was an enormous bronze orange on
the front lawn of the Citrus Museum. It looked like a meteor that had
crash-landed right in front of the small stucco-and-glass building.

Babs dropped me in front of Mount Vesuvius Chrysler-Plym-
outh. I walked in the door and started to wander around looking at
sticker prices. A short dark man in a brown-and-white-checkered
sports jacket came up to me and introduced himself as Bud Grover.

He thrust out his hand. I shook it.

"Hi, I'm Chuck Keats."

"What can I do for you, Chuck?"

"I'm looking for a family vehicle. For a long trip."

"How big's the family?"

"Wife and two kids."

"Dog?"

"Not yet."

"Well, Chuck, you get a Dodge Caravan, you can afford to have two more kids and a dog."

He smiled through a gridwork of tobacco-blackened teeth. "I can put you in a Caravan, set you up with three-point-nine percent APR financing, and throw in a butane outdoor barbecue."

Putting his arm around my shoulders, he led me to the corner of the showroom, where a baby-blue minivan stood modestly in the flat midmorning Florida light.

"That's one gorgeous vehicle, ain't it?"

"Yes . . ."

"Three-point-oh liter, one-forty-two horsepower V-six, four-speed automatic . . ."

"Okay."

"You get twenty-one in the city, twenty-four on the road . . . you got fold-away rear seats if you and the missus want to ditch the kids and go parking." He winked at me.

I winked back. "I'll take it."

" 'Course, you want to drive it, see for yourself how it handles. You'd be surprised what a family vehicle can feel like . . ."

"I want to buy this car."

"You don't have to sacrifice performance . . ."

"Bud, I want to buy this car. Now."

"What's that, Chuck?"

"I want to buy the Dodge Caravan. Right now. This morning. For cash."

"You do?"

"That's right."

It took him a moment to switch gears. Then he said, "Step this way."

He led me to a small glassed-in office with a desk, filing cabinet, and a sign that said THIS BUD'S FOR YOU.

"Have a seat, Chuck."

I sat down on a chair opposite the desk.

"Offer you a cup of coffee?"

"No thanks."

He poured himself a cup from a Mr. Coffee machine, sighed, smiled. "You understand, Chuck, that this is a very popular model. Fact, I only have two left on the lot. And they're both loaded."

I nodded.

"You're getting factory air, AM-FM radio and cassette player, driver-side air bag, drink holder, the whole enchilada. So I don't have a whole lot of flexibility on the price here."

"Fine."

"Ordinarily, I would deal. If you wanted a Le Baron or a New Yorker, hell, I could let you walk off with it for next to nothing. But these babies are back-ordered . . ."

"How much do you want?"

"You go all the way up the interstate to Fort Myers, you won't find another dealer with any in stock . . ."

"Bud, pick a number."

He took another sip of coffee, looked down at his papers, folded his hands like a minister, and said, "I'm going to need fourteen-seven base, with a dealer prep of four-fifty."

"Out the door?"

"With tax and license, you're looking at . . ." He hit a few tiny buttons on his wristwatch calculator, sighed again, and said, "Sixteen thousand, three hundred, and seventy-five dollars."

"Wrap it, Bud."

While Bud was doing the paperwork and prepping the car, I walked down East Main Street to the Kmart. There I bought underwear, jeans, and sweatshirts for the princes, two sets of matching jogging suits for Di and me, toothbrushes, toothpaste, shampoo, and conditioner. I got Miami Dolphins jackets and Florida Marlins baseball caps for the princes. For Di I chose a Kennedy Space Center cap and a pair of Ray-Ban highway-patrol sunglasses to go with her flight jacket.

Across the street at the Foot Locker, I got Reeboks in different colors for the entire family and a dozen one-size-fits-all athletic socks. Then I walked back down East Main Street and stopped into Edie's Diner to wait for my Dodge Caravan to be ready.

I sat at the counter and ordered coffee and an English muffin. The place was empty, with a TV set going at the end of the counter. Edie sat on a stool and watched a young actor with long dark hair tongue-kiss a blond actress in a peignoir.

Suddenly they cut away from the action and flashed NEWS BULLETIN on the screen. There was a garbled signal, some flashes of color, and then a woman standing in front of Buckingham Palace in the rain.

Reading from notes, the reporter said, "I am standing in front of Buckingham Palace, where, just moments ago, a spokesman for Queen Elizabeth announced that Princess Diana and her two sons, William and Harry, have been reported missing. The Princess of Wales and the two young princes had been in the midst of a vacation on the island of Bulba, guests of King Juan Carlos and Queen Sophia of Spain. Yesterday, at approximately noon local time, they departed by helicopter for a shopping trip in Nassau. They were accompanied by an American friend of the family, Leonard Schecter, of Los Angeles, and an officer in the Royal Protection Squad, Sergeant Donald Bellchase, the longtime bodyguard of the Princess and her children. According to Sergeant Bellchase, the four people disappeared from a McDonald's restaurant in Nassau while he was momentarily absent. Officers from New Scotland Yard's Royal Protection Squad and MI6 have flown to Nassau to investigate on the scene. The spokesman declined any further comment."

The reporter slipped her note cards into the pocket of her raincoat, turned three-quarter profile to the camera, and added, "This is all we have officially on this story at the moment, but CBS News has learned that Leonard Schecter has been linked romantically with Princess Diana in recent months, as well as with the Queen's sister, Margaret. Princess Margaret had no comment, nor did any other member of the royal family. In London this is Gabrielle Fredrika reporting live."

We went back to *The Young and the Restless*. Edie got off the stool, turned to me, and said, "I don't know why that girl can't be happy. She's got herself two kids and a castle. What more does she want?"

"Love," I said. The word slipped out of my mouth before I could stop it. Edie considered this for a moment, then nodded slowly and said, "Well, sir, I suppose you got a point there. Refill your cup?"

We checked out of the Naples Howard Johnson's at three o'clock. The baby-blue Dodge Caravan reeked of Naugahyde and vinyl. The princes sat in the backseat in their matching Dolphins jackets and Marlins caps, fidgeting beneath their seat belts. Di was beside me, her hair tucked up inside her cap, her blue eyes shielded by her dark-green highway-patrol Ray-Bans.

Though at a distance we looked like your typical American tourist family, I didn't trust the disguises at close range. At Fort Myers, an hour up the interstate, the princes and I would get haircuts and Di a wig.

When the princes objected, I put my foot down. "No haircuts, no Disney World."

"But we always have Kevin cut our hair," protested Prince Hal.

"Kevin's not available at the moment."

We drove through Fort Myers, a charmless city on the Gulf of Mexico, looking for a beauty-supply store and a barbershop. Kay's Hair Care and Nails was in the back of a forlorn shopping center. I had to talk Di out of going in herself to pick out a wig.

"Just because they didn't recognize you in the McDonald's in Nassau doesn't mean that you won't be recognized here."

"But I look so frumpy."

"Di," I said, "you can never look frumpy."

She smiled, gave me one of her Oh, Leonard looks, and said, "Something dark brown, I should think."

"How about red?"

"I'd prefer not to look like a tart, thank you."

I went into Kay's Hair Care and Nails and told Kay that I was looking for a wig for my girlfriend for a costume party. She led me to a wall display of a dozen wigs.

"What does she want to go as?" Kay asked.

"Cleopatra."

"We don't have a Liz Taylor, honey. We have a Madonna. We have a Joan Collins. We have a Princess Di . . . Did you hear? Poor girl. If I were her, I'd run away, too. Imagine still being married to that son of a bitch, you'll pardon my French."

I bought the Joan Collins and went back to the Dodge Caravan. Di took off the Kennedy Space Center cap and, turning the rearview mirror toward her, fitted the wig on over her hair. She fussed with it for a moment, then turned to us and said, "Well, gentlemen, what do you think?"

We were speechless, all three of us. She didn't look like Joan Collins. But she didn't look like Diana either. She looked like some hybrid creature—a mixed metaphor, a woman created in a test tube. Her fair skin and blue eyes were framed by a dark-brown border, which gave her features a completely different emphasis.

"You look terrific," I said with as much conviction as I could muster.

"Rubbish. I think she looks silly," said Wills.

Di looked back into the mirror for a moment and nodded. "I certainly do look silly." She removed the wig and said, "I can't wear this, Leonard. It's dreadful."

"Di, please. Just until we get to Orlando. It's a big city. They'll have better wigs there."

"If I just let my hair grow and stop highlighting it, it will look completely different."

"I understand, but . . ."

"I'm not a natural blonde, you know. I have mousy light-brown hair. I must get it highlighted monthly."

"We can't wait that long."

"Well then, I shall just stay out of sight."

"But what about Disney World, Mother?" asked Prince Hal. The sound of her younger son's plaintive voice cracked her resistance, and after a moment she silently put the wig back on.

We found a barbershop a few blocks away. Before leaving the car, I told the princes that they should avoid speaking whenever possible.

"And why is that?" said Wills.

"Because of your accents," I explained.

"We don't have accents," Wills pointed out. *"You do."*

"Be that as it may, Wills, we are doing our best not to attract attention to ourselves."

"Don't they hear English spoken correctly in this part of the world?"

"Not very often."

As it turned out, the barber, Tony, and his brother, Giuseppe, didn't speak much English themselves. They chatted away in Italian to each other as they sheared off the princes' long hair. Prince Hal and Wills sat silently watching through the mirror as they were transformed into two American kids with crew cuts.

When they were finished, I took my place in the chair. "Same thing, Tony," I said.

The three of us emerged from the barbershop looking like a marine-recruiting poster. Di's face fell when she saw us. She did her best to put on a happy smile, but you could tell she hated the haircuts.

When I got behind the wheel, I looked in the rearview mirror. Between the crew cut and the burgeoning mustache, I looked like an ax murderer. I started the engine, then turned to my new family and said, "Well, here we are—convicted ax murderer Chuck Keats, his tarty wife, Joan, and their two kids, Spike and Tyke."

Nobody laughed.

CHAPTER

24

I got us adjoining rooms at the Days Inn outside of Kissimmee. I sat in my room waiting for Di to put the princes to bed, watching ESPN with Rivera. I had the Lakers and five points and was down by twelve.

"You going to get laid tonight, *coño?*"

"I don't know. She's kind of tense."

"You're paying for this trip, right? You should at least be getting laid, you know what I mean?"

I nodded.

"You look like an asshole with that haircut."

It was late in the fourth quarter before I heard a soft knock on the door. The Lakers had just scored eight unanswered points and were one up on the spread with two minutes to go. I hurried to the door. Di was in her jogging suit and Reeboks, but without her wig.

I closed the door behind her and said, "You should be wearing the wig."

"Oh, bother the wig."

"Di . . ."

She silenced my protests with her lips. We kissed long and hard under the fire-sprinkler heads of the asbestos ceiling. We kissed for ten full minutes. We were both dizzy with desire. My hands slipped beneath the elastic hem of her jogging suit. She wasn't wearing panties. Her only pair was soaking in Woolite in the bathroom sink next door.

Eschewing the bed as we had on Bulba, Di and I sank down onto the Stainmaster carpet and had at each other, cheered on by the capacity crowd at the Forum in Los Angeles. When it was over, we lay in each other's arms and felt the cool breeze of the air conditioner tickle our skin. She ran her fingers through what was left of my hair and murmured, "Oh, Leonard, my darling . . ."

"Di . . ."

We whispered breathy declarations of love into each other's ears during the postgame interviews in the Lakers' locker room.

Eventually, Di managed to get up, gather her jogging suit, and go next door and check on the princes and her laundry soaking in the sink. While she was gone I went down to the vending machines and got us a couple of Sprites and a bag of pretzels.

When she returned, she had pulled herself together. Her hair was combed, and she had brushed her teeth. I could smell the Crest on her breath as we lay on the bed watching *Notorious* on the American Movie Classics channel.

Di started to cry when Cary Grant and Ingrid Bergman declared their love for each other. Her head on my shoulder, tears streamed down her cheeks and she held my hand tightly.

I remembered what she had said to me the afternoon we'd had tea in the Fulham Road: "I have no one to curl up with in front of the telly."

Well, here we were, curled up in front of the telly in Kissimmee, Florida, while the whole world wondered where we were. We didn't watch the news that night. It would have ruined the sublimity of our evening together.

We drifted off to sleep in each other's arms. Sometime in the middle of the night, I felt her kiss me and heard her whisper, "I love you," before she slipped out and returned to her room next door.

While we slept, MI6 and Interpol agents were combing the Bahamas and the Caribbean for traces of us. They were looking in Nassau, in Freeport, in San Juan, in St. Kitts, even in Bermuda. They were checking the Florida coast, from Jacksonville down to the Keys. They were checking Tampa, Sarasota, and Bradenton. They were looking as far north as Washington, D.C., and as far south as Caracas.

They were not, however, looking for her in the Days Inn in Kissimmee, Florida. Nor would they be looking for her the next day at Disney World in a jogging suit with a Joan Collins wig and Ray-Ban highway-patrol sunglasses.

The princes hounded their mother out of bed at seven-thirty in the morning and then went after me. There was a pounding on my door and a waspish voice shouting, "Come on! Don't be a slugabed!"

We had breakfast together in the Days Inn coffee shop. It was the first real test of the disguises, and, as we sat there, Di kept muttering to me, "This is so lovely. You can't imagine what a delight it is to sit here and have one's breakfast in peace. Even if one does look hideous."

After breakfast, I bought a copy of USA Today and snuck back to my room to read it. The story was front page:

DI AND PRINCES STILL MISSING
WORLDWIDE SEARCH UNDERTAKEN

The search continues for Diana, the Princess of Wales, and her two sons, William and Harry, missing since their disappearance Wednesday afternoon from a McDonald's restaurant in Nassau, the Bahamas. Authorities both in Nassau and in London have confirmed that the missing Royals, as well as their American companion, Leonard Schecter, are the objects of an international search being undertaken by the Royal Protection Squad of New Scotland Yard and agents from the British security service MI6, with cooperation from Interpol and the FBI. Although authorities are being tight-lipped about the progress of the investigation, the possibility of a terrorist kidnapping has not been ruled out. Flight logs in and out of Nassau International Airport are being checked, as are landing manifests at all airports close enough to Nassau for a short- to medium-range airplane to have landed. The U.S. Coast Guard and the Royal Navy are searching the waters surrounding Andros Island for small craft that could be carrying the four missing people.

In London a spokesman for Prince Charles has said that the Prince of Wales is "anguished" by the disappearance of his estranged wife and children. "If it is indeed a kidnapping," he said, "let the kidnappers know that I shall not rest a day in my life until they are brought to justice." Queen Elizabeth and the Duke of Edinburgh have asked for the prayers of the nation and the world in "this moment of great peril to our family."

Authorities would not say whether they believe that the American travel companion, Leonard Schecter, is a suspect or a fellow victim in the disappearance. Reuters is quoting King Juan Carlos of Spain as saying that he is sincerely doubtful that Schecter is anything but a victim. Schecter was a houseguest, along with Princess Diana and her sons, on the King of Spain's private island of Bulba.

Other reports, however, cast a shadow on Schecter's character. There is an outstanding judgment against him in a divorce action in Los Angeles. Several film companies and book publishers claim that Schecter is delinquent with regard to contractual obligations to provide material that he has agreed to write regarding the Royal Family. Renowned British Royal watcher and journalist Rupert Makepeace, who claims to have met Schecter several times, has said that "Mr. Schecter is a devious and dangerous man. He has insinuated himself into the inner sanctum of the Royal Family under the pretense of writing an epic poem about the Windsors. He has managed to infiltrate the Royal Box at Ascot as well as getting himself invited to Balmoral for an intimate weekend *en famille* with the Queen.

Though I cannot speculate as to Mr. Schecter's motives in such an abduction, it is clear to me that this American fortune hunter is no friend of the British people."

In September, there was speculation in some of London's tabloids that the American was romantically involved with the Queen's younger sister, Margaret.

TV personality and journalist Barbara Walters claims to have had long phone conversations with Schecter when he was in London. According to Walters, Schecter and the Princess of Wales are deeply in love. "Their story, to which I hold the exclusive first-run interview rights, is one of the great love stories of the twentieth century."

Schecter's estranged wife, Marilyn Leibowitz-Schecter, has refused to speak with reporters except to say, "Leonard Schecter is a deadbeat who owes me a lot of money."

I picked up the phone, dialed the Togolese embassy in London, and asked for the visa-and-immigration desk.

"Kodjo Kponvi here," he said in his French-inflected, Togolese-accented English.

"Kodjo, it's Leonard."

There was just a momentary pause, and then his cheerful voice said, "Most delighted to hear from you, my dear friend. How are you?"

"Fine."

"And our mutual friend?"

"She's doing great."

"Splendid."

"Listen, I have another favor to ask."

"By all means."

"If I send you some mail, could you drop it in a letter box in London?"

"Most certainly."

"I don't want to cause Charles any more anguish than is necessary. I'd like him to know that his sons are okay."

"Very considerate of you, very considerate indeed."

"As far as she's concerned, I don't think he gives a good goddamn."

"He never has, has he?"

"No . . . Listen, I really appreciate this."

"Of course."

"I'll be in touch."

"I look forward to it."

I got the family into the Caravan, and we headed off to Disney World in good spirits. The princes were gradually beginning to realize that they could go places and do things without detectives and reporters surrounding them. For the first time in their lives they were able to walk around without people staring at them, pointing cameras, and waving flags.

However, for the first time in their lives, they also had to wait in line. Prince Hal became cross when we had to wait with other tourists to gain admittance to the facility.

"Must we really queue up?" he complained.

"Afraid so."

"Don't they have a special gate for important people?"

"They do," I said. "But, remember, we're no longer important people. We're just ordinary people."

We entered the gates of Disney World and began a systematic attack on the facility. The princes were determined to see every square inch. Rigorously following their tour maps, they led the way. Di and I trailed behind, doing our best to keep up.

"It's lovely to see them so excited," said Di.

"How about you? Are you excited?"

"Ecstatic . . ."

I bent down and kissed her. She immediately tensed up, as if she expected a phalanx of photographers to start firing from the hip. When she realized that nobody was watching us, she laughed delightedly.

"Oh, Leonard, this is such fun."

We did Fantasyland, Tomorrowland, and Frontierland, and then stopped for lunch, waiting on line among the Japanese and the

Europeans for our hot dogs and Cokes. Over lunch, I gave my new family its first lesson in speaking American. We made a game out of it. Simon Says. Repeat after me.

"Elevator."

"*Elevator.*"

"Skedule."

"*Skedule.*"

"French fries."

"*French fries.*"

"Is there going to be an exam?" Wills asked.

"Oh, yes. A very difficult one."

"I thought we were on holiday," he protested.

"We're not on holiday," I said. "We're on *vacation.*"

After lunch we continued our trek through the recesses of Disney World, stopping only briefly for tea at four o'clock. Di had to be content with a paper cup of Lipton's and a doughnut. The princes had double scoops of frozen yogurt in sugar cones.

At sundown we gathered on Main Street, along with our fellow tourists, to watch the parade. It must have been a novel experience for Di to watch a parade from the sidelines and not be waving from a carriage.

By the time we were ready to leave, having seen all there was to see, the air had chilled. We piled into the minivan and headed north.

The princes, exhausted, dozed in the backseat, and Di and I held hands as we drove through the monotonous flatness of central Florida, the cloying smell of orange blossoms leaking through the closed windows of the van.

"What a lovely day," she said.

I nodded, squeezing her hand.

"It's peculiar," she went on, "but even though there is no detective in the car, I feel safer than I have felt for a very long time."

"I'm glad."

"And I think the boys thoroughly enjoyed themselves today."

"Apparently."

"Oh, Leonard, this is such a jolly adventure, isn't it?"

.   .   .

At the Holiday Inn outside of Daytona Beach, after a light supper, we had the princes write notes to their father. Di gave them some of her personal notepaper from Smythson's, in Bond Street. She carried this with her at all times, along with her Mont Blanc fountain pen, so that she could write thank-you notes on the spur of the moment.

"Now remember, guys, you can't say where you are," I explained. "Just tell him that you're fine and that there's nothing to worry about."

"May we write in English or must we write in American?" asked Prince Hal.

"You may write in English."

"Perhaps I shall write in French," announced Wills. "Sometimes, my dad faxes me in French."

As I watched them composing their letters, I felt a pang of sympathy for the man back in England with the big ears and the burgeoning bald spot. It was hard enough being cuckolded, even by a woman you no longer wanted, but to have your sons abducted in the bargain must be very difficult. Then I reminded myself that this was the same man who had left Diana alone at the hospital and gone to the opera in Covent Garden while Wills was undergoing surgery, and I didn't feel so bad.

Prince Hal's note read, in its entirety:

> Dear Father,
>
> I am writing to tell you that I am exceedingly well. There is no reason to be concerned about Wills or me. Mother is with us and we are all having a smashing holiday, but I can't tell you where.
>
> Your loving son,
Henry

Wills wrote:

> *Cher papa,*
> *Je me porte très bien. Nous sommes en vacances quelque*

part au monde. Il fait beau. Je ne peux pas vous dire où nous
nous trouvons. Il ne faut pas vous inquiéter.

Amitiés,
Guillaume

We spent the next morning playing miniature golf on a lavish
course replete with intricately constructed windmills, waterfalls, and
aqueducts. The princes did much better than their mother, who
bogeyed every single hole except the eighteenth, which she triple-
bogeyed.

Afterward, we went for a stroll along the beach. The princes
walked ahead, watching the off-road vehicles that sped by on either
side as if the beach were a public thoroughfare, and Di and I considered our next move.

"The sooner we get out of Florida the better," I said.

"I should like to get a decent wig. We shall stop in Dallas. Fergie
will know."

"Can she be discreet?"

"Perhaps not for herself, but she's quite good with other people's secrets."

"Well, I guess the worst that can happen is you get recognized.
And then you'll have to go back."

She stopped walking, turned to me, and looked at me with a
dead-serious expression on her face. "I'm not going back, Leonard.
Not to that life."

I nodded and put my hand on her arm. She went on, building
up emotion as she spoke.

"I am a windup toy. I cut ribbons and plant trees and smile at
people I don't know who are waving flags at me. I cannot walk to
the corner without being photographed. I cannot go to the cinema
or play minigolf or go for a walk on the beach without arranging in
advance for men with guns to be there to protect me. It is no life for
anyone."

"What about your work? All those charities and causes?"

"I shall miss it very much. It is all that keeps me going—that and the boys. I shall go back to it someday, in my own time and in my own way. But I need a holiday from all that now. I need to try something different. Can you understand?"

I nodded.

"I watched Wills and Harry yesterday, eating their hot dogs and queuing up like normal boys, and I realized that they need to learn to be human beings as well as kings. I think it will serve them in good stead."

She paused for a moment, looking out at the gray surf, then said, "I realize that they will have to go back at some point. They are second and third in line to the throne. But before they go back, I want them to know that there is an alternative to sitting on the throne of England. So that they can choose to live the lives they want and not the ones that have been thrust upon them. I've thought this out, Leonard. I've thought this out a great deal, and I know I'm right."

I stood there for a long moment, reacting to the eloquence of her words. She was shaking slightly from the emotion, and I put my arms around her. I could feel her insides trembling, and I held her tight until the last tremor subsided.

Then she said, in her proud-little-girl voice, "We shall not surrender, Leonard, until they have the whole bloody fort surrounded. And then we shall walk out with our heads held high."

CHAPTER

25

Di called Fergie from a public phone at a gas station outside of Daytona Beach. I stood next to her, feeding her quarters, as the Princess of Wales and the Duchess of York had a long chat about wig sizes, among other things. When she hung up, Di said, "She's going to pick up a decent wig for me. Won't that be a relief? You'll never guess who she's seeing!"

"Who?"

"I can't tell you, actually. She swore me to secrecy."

We walked back to the Caravan and got in. In the backseat the princes were immersed in their Game Boys. I had gotten them new cartridges that morning after miniature golf, and we hadn't heard much from them since.

"Boys, guess where we are going?" Di announced.

The princes looked up blankly.

"Texas."

"Is that where they have cowboys?" Prince Hal asked.

"They don't have cowboys anymore," Will corrected his brother. "They have chaps that ride around in Jeeps with walkie-talkies."

We drove inland from Daytona Beach through the Ocala National Forest and up Interstate 75 to Gainesville. The scenery was unremarkable—citrus groves and scrub forest for miles on either side of the highway. To keep the princes interested when they tired of their Game Boys, I taught them how to play Geography.

Wills was a whiz. He had learned the names of all sorts of obscure Welsh villages in preparation for his eventual investiture as Prince of Wales. Di, on the other hand, having flunked geography at school, was hopeless. She had to drop out when she couldn't think of a *K* after Wills stuck her with Gryffdyk. Prince Hal followed, in her place, with Kornwall, and he, too, was gone, though not without a heated argument about the spelling.

Wills and I went down to the wire, and, after a long series of *A*'s, he hit me with Axminster.

I countered with Rancho Cucamonga.

"Oh, stop it," Wills exclaimed. "You made that one up."

"No I didn't."

"I challenge you."

I found it listed in my *Mobil Travel Guide* and showed it to Wills. He sulked all the way to Tallahassee.

We took our time getting to Dallas. We got up late, had breakfast, and hit the road at a leisurely pace. We stopped for miniature golf, amusement parks, ice cream cones, and exercise. At least once a day Di had me turn off onto a small road so that she could go for a jog. We followed along in the Caravan rooting her on.

In Baton Rouge, we went to a drive-in movie, where we saw the international karate star Bobby Mason in a picture about a Macedonian commando who single-handedly wipes out an entire platoon of Serbian irregulars in the hills above Dubrovnik. There were bodies flying all over the place, victims of Bobby Mason's lethal fists. The princes were transfixed, stuffing their faces with popcorn and red licorice. Di sat in the back and read a Jacqueline Susann by flashlight.

I continued to buy newspapers and watch television in my room, but Di remained completely indifferent to the news stories of our disappearance. It was as if it were happening to someone else. "I can't be bothered by that rubbish," she said whenever I tried to bring the subject up.

The princes' letters had reached Charles in London, and he gave a news conference from his office in Clarence House. The American networks preempted their prime-time lineups to carry it live.

Charles read the letters, translating Wills's into English. When asked if he believed the letters were authentic, he nodded and launched into a digression on calligraphy, of which he was apparently a student.

The letters, he said, were mailed from London, at a post office in Mayfair. When asked if he thought his estranged wife and sons were in England, he said that he couldn't imagine how they could have returned there from the Bahamas without being recognized.

He was asked to speculate as to how the letters got to be mailed from Mayfair.

"I suspect it is some sort of ruse," he replied.

He was asked if he knew Leonard Schecter.

"I have never met the gentleman," he said, the words so deep in his throat that it sounded as if he were going to choke on them.

He was asked if he was aware of any liaison between his estranged wife and Leonard Schecter.

"As you know, the Princess of Wales and I are formally separated. Her private life, therefore, is her own concern and none of mine. Nor, I should add, is it any concern of yours."

He glared down at the reporter with his stern, schoolmaster's look of disapproval. At that point, an officer from MI6 took over to answer questions about the progress of the search.

"We are not ruling anything out at this moment," he said,

looking very haggard. He went on to explain how the investigation had been complicated by the number of false spottings of the Princess of Wales and her sons in places as diverse as Sri Lanka and Newfoundland.

"You may rest assured, however, that we are following up every lead we receive. We shall leave no stone unturned in our endeavors to return the Princess of Wales and her sons to safety."

The nightly news shows had crews poking around for stories in Los Angeles. They stood vigil outside my house in Brentwood, a place I no longer lived in but was still paying for, its shrubbery neatly trimmed by a $350-a-month gardener, also on my payroll, the Petitioner's emerald-green Range Rover parked in the driveway. They harassed my lawyer on her way to court with her forensic accountants and their hand trolleys full of check stubs. They got Brad Emprin to say on camera that *Inside Di—The Real Story* had been postponed until the May sweeps. Because of Leonard Schecter's disappearance, he added, there were discussions about replacing him with a hot young writer named Lionel Traven, whom Brad Emprin also represented. They got to Charlie Berns, in baggy khaki shorts and sandals, looking Buddha-like as he emerged from his old Mercedes and walked up the front walk of his house littered with eucalyptus nuts and throwaway papers. When asked if he had heard from me lately, he cupped his hand behind his ear, Ronald Reagan–style, and said, "Who?"

Di and the princes continued to be blissfully unaware of all this media attention. They didn't read the papers or watch the news on television. Di was particularly fond of *Jeopardy* and *Wheel of Fortune*, and the princes were hooked on *Beverly Hills 90210*.

They were tourists in the U.S.A. And they were having a great time. Wills sulked a lot less, and Prince Hal stopped getting carsick. Di adjusted to wearing her wig and Ray-Ban sunglasses. At night she would take off the Joan Collins and show me how her hair was not only getting longer but also browner.

As we drove west into Texas, the season grew shorter, the weather chillier. Di went into a Sears in Beaumont and bought warmer and more fashionable wardrobes for us. We all got sweaters and flannel shirts. Di treated herself to a pair of rhinestone-studded cowboy boots. The princes got ten-gallon hats, which they never took off, even when they went to bed. I got a dozen pairs of Calvin Klein briefs, which Di took particular relish in taking off me at night in our adjoining motel room.

Meanwhile, they were making some progress in their American English lessons. Prince Hal particularly liked the word *doggone.* He said it all the time, to anyone, no matter what had been said to him.

At night Di and I curled up in front of the TV and watched old movies. Then we made tender love and slept soundly, our arms around each other, until some internal alarm clock woke her up and she slipped out of bed to go next door.

On Halloween, we went to the drive-in to see *Friday the 13th, Part 12.* Di hid her eyes, and the princes chewed their licorice intently as the blood and gore filled the screen. Afterward, Prince Hal suggested we go around hitting people up for pennies. "A penny for the old Guy."

Wills pointed out that Guy Fawkes Day was not celebrated on October 31 but on November 5, the anniversary of the 1605 Gunpowder Plot to blow up the Houses of Parliament, and, furthermore, he didn't think they celebrated it at all in the States, and certainly not in Texas.

"Doggone," said Prince Hal.

Sarah Ferguson, the Duchess of York, estranged wife of the fourth in line to the throne of England, and mother of the fifth and sixth in line, was living in a four-bedroom luxury condominium in downtown Dallas. She had moved up from Houston two months before to be closer to the current man in her life, an extremely wealthy and very important individual, who was married and whose identity remained a secret to me.

"We're having dinner with them tonight, and you'll meet him then," Di promised. "Be patient."

"What happened to her financial adviser?"

"Oh, that's been off for a while now. Ever since those dreadful snaps from the south of France."

We were driving on the Central Expressway, heading downtown toward Dealey Plaza to visit the spot where JFK was assassinated thirty years before. This was at Wills's insistence. Though only eleven, Prince William was an aficionado of assassinations.

"He's crackers about them," Di explained. "He knows who shot all your presidents."

I looked through the rearview mirror and saw the future Prince of Wales deeply immersed in his Game Boy.

"Wills," I said, "who shot James Garfield?"

"Charles J. Guiteau," he said without looking up from the Game Boy.

"Do you think Oswald acted alone?"

"Of course not. It was ordered directly by the CIA. A contract job. The Warren Commission was a whitewash."

We visited the crime scene and listened as Wills explained the whole conspiracy, including the ballistic evidence supporting the second shooter. He pointed out the location of the Texas Book Depository, the grassy knoll, the direction of the motorcade.

Afterward, over lunch at McDonald's, I asked him how he had first gotten interested in assassinations.

"I've been keen on them ever since I read a book on Queen Victoria. There were five attempts on her life. Did you know that?"

I shook my head.

"It's a family legacy. Just a few years back they tried to do away with Auntie Anne," he said.

"That was a kidnap attempt, Wills, not an assassination, and must we talk about this over lunch?"

"The man had a gun."

"Yes, but Princess Anne was not harmed."

"Her detective was shot three times . . ."

After lunch we went shopping at Neiman-Marcus. I was still nervous about her disguise, but Di insisted, saying that if we got through Disney World, we could get through Neiman-Marcus.

The princes and I loitered among the racks of designer clothing, as Di looked over the merchandise with a predatory eye. You could tell by the way she went at it that Neiman-Marcus was a treat after shopping at Sears and Kmart. She popped in and out of the dressing rooms, collecting tops, bottoms, sweaters, slacks. The pile of clothes on the counter beside the cash register grew taller.

At one point she called me over and asked me to verify the fit of a pair of studded jeans. Telling the princes to behave themselves, she took me by the hand and led me to the dressing rooms.

"Are men allowed in here?" I asked.

"Why not?"

We entered the air-conditioned cubicle and closed the door. There was a mirror on one wall, hooks for hanging clothes, and a built-in bench. Di slipped out of her jogging pants and folded them neatly on the bench beside me. Then she turned to me and smiled coyly. She wasn't wearing any panties. Blood surged through me like water in the Grand Coulee Dam.

I rose and moved into her embrace. As my lips bit her neck, her hands wandered down my back and slipped beneath the waistband of my jogging pants.

"Di," I whispered, "they've got these things under hidden-camera surveillance."

"Do they?" Her breathing was hot and fitful.

"We could get arrested."

"Oh, bother that . . ."

Fortunately for us, before things got out of hand her salesgirl, Debbi Sue, came back and asked through the door if everything was all right.

"Quite," Di managed, exhaling loudly into my ear and taking her hands out of my pants. I sat back down on the bench and waited for things to calm down.

Di looked at me and sighed. "I've always wanted to do that," she whispered.

"Maybe next time," I whispered back.

It cost me $1,400 to get out of Neiman-Marcus. Weighed down with bags, we got back in the Caravan and headed off to a nearby

Holiday Inn, which had an indoor swimming pool. Di washed her hair and shaved her legs as the princes and I splashed around in the pool for an hour or so. Then I gave them a fistful of quarters for the video arcade and went up to the room to find Di getting directions from Fergie on the phone.

There was a good deal of giggling before Di said, "See you at eight," and hung up.

"Leonard," she said, turning to me, "perhaps we ought to get a baby-sitter for the boys after all."

"I thought we discussed this. They're old enough to stay by themselves."

"Harry is only nine."

"Yes, but Wills is eleven going on forty."

She sat down at the dressing table with a pout on her face. I went over and put my arms around her.

"We'll leave Fergie's number. If there's any problem, all they have to do is call. There's nothing to worry about, believe me."

I was more concerned about being spotted entering Fergie's condo. There might be an enterprising reporter hanging around outside. This time it was Di who reassured me. Fergie had given her the code to her parking garage. All we had to do was drive right in, use the code to open the gate, and park in one of Fergie's four parking spots.

I wore jeans and a flannel shirt and string tie under a denim jacket and cowboy boots. Di wore a long skirt over her rhinestone-studded boots and a cowgirl's vest on top of a $199 Giovanni Grazzianni sweatshirt.

"You look beautiful," I said to her as I unlocked the Caravan door and helped her in.

"One does one's best."

Di removed the wig and glasses as soon as we entered the elevator in the parking garage of Fergie's building.

"What if someone gets on with us?" I said.

"I shall smile and say howdy."

She pronounced *howdy* with too much emphasis on the last syllable. I had been doing my best to teach her and the princes to stop enunciating so clearly, but it was an uphill battle.

"What about Fergie's help?"

"I can assure you, Fergie's servants are the soul of discretion. When you see who's joining us for dinner, you'll understand."

The elevator took us up to the penthouse, opening onto a small private hallway. The front door to the apartment had faux Doric columns on either side. There was a large gilt-edged mirror facing us and a pewter standing ashtray and matching umbrella stand.

"Just like Sunninghill Park," I said as we rang.

"Please, Leonard. She's very sensitive about her decorating."

We were ushered in by a Korean butler and led into an enormous living room with a view of downtown Dallas. There was a sunken conversation pit large enough to accommodate twenty, a couple of fireplaces, glass and marble everywhere. The furniture was all black and white leather. The floor was covered by very expensive-looking deep-pile white carpeting, the type that Playmates of the Month used to frolic naked in.

Easy-listening music gurgled from the huge speakers flanking an entertainment center with every conceivable type of state-of-the-art electronic device. There was a giant-screen TV, three VCRs, a tape deck, a CD player.

"Andrew would love this place," I whispered.

"Shhh," Di said.

The easy-listening music switched to the Tara theme from *Gone With the Wind*, and, as if on cue, Sarah Ferguson swept into the room. There was a loud squeal from both of the women, and they ran into each other's arms.

Fergie and Di hugged and kept repeating, "You look smashing. Just smashing."

When this effusion was over, Di presented me to the Duchess.

"Awfully glad to meet you," said Fergie, offering her hand.

We shook. "My pleasure."

She was wearing beige silk lounging pajamas and very high heels. Enormous jade earrings dangled from her ears. Around her neck was a large silver pendant that clanked when she walked. It was a Navajo good-luck talisman, she explained. "A present from my sweetheart," she said.

Fergie took us on a tour of the 5,400-square-foot condominium. Every room had lush carpeting, acoustical tile ceilings, central air, piped-in stereo. Princess Beatrice and Princess Eugenie—who were with their father in England at the moment—each had a bedroom and bathroom in preparation for their visits over Christmas and summer holidays. There was a gym, with a StairMaster, Nautilus circuit, rowing machine, and sauna. The master bedroom had an enormous circular bed, recessed lighting, and a large-screen TV that hovered over the foot of the bed, suspended from the ceiling like the Angel of Death.

We returned to the conversation pit for drinks. The butler served Di her Perrier with a twist. I asked for a gin and tonic. Fergie drank Jack Daniel's on the rocks.

Di recounted the story of our escape from the McDonald's in Nassau. Fergie laughed uproariously.

"I can just see old Donald with his sack full of sanitary towels..."

Di modeled her Joan Collins wig, and then the two of them went off into Fergie's bedroom to see the new wig that Fergie had gotten for Di, leaving me alone in the cavernous living room. I went over to the entertainment center and switched on the TV.

I was sitting there watching CNN when the butler returned with a short man in a very expensive suit. He had wire-rimmed glasses and very prominent ears.

"Hi there," I said.

"Howdy," he said.

We had dinner in the speckled marble dining room, the four of us at a very large glass table set with Duchess of York Wedgwood, a wedding present from the Queen Mother, Fergie explained. "Andrew and I would throw the odd piece at each other when we had a row," she said gaily.

The dinner was catered French with a down-home touch. We had escargots and biscuits. Ross drank Coors Light at the table. Di stuck with Perrier. Fergie and I shared a bottle of overripe zinfandel.

Ross told us about his lunch with the Sultan of Brunei, who was in Dallas for an operation.

"This is confidential, but he's going to get a hemorrhoidectomy on Friday. I told him, 'Sultan, you came to the right place. We got the best rear-end man in the world over at Rice Memorial.' "

Di put down her escargot fork and took a long sip of Perrier, looking as if she were going to be ill.

"So, Ross," I said, quickly changing the subject, "you going to run in '96?"

"Let me tell you something, Mr. Spector. The way this country is run, there may not be a country to be president of in 1996, you follow my drift?"

"It's that bad, huh?"

"You understand how a suction pump works?"

We all shook our heads. He took his wine goblet, his butter plate, and his coffee spoon and arranged them on the table like a schematic drawing.

"Now, you see this pump here creates a pressure vacuum and draws air from the outside into the system here." He pointed to the butter plate, which had a half-eaten roll on it. "In order for the system to operate, however, you need to have air to suck in. You got no air, you got no system. That's what's going on up there in Washington these days. They're sucking the system dry. And you know who's paying for it?"

"Well, *I'm* not," said Di.

"No, ma'am, you're not. However, you're paying for every Pakistani and Nigerian who wants to get a root canal on the National Health. You want to talk about a suction pump?"

The main course was barbecued coq au vin, with a glazed Madeira sauce and okra. Fergie sat there drinking in everything Ross said. He blew her kisses. They acted like honeymooners.

"We're going to sneak off to Hawaii for a weekend in December," Fergie announced. "Ross owns a little island near Kahoolawe. It's absolutely deserted. You can go skinny-dipping in the ocean."

"Do be careful," Di said.

"Oh, there's nothing to worry about. Ross's security people don't let anyone near the island."

"They have these long-range cameras now. It's dreadful."

"Anybody tries to get a picture of the Duchess bare-assed is going to be on the wrong end of a .357 high-velocity shell. Go right through them and halfway to China before they know what the hell hit them."

We had dessert and coffee back in the living room. *Oeufs à la neige* and decaf. Johnny Mathis oozed through the speakers as we sat there and watched the fire.

I asked Ross how he managed to dodge the paparazzi.

"I got a man does nothing all day long but work on that problem. He's what I call a privacy engineer. He gets up in the morning, goes to his office, and spends his entire day figuring out how to get me from Point A to Point B without anyone knowing about it except him and my security people."

"Can I hire him?"

"Mr. Spector, you can't afford him."

"What makes you think that?"

"I pay him seven hundred and fifty thousand dollars a year. Plus a medical plan. You got that type of money?"

Fergie went to the CD player and put on some Elton John. Then she and Di dragged Ross and me up to dance. We did our best, but eventually we left Di and Fergie to dance together, and we sat back down and talked about football.

"You know why a team wins?" he said. "They execute. That's the whole trick—execution. It's what we, the fans, deserve. Because we pay their salaries. They work for us. And public servants should either execute or get the hell off the pot."

At ten o'clock, Ross's security people came in and huddled with him. He nodded several times, turned to Fergie, and said, "Duchess,

I'm going to have to skedaddle. Got to be in Houston first thing in the morning. Terrific meal."

He went over to her, kissed her on the lips with great gusto, then pinched her ass. He turned to Di and extended his hand. "Princess, it's been an honor."

"A pleasure to meet you, sir."

"Keep an eye on that suction pump."

He winked toward me and said, "Mr. Spector, take good care of the little lady."

"I will."

"You don't, and you're going to hear from me personally, you understand?"

"Yes, sir."

And with that he was swept out of the room by his security men. Though he was a little man, the room felt a great deal larger after he left.

Di and I rode down in the elevator necking like teenagers. We were still kissing when the door to the parking garage opened. In the split second it took us to disengage, the flash went off, filling the dank garage air with explosive light.

Reflexively, we turned toward the flash. The photographer caught us in three-quarter profile, one arm still around each other, the other leading toward the open elevator door. In the picture that would soon appear on every front page in the world, it looked as if we were mambo dancers about to do a break.

Di was not wearing her wig. He got her bare-assed. I went after him, but the man was young and wearing tennis shoes. I could barely walk in my cowboy boots, let alone run. He was out of the garage, into his car, and gone before I could stop him. As Ross would say, I didn't execute.

Di had been a target of hit-and-run paparazzi for so long, she was not overly upset by the incident itself. She got into the Caravan, reached into her pocketbook, and took out her new wig.

"As my dads would say, this is letting the dogs out after the fox has gone, I suppose."

She carefully put the new wig on, angled the rearview mirror toward her to make sure it fit right, then turned to me for approval.

"You look fabulous," I said.

"Do I really?"

"Absolutely."

She looked away for a moment, then said, with a note of plaintiveness in her voice, "Oh, Leonard, what shall we do?"

"I think we better get out of Texas."

CHAPTER

26

We went back to the hotel and woke the princes up. They were very cranky when we told them we were leaving.

"But it's the middle of the night," protested Prince Hal.

"Of course, sweetheart, but it's a lovely night for a drive," Di said. "Won't it be fun?"

Di went through the room gathering their things and putting them into our Kmart luggage. In fifteen minutes, we were in the Caravan, heading north out of the city.

It was a little past midnight. We were about an hour from the Oklahoma border. According to my *Mobil Travel Guide*, we could be in Wichita, Kansas, by dawn. I would feel a little safer with a one-state buffer between us and Texas.

I figured we had about a sixteen-hour head start on the posse. The photographer would not call the FBI immediately. First he would sell his photo to the highest bidder and then let the news leak out.

We would probably make the six o'clock news. By eleven, we'd be coast-to-coast.

The princes soon fell back to sleep in the rear seat, and Di and I drove through the starry northern Texas night listening to country music on the radio. I kept the speedometer at sixty-five and watched the mileage signs fly by.

After a while Di said, "Would you like me to drive?"

I shook my head. "This is probably not the best time for you to get used to driving on the right side of the road."

"You must be tired."

"I'm all right. Talk to me. It'll help keep me awake."

"About what?"

"I don't know—tell me about what it feels like to walk down the aisle of St. Paul's Cathedral with five hundred million people around the world watching you."

She looked at me peculiarly, as if surprised by my question.

"You almost never talk about the past," I said.

"It all seems so long ago. As if it were another lifetime."

She turned away for a moment, looking out at the blackness surrounding us. Then she began to a speak in a quiet, wistful voice. "I was so young. You have no idea how young I was, Leonard. The first time I spoke to Charles I was barely seventeen. We were house-guests together in the country. It was one of those dreary English weekends when the sky is continually gray and one has to be bundled in sweaters all the time to keep warm. I was tagging along for the weekend with my sister Sarah. She was the one who had set her cap for Charles. I was being saved for Andrew, actually . . ."

She laughed gently as she said this. "Poor Andy. Fergie has given him quite the runaround, hasn't she? In any event, I was having a perfectly dreadful weekend, spending most of the time reading in my room, and being royally ignored by everyone. On Sunday, they had all gone shooting, and I went out for a walk across some plowed fields. I was walking with my head down, not minding where I was going, when I suddenly saw him across the field. He looked so alone, so sad, that I felt this enormous surge of compassion for him.

"Well, he turned and noticed me. And he started walking toward me. I was mortified. I was wearing mud boots and my sister's mac and had no makeup on whatsoever and looked perfectly hideous. He came up to me and asked me how I was. I said I was fine, and then I asked how he was. When he didn't answer right away, I blurted out this rubbish about how sad he looked and then, I don't know why I said it, but I said that he looked like he needed someone to love him.

"He tilted his head, then smiled and thanked me. Very seriously. As if I had said that he looked like he'd had a good shoot or a good polo match or what have you. I don't remember what happened after that, but I was so mortified I said nothing more the rest of the weekend. To anyone. Later, Charles told me that was the moment he fell in love with me."

"Did you fall in love with him as well?"

She didn't answer immediately. The question seemed to perplex her. When she spoke, there was a jaded tone to her voice, replacing the romantic young girl's voice that had recounted the story of the meeting in the fields.

"He was the Prince of Wales. He lived in a castle. His mother rode in a carriage to open Parliament. He played polo and spoke twelve languages . . . If I loved anything, I loved his ears."

"His ears?"

"Yes. They made him look vulnerable. Even now, after all we've been through, I feel something when I see his ears."

Her talking about Charles's ears gave me a twinge of jealousy. "You still have feelings for him?"

"I should say not. He's a perfectly dreadful man. I was merely talking about his ears. And besides, Leonard, I'm in love with you. Hopelessly."

I reached over and took her hand, squeezing it gently in mine. We passed a sign that said WELCOME TO OKLAHOMA, THE SOONER STATE.

Soon after that Di drifted off to sleep, and I was alone at the wheel, speeding through the American night. I put the Caravan on cruise control and settled in for the long haul.

"You really stepped in it now, *coño.*"

I looked over and saw Rivera riding shotgun. Di was asleep, her head on his shoulder. He was eating sunflower seeds and spitting the shells out the window.

"You going to find yourself doing three to five in Atascadero because of her," he said.

"I'll change cars in Wichita."

"She worth it?"

"I'd drive to the ends of the earth and back for her."

"That's a long way, man."

It was 7:30 A.M. when we reached the outskirts of Wichita. As we drove through the morning commuter traffic, I looked out at the people around us on their way to work—listening to the radio, chatting among themselves in hushed morning tones, sipping coffee, and putting their mascara on—and envied them the banality of their lives. They had not driven all night in a minivan whose Florida dealer plates would soon be on every police computer in the country, carrying forged Togolese passports and over $800,000 worth of advances against undelivered material, nor were they fugitives from family law courts in both Los Angeles and London.

Di and the princes had slept through the night and were now awake and chirpy.

"Are there Indians in Kansas?" Prince Hal asked.

"They've herded them all onto renovations," Wills said.

"You mean reservations, don't you?" I corrected.

"I challenge you," Wills said.

"We'll check it as soon as we get to a dictionary."

I got off the interstate at the McConnell Air Force Base exit and pulled into a Ramada Inn. I deposited Di and the princes in a room, then shaved off my burgeoning mustache, put on a baseball cap and dark glasses, and headed downtown.

I parked the van in an underground garage in the Mutual of Kansas building on Broadway, then removed the dealer plates, leaving the keys in the ignition. If I was lucky, someone would steal it.

This time I decided to go with a Ford. There was a dealership on Seneca Street, and I let Big Bill Ardmore sell me an Aerostar minivan loaded for $18,450.

"I'm losing money at that price," he said.

I offered him $20,000 even, but he wouldn't take it.

"A deal's a deal," he insisted, and threw in a set of steak knives.

It was two in the afternoon before I was able to drive the Ford off the lot. I turned the radio on and fiddled with the dial until I found an all-news station.

". . . in the underground parking garage of the exclusive downtown Dallas building where the Duchess of York has a condominium. The picture shows a woman, clearly the Princess of Wales, getting out of an elevator with a man who has been identified as Leonard Schecter, the screenwriter from Los Angeles with whom Diana and her sons disappeared from Nassau in the Bahamas three weeks ago. The Duchess of York has refused any public comment, but FBI agents have been seen entering her building. To repeat the hour's top story: Princess Diana was spotted leaving the Duchess of York's condominium in Dallas at approximately eleven-thirty last night. She and a man, identified as Leonard Schecter of Los Angeles, were photographed by a freelance photographer as they left the elevator to the parking garage. We will keep you posted as developments occur. . . . In other news, Bosnian forces clashed with—"

I turned the dial, looking for more news. Every station had pretty much the same story. I was sure that the picture was already on TV. We were only 356 miles from Dallas. We would have to put more distance between us and Fergie's condo.

When I got to the Ramada, I told Di to wake me at 6 P.M. We would travel again under the cover of night. The princes weren't happy about this, but I promised them that we would do it for only one more night and then we would visit an Indian renovation the following day.

Di came to my room with me to tuck me in. I was overtired and irritable, but she insisted on giving me a back rub. It would help me fall asleep, she said.

She undressed me as if I were a drunk and laid me down gently on my stomach. I closed my eyes and tried to drift off under the soft touch of her fingers.

It wasn't long before we were going at it on the floor again. We had to put our hands over each other's mouths to muffle the cries. When we were finished, she helped me back up onto the bed, put the covers over me, kissed me gently on the lips, and whispered that I'd see her in my dreams.

Sometime around two in the morning we crossed over the Colorado line. Di and the princes were asleep, having dropped off after we'd passed Dodge City. Wills had hung in till after midnight, playing head-on Geography with me, before nodding out on Alcatraz. As soon as he was asleep, I turned on the radio for news.

The Duchess of York had made a statement. It was the major development since the afternoon. She admitted to having had us for dinner but claimed that she had no idea where we were headed. There was a taped sound bite that had Fergie saying, "Diana seemed in marvelous health and smashing spirits. I believe that they're very much in love."

Playing with the radio dial, I got an all-night call-in radio station out of Albuquerque. Barbara from Truth or Consequences was saying that, as far as she was concerned, Princess Diana should be allowed to live wherever she wanted with her children and the man she loved.

"I mean, Charles never was much of a father to those two little boys anyway. She takes them everywhere—to the movies, to McDonald's, everywhere. And later, if they want to come back and be King, fine, that's their business. But Diana deserves some happiness in her life after all she's given to AIDS and homeless people, you know what I mean?"

Mike, an attorney from Placitas, said, "I don't care what you call it. It's kidnapping. She's taken those kids away from their father without his permission. She ought to be arrested and extradited to England."

Peggy from Rio Rancho said, "I think she's right and he's wrong. For example, he went to the opera when the older one, what's his name, William, was in the hospital with a golf club in his head and she stayed up all night at his bedside worrying. I'm a mother of six and I know how it feels to stay up all night with a sick child and no husband around to give you support when you need it."

Madge from El Quatro said, "The guy she's with, Spector, I hear he left his wife in L.A. without a dime and she's living on the street in a shopping cart."

The vox populi. I listened to it with detachment, as if Di and I weren't, in fact, the subjects of all this talk. It seemed like everyone in America was talking about us. Twenty-four hours a day.

When Albuquerque faded into the night, I turned to a country-music station and left it there. I'd had enough of people's opinions of us. Instead, I listened to the comforting homilies of the jukebox poets as I drove west into the Rockies, looking for the posse in the rearview mirror.

By four in the morning I was starting to hallucinate. I stopped for gas and let Di take the wheel. It was either that or stop for the night, and I still didn't feel like we were far enough from Dallas to rest the horses. We put the princes in the front seat with her, giving me the entire backseat to stretch out and sleep.

Before dropping off, I said, "Set it on cruise control at sixty-five, slow down when they tell you to, don't pass on the right, and keep your wig on."

I went out like a ten-watt bulb and slept as Di navigated the Aerostar across the Continental Divide. I dreamt of being chased around the parking garage of the Mutual of Kansas building by men with golf clubs. When I woke we were nearly in Utah.

We stopped in Grand Junction for breakfast. As we walked into the coffee shop, my eye caught the headline of a newspaper: BENCH WARRANT OUT IN CALIFORNIA FOR LEONARD SCHECTER. I deposited Di and the princes in a booth and went back and bought the paper.

In a stall in the men's room, I read that the Petitioner had gotten the judge to issue a contempt citation for my failure to respond to her various subpoenas. So I was now wanted for contempt as well as for accessory to kidnapping.

I dialed my lawyer's number from the pay phone in the corridor outside the restrooms.

"Leonard?"

"Yes."

"You are in deep shit."

"Is that a nice way to say hello?"

"Where are you?"

"Is this a privileged conversation?"

"Only on the divorce action. As far as the accessory-to-kidnapping charge is concerned, I could be deposed."

"What if I hired you to represent me on that charge?"

"I don't do kidnapping. By the way, there's also a number of breach-of-contract suits piling up on my desk. I seem to be the only place where people can go to sue you. And, believe me, there are many people wanting to sue you."

I stood there among the plastic cactus plants in the hallway of a roadside coffee shop on the Colorado-Utah border and listened as my lawyer went down the list of aggrieved parties suing me for nonperformance, breach of contract, fraud, conspiracy to commit fraud, and so forth.

"Is that all?"

"I'm preparing papers for nonpayment of fees."

"What?"

"Leonard, you owe me twelve thousand dollars."

"For what?"

"For filing ex parte motions to keep you out of jail."

"Look, I'll pay you the money, okay?"

"When?"

"It's a little complicated. I don't have a bank account. But I have lots of cash."

"So I gather. According to the complaints, you've accepted

close to a million dollars in advances. That money is reportable to the court as a basis for spousal support. You're lucky the judge only threw a contempt at you and didn't hand you over to a grand jury."

I didn't say anything for a moment. Then, in a controlled voice, I asked, "What is your advice, counselor?"

"Go to a post office, write me a money order for twelve thousand dollars, send it to me Federal Express, and call me in the morning."

We finally stopped to sleep in a Motel 6 outside of Richfield, Utah. Di put the princes to bed, then came next door and lay down beside me on the bed. She took off her wig and shook out her hair, now long and brown.

We lay back together against the headboard. I put my arm around her, and she settled in with her head in the crook of my shoulder. After a moment, she said, "Leonard?"

"Hmnn . . ."

"Where are we going?"

"West."

"Yes, so I gather. What happens when we get there?"

"I don't know."

"I've been thinking . . ."

"Yes?"

"I've been thinking that we need some sort of plan."

"Plan?"

"Yes. Otherwise we shall be caught."

"And then we'll walk out with our heads held high. Isn't that what you said?"

"Yes, but I'd rather we didn't walk out at all."

"I don't know if that's possible."

"Look how far we've already gotten. Who would have thought that we'd be in Utah with the boys and without a detective and with the whole world looking for us? Isn't that extraordinary?"

I nodded but without enthusiasm. The night driving and the

miles and the wigs and the sunglasses were all beginning to take their toll on me.

"Do you think it would be possible to find a nice quiet town and live there—just the four of us?"

"Without being discovered?"

"Of course."

"Di, do you really want to spend all your time in a wig and dark glasses?"

"What if I did something permanent to disguise myself?"

I sat up and looked at her, suddenly alarmed.

"What are you talking about?"

"Plastic surgery."

"Oh, no . . ."

"I have never been terribly fond of my nose."

"I love your nose."

"No, you don't."

"Yes, I do. It's just like the way you feel about Charles's ears."

We talked for hours. I argued with Di about getting her nose fixed, but, as I was to learn, once Di has her mind set on something, she is difficult to move. Gradually, she made me understand that the nose job was just another way of shedding the persona of the Princess of Wales.

"Don't you see, Leonard," she said, "I don't want to be Princess Di anymore. It's been twelve years. I'm fed up. I want to live a real life. With you. And the boys. Is that too much to ask?"

I didn't know what to say. I had no arguments to convince her otherwise. She was right. I realized that I hadn't fallen in love with Princess Di. I had fallen in love with Sandy Keats, who was lying beside me with her mousy brown hair falling in her eyes, which were moist with tears.

I bent over and kissed her eyes, sponging up the tears with my lips. My fingers caressed the side of her face, then wandered to her nose. I would learn to live with a different one. If this was the price of love, I would pay it.

. . .

It was time to share some of these thoughts with the princes. Without going into extraneous detail, we explained that we would find a nice place to live in America. They would go to school and learn to play baseball. We would be Chuck, Sandy, Timmy, and Jimmy Keats, and we'd go to drive-in movies and play miniature golf and wouldn't have to worry about photographers and detectives.

"You mean, we'd be Yanks?" said Prince Hal.

"We'd always be English, sweetheart, but we'd live here in America. Don't you like it?"

"I wish they had scones."

"We'll find some, don't you worry."

Wills was sitting there developing a deep scowl. Di looked at him and said, "What do you say, Wills?"

"What about Dad?"

"We shall continue to write him, and then after a while, when it's all been sorted out, you can go and visit with him for holidays and such."

"Is Leonard going to be our dad?"

"No. Leonard's our friend, but he's not your dad. Charles is your dad, and he always will be."

"Can we get faxes from him?"

"We shall try to arrange that."

There was another long moment of silence. Then Wills asked, "Where shall we live?"

"Anywhere we want to," I replied.

"How about Rancho Cucamonga?"

CHAPTER

27

We did not visit the Grand Canyon, though we were only a few hours' drive from it as we headed southwest on Interstate 15 through Utah and into Nevada. Nor did we stop in Las Vegas. As far as I was concerned, the sooner we got off the road the better.

At three in the morning, I woke up Di and the princes to look at the Vegas strip. They peered through sleepy eyes at the extravagance of neon, and yawned.

"Who's Engelbert Humpernickel?" Prince Hal asked.

"It's Engelbert Humperdinck," Wills replied, "and he was a nineteenth-century German composer, a contemporary of Wagner."

"What is he doing here in Las Vegas?"

"I wouldn't know."

Di drove the Aerostar across Death Valley as I dozed fitfully in the backseat among the potato-chip crumbs and sacks of dirty laundry. We hadn't done a wash since Dallas. We were gypsies, making our campfire wherever night found us, heading west toward the Pacific and the unknown.

Rancho Cucamonga might as well have been Antarctica. To me it was just the punch line of a lot of bad jokes, the West Coast equivalent of Canarsie. I had never been there and wasn't even sure where it was until I found it in the *Mobil Guide*—in San Bernardino County, about forty-five miles from Los Angeles.

I drifted off to sleep among images of grand-jury vigilantes from Section 29 of the Los Angeles County Superior Court roaring across the county line on Harley-Davidsons to apprehend me. At the head of the column of bikes was my lawyer, a briefcase of lawsuits strapped to her back, an extradition order clenched between her teeth like a dagger.

I was awakened in the parking lot of a Taco Bell outside of San Bernardino. Prince Hal nudged my shoulder and said, "Come on, now. Step to it."

"Step on it," I corrected.

"Sorry?"

"That's what Americans say—step *on* it, not step *to* it."

I climbed out of the minivan, slowly uncoiling my legs and flexing my cramped back. I peered through the hazy morning sunshine at the snow-peaked San Bernardino Mountains and felt the familiar hot, dry desert air on my face. Welcome to California, the Golden State.

We sat on the terrace and ate taco grandes and watched the cars speed by on the freeway off in the distance. We were strangely quiet, the four of us. Even the normally voluble Prince Hal had nothing to say. He was blowing Pepsi bubbles through his straw and making faces. Wills had his Game Boy out but didn't turn it on. He was alone with his thoughts, his hands folded neatly in his lap, his cowboy hat pulled down over his eyes.

For her part, Di seemed to be meditating behind her Ray-Bans. From time to time she would go off into trances and be completely absent for ten to fifteen minutes. I had learned not to disturb her during these periods of detachment.

And so we sat there, with the pigeons eyeing the remains of our tacos, each of us lost in private thoughts. There was something sobering about the end of the road. We were pitching our tent, settling in for the winter in a place we didn't know, except as a name on a map. We were circling the wagons around us.

We got off the freeway at the exit marked RANCHO CUCAMONGA and drove up and down a series of long avenues with occasional traffic lights and gas stations. There were miles of scrub oak and cactus on either side of the road, disappearing into the wind-blown wilderness beyond, but no town.

"Where is it?" Wills asked after a while.

"It must be here somewhere," I said, no idea where it was.

I headed back toward the mountains, driving for miles, until some houses appeared on the side of the road. Eventually, there were more houses. They were small stucco houses with fruit trees in the yard, pickups and dirt bikes in the driveways, American flags on the front doors.

"Isn't this charming?" said Di.

"This is America," I said somewhat ponderously.

"Lovely."

As we got closer to the foothills, the town began to emerge from hiding. We passed the Freedom Mall, on Eucalyptus Avenue, and the Millard Fillmore Middle School, a Spanish colonial-style building with a marquee in front of it that said BEAT SAN BERDOO.

We drove down San Bernardino Boulevard, a clean, sparse street with diagonal parking, palm trees, and chain stores. There was an old movie theater, a bowling alley, a library, and a number of Mexican and Chinese restaurants.

I drove slowly, as Di and the princes gazed out the windows.

"Is this the high street?" Prince Hal asked.

"I think so."

"It's terribly clean," he said.

"Isn't it, though?" said Di.

"Do you suppose they have a minigolf?"

"I'm sure they do."

"What about a McDonald's?"

We found one in the Freedom Mall. It occupied a prominent space on the ground floor of the mall, between a Crown bookstore and a Radio Shack.

It was a western-themed McDonald's, with pictures of movie cowboys on the wall, plastic cactuses, and a play area for kids. Over the door was a big sign that said HOWDY. Western-style Musak drifted down from the ceiling, and the counter help wore bandannas and cowboy hats.

As I waited on line to have my order taken, I noticed a small sign behind the cash register: FRANCHISE FOR SALE. SEE MANAGER.

It was late that night, lying in bed with Di in my room at the Cucamonga Holiday Inn, that I mentioned, off-handedly and in a completely different context, that the McDonald's franchise at the Freedom Mall was for sale.

"Really?"

"Yes."

"Extraordinary."

I thought she would leave it at that. But a moment or so later, she said, "Do you suppose they're very dear?"

"Dear?"

"A McDonald's restaurant."

"I have no idea."

She sat up and reached for her pocketbook on the night table. As she spoke, she tweezed her eyebrows with the aid of the small mirror in her compact.

"Do you like this town, Leonard?"

"Sure."

"I like this town a great deal. It is small, it is quiet, it is lovely. There is snow in the mountains. It has a nice-looking school. There is a mall with everything one needs and houses with lemon trees in the yard. People drive courteously. There are no reporters lurking about. And there's a McDonald's restaurant for sale."

It took me a moment to digest all this. She went on tweezing her eyebrows fastidiously as I let it all slowly sink in. The Princess of Wales running a McDonald's in Rancho Cucamonga? It was preposterous. And it made perfect sense.

This was what curling up in front of the telly with someone ultimately meant. This was Cinderella backward. This was what she had been telling me all these months as we made love in our little room in the Togolese embassy in London, and then fled west together from the swamps of Florida.

Ever since that first time we danced together to "Embraceable You" and she looked at me with those get-me-away-from-here eyes, she had wanted to flee, to live her life simply—away from the reporters and the detectives and the Germans with their horses and hounds and drafty stone castles.

And here we were. Just the two of us and the princes, with new identities and enough money to start a new life. Or at least I thought so. I had no idea how much a McDonald's franchise cost, but I suspected they wouldn't go cheaply.

"I'm not sure I have enough money," I said at last.

"Do you know how much my tiara is worth?"

The next morning I went alone to speak to Pete Kelleher, the manager of the McDonald's at the Freedom Mall. We sat in the quiet of the postbreakfast rush, with coffee and Egg McMuffins, and he explained that he was getting out of the business because he'd made too much money. He wanted to buy a Winnebago and live off the fat of the land.

"Always wanted to see Costa Rica, and at my age, you ought to get going or you might never get there."

He had one of those leathery California suntans, which was strange for a man who spent his days in a restaurant.

When I asked him how he got his tan, he said, "You set this place up right, you can spend a lot of time out in back with a chaise lounge and a reflector. Get yourself some Mexicans, give 'em a dollar more than minimum an hour, free lunch, and a Christmas bonus, and in five years you'll be on your way to Costa Rica."

"What's it going to cost me to get in?"

"An arm and a leg. But you'll get it back. And then some. Believe me, it's a license to print money. 'Course, you're going to have to go to Hamburger University and learn how it's done. Otherwise, they won't let you have the franchise."

"You've got to go to school to learn how to make hamburgers?"

"These aren't just hamburgers. These are McDonald's hamburgers. One bad hamburger, and the whole chain is affected. That's what you learn out there in Illinois—you're only as good as your worst hamburger."

"How long do you have to spend out there?"

"Two thousand hours."

"You're kidding!"

"Nope. But as long as you've got graduates running your shifts, you yourself don't have to go out there right away. They give you eighteen months to get your BH."

"BH?"

"Bachelor of Hamburgerology."

I finished my coffee and Egg McMuffin and said, "Approximately how much is an arm and a leg?"

"A million two."

"One million, two hundred thousand dollars?"

"Out the door."

That afternoon, as the princes swam and played Ping-Pong in the Holidome, Di sat in the room with a pad of paper and made a list of things to do. I paced back and forth guzzling diet Coke.

"One must prioritize," she said. "Otherwise, one gets nothing accomplished."

She wrote down the following:

1. Buy house.
2. Put boys in school.

3. Sell tiara.
4. Buy restaurant.
5. Get nose done.

"Not necessarily in that order," she explained.

She was wearing spandex pants and a bra, her feet tucked up beneath her. She rubbed her cheek with the eraser end of the pencil. I had still not reconciled myself to the nose job.

"Di, are you sure you want to do this?"

"I'm very sure, thank you. I rang Fergie this morning while you were out at the mall. She will find out just who the best plastic surgeon in this part of the country is, and we shall make discreet inquiries. Perhaps we could get the one who does Cher . . ."

I began to protest again, but she wasn't listening.

"Now, as far as the house is concerned, I should like something small, with a garden and some fruit trees and a view of the mountains. And a swimming pool. So I can swim laps. The one thing I haven't the foggiest notion about is how to sell the tiara. I suppose one doesn't just put a notice in the paper, does one?"

"One doesn't," I said. "Just out of curiosity, does it belong to you or to England?"

"Oh, this belongs to me. It was a present from King Hussein. I suspect it's worth a tidy sum."

It was comforting to know that I wasn't going to add disposing of stolen property to the growing list of crimes I had committed. Still, I had no idea how you fenced a diamond tiara.

There was only one person I could think of to call who just might know the answer to the question and who I felt, for some strange reason, wouldn't set the FBI on me. On a hunch, I picked up the phone and asked for information for Beverly Hills.

He sounded, as usual, as if he had been woken out of a deep sleep. It was two-thirty in the afternoon, but my first question was "Charlie, I'm sorry. Did I wake you?"

There was a long silence, then, "Leonard, how are you?"

"Fine."

"Nice to hear your voice."

"Thank you . . . Charlie, listen, I need a favor."

"What else is new?"

"Sorry. I'm in kind of a tight spot."

"You sure are."

"Charlie, I need to fence a diamond tiara worth several million dollars."

There was more silence, then I heard something that sounded vaguely like a laugh. When it subsided, he said, "Leonard, tell me something—why in god's name did you think I would know how to do that?"

"I don't know. You ran away and made a film without the studio knowing about it and wound up winning an Academy Award. I figure that anybody who could pull that off could find out how to fence a diamond tiara."

"Is that so?"

"Uh-huh."

He laughed some more, then said, "Where are my pages?"

"You want me to bullshit you, Charlie?"

"No."

"I'm living the pages instead of writing them. Maybe someday I'll write about this, but it's not over yet. I need to find out what happens."

"Hell of a story."

"You don't know the half of it."

"Worldwide rights . . . first refusal?"

It was my turn to laugh. Good old Charlie. Still working the room.

"Why not?"

"Gentleman's agreement?"

"In this business?"

This time we both laughed. He told me to give him a day and then hung up. Like Kodjo Kponvi, Charlie Berns never asked me where I was.

As we drove down San Bernardino Boulevard looking for a real estate office, I told Di about Charlie Berns.

"He was making a karate movie in Belgrade with Bobby Mason when his star was kidnapped by Macedonian separatists. So you know what Charlie Berns did? Instead of shutting down, he recast, sneaked off to Zagreb, and made a completely different movie about Benjamin Disraeli and William Gladstone without telling the studio what he was doing."

"Did he?"

"Uh-huh. And he wound up with the Oscar for Best Picture. It was called *Dizzy and Will.*"

"I adored that movie. We had a screening at Buckingham Palace for the Queen. Jeremy Ikon was there, and afterward, we had a lovely chat."

Soon we were sitting across the desk from Patti Duc, a real estate broker of Vietnamese origin, looking at photos of houses for sale.

"Good time to buy," Patti Duc said. "Lots of houses on the market. You come in with good offer, lots of cash, and you get very good deal."

"How about all cash, fast escrow?" I said.

"You steal the house."

"Well, I'm not sure we want to do that," Di said.

"Figure of speech," Patti Duc explained.

Patti Duc took us around in her Jeep Cherokee, showing us a dozen houses before the afternoon was over. Compared to Los Angeles real estate, the prices in Rancho Cucamonga were very affordable. I could have bought several of them with what I had stuffed in my shoulder bag.

The princes and Di had their hearts set on a swimming pool, which got us up over $200,000.

"Don't worry. You make offer in high ones," Patti Duc said, "it flies."

The sun was just starting to set when we drove up to the yellow-and-green stucco house on Persimmon Avenue. A lemon tree, pregnant with ripe fruit, stood in front of the house, and a basketball hoop was attached to the garage. There were rosebushes climbing vagrantly on a trellis that led to the yard.

We walked in back and saw the pool, green with neglect, in the middle of a large yard with a gazebo and a picnic table. In the distance, there was a stunning view of the San Bernardino Mountains, now a deep golden orange in the refracted glow of the sunset.

Di and I stood there and watched the light play off the mountain, breathing the fragrance of jade and oleander that rose in the cooling desert air. It was dead quiet but for the sound of birds.

I felt her hand squeeze mine. I squeezed back.

Patti Duc had been in real estate long enough to recognize the symptoms.

"I get you a twenty-one-day escrow. You in by Christmas."

We signed papers that evening at Patti Duc's office. I gave her $30,000 as a deposit and told her that we wanted to take title as Chuck and Sandy Keats, joint tenants.

"I'm sure you going to be very happy," Patti Duc said.

"We already are," I replied.

"You very pretty," she said to Di, or what she could see of her behind the Ray-Bans. "You look like movie star."

"Really?"

"Yes. Helen Keller."

"Thank you."

CHAPTER

28

Di insisted on going on a tour of the Millard Fillmore Middle School with the princes before enrolling them. Though the wig she got in Dallas was terrific and though she was very good about never taking off the Ray-Bans in public, I was still nervous about her being recognized.

"I'm sorry, Leonard, but I shall not put my sons in a school that I have never seen."

That was that. We called for an appointment and were taken through the facility by Phyllis Montecito, the assistant principal, a six-foot Hispanic woman with a great deal to say about education. She told us about test scores and curriculum-enrichment programs as she led us through the hallways, the auditorium, the gym, the lunch-room, the computer center.

Di asked a lot of questions, doing her best to speak in an American accent. She didn't sound American, but then she didn't sound English, either. She sounded like some sort of Scandinavian who'd had a little too much to drink. The princes were much better at it. They had picked up a lot from television and could be very convincing in short bursts.

When Ms. Montecito showed us the computer center, Prince Hal said, "Holy cow."

The school was clean, well equipped, and spacious. Di gave her approval, and we went into the office to enroll Timmy and Jimmy. I explained to Ms. Montecito that I was with the State Department, having recently returned from a long tour of duty in Togo, and that I was in the process of having the boys' school records transferred here.

"Togo?" she said. "In Africa?"

"Yes."

"How fascinating. Perhaps Timmy or Jimmy could do a report and tell their new classmates all about their adventures living in Togo."

Later, in the car, Wills said, "What shall we do if they ask us about Togo?"

"Tell them that it's all classified information and you can't talk about it."

We stopped off at the mall, and while Di and the princes shopped for school supplies, Pete Kelleher and I talked turkey. He set me up with a chocolate shake, and I got right to the point.

"I want to make an offer."

"Shoot," he said.

"It's a very clean offer."

"How clean?"

"So clean you could eat off it."

He laughed like a submachine gun, in short staccato bursts. It would go over well in his trailer park in Costa Rica. I laid out the deal for him on a napkin.

"This is it," I said, writing the number down and folding it over. "The number on this napkin is a firm offer. In cash. No banks. No qualifying for loans. No inspection contingencies. The only thing you've got to do is sell us to McDonald's. You do that, and you're on your way to Costa Rica."

I handed him the napkin. He opened it and read the figure: $1,250,000. I've always believed that generous tipping is worth it in the long run. He folded it back up again, as if it were a legal document, put it in his shirt pocket, looked at me carefully.

"You a convicted felon?"

"No."

"Drug addict?"

"No."

"Abortionist?"

"No . . ."

"Because I won't sell to anybody who doesn't respect the sanctity of human life."

I gave him our names, the address of the house on Persimmon Avenue, and Patti Duc and Phyllis Montecito as local character references, and told him to lobby it through McDonald's.

"We're a family of four, we've got two kids in the local school, we own a home in the neighborhood and a paid-off Ford Aerostar, and we've got money in the bank. This should be a slam dunk."

I found Di and the princes in the Thrifty drug and discount store with a cartful of school supplies.

"They don't have rubbers," said Wills.

I looked at him strangely. He was only eleven years old. Then he picked up a pencil to show me that it didn't have an eraser. I breathed a sigh of relief and said, "In America we call them erasers, Wills."

When we got back to the hotel, I had them both write to Charles. They were allowed to say they had bought a house and were going to school, but couldn't say where. I read the letters carefully, making sure that there was nothing in them that could trace us to Rancho Cucamonga, then sent them to Kodjo Kponvi in London.

That night we had dinner at Pizza Hut. Di and I split a mushroom pizza. The princes had sausage and pepper. They were nervous about fitting into their new school.

"What if I forget and say *rubber* instead of *eraser*?" Prince Hal worried.

"Just explain that in Togo they speak English English instead of American English."

"They speak French, actually," Wills corrected.

"But I don't speak French," said Hal.

"Well, you ought to. If you're going to succeed me as King, you'll need to speak French. How else can you talk to Mitterrand?"

"Boys," Di said. "Let's not forget that for the moment we are the Keats family. You're Timmy and Jimmy Keats."

"I want to be Timmy, not Jimmy," Prince Hal said.

"Sorry. I get first choice, and I'm Timmy."

When we got back to the Holiday Inn, Di spent a long time getting the princes to bed. They were jumpy about school, and Di, always the devoted mother, stayed with them until they were asleep.

It was after eleven before she came next door. I was lying in bed watching the news. We were no longer the lead story, upstaged by a disgruntled Toys "Я" Us employee who had terrorized an entire section of the Long Beach Freeway for hours with a homemade antipersonnel bomb assembled entirely with ingredients bought at his local Builders Emporium.

In fact, for the first time since we left Dallas, there was no mention at all of us. No statements from Buckingham Palace, or from Charles, or from MI6. No reported Di spottings or interviews with royal watchers.

Di lay down next to me on the bed, snuggling into my arms. We watched firefighters battling a brush fire in Hesperia. Then we watched the weatherman tell us that rain was expected over the next several days.

"Rain? Does it actually rain here?" Di asked, surprised.

"Only in the winter."

"Oh, how jolly. I shall have to pick up macs for the boys."

"Raincoats," I corrected.

"Will I ever learn this bloody language?"

"*Damn* language . . ."

She punched me playfully on the arm, then turned over and put her lips on the side of my neck. She liked to chew on the side of my neck. I put my arms around her and let my hands wander down to the small of her back. I pulled her in tight and felt her stomach hard against mine. She exhaled deeply and issued a long, low moan. I recognized that long, low moan as my cue, and eased her off the bed and onto the floor.

Two days later I was on my way to Los Angeles. I had two appointments within a few hours of each other and, fortuitously, within walking distance of each other as well. Harvey Kilkus, M.D., had offices on Bedford Drive in Beverly Hills. Karim Hashnani, president and chief operating officer of the Hashnani Import/Export Company, was in the Wells Fargo Bank Building around the corner on Wilshire.

Di had gotten Kilkus's name from Fergie, who said that, according to her sources, he was the top man in town. Besides Cher, Kilkus had done Jane, Liz, and Michael. The Duchess herself was thinking of having a little tightening done in the spring.

"Tightening what?" I asked Di.

"None of your affair," she replied.

The idea was for me to see Kilkus first and assure myself of his discretion. When I called, I was told by his receptionist that the first available appointment was in mid-January.

"I've been referred by the Duchess of York," I said huffily.

"One moment please . . ." She put me on hold, then got back on almost immediately to say, "How about tomorrow morning at eleven?"

Getting an appointment with Hashnani was more circuitous. Charlie Berns had given me explicit instructions. I had to call a certain number at noon precisely, identify myself as Mr. Phillips, and leave a number where I could be reached.

"Mr. Phillips?"

"They're Iranians," Charlie Berns said, as if that explained everything.

When I called the number, I got an answering machine with a mellifluous voice asking me to kindly wait for the tone and leave my name and number. An hour later the phone rang, and a man who did not identify himself asked if I would be good enough to bring the carpet samples to his office at two o'clock the following afternoon.

So here I was, driving west on the San Bernardino Freeway with Di's tiara in a shopping bag beside me. There was a thick cloud cover hanging over the San Gabriel Valley that would burn off by noon. You could taste the ozone on your tongue.

It was without emotion that I crossed over the dry L.A. River bed and headed north to the Hollywood Freeway. I had left this city six months ago without regrets and was not particularly happy to be back. I drove past the Temple Street exit, right by the Criminal Courts Building. Within those granite walls were a number of writs, orders, subpoenas, and citations with my name on them.

I got off the Hollywood at Sunset and drove west in midmorning traffic, noticing the increasing number of homeless people standing at traffic lights with cardboard signs. They looked shell-shocked, almost catatonic, as they slouched at intersections with their crudely lettered pleas for help.

I parked in the underground garage on Bedford and took the elevator up to the fourteenth floor. On the door was written HARVEY KILKUS, M.D., A MEDICAL CORPORATION. Pushing open the floor-to-ceiling door, I found myself in a waiting room that looked more like an art gallery than a doctor's office. There were abstract paintings and sculpture everywhere, plants, and even a small fountain in the middle of the room. There was a woman sitting with a bandage over her nose, another one in dark glasses.

The receptionist asked me to fill out a form while I waited. I wrote: JOHN KEATS, POET, LONDON, ENGLAND. IN CASE OF EMERGENCY, CONTACT PERCY BYSSHE SHELLEY, NO PHONE.

A half hour later I was ushered into Dr. Kilkus's office. There was a carved walnut desk, Italian chairs, African violets, and more art. Pachelbel's *Canon* gurgled softly from the CD player.

Dr. Kilkus was in his thirties, with a bushy mustache and an earring. He was wearing an Armani suit with no tie and an AIDS ribbon on his lapel. He looked at me carefully, trying to figure out who I really was and just what part of my anatomy needed his attention.

"Mr. Keats?" he said with a supercilious smile.

"Hi."

I sat down in one of the minimalist Italian chairs and crossed my legs. It was terribly uncomfortable, with a hard seat and no back support.

"You realize, of course," he said, "that I'll need to know eventually who you really are."

"It's not for me," I said.

His features clouded over and he sighed. "I really dislike wasting time like this. Unless a person has enough confidence in my discretion . . ."

"I represent the Princess of Wales."

This stopped him in his tracks. He stared at me for a moment to see if I was kidding, then said, "Diana?"

"Yes."

"I thought she was missing."

"She is."

"Wait a second . . ." A look of revelation came across his tanned, taut face. "You're the guy, what's his name . . . Spector . . . the guy she ran away with . . ."

I said nothing. He went on, beaming as he spoke. "Hey, listen, as far as I'm concerned, more power to you. Frankly, I think Charles is a real stiff."

"You are familiar with her nose, I assume?"

"Who isn't? The redeeming feature in an otherwise flawless face. Without that nose, she would have been Grace Kelly."

"She doesn't want to be Grace Kelly. She wants to be unrecognizable."

He leaned back in his chair for a moment, and stroked his mustache. "Not easy," he said.

"We realize that. That's why we came to you."

"Interesting problem. You want her unrecognizable and still beautiful, I assume."

"She'd be beautiful to me without a nose."

"That's a lovely sentiment."

"I'd like to bring her to see you. But it has to be in secret."

"Of course. There is no one but my patients and my nurses in my waiting room."

"This would have to be at night. With no one around. Not even a nurse."

"I'm sorry but I don't work at night . . ."

"Then I guess the Princess will have to find someone who will. Thank you for your time."

I got up and started for the door. He let me get my hand on the door handle before saying, "Spector?"

I turned around slowly and faced him, my hands casually in my pockets.

"Would Friday at eight be convenient for her?"

I had lunch at a McDonald's on La Cienega. It looked to me like Pete Kelleher had been right when he'd said it was a license to print money. There were long lines of people waiting for their hamburgers, another long line of cars snaking past the drive-up window.

I ordered a Quarter Pounder with cheese, large fries, and a chocolate shake. Under my food was a tray liner with a number of facts about McDonald's. I learned that a new McDonald's restaurant opened every fifteen hours. I learned that in their first thirty years, McDonald's has employed 7 percent of the country's entire work force. I learned that more than thirty-six thousand McDonald's management employees have graduated from Hamburger University in Oak Brook, Illinois.

All of this was very interesting, but first I had to unload a tiara. I arrived at the Wells Fargo Bank Building at five to two and took the elevator up to the Hashnani Import/Export Company, carrying my carpet samples in a Broadway shopping bag.

Inside there was a small waiting room with no receptionist. There was expensive rented furniture, some potted palms wilting in the air-conditioning, and movie posters in Persian. I sat down on a leather couch and waited. It was deathly quiet. And freezing. They had the air-conditioning on arctic.

I picked up one of the two old issues of *Time* magazine and leafed through it. A half hour went by. Nobody came out to see me. I got up several times to look down the long corridor, but saw nothing but closed office doors.

I recognized this as a classic Middle Eastern negotiating tactic. Make them wait. Put them on the defensive. Charlie Berns had not gone into detail about these people except to say that they were in the film business. I did not find this comforting.

At 2:40 a man emerged from the corridor. He was short, dark, well dressed, and immaculately groomed and wore a carnation in his lapel. He looked to be in his sixties, give or take ten years. Bowing slightly, he offered his hand and said, "Dr. Mezrayd, at your service."

His breath reeked from Tic Tacs. We shook hands, and he beckoned me to follow him down the corridor. I walked behind him past the closed doors to one at the end of the corridor. Holding it open for me, he ushered me inside.

There was no desk in this office—only a long leather couch, a coffee table, some urns, and more potted palms. Like the waiting room, it was freezing. Seated on one end of the couch was a man younger than Dr. Mezrayd, wearing a silk shirt, trousers, and five-hundred-dollar Italian shoes.

He did not get up, merely nodded in my direction. Dr. Mezrayd said, "Mr. Hashnani is pleased to make your acquaintance."

"Likewise," I replied.

"Please sit down, sir." Dr. Mezrayd beckoned toward the middle of the couch, and he himself sat down on the other end.

I sank into the contours of the leather couch, feeling it envelop me on all sides. Surrounded by Iranian film moguls, I kept the shopping bag clutched in my lap. As if on cue, another door opened, and a young man entered with three cups of coffee and some dough-nuts.

"I took the liberty of ordering coffee," Dr. Mezrayd said, his voice unctuous. "Would you care for cream and sugar?"

"Yes, please."

He snapped his fingers, and the young man hurried out, return-ing in a few seconds with a jar of Cremora and some packets of Sweet'n Low.

I mixed my coffee, took a sip, and had a bite of a stale glazed doughnut, as the two men sat impassively and watched. My teeth chattered from the cold. I felt like we were in a meat locker.

"Are you from out of town, Mr. Keats?" Dr. Mezrayd asked.

"I'm from Togo."

"I see. And have you been in the carpet business long?"

"No. Actually, I'm an epic poet."

Karim Hashnani continued to say nothing, but his eyes never left the shopping bag.

"And you are interested in disposing of some property?" Dr. Mezrayd continued in his slow, rhetorical manner.

"I'm just a little hard up at the moment and forced to divest myself of some family heirlooms. The epic-poetry market's a little flat."

No reaction from either of them. It was clear that my material wasn't playing to this room, so I decided to get to the point.

"Look, can we cut to the chase here?"

"The chase?"

"I thought you were in the film business."

"We are in distribution."

"Do you distribute diamond tiaras?"

"Why not?"

I opened up the bag, took out Di's tiara, and put it on the coffee table. Dr. Mezrayd did his best to cover his reaction, but it was difficult. He had a four-foot hard-on.

"May I?" he asked, reaching for the tiara.

"Certainly."

He picked the piece up gingerly and examined it closely. Then he reached across me and handed it to Karim Hashnani, who took out a jeweler's loupe and examined each stone in the tiara with great care. Finally he handed it back to me.

They exchanged several terse sentences in what I took to be Farsi. Then Dr. Mezrayd smiled at me and said, "Mr. Hashnani regrets that the stones are not loose. He believes it creates a marketing problem."

"I wouldn't know."

More Farsi, then: "Mr. Hashnani has reason to believe that this tiara would be highly identifiable as is and, therefore, difficult to market."

"That's your department."

"Mr. Hashnani has no way of knowing that this piece isn't stolen."

I turned to Karim Hashnani and said, "You know very well that the stones can be separated and sold individually. You know how and where to do it. And you know how to speak English, so can we cut the bullshit out and discuss a price?"

He looked at me for a very long moment, then said, "One million dollars."

"Sorry. It doesn't cover my costs."

"How much do you need?" Karim Hashnani asked.

"Two million."

"I'm afraid that's impossible."

"Well, sorry to have taken up your time." I put the tiara back into the Broadway shopping bag, got up, and headed for the door.

This time I got as far as the elevator. I had already pressed the button when Dr. Mezrayd hurried down the empty hallway to intercept me. The elevator arrived, and I stood there holding the door open as he came up to me, out of breath from his exertion.

"Mr. Keats, we have reconsidered."

"How much?"

The elevator-door warning buzzer went off. He looked around him to make sure we were alone, then he whispered, "A million five."

"Out the door?"

"Out the door."

I drove back across town through the early rush-hour traffic, feeling ebullient. It had been a very productive day. A million five would get us a McDonald's franchise and leave us with enough pocket money to carry us over until we could start printing money. I decided this called for a small celebration.

I got off the freeway downtown and parked in front of the Ensenada Lounge on the corner of Alvarado and Sunset. I found Rivera at the end of the bar putting back straight shots of tequila.

"How's it going?" I asked.

He looked at me and shook his head, then motioned with his finger for the bartender to refill his glass.

"That bad, huh?"

"She got a new lawyer," he said. "Some hotshot Mexican named Rodriquez. He found out I got a new TV set. Forty-eight-inch color big-screen. The judge says I got to sell it, give her half."

"Tough break."

"Why don't we hire a guy, hit both of them. Two jobs for one. We get a price."

"I'll look into it."

"So what're you doing, *coño*?"

"I'm buying a McDonald's out in Cucamonga."

"She got you selling fucking hamburgers?"

"It's nice out there. Quiet, clean, good schools. We bought a house with a basketball hoop on the garage."

He put down another shot of tequila and muttered, "Jesus Christ."

CHAPTER

29

Di got her nose job on December 10 in a private clinic in San Marino. Their track record for discretion with these sorts of operations, Kilkus assured us, was exemplary—all the way back to the Duchess of Windsor, who, apparently, got tidied up there in the fifties.

All the paperwork was done under the name of Sandy Keats, and Di entered and left at night, with only the clinic's anesthesiologist and Kilkus's personal nurse attending, both of whom, Kilkus assured us, wouldn't talk under torture or sodium pentothal.

During the operation, I paced the empty waiting room like an expectant father. The two hours felt like two days. I kept wondering if we had gone too far. It was one thing to elude DEA radar and land illegally in Florida, but this was irrevocable. We were altering the world's best known and best loved face.

When it was over at last, Kilkus came out to announce that it had gone superbly and that we would be thrilled with the results.

"More beautiful than Grace," he said.

He led me into the recovery room to see her. She was lying there unconscious, her nose wrapped in bandages.

"How much longer will she be out?" I asked.

"A half hour, maybe."

I took her hand and waited as she fought her way back up through the anesthesia. When she finally opened her eyes, I smiled at her and said, "Good morning."

She blinked, then smiled back and squeezed my hand. But when she saw herself with her nose wrapped in bandages, she started to cry. I held her in my arms and told her how much I loved her and how courageous she had been.

"Oh, Leonard, what if I look hideous?"

"You could never look hideous," I assured her.

The princes did their best to be supportive, but Prince Hal couldn't keep his mouth from dropping when he saw his mother.

"What a nasty bruise, Mother," he said.

I got her a dozen Danielle Steels for her convalescence. She lay in bed reading and watching daytime soaps, while I drove the princes back and forth to school and arranged for Abbey Rents furniture for the new house. It would have to do until Di was up to decorating.

True to her word, Patti Duc got us into the house before Christmas. We closed on the twenty-third and were moved in by Christmas Eve. I picked up a small tree and some decorations and strung up lights over the basketball hoop.

It was a quiet Christmas. I got the princes a state-of-the-art Super Nintendo and Di a videocassette of *Love Story* and some costume-jewelry earrings. Prince Hal gave Di a pot holder and me a clay paperweight that he had made in school. Wills wrote us Christmas cards in French. Di gave us each an IOU and a little poem.

Mine read:

> *Each day I love you more and more,*
> *The way you smile through darkest night,*
> *The way you kiss and hold me tight,*
> *The way we dance upon the floor.*

I admired the irregular *abba* rhyme scheme and the racy double entendre in the last line. And I told her so very late Christmas night, after we had inaugurated the floor of our bedroom. We'd had to be a little more subdued than usual due to the still-delicate condition of Di's nose.

"Well, you're not the only poet around here, you know," she said.

"Sweetheart," I said, "as much as I love your poem, I think you should keep your day job."

"Sorry?"

"Never mind."

"Speaking of poetry, are you getting on with *The Dianiad?*"

"I'm afraid I haven't had much time to work on it of late."

"Well, you are going to finish it, I trust?"

"Absolutely. I've written six cantos. I'm all the way through the birth of Hal."

As I lay there on the floor, cuddled up with Di, I reflected that she was one more person I owed pages to. I hoped to finish *The Dianiad*, but for the moment I was trying to get into the hamburger business.

I had asked Pete Kelleher to set up our interview with the McDonald's people for after the first of the year. By then the bandages would be off, and Di would not have to wear dark glasses.

Meanwhile, the money was put in escrow, conditioned on our being approved as franchisees. With the exception of two nocturnal visits to Bedford Drive for Kilkus to check on the progress of the healing of Di's nose, we hung around the house during those last days of December.

The princes, on school vacation, played *Super Mario Bros.* and shot baskets in the driveway. At night we ate takeout and watched videos. I did my best to interest them in American football, but it didn't take.

"They just bang into each other and these blokes with zebra shirts blow whistles," said Wills. "Don't they ever get on with it?"

On New Year's Day we were back in the news. Carl Webb finally spilled his guts. There were clips of him being interviewed beside his Cessna, describing how we flew in under the DEA radar and popped up over Marathon and put down on the abandoned landing strip outside of Naples. He made it seem like *Raiders of the Lost Ark*. When he was asked if he thought that I had abducted Diana and the princes, Carl Webb laughed his boozy laugh and said, "You kidding? They couldn't keep their hands off each other."

Buckingham Palace had no comment on Carl Webb's story. But Rupert Makepeace was on *Geraldo* along with three other prominent royal watchers. He compared me to Rasputin, saying that I had an unnatural influence over Diana.

Hell hath no fury like a journalist scorned.

On the crawl at the end of the show there was the name of the hotel where guests of the *Geraldo* show were put up. I took a shot and dialed the hotel.

"One moment, please," the hotel operator said when I asked for Rupert Makepeace.

"Yes . . ." The voice bellowed forth into the earpiece, and I quickly moved the phone a safe distance away. It had been months since I'd spoken to him, and I had forgotten to take the precaution.

"If I'm Rasputin, Rupert, who does that make you—Nicholas?"

"Sorry?"

"No, Charles would be Nicholas. You could be Trotsky . . ."

There was a long silence, punctuated by heavy breathing. Then, "I should warn you that there is more than adequate security in this hotel."

"Unlike some individuals I know, I do not break into hotel rooms and terrorize people."

"Is this on the record?"

"Sure. Why not?"

"Where are you?"

"I'm in my apartment in St. Petersburg, with my Ouija boards and samovar, plotting the overthrow of the czar."

"It was just a figure of speech."

"An unfortunate one."

"Can we meet?"

"Why would I want to do that?"

"So I can tell your side of the story."

"You've been doing a swell job of that so far."

"You abused my confidence. What do you expect?"

I could see him there in his Burberry and cap, chain-smoking in his comped hotel room.

"I'll tell you what I'm going to do, Rupert. And I'm going to do this only because we once sat together in a pub in Norfolk and talked about Diana like two men in love with the same woman. I'm going to send you the whole story. In verse."

"What?"

"I am in the process of writing our story, the story of Diana and Leonard. It is an epic poem called *The Dianiad*. I've written six cantos and hope to have the rest completed in a few more months. Then I will send it to you in London, and you may publish it. It will all be in there. In iambic pentameter."

"You are having me on, Leonard."

"On the contrary, Rupert. I have never had you on, whatever the fuck that means."

"Really?"

"Happy New Year," I said and hung up.

The unveiling took place on January 10, one month to the day after the operation. We drove up to Kilkus's office after dinner.

Di was as nervous as I'd ever seen her. She kept her hands folded tightly in her lap and drifted into one of her meditative trances, staring blankly out at the dark lunar landscape of the San Gabriel Valley.

We parked on the street and walked down an alley to the back of the medical building. Kilkus had left a block of wood in the service entrance door, as he had done on the other occasions we'd been to see him at night. We took the service elevator to the fourteenth floor, got off, and walked down to the large door marked HARVEY KILKUS, M.D., A MEDICAL CORPORATION.

We entered the empty waiting room, crossed to the closed opaque glass of the receptionist desk. I knocked softly on the glass while Di sat down and picked up a copy of *Vogue* and leafed through it.

A moment later Kilkus came out to greet us. He was wearing a beige cashmere sweater and wingtips.

"Hey, how're you doing?" he said.

I nodded, and Di got up silently and walked past him to the examining room. I followed and took a seat on a small stool. Di propped herself up on the table.

"So, you ready?" said Kilkus, as he probed the bandages with his fingers.

"Quite," said Di.

"There'll be some skin discoloration due to the bandages, but it will disappear in no time."

"Yes, of course," she said.

Slowly he began to peel the bandages off. It seemed to take forever before the nose was completely exposed. She looked dramatically different. But I was at a loss to say exactly how. The new nose was narrower, finer, more severe.

"Amazing how the changing of one feature can completely alter the face," said Kilkus, handing Di a mirror.

She stared at herself in the mirror for a long time, turning her head both ways to check out the profiles.

"It's beautiful," I said, not sure it was, but knowing that I would love her regardless of whatever they had done to her.

She ran her fingers along the ridge, feeling the contours, exploring this new part of her body. Finally, she handed the mirror back to Kilkus and said, "Well, I suppose I shall just have to get used to it, shan't I?"

Getting down off the table, she offered her hand to Kilkus. "Thank you, doctor. Well done."

Then she turned to me and said, "Let's go home."

"If there's any problem, give me a ring . . ." said Kilkus. I handed him an envelope with a hundred one-hundred-dollar bills, and we shook hands.

In the car she didn't bother putting her wig on. She didn't have to. She was a dead ringer for Sandy Keats.

"These cookies are delicious, Sandy."

"Thank you, Blanche."

"You must give me the recipe."

"Of course."

Di had bought the cookies in the bakery section of the Alpha Beta, but she didn't tell that to Blanche Moranis and Bob Cooper, the Los Angeles–area franchise managers for McDonald's, who had driven out to interview us.

"Sandy makes up a whole batch and sticks them in the cookie jar. And then when Timmy and Jimmy come home from school, they dive right in," I said.

"Right," said Bob Cooper with a big, cholesterol-rich smile. "That's just what my mom used to do. She'd be going on about how we could only have two after school so we wouldn't ruin our appetites for dinner, but we'd sneak back into the kitchen when she wasn't looking and grab a handful."

We all laughed—Blanche, Bob, Sandy, and I. We were sitting around the kitchen table, having coffee and cookies on plastic place mats, as the sun set in the west and the lunch dishes dried themselves in the dish drain.

"More coffee, anyone?" Di asked with her drunken Scandinavian accent.

"No thanks, Sandy," said Bob, covering his coffee mug with his large flabby hand.

"So you grew up in Denmark, Sandy?" Blanche Moranis said, referring to our application form in an open folder in front of her.

"Yes," Di said. "Daddy was in the air force. I learned Danish from my governess. It was my first language."

Di and I had worked out her biography to explain her peculiar speech patterns. She had her long, mousy-brown hair tied up in a bun for the Scandinavian look.

"Really?" said Bob Cooper, all smiles. "That should be useful in dealing with tourists."

"Yes," I said. "There are an increasing number of Danish tourists in the States these days."

"They can schedule Cucamonga right along with Solvang," Bob Cooper, good cop, said.

We all laughed some more.

"So, Chuck, you've been working for the State Department?" Blanche Moranis, bad cop, said.

"Yes."

"Most recently in Togo?"

"Uh-huh."

"What were you doing over there?"

I looked at her intently and lowered my voice. "I'm really sorry, Blanche, but I can't talk about it."

"Of course."

"He can't even tell me," Di added.

"I bet you have your methods for finding out," said Bob Cooper with a wink.

The innuendo hung in the air like stale cigar smoke. Outside, the school bus stopped in front of our house. The princes entered and went right for the cookie jar, as rehearsed. We introduced them to Blanche and Bob, and they stood there—Timmy and Jimmy Keats, in their marine-corps crew cuts and Gap jeans, muttering replies with cookie-filled mouths, before heading for their room to play Nintendo.

"Nice-looking kids," said Bob Cooper.

"Thank you," I said. "If you're not careful, though, they'll eat you out of house and home."

"Kids these days, I tell you," said Bob Cooper. "My youngest said the other day that he wants to be president of McDonald's when he grows up."

"That's nothing," I said. "Timmy wants to be King of England."

I couldn't resist it. Di flashed me a look.

"Does either of you have any experience running a business?" Blanche Moranis asked.

"We're reading everything we can on the subject," I said.

"What made you want to become McDonald's franchisees?"

There was a moment of silence before Di said, "We like to work with people. It's the most gratifying thing one can do, isn't it?"

There was a look of perfect sincerity on her face. She could have been addressing Parliament. I wanted to get up and hug her, right then and there.

We made some more small talk, but by the time Blanche and Bob got up to leave, I was convinced we had passed the audition. Di and I walked them out to their car.

"Been great talking to you," said Bob Cooper as Blanche Moranis got behind the wheel.

"Likewise," I said.

"Cheerio," said Di. It didn't matter. We had already bought the ranch.

CHAPTER

30

Our application was approved by Oak Brook on February 1, and we closed with Pete Kelleher a week later. He took us around and introduced us to the staff, some sixty odd people working three shifts. They were organized like a military operation, with a rough hierarchy of rank, beginning with maintenance workers, who cleaned the bathrooms and mopped the floors, to counter help, who served, to grill people, who cooked, to quality-control supervisors, who oversaw the cooking, to shift managers, who ran the show.

As franchise owners, Di and I were essentially feudal lords. We collected our rents and looked over our domain with a beneficent eye, settling disputes and dispensing justice when necessary. But if we were feudal lords, we were hands-on feudal lords. One of us was almost always there.

Di took the morning shift, while the princes were at school and I was working on *The Dianiad*. I would meet her for lunch, and afterward she would go home in order to be there when her sons returned from school. Sometimes the princes would bring their home-work to the restaurant, and when they were finished, they would take a turn making milk shakes for the drive-up window or running to the stock room to get more napkins.

The staff adored Di right from the start. She immediately put them at ease by rolling up her sleeves and working alongside them when things got busy. She learned all their names and had a good word for everyone, a compliment or supportive remark. When Delia's boyfriend left her for a salesgirl at Miller's Outpost, Di consoled her as she cried her eyes out in the ladies' room. When Manuel lost his grandmother, Di sent flowers to the funeral home with a personal note.

The princes were a big hit with the staff as well, especially Prince Hal, who was sounding more and more American every day. He would walk into the restaurant with his book bag, wave to everyone, and shout, "Hi."

"Hi, Jimmy," they would reply. "How are you?"

"Can't complain," he would reply and go over and make himself a milk shake.

Over the next few months, we got two letters of commendation from undercover McDonald's inspectors and a certificate of excel-lence from the Rancho Cucamonga Chamber of Commerce. We were featured in *Mall News*, the giveaway newspaper that was distributed when you entered the Freedom Mall.

Meanwhile, the princes were doing very well in school. Com-pared to Ludgrove School, the Millard Fillmore Middle School was a cakewalk. Wills got a job on the school newspaper, *The Beacon*, writing under the nom de plume of T. W. Keats. He wrote a hard-hitting article on the problem of cafeteria noise, arguing that "a refectory should be a haven of peace and quiet amidst a sea of *sturm und drang*."

Prince Hal played Tiny Tim in the fourth grade's Easter produc-tion of *A Christmas Carol*. Di's eyes watered as her youngest son said, in a perfect Cockney accent, "Will ye be 'aving some goose with us, Mr. Scrooge?"

Di joined the PTA and organized a bake sale for the underfunded public library. She hosted a group of Persimmon Avenue neighbors for a coffee-and-cake get-together to discuss putting up a stop sign on the corner of Persimmon and Oleander. She sent the princes off to school with canned goods for the local homeless.

Every Tuesday night Di and I went down to the El Contento Lanes, on San Bernardino Boulevard, and bowled in a league made up of other Freedom Mall business owners. So that she wouldn't be embarrassed by having to wear shoes with the number ten written prominently on them, I got Di her own bowling shoes. With her hair tied back in a ponytail, her long legs encased in spandex, a bowling shirt with SANDY written on the back, she looked delectable. Each time she bowled a strike, she would turn around and make a thumbs-up sign, and I would want to spread her out across the foot-foul line and take her right there on Lane 24.

And so we lived, Di and I, in our little house at the edge of the desert, lovers and McDonald's franchisees, expatriate Togolese, insanely happy. The days passed in their peaceful rhythm of work and love and bowling. Winter drifted into spring. The wildflowers bloomed and died and bloomed again.

By early April I had completed the last canto of *The Dianiad.* Twelve cantos, twelve hundred lines. I printed it out on my Hewlett Packard Desk Jet printer and gave Di her copy in a pink leather folder, with the words TO MY MUSE written on the inside cover.

She took it to bed with her that night, and as I slept the sleep of the depleted, she read of her life and our love in verse. At three in the morning, she woke me with a kiss, then gently pulled me off the bed onto the floor, where she bestowed upon me my poet's purse.

I sent it off to Rupert Makepeace, via Kodjo Kponvi. The poem covered Di's life as far as Dallas and the paparazzo in the parking garage of Fergie's condo, omitting any mention of Ross. In the earlier cantos, I had also omitted mentioning our facilitator, Kodjo Kponvi, by name, referring to him only as Friar Laurence, and our beard, Gwen Poulstice, was known as Lady Cecil, in honor of her dog.

I did not, however, omit identifying my spiritual brother and fellow victim of Section 29 of the Los Angeles County Superior

Court, Jesus Rivera. He figured prominently as a sort of Mexican Greek chorus, commenting tersely on the events as they occurred.

With the publication of *The Dianiad,* the story, which had lain dormant since early January, exploded back into the headlines. The poem was printed and reprinted in newspapers and magazines worldwide. It ran on the first page of the *San Bernardino Telegram* with the banner headline DI AND LEONARD: A LOVE STORY IN VERSE.

The publication of *The Dianiad* was, in a sense, our salvation. In spite of the strictures of the British family-law system, or of Charles's legitimate rights with regard to his children, our love story conquered the world. We were Romeo and Juliet, Bonnie and Clyde, Ed and Wally. And when we were finally tracked down, we would have worldwide public opinion to use as leverage in our negotiations with the royal family.

In the time between the publication of *The Dianiad* and the fatal phone call from Charles at the Cucamonga Holiday Inn on the night of Di's thirty-third birthday, we were the subject of countless articles, stories, plays, and poems celebrating the power of love. Rupert Makepeace went back on *Geraldo* to claim, this time, that he had aided and abetted our love affair. I was no longer Rasputin, the evil conniver, but Sir Tristan, the Valiant, rescuing the fair Isolde from her castle in Ireland.

I left a one-word message on his voice mail: "Bullshit."

Charles and the Windsors did their best to swim against this current, concentrating their arguments on the missing princes and the denial of paternal rights. But once again the world sided with Di, as they had throughout the Wales's marriage and separation.

I was actually beginning to feel a little sorry for Charles. As Jesus Rivera would have said, the guy was getting pussy-whipped in front of the whole world. He was, in a sense, a fellow victim of the divorce wars, trying to deal with an estranged wife, though this particular estranged wife wasn't going after him for half the Duchy of Cornwall, which she could go after if she ever decided to abandon her life in Rancho Cucamonga and return to England to take him to the cleaner's—a thought that, as far as I could tell, never occurred to Sandy Keats.

And so we drifted through the months of May and June, printing money in our McDonald's, decorating our house, raising our bowling average. The ephemeral Southern California spring came and went, and Di planted the yard with profligate rows of daisies and chrysanthemums.

We harvested our lemons. I repaired the backboard of the basketball hoop and painted the trellises. We looked through catalogs for spas to adjoin the pool, where Di swam fifty laps every morning before going to the mall.

Wills celebrated his twelfth birthday in June. I got him a small dirt bike, and we went off together into the desert and rode around playing macho. He was beginning to creep up on the leading edge of puberty. I saw him at the restaurant giving lingering looks to the high school girls.

"Do you think I should talk to him?" I asked Di.

"Talk to him?"

"Yes. In case you haven't noticed, your son is starting to take very long showers."

She looked at me blankly. I realized that she hadn't a clue what was going on with Wills. She had a blind spot when it came to her own son's sexuality, though I noticed her reacting viscerally one day when a tall, leggy countergirl named Cheryl invited Wills to go to the stockroom and help her carry ketchup cartons.

So on one Sunday dirt-bike outing, I asked him, "Your dad ever talk to you about sex?"

We were sitting on a little bluff overlooking a slope of cactus, eating subway sandwiches and drinking homemade lemonade from the tree in our yard.

"Sorry?" he said. I was convinced he'd heard me perfectly well, but I repeated the question. His features tightened and the color rose in his cheeks.

"Of course," he said.

"What'd he tell you?"

"Well, he . . . pointed out that it would one day be my duty to provide an heir to the throne."

"I see. And did he also point out how you went about providing heirs?"

"Oh, yes. Quite."

"So you don't have any questions, I take it."

He shook his head, then added, "In any event, given that we are living here incognito, the question appears to be academic, doesn't it?"

We left it at that. Later, when I reported the conversation to Di, she asked, "Do you think he resents me?"

"For what?"

"For taking him away from England and the succession to the throne."

"I don't know."

We didn't discuss it further that night, but I sensed that Di was feeling guilty about the princes. I am convinced that these feelings made the future easier for her to face. Whenever the fatal moment came, as we both knew it would, she would have already resigned herself to the inevitable.

During the last week of June I telephoned Kodjo Kponvi to find out if there was a secure fax line so that I could start faxing the princes' letters. He told me how much he liked *The Dianiad.*

"Splendid job," he said.

"Thank you."

"The ambassador is quite tickled that you mentioned the embassy in Canto Nine."

"That's where we met. I'm sorry I couldn't mention you by name, but I didn't want you to be bothered by the police."

"Most considerate of you."

"We both really appreciate all your help."

"*C'est le moindre des choses, mon ami.*"

That phone call was on June 27. Four nights later, on July 1, we were at the restaurant late celebrating Di's birthday with the staff. We had a cake with candles. We sang "Happy Birthday." The staff gave Di a new bowling ball and an apron with her name on it. She went around and thanked everyone personally.

At eleven, we closed the restaurant and drove home. The princes dozed off in the car on the way. Di carried Prince Hal inside the house, while I gathered the bowling ball and Wills.

We put the princes to bed, and Di got into our big four-poster with her Danielle Steel, while I took a shower. By the time I got out, she had fallen asleep. Naked, I tiptoed out of the bedroom and down to the kitchen to get a drink of water.

As I stood there in the kitchen drinking a glass of water, looking out the window at the moonlit summer night, letting the desert breeze dry me, I felt an overwhelming sense of well-being. It was an exquisite night—dead quiet except for the cicadas and the occasional yelp of a far-off coyote. My house was safe and quiet. Di and the princes were asleep. Soon I would crawl in beside her, put my arms around her, and drift off with her into separate dreams, and we'd lie together, side by side, till morning.

And it was at this moment, as I wallowed in the *gemütlichkeit* of my life, that the phone rang.

I grabbed it quickly so as not to wake Di and the princes.

"Hello?"

"Yes. This is Charles speaking."

There are a lot of Charleses in the world, but there was never any doubt in my mind which one this was. I sat down on a kitchen chair and twirled the phone cord around my little finger. I looked out the window to the lone lemon tree, standing sentry in our front yard, and beyond it to the street, where a Ford Taurus was parked, two men in the front seat.

There was no one else around. Persimmon Avenue was sleeping blissfully in the summer night.

"Your Royal Highness," I said, in as civil a voice as possible, "good of you to ring . . ."

CHAPTER

31

RANCHO CUCAMONGA,
JULY 2, 1994,
2:07 A.M.

"Are you there?"

I am here, but I don't answer. He repeats the question, his voice taut with impatience. I look over at the dangling receiver and chuckle to myself at the sight of the Prince of Wales hanging upside down in my kitchen.

I take a long hit off the Coors can, reach over and take the receiver, put it to my ear.

"You were saying, sir . . ."

"You *are* there . . ."

"Yes. I was just getting a beer."

"I really believe it would be fruitful if you and I were to have a chat face-to-face."

"So you've said."

"I believe it would be in our mutual interest."

"Really?"

"Yes."

"All right," I reply. "There's a twenty-four-hour Denny's on La Jolla and First."

"Sorry?"

"Denny's. It's a restaurant. Neutral territory. In the meantime, call the two gorillas in front of my house on their car phone and tell them to drive me there and to wait for me while we talk."

"Yes . . ."

"I must caution you, sir, that if anyone enters the house or disturbs Di or the princes while I'm there, I will guarantee you that the most intimate details of your family's life will be smeared across newspapers and magazines around the world. For a very long time."

"La Jolla and First, you say?"

"Yes. Fifteen minutes."

I hang up and go get some clothes from the bedroom. Careful not to wake Di, I take the clothes down the hallway to the kitchen to put them on. Then I go out the front door, double-locking it, and walk across the lawn to the Taurus.

The guy riding shotgun gets out and opens the back door for me. He is thin, with a receding hairline and a maroon sports jacket. The last time I saw him he was entering a drugstore in Nassau.

"Donald," I say cheerfully, "good to see you again."

"Good evening, sir."

I get in the backseat, and he gets in beside me.

"SOP, huh?"

"Sorry?" says Donald.

"Standard operating procedure. Put the suspect in the back with one operative, while the other drives. I hope you're not going to put cuffs on me."

"No, sir, we're not. Where is La Jolla Avenue?"

"Turn right at the corner, go three blocks to La Crescenta, hook a left, and it's your first light."

The driver starts the engine and takes off down the quiet street, pausing at the stop sign that Di was instrumental in having installed.

"You realize, Donald, that it was nothing personal."

"I beg your pardon?"

"Leaving you holding the Tampax in Nassau," I say, unable to resist a bit of nostalgia at his expense. "I mean, I felt bad after all we had been through together, but it was our only shot. You *do* understand?"

"Yes, of course."

We ride in silence the rest of the way. In front of Denny's, Donald gets out and opens the door for me.

"Remember," I say, "you don't touch her or the boys."

He gives me one of his minimalist nods, and I head toward the entrance.

As soon as I walk in the door, I see him. He's sitting alone in a corner booth, wearing a blue blazer, a red striped tie, and sunglasses. He might as well have skipped the shades. The ears are a dead giveaway. Fortunately, however, there are only three people in Denny's at this hour, and none of them recognize the Prince of Wales.

I slip into the booth opposite him. We don't shake hands. A cup of tea sits in front of him, the teabag lying in the saucer.

"Thank you for coming," he says.

"My pleasure."

"You understand that my main concern is the welfare of my sons."

"Yes."

"I appreciate your having gone to the trouble of having the boys' letters sent to me."

I look at him quizzically, not sure how much he knows.

"The chap at the Togolese embassy, Mr. Kponvi, did not betray you. We analyzed the paper on the envelopes he used to post the letters, traced it to a stationer in Mayfair. It was painstaking, but we eventually got the match and put a tap on Mr. Kponvi's phone. Had you not rung him, of course, we may not have found you."

He reveals these facts to me without any particular sense of triumph.

"Has the story broken?" I ask.

"No. We have kept a very tight lid on it."

"Good. Maybe we can make a deal."

"I would very much hope so."

A waitress comes over to ask what I want. I order an English muffin and a glass of tomato juice. She asks Charles if he wants a refill on his tea, and he says, "Thank you so much."

The waitress looks at him uncomprehendingly. I translate. "He doesn't want any." After she's gone, I ask, "Are U.S. Marshals really on their way?"

He hesitates for just a moment, then shakes his head. "We thought it would be preferable not to involve them if we didn't have to."

"So no one knows but you, me, Kodjo Kponvi, Donald, and a couple of operatives of MI6?"

"That is correct."

I've been thinking about this deal for weeks. It's crazy and probably unworkable, but it's the only deal that Di will accept. I'm sitting there with a very small gun in my pocket, but I take it out and put it on the table anyway.

"Okay, here's the deal. The boys return to England at the end of their school vacation. They spend their school terms at Ludgrove, weekends with you. They return here for school holidays and the entire summer. You never reveal where they were or where Di is, and I never say a word to anyone about what happened."

He takes a sip of his tepid tea and sits there considering while I look outside to make sure the Taurus is still parked in front.

"Audacious," he says finally.

"Yeah."

"Do you suppose we can pull it off?"

"Hey, if your guys could trace us from an envelope, they can certainly figure out how to get two kids back and forth between Rancho Cucamonga and London without a lot of people knowing."

Then, with a perfectly straight face, he says, "I suppose that this . . . arrangement . . . would terminate if Wills were to become Prince of Wales?"

I laugh. I can't help myself. The idea of the Prince of Wales spending his summers flipping hamburgers in Cucamonga is hilarious. In spite of himself, Charles finds himself laughing along with me.

We share a good laugh, and then I say, "Look, who knows how long this is going to work? It depends on Wills and Harry themselves, not to mention Di. Why don't we take it one year at a time?"

"All right."

He reaches into his blazer pocket, takes out an envelope, hands it to me.

"I thought you might want to have these."

I open the envelope and find a bunch of negatives. I hold them up to the light, and it takes me a moment to recognize the photos that Rupert Makepeace's photographer snapped of me naked at the Dorchester.

"Fortunately, we were able to seize them before publication," he explains.

"Thank you," I say.

"You're quite welcome."

He takes another sip of tea, then asks how the princes are.

"They're terrific," I say. "Healthy and happy. They both did very well in school this year. And they've been helping us part-time at the McDonald's."

"The McDonald's?"

"Yes. Di and I bought one."

I tell him all about the restaurant and the bowling league and the dirt bike and the facts-of-life conversation. He listens intently, fascinated by the details of the Keats family's life in Rancho Cucamonga.

I invite him to spend the day tomorrow with the princes around our pool. I explain that there'd be too great a risk of his being recognized if they came to the hotel.

"How is it that she hasn't been recognized?" he asks.

"Nose job," I say.

He looks at me incredulously. "She agreed to have plastic surgery on her nose?"

"She was the one who suggested it."

"Really?"

"Yes."

"Extraordinary."

By the time I am ready to leave, we are getting on quite well. I promise to call him as soon as I talk to Di and the princes.

He gets up and offers his hand. We shake.

"Thank you, Leonard," he says.

"You're welcome, Charles."

As I drive home through the awakening streets of Rancho Cucamonga, I suddenly feel exhausted. It's been a long ordeal. And it's not quite over yet. I still have to sell the deal to Di, though I have little doubt that she will buy it.

Donald sits beside me impassively as the driver retraces his route, this time running the stoplight on Persimmon. They drop me in front of the house.

"Good night, Donald," I say, as I get out of the car.

"Good morning, sir," he says, literal to the end. I watch them pull away, then turn toward my house.

On the lawn beside the lemon tree, Rivera is waiting with fresh horses. He is wearing a black sombrero and has two ammunition belts across his chest and a red bandanna around his neck. In one hand is a Dos Equis, in the other a nickel-plated six-gun.

He looks at me and says, "If we ride hard, *coño*, we can make the border before dawn."

I hesitate just a moment, then shake my head. Inside the house is the woman I love. I am going to crawl into bed beside her and sleep until the sun comes up. Then I'll kiss her and tell her what happened.

ABOUT THE AUTHOR

PETER LEFCOURT lives in Los Angeles, where he writes TV and movie scripts in addition to novels and plays and the occasional epic poem. He is no relation to the British royal family.

ABOUT THE TYPE

The text of this book was set in Palatino, designed by the German typographer Hermann Zapf. It was named after the Renaissance calligrapher Giovanbattista Palatino. Zapf designed it between 1948 and 1952, and it was his first typeface to be introduced in America. It is a face of unusual elegance.